Wild
on my
Mind

Laurel Kerr

Published by Sourcebooks Casablanca, an imprint of Sourcebooks, Inc.
P.O. Box 4410, Naperville, Illinois 60567-4410
(630) 961-3900
Fax: (630) 961-2168
sourcebooks.com

Printed and bound in the United States of America.
OPM 10 9 8 7 6 5 4 3 2 1

Chapter 1

THE INCREASINGLY INSISTENT SQUEAKS BROKE through Katie Underwood's intense concentration. Cocking her head to the side, she paused in her drawing. The chirping grew more and more demanding, the sound bouncing off the sandstone rocks surrounding her. At first, Katie thought a flock of birds was scolding her for invading their sanctuary, but she didn't spot any flying overhead in the waning light.

She started to turn back to her sketchbook, intent on taking advantage of the last rays before the sun dipped below the horizon, but something stopped her. The squeaking had the plaintive quality of an animal calling for help, and Katie had never been able to resist a wounded critter. Shoving her art supplies in her backpack, she followed the direction of the sound. Climbing a few feet above the ledge where she'd been sketching, she realized the cries originated from a cave that she remembered from childhood games with her four brothers.

Dropping to her hands and knees, Katie peered inside the crevice, wishing she had a flashlight. The pearly glow of twilight barely reached the back of the small alcove. She would have crawled inside, but both cougars and wolves haunted this sandstone promontory. As much as Katie loved wild creatures, she did not wish to encounter a wounded predator in a tight space.

Once her eyes finally adjusted to the gloom, Katie's heart simply melted. Tucked into a corner lay three squirming cougar cubs. One of the disgruntled fluffs chose that exact moment to howl its displeasure. A tiny pink mouth, framed by delicate whiskers, opened wide as the kit mewed in frustration. Katie could just barely make out the black spots peppering its grayish-brown fur.

She started to crawl forward and then stopped. Katie didn't know what would happen if she got her scent on the little guys. Resting on her haunches, she debated her next step. The mother might return, but Katie couldn't shake the feeling that the kits were either orphaned or abandoned. A neighboring rancher had recently been complaining about attacks on his livestock by pumas, which is what he called cougars or mountain lions, and he'd been known to shoot them in the past.

Katie reached for her cell phone. No signal. She would need to climb down to the old homestead and use the landline. Before she left, Katie stared back into the crevice where the cubs clumsily toddled in search of milk. "Don't worry, babies," she promised. "I'll be back with help."

As Bowie Wilson made the sharp turn onto the old Hallister spread, the suspension of his ancient pickup groaned loudly. He had a hell of a time keeping the vehicle running. The zoo sorely needed a new truck, but funds were tight and getting worse. They'd barely staved off foreclosure this past winter, and attendance hadn't picked up this spring. They were down to just a handful of volunteers and staff—a far cry from the animal park's heyday.

Pulling up to the old homestead, Bowie cut the engine and turned to wake his passenger, the former owner of the zoo. The eighty-year-old had fallen asleep on the twenty-minute drive to the ranch. Bowie had debated whether to bring Lou, since the older man generally headed to bed about now. But, unlike Bowie, Lou was a trained vet, and he could immediately start treatment on the cubs if they were seriously dehydrated or malnourished.

As Bowie waited for Lou to descend from the pickup, the front door to the old ranch house banged open. A woman, backlit by the porch light, waved. Although Bowie couldn't make out her features, he could easily spot the flash of her fiery-red hair. As she stepped out of the brightness and moved closer, the moonlight washed over her and gently illuminated her face. Her brown eyes widened at the sight of him.

Bowie couldn't quite read her emotion. Shock? Dismay? Recognition? Considering the size of their town, the latter was likely, but despite the fact that she seemed vaguely familiar, he couldn't place her. And he was pretty certain he'd remember a woman like her: all curly auburn hair, curves in the right places, and expressive chocolate-brown eyes. She exuded an earthy sexiness that appealed to him, awakening sensations that had lain dormant for far too long. Between his responsibilities as a single dad with an eleven-year-old daughter and his duties at the zoo, Bowie hadn't been with a woman in years.

Unfortunately, he had no time to appreciate this one. At least not now. Not with abandoned cougar cubs to rescue.

The woman focused her attention on Lou. "My parents are inside if you want to wait with them. It's a pretty difficult climb to the cubs."

Lou thanked her and headed to the homestead. The woman waited until he had disappeared into the house before she whirled back to Bowie. She thrust a headlamp in his direction, smacking his chest in the process.

"Here, take this. You'll need it to see," she bit out before she turned and strode gracefully toward the rock promontory silhouetted against the starry sky. Something about her gait reminded him of an Amazon warrior. An irate one. Although he'd spent most of his youth with adults angry at him—some with cause, some without—Bowie wasn't accustomed to facing a hot blast of fury anymore. He lived a quiet life now, and he had no idea what he could've done to upset this particular woman. It would be his crappy luck that the one female who attracted him also instinctually hated his guts.

When the woman reached the base of the rock formation, she bounded up the lower boulders with the surefootedness of a mountain goat. Even if she had taken an immediate dislike to him, Bowie found his eyes following her lithe shape in the dim light. She moved with a combination of fluidity and unbound energy that made him wonder what she'd be like in bed.

Forcing those unprofessional thoughts from his mind, he concentrated on finding footholds. It wasn't easy keeping pace. His reluctant guide clambered up the cliff almost as quickly as she walked. Bowie figured she must know the land pretty well, since only moonlight illuminated the landscape, and she hadn't turned on her headlamp.

"I guess you've climbed here before," he said.

She nodded, but she still didn't seem too happy. "Yes. My mom's folks, the Hallisters, lived out here, so I grew up playing on these rocks with my brothers. My parents moved out here after my dad's retirement."

That could explain why she looked vaguely familiar, but not her anger toward him. Perhaps he'd seen her around as a kid when she'd visited her relatives. She looked close to Bowie's age, and in his early teens, he'd worked on a ranch nearby. That was until he'd broken his leg and the rancher, who'd been his foster parent, had thrown him right back into the system. Bowie had never known a real home before Lou and his late wife, Gretchen, had taken him in after yet another guardian had kicked him out on his eighteenth birthday when the reimbursement checks stopped.

Deciding to try one more time to befriend the woman, Bowie asked, "So did you come to Sagebrush Flats a lot as a kid?"

She gave a snort of patent disgust. Even though the climb had just become more difficult, the woman picked up speed. Confused as hell, Bowie had no choice but to follow her up the cliff.

<hr>

If the lives of baby cougars hadn't hung in balance, Katie would have left Bowie Wilson stranded on the rocks until morning. After all, he'd done a lot worse to her back in high school. And despite all his horrible pranks, he'd apparently forgotten that she had ever existed.

That angered Katie more than anything. With all that Bowie had made her endure, she deserved at least a sliver of room in his memory. Even after high school graduation, she would wake up in her dorm, dreaming of her old classmates laughing at her. Because of Bowie.

Oh, she knew Bowie was the mastermind behind all the awful tricks. His high school girlfriend, Sawyer Johnson, might have taunted Katie since elementary school, but it had never amounted to more than snide and not very clever remarks before Sawyer had started dating Bowie. Sure, some of Sawyer's comments had hurt, but they hadn't scarred and certainly hadn't caused the all-consuming humiliation that Bowie's pranks had.

And what horrible thing had Katie done to Bowie to warrant such malicious attention?

She'd had the temerity to form an innocent, school-girl crush on him. That was all.

Katie had never even acted on her feelings. She doubted that Bowie would ever have noticed her if Sawyer hadn't pointed out Katie's secret infatuation. Through the years, Katie had never been able to figure out exactly why Bowie had decided to target her so viciously. Sawyer had never liked Katie, and Bowie might have just enjoyed making other people suffer. Either way, she'd become his favorite mark. And it had all started in the worst way possible.

Bowie had duped Katie into believing that he returned her feelings. For two weeks, Katie had lived in euphoric bliss, oblivious to the fact that Bowie was dating Sawyer. In retrospect, Katie should have realized that the cute bad boy would have had no interest in the nerdy girl. However, teen TV shows told a different story, and she'd stupidly believed the fantasy they peddled.

Which was how Bowie had managed to trick Katie into kissing a pig in the janitor's closet. Even worse, Sawyer had filmed the entire horrifying episode and slipped a clip of Katie puckering up to the hog into the student-run morning announcement program that ran on the televisions anchored at the front of each homeroom. For the rest of her high school career, she'd become known as "Katie the Pig-Kisser." That is, if they weren't calling her the oh-so-creative "Katie Underwear," a name Sawyer had coined in the first grade.

When Katie had left Sagebrush for college twelve years ago, she'd been more than happy to leave high school behind. Unfortunately, her escape hadn't turned out quite as she'd dreamed. She'd planned to become an artist, maybe in New York, LA, or even Tokyo. Instead, she'd traded a small town with tumbleweed for one with trees. Worse, she'd found herself the oddball out again in the male-dominated mulch plant in Minnesota where she'd worked designing packaging and performing the secretarial tasks that her boss assigned to her instead of her more junior male counterpart.

All told, it hadn't been hard to quit her job when her father, a retired police officer, was shot by an ex-con, Eddie Driver. Even if Sagebrush didn't offer many career opportunities, Katie's family had needed her. Her mother had never handled crises well, despite being the wife of a former chief of police, and Katie's four brothers couldn't handle their mother in a crisis.

Unfortunately, Katie hadn't counted on running into Bowie again. As wild as he'd been as a teenager, she'd figured he would have left their dusty hometown long ago. But it appeared that he hadn't. She knew one thing for certain, though. After publicly humiliating her and effectively ending any chance of her dating anyone else in high school, Bowie Wilson had simply and utterly forgotten her.

"Uh, ma'am? Where exactly are we headed?"

Ma'am? Really? Although she supposed it *was* better than Katie Underwear.

"Up."

"I see that, but where did the mother cougar leave her cubs?" The patience in Bowie's tone irritated Katie even more. How dare he act like *he* was the rational one?

She whipped around to glare at him. Even in the harsh light of the LED lantern, Bowie was a handsome man.

"We're headed to a cave," she bit out.

Twelve years ago, Bowie could have doubled for a teenage heartthrob with the shock of jet-black hair that had always dangled over his piercing gray eyes. Now, with that hair neatly trimmed and a five-o'clock stubble dusting his jaw, he looked like a model posing for an outdoor magazine. As an immature youth, he'd possessed a bad boy prettiness that appealed to girls—even self-proclaimed geeks like her. The years had toughened his features, hardening his male beauty into something more alluring and dangerous, even to a woman who should have known better.

Much better. Darn the man if he still didn't have the capacity to make Katie's hormones dance a happy little jig.

She steamed. If time hadn't mattered, she might have taken them on a more difficult path. Even then, she doubted that it would have fazed Bowie. Despite never climbing on this particular rock face before, the man moved like a machine. She could just imagine his muscular forearm extending as he reached for the next hold. His bicep would flex as he hoisted his body…

Katie cursed at herself. Sometimes she found her vivid imagination more of a burden than a gift. It had certainly brought her more difficulties than successes.

Thankfully, they quickly arrived at the small cave. Katie started inside, but a warm hand rested on her shoulder. Even through the fabric of her T-shirt, she could feel Bowie's heat and the strength of his fingers. An unbidden shiver slid through her.

"Let me go first." Bowie's breath caressed the sensitive skin on the back of Katie's neck, and she had to fight to suppress another shudder. "The mother cougar may have returned."

Bowie dropped to his knees and used the light from his headlamp to scan the cave before crawling inside. With his larger frame, it took him a few seconds to wiggle through the narrow passage. As soon as Bowie moved far enough into the alcove for Katie to enter, she crawled over to the cubs. They moved clumsily about, searching for milk and their mother's warmth. One yawned. Its tiny whiskers flexed as it emitted a long squeak. The others followed suit. Katie's heart squeezed. She resisted the urge to gather the little fluffs against her chest. She still didn't know the protocol on handling kits this small, and she didn't want to harm one inadvertently.

"Their eyes aren't even open yet!" she said.

Bowie nodded. "Nor are their ears at this stage. They must be less than ten days old." The awe in his voice caused Katie to turn sharply in his direction. He appeared just as infatuated with the cubs as she was. Was this the same man who'd once tied granny panties to the undercarriage of her car along with the sign HONK IF YOU SEE MY UNDERWEAR?

Bowie reached for one of the mewling cubs and cradled it against his muscular chest. The little guy burrowed against him, and Katie's hormones went crazy again. Just when she thought the scene couldn't get any sweeter, the kit yawned, showing its miniature pink tongue. Then with one more nuzzle against Bowie's pecs, it heaved a surprisingly large sigh as it fell asleep. Bowie's handsome features softened into a gentle smile as he stroked the baby cougar's spotted fur with one callused finger.

If Katie hadn't suffered years of Bowie's cruel teasing, she would have found herself halfway in love with him. He'd appeared to be the ideal boyfriend once before, but it had all been a veneer, the perfect trap for a geeky girl with silly dreams of romance. And Katie, the woman, would not fall prey to his outward charms again.

"Can I pick up one of the cougars too?" The cuteness of the cub would serve as a nice distraction from her unwanted feelings.

Bowie nodded. "They'll need to be hand-reared,

so they're going to end up imprinting on humans anyway. Unfortunately, we won't be able to reintroduce them to the wild, but we can save them."

Katie lifted one of the furry bundles, marveling at the softness of its fur. The little guy emitted a small, contented sound and immediately snuggled against Katie's warmth. She could feel a cold, teeny nose against her skin as the cub rested its head in the crook of her arm. And right then and there, Katie fell in love. With the tiny kit. Definitely not with the man.

Although she hated putting the baby puma down, she knew the little trio needed more than just a warm cuddle. "Did you bring something to carry the cubs back down the mountain with?"

Bowie grimaced and shook his head. "I didn't know the climb would be so steep."

And, Katie realized, she hadn't given him time to grab something from his truck either. To her surprise, Bowie was too polite to point that out.

"Do you want me to run back to the house to get a backpack?" she asked.

Bowie shook his head. "We'll have to improvise. I'm not sure how long the cubs have been without milk, and we need to get them out of this cave as soon as possible."

Katie scanned the dirt floor of the alcove and saw nothing—not even a twig. She turned back to ask Bowie what he planned on using and stopped. He was halfway out of his shirt. Normally, Katie wouldn't blatantly ogle a man, but…those abs. And pecs. His biceps flexed as he ripped his shirt down

the middle so it made one thick band. Bowie Wilson
might be just as bad for Katie as an entire carton of
rocky road ice cream, but he looked just as temptingly
scrumptious.

Bowie froze as he lifted his head and found the auburn-
haired woman watching him as if she wanted to lick him
all over. Something equally hot and elemental whipped
through him. He'd never had this much of a visceral
response to any woman. If it weren't for the baby mountain lions, he might have been crazy enough to accept her
unspoken offer...even if he didn't know whether she'd
jump him or push him down the cliff.

The lady—who he'd mentally taken to calling Red—
might be showing an attraction to his body, but she didn't
appear to like him. At all. She reminded him a bit of the
zoo's honey badger, Fluffy—all snarls, bad temper, and
teeth. In the wild, Fluffy's relatives were known to take
down king cobras, and Bowie couldn't shake the feeling
that Red viewed him as one giant snake.

Still, Red had looked soft, sweet even, while cuddling the runt of the litter against her breasts. Sugar
and spice—that was Red. And damn if the combination
didn't intrigue him.

As a single father, Bowie should know better than
to lust after a woman who was all fire one moment and
pure honey the next. If he ever started dating seriously,
he'd need an even-tempered partner who could handle
the ups and downs of parenthood. He'd already dated
one female chimera and learned a lesson about falling
for someone with a dual personality. His high school

girlfriend, Sawyer, had been classy and elegant with an outward poise that had impressed and intimidated the hell out of his teenage self. But inside, she had a childish mean streak that could strike at any time. She had never wanted anything to do with their daughter, and for that, Bowie was actually grateful. He loved his baby girl and wanted to protect her from the Sawyers of the world for as long as possible.

"Is that going to work?" Red asked, jerking her head toward his ruined T-shirt. She still snuggled the kit to her breasts as she peered at him.

"It should," Bowie said, withdrawing his Leatherman from his pocket. He cut two slices near the bottom of his shirt and then tore them off to use as bindings. With the zoo's piss-poor budget, he'd learned to find creative solutions with the supplies on hand. Within a few moments, he had jerry-rigged a semblance of a bag. He tested it with a few rocks first. Satisfied it would hold three pounds' worth of wiggling cubs, he carefully placed the babies inside, including the one in Red's arms.

"You always were smart."

Bowie glanced up at Red. That hadn't sounded like a compliment, but it wasn't the only thing that confused him. She certainly acted like she knew him, but he still couldn't place her.

"How do we know each other?" he finally asked.

She glared, looking every inch like an irate Fluffy during one of his particularly bad moods. "Think a little harder."

Somewhere, a memory flickered. A fleeting

glimpse of red hair. But then the recollection floated away, out of reach. Bowie shook his head. "Sorry, ma'am. You seem familiar, I promise, but I just can't remember from where."

Rather than mollify Red, his words only fanned the flames shooting from her eyes. Still on her haunches, she spun around and then scrambled out of the cave. Sighing, he gathered his bundle of cubs and followed.

Bowie noticed that Red moved slower descending the cliff than she had going up, probably out of consideration for the cougars that he carried. When they reached the bottom of the rock formation, Bowie spotted Lou standing under the porch light next to a lady with the same fiery mane as Red's. Instead of Red's flowing cascade of curls, though, this woman's hair formed a frizzy halo about her cherubic face. Something jangled in the back of Bowie's brain, but before he could zero in on it, the older woman called out to Red, waving her hand cheerfully.

"Sweetheart, I was just telling Lou how you came back home to help out your father and me and that you're looking for work."

Red shot Bowie a sidelong glance and then spoke through gritted teeth. "I do have some paying projects, Mom."

Lou, always the peacemaker, quickly added, "Helen was also telling me that you're designing labels for Clara Winters's granddaughter's new jam business."

So, Red was acquainted with June Winters, Bowie thought, although that clue didn't help him much, since everyone in Sagebrush Flats knew June. The woman had breezed into town a little less than a decade ago and revitalized her family's tea shop. What used to be the domain of little old ladies after Sunday church had become the local hot spot. Even the most taciturn ranchers stopped by for the fussy desserts and fancy drinks. Although June's cooking was the best in town, the food wasn't the only draw. It was the woman herself. June had long blond hair and eyes as green as the grass during the month after which she was named. But unlike her surname, Winters, her personality was as bright as a summer's day. Bowie had stopped by the tea shop himself, but he much preferred Red's earthy sexiness to June's more classic elegance.

In response to Lou's comment, Red's mother bobbed her head like the zoo's cockatoo, Rosie, when the bird was shaking her plume in time to her beloved punk rock. "Yes, and I told Lou how you redid the menus for June's tea shop and that the Prairie Dog Café agreed to use the place mats you're designing—the ones with ad space for local businesses."

"Your mother thought you could help us with the zoo's website and our general marketing strategy," Lou said, looking first at Katie before he turned to address Bowie. "What do you think?"

"Well, it hasn't been updated since before I started," Bowie said carefully. Red looked like the zoo's camel, Lulubelle, right before the animal spit. Clearly, Red didn't appreciate her mother's interference. Keeping his voice neutral, Bowie decided to give her an out. "How high are your fees? Our budget is pretty tight."

Honestly, Bowie wouldn't mind improving the zoo's internet presence if he could do it at a reasonable cost. He and Lou needed something to draw folks through the gates. He'd never really had much of an artistic side, and unlike most of his generation, he sucked with computers. Except for the occasional use at school, he hadn't had much access to them growing up. He certainly didn't know anything about web design. But Bowie didn't want to strong-arm Red into helping him, even if it would benefit the zoo.

"I'm sure my daughter would give you a discount," Red's mom said. "Wouldn't you, sweetheart?"

Red's jaw clenched, and she was back to looking like a mulish honey badger. "Mom, Bowie and Lou haven't even seen my work."

"I'm sure it's wonderful," Lou said quickly. Too quickly. Bowie barely prevented a groan from escaping his lips as he turned from Lou to Red's mom and then back again. This wasn't just about building Red's business or getting low-cost marketing advice. It was a matchmaking scheme, plain and simple. And from the way Red's shoulders stiffened, she recognized it too.

Before Lou and Helen drove Red into finally losing her temper, Bowie turned to her and asked, "Why don't you stop by the zoo tomorrow and bring some samples of your work? We can see if it will be a good fit for both of us."

Before she could answer, her mother beamed. "That sounds like an excellent idea! Doesn't it, sweetheart?"

Red made a sound that Bowie figured was supposed to be noncommittal, but it came out like a honey badger's snarl.

Sensing the need for a diversion, Bowie turned to Lou and gestured to the bundle of squirming mountain lions. "Lou, do you want to check on the cubs?" Bowie asked. "I think they're all right other than they'll need milk as soon as we return to the zoo." After Lou took the bundle from him, Bowie turned to Red and her mom to explain, "These little guys are going to need formula about every four hours."

"Ooo," Red's mom said, "that sounds like a lot of work. Will you be looking for volunteers?" She turned to Red. "What do you think, sweetheart? Would you like to help care for them? You've always loved taking in strays."

"Mom, I'm here to help you with Dad."

Helen waved a hand dismissively. "He's stronger now, and you've been so much help. It's time you took a break and did something for yourself. We'll be fine. You could even work on the zoo's marketing while you watch the cubs."

"Uh, we can talk about that tomorrow as well," Bowie said as he quickly swiveled in Lou's direction. "Are the cubs in good enough shape for the return trip?"

When Lou nodded, Bowie placed his hand on the older man's upper arm and gently steered him to the truck before either he or Helen could attempt more matchmaking. Considering the zoo's skeletal staff, Bowie couldn't afford to turn down volunteers, but if anyone pushed Red further tonight, she would explode. Although he wouldn't mind watching the fireworks from a safe distance, Bowie was a little too close to the danger zone. Plus, he and Lou really did need to get the cubs back to the zoo.

Waiting until Lou got settled in the truck, Bowie helped arrange the bundle of kits on his mentor's lap. As Bowie climbed into the driver's seat, Lou yawned and said, "Nice, sweet girl. Good family."

Bowie grunted. He really wanted to learn Red's name and hear what had brought her back to Sagebrush Flats, but he was afraid that any interest would just encourage Lou and Helen's matchmaking. Maybe if he kept Lou talking, the information would come out naturally. As Bowie considered how to dig innocuously for more details, he heard a snore. A fond smile crossed Bowie's face when he glanced over at Lou and realized the eighty-year-old had fallen asleep again.

Oh well. Regardless of who Red was, Bowie had a feeling that tomorrow's meeting with her was going to be interesting.

———ᜋᜋ———

Fluffy, the honey badger, stirred inside his man-made den. Night had fallen, and Fluffy preferred the dark to day. Light hurt his eyes, but that didn't always stop him from leaving his enclosure to spy on the pesky humans when they were most active.

Fluffy didn't mind the bipeds…much. The Black-Haired One did bring him lovely insects. Although the Gray-Haired One tended to poke and prod him, which Fluffy did *not* appreciate, he occasionally received a honey-covered bee larva for the annoyance. All in all, the humans were tolerable…not that Fluffy would ever admit it. He did like the Wee One. She always snuck him treats. True, she had saddled him with his ridiculous name, but she'd been a little thing back then, so he could forgive her.

Just then, Fluffy's ears perked at an unusual noise

for this time of night: the crunch of tires on the gravel path winding through the zoo. A loud sound bellowed through the air. Fluffy hissed. It was the Black-Haired One's truck. It always made the most horrendous noises.

Fluffy stretched his long body, digging his claws into the dirt. Once his muscles felt suitably limber, he darted into his enclosure. The Black-Haired One had dug a large run and then cemented the sides to prevent Fluffy from climbing out. The silly biped thought that he could corral Fluffy when honey badgers were clearly much, much more clever than mere humans.

The Black-Haired One was in the process of digging the already four-foot-deep concrete barriers lower, but he hadn't reached the west wall. Fluffy scampered over to that weak point and began to dig. It was not the most brilliant strategy, but it was effective. He tunneled quickly through the dirt, popping out on the other side. Keeping his flat, furry tail low, Fluffy scurried through the deserted zoo.

Most of the animals lay asleep, snug in their dens. He heard Lulubelle, the camel, snoring loudly above the llamas as he passed by their paddock. Making a hard right, he ran alongside the enclosure of Frida, the bear. The grumpy old grizzly growled when she caught wind of Fluffy. Fluffy grinned. He liked irritating the elderly bruin. Frida needed a bit of excitement to keep her spry…even if she didn't always thank Fluffy for stealing pieces of her meat and poaching the berries that the Wee One brought.

Fluffy, however, had more important matters

than just Frida tonight. A warm glow seeped from the
zoo's maintenance facility that housed both the feed
and the animal hospital. Due to the presence of treats,
Fluffy had a long history of invading the building.
Climbing up the downspout, he hopped onto a narrow
ledge. Slipping his sharp claws between the loose
frame, he worked the window free and then wiggled
through the small space he'd created. The silly human
hadn't figured out yet that the window was broken.
Clinging to the drapery, Fluffy silently lowered himself to the floor and headed toward the light. Carefully,
he peeked around a doorframe and spotted the Black-
Haired One sitting cross-legged on the floor. Two little
sausage-shaped fur balls crawled on the biped as a third
cub drank greedily from a bottle. Fluffy could hear the
hungry sucking sounds from across the room.

He watched with interest, his little black nose twitching. It wasn't the kits that drew his attention, though.

No, it was the expression on the Black-Haired One's
face. He looked the way Fluffy felt when facing a challenge—a challenge with honey at the end of it.

Chapter 2

"AND THEN SHE OFFERED A DISCOUNT. A DISCOUNT! To my high school nemesis!"

"Katie," June drawled in her Southern accent as she turned from the pot of jam on her stove, "you're a grown woman. You don't have nemeses. You are not a comic book character fighting aliens."

"Well then, what do you call a guy who made your life miserable for three years?" Katie asked.

June smiled wickedly as she added fresh raspberries to the boiling mixture. "Why, I'd say he was just a peach, bless his little heart."

Katie glared good-naturedly at her best friend. Even wearing a ridiculous hairnet, June looked radiantly regal with her perfect blond hair and tall, willowy body. June simply did not understand the cruelty of high school. She'd somehow avoided the awkwardness of the teenage years. Katie knew— she'd seen the photographic evidence. Despite June being a military brat, or maybe because of it, she had managed to become prom queen two years in a row at two different schools in two entirely different parts of the country.

It wasn't just June's looks either. As she would say in her Southern drawl, June just drew people like ants to molasses. The child of a second-generation airman, she had grown up all over the world—her mom's home state of Georgia, then North Dakota, South Korea, Colorado, Germany, Florida, and New Mexico. She had a chameleonlike ability to blend into her surroundings and a way of putting all people at ease, no matter their backgrounds.

If Katie's gran and June's grandmother hadn't arranged for them to be college roommates, Katie doubted they would ever have met. She certainly wouldn't have attended the parties that June had dragged her to. In fact, her whole college experience would have been entirely different, since Katie would've spent it holed up in her dorm room. When June had convinced Katie to try a makeover, she'd done more than introduce Katie to the wonderful but complex world of hair product and conditioner. June had helped Katie discover her confidence.

Back in high school, Katie had looked a mess. A geek since the first grade, she had ended up clinging to the role as if it defined her. She'd never attempted to dress the way the popular girls did. And her hair, before June had taught her to tame it, had looked like a flaming bush, as Bowie and his girlfriend used to tease. It wasn't until she met June that she realized a girl could be both nice to others *and* well dressed.

"Here, taste this." June handed Katie a spoon filled with hot jam. Katie took it and blew on the mixture before popping it into her mouth. Decadent sweetness with a hint of tart heat exploded on her tongue. June had the same way with cooking that she had with people. She could combine the most unexpected ingredients to make something extraordinary.

"What's in this one?" Katie asked.

"Fresh raspberries, my great-grandmother's berry

cordial, and a smidgen of cayenne pepper." June leaned her elbows on the counter where Katie was sitting. "What should I call it?"

"Drunken Fire Berries," Katie said, the image for the label already springing to her mind. She'd draw two reclining raspberries drinking from champagne glasses with little flames over their heads.

June clapped her hands. "I love it. I knew there was a reason I keep letting you into my kitchen."

"Har. Har. Har," Katie said, reaching for her sketchbook to create a mock-up of her idea for the tag.

"Do you want more jam for inspiration while you work?" June asked, putting some extra liquid into a bowl. Katie waited until the sample stopped steaming and then took a huge mouthful.

It was then that June made her strategic move. "You know, Katie, your mother may have a point."

Unable to form a retort with warm jam filling her mouth, Katie glared at June.

"If you want to make a go of freelancing, you'll need more clients than me and the Prairie Dog Café."

Katie swallowed the jam. "I'm just looking for short-term work, since I don't know how long I'll stick around. This is my chance to start fresh and find a new job—somewhere more impressive and exciting than a mulch factory."

"And, honey, you will," June said, "but you need something to tide you over in the meantime."

Katie frowned. June had a point, but Katie really didn't want to concede it.

"You're giving me a cut of your jam sale proceeds."

June smiled. "Katie, as much as I do appreciate your faith in me, I've only got the local supermarket stocking my jellies. I'll be selling at local farmers' markets and festivals this summer, but it's going to be a while before we turn any profit. You know that."

Katie stabbed her spoon into the bowl. "But that means I have to make nice with Bowie Wilson."

June shrugged. "Would it be any worse than dealing with your old boss?"

Katie swirled the raspberry liquid with her spoon as she thought about June's question. She'd worked for almost a decade in Minnesota and had never once received a promotion. Her supervisor—a closet chauvinist—had either dismissed her ideas or taken credit for them.

"Debatable," Katie finally managed. "Both men are terrible, but in different ways."

June grabbed Katie's hands. "Katie, honey, this is your chance. Think of all the ideas you could come up with. People love animals. You love animals! I have no doubt that you can come up with a marketing campaign that'll go viral. This time, you'll get recognition, and you can build your portfolio like you're always jabbering about."

Katie sighed. When June put it that way, it did sound like the perfect opportunity. The only drawback: her former high-school bully.

"But that means I'll have to work closely with Bowie," Katie said. "You know he didn't even recognize me?"

June patted her hand before returning to the stove. "You said it was dark last night when you met again, didn't you?"

Katie nodded glumly. "And I look like I have a pound less hair than I did in high school. But the thing is, I don't really want him to recognize me."

June laughed. "I thought you were angry that he didn't know who you were."

"I am, but also glad in a way. I always had this fantasy that I'd come back to Sagebrush Flats as this wildly successful woman and make both Bowie and Sawyer, his old girlfriend, sick with pure jealousy. Instead, I'm jobless, practically broke, and living in my parents' home."

June turned to reach into the refrigerator. She pulled out a custard bowl and set it in front of Katie. "Eat some of this. It will chase away your sorrows."

"What is it?"

"Lime curd with graham cracker layers—my riff on lemon curd and key lime pie. I'm planning to offer it at the tea shop next week. If it sells well, I'll add it to the jam collection, so I'll be needing a name for that as well."

June's creamy concoction was the perfect blend of sweet and sour. Katie closed her eyes as the silky dessert slid down her throat. When she opened them, June had a no-nonsense expression on her face.

"Now that you're in a better frame of mind, let's discuss what you just said. First, you were *not* fired from your job. You quit with your head held high to help your mom after your dad was shot. That doesn't make you a loser. It makes you a good daughter."

"Sacrifices like that wouldn't impress people like Bowie and Sawyer."

"Well, it impresses me," June said. "Second,

you have drummed up business in sleepy old Sagebrush Flats already, so you have some income. Third, you're not living in your parents' home."

Katie rolled her eyes. "I'm living in a small house only fifty yards away from the main homestead."

"But it is a charming little geodesic dome," June said. "That has to count for something."

"It looks like a mouse house," Katie corrected. "And my grandparents ordered it prefab from a catalog in the sixties when they were newlyweds—not a real selling point."

"It's a classic."

"For a sci-fi movie setting maybe."

June nudged the lime curd in Katie's direction. "Eat more of this."

"I don't know if it's still going to work to distract me, but it is delicious." Katie shoveled another large bite into her mouth.

"I think you may be missing a golden opportunity."

"I know. I know," Katie grumbled. "Cute animals. Awesome artwork for the portfolio."

"I don't just mean for your career. I'm talking about revenge."

Katie scrunched her brow—a habit her mother had always tried to break her of. "I don't see how helping Bowie would count as payback. It's the exact opposite."

June delivered one of her most mischievous grins. "Honey, you have got to start thinking more deviously. Didn't you say he used to pull pranks on you?"

Katie nodded. She'd never gone into the painful details with June, but she had mentioned that she'd been bullied in high school.

"Did any of his practical jokes involve animals?"

Katie couldn't stop her automatic wince. "He tricked me into kissing a pig."

June laughed in delight. "Why, that's just perfect!"

Katie did not share in her mirth. "I'm glad that at least you're amused. It was probably the most embarrassing moment of my life."

June's mouth quirked into a devious grin. "Think about it, Katie. Bowie Wilson has stopped by the tea shop once or twice. He is quite the attractive package. Make a video of him smooching a pig, and you'll have a hit on your hands. Women will love it."

Katie froze, a spoonful of lime curd halfway to her mouth. "June, that's absolutely brilliant."

"I know," June said proudly.

Then reality punctured Katie's excitement. "But how would I convince him to do it?"

"Come up with a brilliant marketing plan, and sweeten the pot by volunteering to help raise those adorable cougar cubs you were telling me about."

It just might work, but Katie had to think practically. Fantasizing about Bowie Wilson was what had gotten her into trouble in the first place—even if the daydreams were of an entirely different nature. "What about my dad? He's still recovering."

"He is on the mend," June pointed out. "Your mother even went line dancing two nights ago. You can be away from the house at night to babysit cougar cubs."

Katie huffed out a breath. "It might just work."

"Of course it will work. I came up with the plan."

Katie allowed a satisfied smile to curve her lips.

June was right. She needed to think about this strategically. This might be a fun summer after all.

———————

"Your website definitely needs an overhaul. Nobody uses scrolling banner headlines anymore or flashing GIFs. And the fonts are an old-fashioned mess," Red said. "It looks like it was done in the early 2000s."

"It probably was," Bowie replied as he watched Red from across his desk. The evening rays filtering through the glass-block window caught her auburn curls, making them shimmer. Her chocolate-brown eyes were slightly large for her face, but he liked that about her. And they suited her—those wide eyes full of energy and intelligence.

Sometimes, when she cocked her head in a certain direction, a glint of memory winked at Bowie. However, he couldn't quite hold it in focus long enough to remember her. He'd vaguely recognized her mom from town but couldn't recall her last name either. Bowie had never been very sociable.

He debated about asking Red for her name, but that might set her off again. She sounded like she knew what she was doing when it came to marketing, and he didn't want her storming from his office. He figured she'd have to tell him her name eventually, even if just for the check.

"Here are some mock-ups I threw together this morning." She handed him a couple of printouts. Leafing through them, he raised an eyebrow. They were good. Very good. Better than anything he could have created.

"I'd also like to do a new logo for the zoo, but I need to see the animals first. That way, I can personalize it and highlight the species you have here. Right now, your brand has a real seventies vibe."

"That would be because Lou and his late wife, Gretchen, founded the zoo then." Lou had grown up in Sagebrush Flats. After leaving the state to get doctorates in zoology and veterinary medicine, he had worked for several major zoos before he and Gretchen had returned to his boyhood home to start their own animal park. When it opened, the place had generated a healthy stream of visitors and had a great reputation as a sanctuary for animals that could not survive in the wild. Through the years, attendance had dwindled as kids preferred watching animals on YouTube to visiting them in person. The stream of volunteers had turned into a trickle, forcing Lou to cut back on the number of rescues.

"The logo isn't the only thing you should change to bring the zoo into this decade," Red said. "You don't have any animal cams. You'll want one for the cougar cubs, but you need more than that. Since every zoo has them now, you should have a hook, something for people to anticipate. The kits' eyes aren't open yet, so I think we can use that to get people to watch."

Bowie straightened in his chair. "That might work, although we'd have to get a webcam right away, since their eyes could open any moment now. We could also have a countdown clock for when the cubs can go on exhibit. That will be in about nine weeks, so it gives us plenty of time to build momentum."

Red nodded enthusiastically. "That's a perfect idea! I also thought we could do a video profile of each animal—maybe even post one weekly. Then we could archive them on the site."

"I like how your mind works, Red." His nickname for her slipped out of his mouth. He realized his mistake as soon as he saw her features harden.

"Don't call me that." As she spoke, her brown eyes flashed with anger and something else. Hurt, maybe? Something nudged at Bowie's memory. An image of a wounded brown gaze started to form in his mind. It had just begun to crystallize when Red folded her hands neatly on her lap and said, "Now, we need to talk money."

"I can't afford much," Bowie admitted, "especially with all the work you're proposing. Our numbers aren't good."

"I'm willing to work for a small up-front fee. If the marketing campaign brings in more foot traffic, then you'll need to pay the rest when the zoo can afford it. Of course, I want credit on all the work I do, since I'm in the middle of a job search and need to keep my portfolio up to date."

"That sounds fair." More than fair, actually.

"And I'll even volunteer to help with the cubs at no cost."

Bowie forcibly schooled his face not to show his reaction to her words. He couldn't believe her generosity. Other than his good fortune with Lou and Gretchen, things like this didn't happen to him. If anything, people in his past had shown more interest in tearing him down than in lending a helping hand. He didn't quite understand why Red was being so accommodating, especially since he still got the sense that she didn't much like him.

"There's just one thing I want you to do," Red said. "In fact, it'll even be part of the marketing campaign."

At the challenging glint in Red's eyes, a trickle of unease started to spread through Bowie. He felt trapped in those brown depths, but he couldn't retreat. The zoo couldn't afford it. Hell, *he* couldn't afford it. He needed help desperately with the cougar cubs, and the place wasn't exactly crawling with volunteers. Two of his high school helpers had come down with mono, and the intern that he'd lined up for this summer had gotten a better offer at the last minute. Whatever Red wanted couldn't be that bad. Could it?

"Sounds reasonable," Bowie said cautiously.

"Good." Red smiled. Wickedly. "I want you to kiss a pig."

The words hung in the air as recognition finally slammed into Bowie with the force of a stampeding rhino hopped up on amphetamines. Crap. Crap. *Crap.*

Red wasn't a stranger after all. She was Katie Underwood, the girl Bowie had mercilessly teased and tricked into kissing a pig.

The years had changed Katie—for the better. Her bushy red hair had darkened and been tamed into a cascade of silky auburn curls. Instead of hiding her surprisingly tight body beneath baggy clothes, Katie now wore curve-hugging jeans and a little T-shirt that clung to all the right places. Unlike in high school, there were no thick glasses or static-cling hair to detract from her cherubic features and brown eyes.

Clearly, Bowie had not only been a jerk in high school, but an utter moron. Considering the things that he had done to Katie, he was lucky she hadn't kicked him straight in the balls. But, he had to admit, the shock of seeing her felt pretty darn similar to a knee to the groin.

"Katie Underw—" he heard himself say before cutting himself off. *Shit*. He'd almost slipped and called her Katie Underwear. "Underwood."

Katie stiffened, and he knew she'd realized the reason for his hesitation. *Crap*. This wasn't going well. He should have arranged for Lou to meet with her instead, especially since he'd sensed Red's hostility. But he'd wanted this time with her. Something about this woman fascinated him, and he'd…well…he'd hoped maybe he could charm her into agreeing to a casual date. Obviously, that wouldn't happen now. Bowie was fairly certain that if he attempted to even wink at Katie, she would castrate him.

Not that he blamed her.

As his brain madly scrambled for a way to salvage the situation, he said the first thing that popped into his mind. "Would a red river hog do?"

Katie blinked. Clearly, she hadn't expected that particular response. "Excuse me?"

"You told me to kiss a pig. I don't have one handy, but we've got two resident red river hogs. I don't think Daisy, our sow, will mind. Boris, the boar, might, but I'll let him know it's for the good of the zoo."

"Are you *mocking* me?" Katie drew an irate breath. When she did so, her chest jutted in Bowie's direction. He tried very hard not to notice that.

"No, ma'am," he told her. "If you agree to volunteer with caring for the cougars, I will kiss Daisy."

Katie's anger faded into speculation, and it took all of Bowie's talent at bullshitting through life not to drop his grin and shift uncomfortably. He'd engineered quite a few tricks against her, and he'd just exposed his willingness to perform stunts in return for her services as a volunteer.

"You'll kiss the hog in public?" Katie asked.

Bowie nodded solemnly. It wasn't as if they would draw a crowd. Hell, if it did, he'd kiss Daisy every day.

"And post a video of it on the internet?"

He paused, trying to decide if that could negatively impact the zoo. Katie's mouth immediately drew into a smug line. "Well then, I'm not sure if our deal will work." She started to rise from her chair.

"Wait!"

Katie pivoted. She crossed her arms and watched him expectantly.

"Give me a minute to think. It might look odd for a zoo director to start posting videos of himself kissing animals."

Katie shrugged nonchalantly. "Not if it's for a fund-raiser. If you agree to the video, June Winters will sponsor it for $250. We'll just need to give her tea shop and new jam business a plug at the end. She and I are hoping the video will go viral."

Bowie didn't know how to feel about June Winters's involvement or about a viral video of him making face time with a sow, but he didn't have much choice. If the video was watched by tons of people, it could help the zoo. "So, if I kiss Daisy and post it on the internet, you'll volunteer?"

"I'll volunteer for a week."

He bit back a sigh. "Then what?"

A devilish smile played at Katie's lips. "Oh, I think I can come up with another 'fund-raiser.'"

Bowie just bet that she could. It was going to be a long summer.

"Deal."

Katie's wicked grin grew broader, and he wondered what he'd just committed himself to. Bowie recalled the quote he always told his daughter when the kids at school picked on her: "Be nice to nerds. Chances are you'll end up working for one." In Bowie's case, he'd just become indebted to the one geek he'd been down-right cruel to. It didn't matter that he regretted how he'd treated her. Hell, he hadn't particularly liked picking on her in high school—not that Katie would ever believe him. How exactly could he explain his motivation when he didn't fully understand it himself?

Gee, I was so desperate to impress my hot, rich, popular girlfriend that I made your life hell for over two years. Sorry, but I had a crappy home situation, and I wanted to fit in so badly, I didn't care who I humiliated in the process.

Yeah, those excuses sounded great. He'd had no right to treat her or anyone like that, no matter his sorry-assed reasons.

"Deal," Katie echoed.

"When can you start?" Bowie asked. He might sound desperate, but at this point, what did it matter? Katie clearly knew who wielded the power in this relationship. He couldn't keep caring for the cougar cubs and running the rest of the animal park without more help. And they didn't have the funds right now to hire more staff, no matter how much the zoo needed several more pairs of hands.

Katie gave him a dry look. "How soon can you kiss the pig?"

"I can do it right now, but if you want a bigger audience, Saturday is the day," he told her. If he was going to kiss Daisy, he might as well try to wrangle more interest in the zoo.

"Then I guess I'll start Sunday."

That was six days away, and he didn't want to wait that long. "How about a compromise? I'll post the upcoming event on the website today. That way, I can't back out, and you'll get more people to witness me kissing Daisy."

Katie eyed him suspiciously, and Bowie held up both of his hands. "I promise, Katie. I will kiss a pig for you. You can check the site before you start."

"Fine. I'll come tomorrow, and if you buy a webcam, I'll get it set up then too. What times do you need help?"

Bowie almost laughed at the question. Ideally, they'd have a list of trained volunteers who could help out when an orphaned animal arrived. Unfortunately, interest in the zoo had been slowly dying since its heyday in the seventies and eighties when Lou had run one of the more well-regarded sanctuaries for orphaned animals. Bowie needed at least five more workers 24/7, but he was lucky to find one, considering the small size of Sagebrush Flats. Instead, he only said, "An eight-hour shift would be great, but I understand if you can't commit that much time. Any little bit will help, and we can be flexible with your schedule."

"I can generally start at eleven at night and leave early in the morning, but I'll stop by around seven tomorrow to get oriented."

He stared at her in disbelief. "You want the graveyard shift?"

"My mom still needs help with my dad during the day. Plus, I've always been a night owl who doesn't require much sleep."

Something else clicked in Bowie's brain. Katie was the daughter of Chief Underwood, the man who'd been shot in the chest by a former convict. No wonder she was back in town.

"I was sorry to hear about your dad."

At the mention of her father, Katie's expression softened. "Thank you."

"How's he doing?"

"Okay, considering everything that happened. His physical therapy is going well. In fact, I'm driving him there tomorrow morning."

"It's nice of you to help your folks out."

Katie nodded again, and Bowie took a deep breath. He hated to derail the conversation now that it was going relatively well, but he couldn't ignore the tension brewing beneath the surface. The woman didn't like him, and he didn't blame her. Not after what he'd done. If they were going to establish a meaningful rapport, he needed to apologize.

"Katie, about what I did back in high—"

Her entire body stiffened, and her eyes flashed just as they had the night before. "The only part about the past that I want to discuss is how you're going to kiss that pig."

"Okay," Bowie said in the tone he'd use with a skittish animal.

Katie swallowed as she clearly reined in her temper. "Okay. I'm glad we're clear on that now." Then, with the same Amazonian grace he'd witnessed last night, she strode from his office. She didn't slam the door, but the way she shut it showed that she hadn't forgotten all the tricks he'd played on her.

Bowie stared after her for a moment before groaning and dropping his head into his hands.

What the hell had he just gotten himself into?

Fluffy watched the redheaded female human with interest as she left the zoo's office. She wore a triumphant smile, which Fluffy easily recognized. He spent most of his existence pleased with himself, but he wasn't sure how he felt when others experienced that emotion. But since he was feeling particularly self-satisfied at the moment, he decided he wouldn't begrudge the biped her victory.

Fluffy had escaped his enclosure in record time since the Black-Haired One had forgotten his shovel after he'd finished digging the trench to deepen the west wall. Fluffy had very quickly dragged the tool to the wall so that it formed a ramp. Within seconds, he'd scurried out of his enclosure. He'd already snagged a nice chunk of meat from Frida's bowl. The old girl had taken a swipe at Fluffy, which he'd quickly dodged. He'd noticed that Frida hadn't tried too hard to hit him. After all, their games were the most fun Frida had all day. Fluffy, though, had other adventures.

Like this one.

He fully planned to get into the general feed supply again. The redheaded biped had not properly shut the door. Fluffy nudged it open with his nose. He was just about to dart inside the storeroom when he noticed the Black-Haired One sitting at his desk. The human held his head between his hands, and he looked bone-weary.

Fluffy cocked his own head. He enjoyed irking the Black-Haired One. He did not, however, like his human to appear so tired. It might delay the morning meal. The Black-Haired One suddenly straightened. Fluffy tilted his head to the other side. If he was not mistaken, he detected a bit of excitement shimmering beneath the Black-Haired One's exhaustion.

Fluffy smiled and thought of the redheaded female. Perhaps the Black-Haired One needed a challenge as much as Frida did. The idea pleased Fluffy. He would not mind if the Black-Haired One found a mate. They would produce more like the Wee One, which, in turn, meant more treats.

———

"So, your mom tells me you're going to be working at the local zoo."

Katie glanced over at her dad as she drove him to his physical therapy appointment. Although Chief Underwood had improved since Eddie Driver had shot him, car rides, especially longer ones like this, wore him out. Katie knew from experience that he'd spend the trip home fast asleep. Even now, his lips were pinched from the effort of getting from the house to the car. But she knew better than to ask how her father felt. He hated the fact that he couldn't force his body to heal faster, and he didn't like to rely on his wife and children.

Katie nodded in response to her dad's statement as she turned onto the highway. "I'm heading over there tonight to watch over the cougar cubs I found two evenings ago."

Her dad frowned. "Don't wear yourself out, Katie. You shouldn't be hauling me around if you're going to be watching baby animals all night."

"I have time to take a quick nap between your appointment and when I have to leave for the zoo."

Her dad made a *hrmph* sound in the back of his throat as he sank into the passenger seat. If Katie hadn't been driving, she would have leaned over and kissed him on the cheek. Her ability to charm her dad had always irritated Katie's four brothers. While growing up, she'd wanted to trade one of the twins for a sister, but there'd been advantages to being the only girl.

"You're working too hard taking care of me," her dad grumbled.

"Dad, I'm glad to get out of the house and Sagebrush for a little bit. While you're doing physical therapy, I'll be having fun shopping. Besides, it's always good to have some father-daughter bonding time."

Her father's chuckle turned into a cough and then a wince of pain as he folded his arms over his chest.

Katie jerked her head in his direction but quickly returned her attention to the road before her dad could catch her. He hated when she and her mother hovered. It invariably led to a declaration about him not being a wounded animal to fuss over. Since it wasn't good for his healing body to get worked up, Katie just gripped the steering wheel tighter.

When her father spoke again, his voice sounded a little strained. "After all the time you've been spending with me, you'd need a crowbar to pry us apart if we bond anymore."

Katie shook her head. "Dad, I've been gone for over a decade. I'm glad for this chance to catch up with you and Mom, even if it didn't start under the best circumstances."

Her dad carefully cleared his throat. "It was a good thing that you did for your mother and me, moving back here. I don't know how we could have gotten through this without you. I know it wasn't easy when I first came home—all those bandages you helped your mother change and the errands you ran for us."

"It's nothing, Dad," Katie said. "You and Mom have always been there for me and the boys. It's time we did our parts."

"I wish you hadn't had to quit your job."

Katie sighed. This wasn't the first time she'd had this conversation with her father. She knew it bothered him that she'd dropped everything to take care of him. She couldn't quite get through to him that there hadn't been that much *to drop*. "Dad, I could have taken FMLA leave, but it was time for me to move on. That job hadn't made me happy in years, and the shooting…it gave me the push that I needed. I should have done this years ago."

Her dad was quiet for a moment before he spoke.

"Have you thought about sticking around? Your mother and I will be happy with whatever you decide, but it's been nice having you here, even if I don't like being the reason."

"I don't know," Katie said truthfully. "There isn't enough work in Sagebrush for a business. I'd have to get other clients over the internet."

"Katie, you always could do anything you put your mind to."

To her horror, Katie felt tears sting the back of her eyes before she chased them away. Her dad had always believed in her, and so had her mom. But for years now, Katie had felt like she'd let them down. She'd done so well at Sagebrush High and then in college, but her life had stalled while working at the mulch plant.

"I thought I'd be living in a major city by this age," Katie admitted.

"Have you tried sending out your résumé?" her dad asked.

Katie nodded. "Every now and then, I take a look at job postings, but I haven't really buckled down and submitted tons of applications. That changes now. I'm planning to build up my portfolio this summer and then start to look for a job in earnest this fall. That will give me plenty of time to research what advertising firms I want to apply to."

"Have you tried talking to Josh?" her dad asked, referring to Katie's other best friend from college. "Isn't he some tech wiz? Maybe he could put in a good word for you with some of his clients. Don't you do some work for him?"

"Yes," Katie said. "I draw a comic that he posts on his cybersecurity firm's website. His clients enjoy it."

"Then you definitely should see if he has any connections you can use."

Katie sighed. "I don't know, Dad. It feels like cheating."

Her dad chuckled again, but Katie noticed he did so cautiously. "Most police chiefs' daughters try to rebel a bit. You always went the opposite direction."

Katie shrugged. "I like rules. Rules are safe."

"Katie, I may have spent my whole career on the same police force, but even there, we had politics. People network all the time. It's no different than neighbor calling upon neighbor here in Sagebrush. Talk to Josh. See if he can help you."

Katie thought about her dad's suggestion. Josh had offered in the past to do just that. Maybe it was time to let him.

Her father paused a beat and then asked, "Are you sure, kiddo, that you want to live in a place like San Francisco or New York?" The serious note in Chief Underwood's voice caused Katie to stiffen. She felt her eyebrows draw down.

"Yes," she said. "I've been dreaming about it since high school."

Her dad didn't speak for a moment. When he did, his tone was thoughtful. "I've always heard you talking about big cities like they were prizes, not places where you wanted to live."

"What do you mean?"

"Did you know that I once was offered a job as a policeman in Denver?"

Katie swung to her dad in surprise. "No, I didn't know."

Her dad shrugged. "It happened before you were born. Luke was just a baby. Your mom said I could take the position even though it meant living away from both our parents. And I almost did. But then I realized something. I didn't want to be a big city cop. I just wanted to say I was a big city cop."

"Ahh," Katie said as her dad's point became clear.

"Once I figured that out, I never regretted my decision to stay."

"Do you think you would have enjoyed living in Denver?"

Her dad gave that careful chuckle again. "Hell no. Sagebrush is home for me and your mother. Always was. Always will be. That doesn't mean it has to be for you, but I don't want you dashing off to a big city just because you think you have something to prove."

Katie fell silent as she mulled over her dad's words. She'd never really thought about why she wanted to live in a West or East Coast city. Whenever she'd headed to downtown Minneapolis, she'd always felt a thrill of excitement—this sense that she'd arrived. But how long would that feeling last if she moved to a place like that? Was her dad right? Was she just chasing after a flashy piece of fool's gold?

Her dad reached over and patted her arm. "Think it over, kiddo. You're starting with a clean slate, and you might want to give some thought about exactly what type of picture you want to draw."

Katie nodded. Regardless of the path she ultimately chose, her short-term goal remained the same. She needed to improve her own brand. Prospective employers and clients would want to see her work, and she needed to find opportunities in Sagebrush right now... even if that meant working closely with Bowie Wilson.

—⁓—

Katie managed to grab an hour nap after she and her dad returned home from his physical therapy. Her mom, being her mom, had packed Katie a snack to take with her for her first night with the cubs. As Katie walked across the zoo grounds, she felt transported back to grade school. The place hadn't changed much. While not run-down, it teetered on the edge. Even back in the nineties, the buildings had felt like outdated throwbacks to the seventies. Only the obvious care that went into the upkeep saved the zoo from being a ramshackle mess. Someone had planted cheerful, inexpensive impatiens in big barrel-shaped planters, and the grass was meticulously mowed. Although the facilities might not have been freshly painted, there were no unsightly signs of disrepair.

The zoo, at least, didn't lack for space. The animal enclosures might look simple and utilitarian, but they weren't the small cages Katie had seen in history books. She spotted several llamas and a camel chowing down on hay. At her approach, they all turned simultaneously to stare at her, but they didn't pause in their chewing. Instead, the six of them stared at her with their liquid-brown eyes as they continued to move their lower jaws side to side in perfect unison. Bits of straw dangled from their mouths as they watched her intently. Although the llamas remained otherwise as still as sentries, the camel emitted a rumbling grunt. With a silly smile on its long face, it ambled over to Katie on long, knobby legs.

"Hi there," she said softly, pausing by the wooden rails of its pen.

The camel blinked its long lashes at her. As if in greeting, it rolled back its lips and made a raspberry sound. Then, it stuck its chin over the top of the fence in clear demand. Katie reached out and scratched the animal on its fuzzy head, its fur coarse beneath her fingers. The animal breathed out a contented sound before it shuffled back to the hay bale. Katie waved goodbye, but the camel's attention had returned to its food.

When Katie next walked past a grizzly, the bear lifted her massive head and emitted a half-hearted sound between a grunt and a growl. The fur around her face was white, and one eye had gone rheumy. She looked so much like a grumpy old dog that Katie had to resist the urge to scratch the displeased bear between her ears as she'd done with the camel. Katie didn't think the grizzly would appreciate the gesture, though. As soon as Katie passed the fence, the old gal laid her head back on her enormous paws with a beleaguered sigh.

Behind the bear's enclosure stood the main zoo facility. Via an earlier text message, Bowie had directed Katie to a small building attached to the back. Pulling back the door to the structure, she found a gangly, preteen girl sitting cross-legged on the floor. In the volunteer's arms was one of the cougar cubs, eagerly sucking on a bottle. The other two snuggled against a medium-sized animal that looked rather like a plump kidney bean on stubby legs.

The girl glanced up at Katie's entrance, and

immediately, a wide smile spread across her elfin face. For some odd reason, the child looked vaguely familiar to Katie, which made no sense. The girl would have been born shortly after Katie had left Sagebrush Flats for college. Since Katie had rarely visited in the intervening years, she would have had little opportunity to meet the youngster.

"You must be Ms. Underwood," the girl said cheerfully. "I'm Abby."

Ms. Underwood? Now she really felt old. "You can just call me Katie," she instructed.

The girl nodded and inclined her head to the cougar cub in her arms. "This is Tonks. Fleur and Dobby are sleeping on Sylvia the capybara. Sylvia likes to cuddle all the orphans."

Katie blinked at the rapid fire of information. Her brain settled on the first tidbit the girl had lobbed at her. "The cubs are named after Harry Potter characters?"

The girl beamed brightly. "You're a Harry Potter fan too!"

Katie nodded. "One of the originals."

"I love the books," Abby gushed. "My dad used to read them to me when I was little, but I've read the whole series myself tons of times."

"Who named the cubs?" Katie settled down next to Abby, who she guessed was about ten or eleven.

"I did," the preteen said proudly.

"They're good choices."

The girl beamed, but before she could respond further, one of the sleeping cubs began to stir. Its tiny nose twitched as it began to root against the capybara in a fruitless search for milk. Although almost two days had passed, the cubs' eyes remained closed. The poor

little tyke had trouble finding traction on the lino-
leum floor, and his hind legs splayed out behind
him. Sylvia lifted her head and gently nuzzled the
small kit. The baby puma quieted for just a moment
before opening its pink mouth to utter a demanding mew. The capybara swung her large head to fix
Abby with an imploring look.

Abby laughed. "Dobby is hungry now too.
Would you like to feed him? I helped Lou mix up
the bottle sitting on the counter."

"I'd love to," Katie said, quickly rising to her
feet. She lost no time grabbing the bottle and scoop-
ing up the wiggling little fur ball. Katie settled down
beside the girl, and the preteen showed her how to
hold the cub properly. As soon as Katie placed the
rubber nipple in the kit's mouth, he began to suck
eagerly, the sound echoing in the utilitarian room.
Katie laughed as Abby giggled.

"You must volunteer here a lot," Katie said.

Abby nodded solemnly. "I help out all the time.
I want to be a veterinarian or a zoologist."

"Ah, you're an animal lover then," Katie said.

"I love them! I'm glad it's summer, so I can
hang out here more. I like school okay, but the
other kids..."

Abby suddenly trailed off as if realizing what
she was about to admit to a stranger. When Abby
shot her an embarrassed look, Katie recognized the
expression, because she had felt it too. Too many
times to count, in fact. The pain of not fitting in,
no matter how hard she'd tried. Of always saying
or doing something that set her apart. Of just not

understanding what seemed to come so naturally to everyone else.

Instantly, Katie realized the reason for part of Abby's passion for animals. In some ways, it wasn't much different than what had driven Katie to sketch daring princesses and heroic princes in her school notebooks as she dreamed of escape.

"You know, when I was your age, I preferred drawing to hanging out with other kids."

Abby leaned forward as if Katie had just spilled a shocking secret. "You did?"

"Yeah," Katie said, holding the younger girl's gaze over the nursing cougar kits. "The characters in my sketches never picked on me or called me names. They were easy to interact with. No secrets, no whispering, no mean jokes. Animals are pretty much the same, aren't they?"

"You were made fun of too?" Abby asked. "For being smart?"

Katie nodded, but Abby didn't seem entirely convinced. "You don't look like you'd be picked on."

Katie laughed and had the strange urge to ruffle the girl's hair. "Are you saying that I don't look smart?"

Horror crossed Abby's face, and she quickly shook her head. "No, it's not that. You look pretty, like a popular girl."

Katie shrugged. "Well, you know the story *The Ugly Duckling*? That could have been about me."

"When I was little and the girls in first grade were mean, Dad read me that book. I don't think I'll turn into a swan. I think I'll stay ugly forever. Dad says I'm pretty, but he has to. He's my dad." When Abby spoke, she focused on Tonks, gently stroking the kit's grayish-brown fur.

"My dad always told me the same thing. It turns out he was right, and your dad is too," Katie said. Abby looked like any other cute eleven-year-old girl with petite features, jet-black hair, and gray eyes. Her problem was the same Katie's had been. She simply didn't care about her appearance. Although Katie didn't know much about preteen fashions, she highly doubted oversized T-shirts and baggy, boyish jeans were popular. The girl's short bob was too bluntly cut and her glasses a touch out of style.

Abby made a face. Clearly, she didn't believe Katie any more than she did her father. "I don't care if I don't turn into a swan. I'd rather be successful. Dad always repeats a saying about being nice to geeks 'cause you might work for them. I like that better than *The Ugly Duckling*."

"So did I," Katie said, and then she leaned in conspiratorially, "but you know what? You can be the pretty girl *and* the smart one."

Abby frowned skeptically. Katie didn't blame her. She sensed in Abby a true kindred spirit. "All through public school, I believed that I had to choose between being intelligent or being popular. Then I met my college roommate, June Winters, and she showed me that I could be smart and have fun wearing girlie clothes."

Abby bounced with excitement, almost upsetting the cougar cub in her lap. Tonks emitted a disgruntled squeak but calmed when Abby brushed a hand over the kit's fur.

"You're friends with Miss Winters? She comes to my Girl Scout troop to give talks about the places she's been. When she was little, she grew up all over the world 'cause her dad was in the air force. She has all this cool stuff from Korea and Germany!"

Katie nodded, unable to hold back a grin at the girl's obvious excitement. "Yep. The one and only June Winters."

"I love her stories," Abby practically shouted as she clutched the little cougar to her chest. "Someday, when I grow up, I'm going to visit those places. My dad and I don't have a lot of money, but he says that it shouldn't stop us from experiencing other cultures. When there's a place that I really like where Miss Winters lived or that I learn about in school, my dad and I look it up on the internet or get books out of the library. We find recipes from there and try them out. My dad does most of the cooking. He's really good at it."

Abby's dad was starting to sound more and more interesting. Since Abby had mentioned her father several times and not her mother, Katie suspected that Abby's mom wasn't in the picture. Now, why couldn't Katie's mother try to set her up with someone like Abby's dad? Someone who read his daughter Harry Potter books and cooked her international dishes so she could explore the world even when stuck in Sagebrush Flats. Now that was the kind of man who would interest Katie.

"Dad!" Abby sang out just as Katie heard the door open behind her. "Katie came early. Oh, and she told me to call her Katie, not Ms. Underwood."

Katie swung around, eager to meet Abby's father—only to have her eyes fall upon Bowie Wilson.

Chapter 3

KATIE GLANCED QUICKLY BACK AT ABBY IN confusion. Then suddenly, everything gelled in her mind. No wonder Abby looked familiar. She was a perfect blend of Sawyer Johnson and Bowie Wilson. If Abby hadn't inherited Bowie's coloring, she would be an exact doppelgänger of Sawyer. Of course, even at eleven, Sawyer would never have worn such frumpy clothes. She would have painted her nails, styled her hair, and accessorized.

Any daughter raised by Sawyer would look like a fashionista. Abby did not. That, even more than Abby's stories, left Katie with no doubt that Sawyer had absolutely no part in Abby's life. That didn't surprise Katie. She had known Sawyer for thirteen years, and nothing in her character had indicated that she would put her life on hold for an unexpected teenage pregnancy.

What stunned Katie was that Bowie had. He was obviously doing an excellent job at single parenting. Sure, she had only spent a handful of minutes with Abby, but anyone listening to her talk about her dad could sense the solidness of their bond. Abby might have trouble fitting in at school, but she possessed the confidence of a child who'd grown up in a stable environment, who simply accepted her parent's love as automatic and natural.

Katie couldn't reconcile the boy who'd tormented her with the father who stood before her now.

"Katie's really nice," Abby told her dad cheerfully.

"Is that so?" Bowie shot Katie a warm smile.

Her stomach flip-flopped—the traitorous organ. She really should have developed an immunity to Bowie's charming good looks, but at the age of twenty-nine, she couldn't blame teenage hormones this time.

Abby nodded. "We're a lot alike. She says kids teased her in school too."

Bowie's gaze flew to Katie. His look—both panicked and protective—seared her. Over Abby's head, Katie gave a quick negative shake to indicate that she had not exposed him as her bully. A tick of irritation struck her. Did the man really believe she would use a child to enact revenge?

Bowie relaxed marginally and turned his attention back to his daughter. "It's getting late."

Abby treated her father to a look that only a preteen could achieve with such perfection—the adorable pout. "Can I stay with the cougars a little longer, *puh-leese*? I think Sylvia needs a break, and I don't mind cuddling the babies for a while." As if on cue, the capybara lifted her head a couple of inches from the floor as if she didn't have the strength to raise it any farther. Her huge, almond-shaped black eyes mirrored the pleading look in Abby's. Tonks, the cub on Abby's lap, emitted a sigh-like sound as it nestled closer to the girl.

Katie probably would have caved. Bowie didn't. Instead, he reached out and ruffled Abby's hair. "Sorry, kiddo. No can do."

"Will you at least read me a story tonight?" Abby asked.

Katie could see by the slight change in Bowie's expression that this question affected him.

"Not tonight, sweetheart. Lou will have to put you to bed again. I can't leave Katie alone with the cubs on her first night. I promise, though, that I will tomorrow."

Abby looked a little crestfallen, but she didn't argue. "Pinkie swear?"

Bowie crouched and crooked his little finger. "Pinkie swear."

Then, in what had to be one of the top ten surreal moments of Katie's life, she witnessed her high school's biggest jerk pinkie swear with his adorable daughter. Was this the same man who had run Katie's bra up the school's flagpole after his girlfriend had stolen it from her gym bag? Bowie wasn't just the fun parent either. The dispute about Abby's bedtime showed that he set rules for his daughter and enforced them. The scene grew sweeter as Abby laid Tonks back down on Sylvia and flung her arms around Bowie for a good-night hug. He planted a quick kiss on the girl's head before she skipped out of the building.

"If you need to walk her home, I'm sure I'll be fine with the cubs for a little bit," Katie said.

Bowie shook his head, and Katie thought his voice seemed a little strained when he said, "No need. We live on the property, and Lou's expecting her."

She was about to ask where on the property they lived when Bowie whirled on her. Like heat lightning in July, anger flashed over his features, and Katie realized why his voice had sounded odd—constrained ire.

"What the hell game are you trying to play?"

Katie met his blast of fury with icy indignation. "I don't know. The kind where I volunteer to help you and your zoo?"

Bowie took a threatening step toward her. "Look, I'll do practically any humiliating thing you ask me to do. I probably owe you that, but keep my daughter out of this."

Katie didn't back up. In fact, she moved forward. Although she wasn't a short woman, Bowie still had a few inches on her. That didn't matter. She jutted her chin and met his angry expression with one of her own.

"I think you've forgotten who is the master at manipulation and mind games," she shot back at him. "I'm not so twisted or vindictive that I'd prey on a little girl's emotions."

"Then why did you bring up high school?"

Katie didn't even try to stop her aggravated sigh. "I didn't bring up high school! Do you think I go around terrifying elementary students with how horrible middle school and high school can be? 'Hey, kids, you think getting picked on now is bad, wait a couple of years and that boy you like will steal your journal so that his girlfriend can read your most private thoughts aloud during a school-wide talent show.'"

Bowie had the grace to wince, but he didn't back down. "Why did you tell her about being picked on?"

"First of all, I didn't know she was your daughter."

That news calmed him slightly, but he didn't appear convinced. "She looks like Sawyer and me."

Katie delivered her driest expression. "I see that now,

but I wasn't expecting you to have a kid. Sure, she looked familiar, but I couldn't place her. It's been over ten years since I last saw Sawyer."

Bowie's muscles started to uncoil. He rubbed his hand over the back of his skull—a tic that Katie remembered from high school. All through her freshman and most of her sophomore year, she used to covertly watch him make that gesture and imagine running her own fingers through his hair.

"Why did you bring it up?"

Katie exhaled. "I didn't... At least I wasn't the one who introduced the topic. Abby indicated that she liked working with the animals because they didn't make fun of her like the kids at school. I saw a fellow nerd, and I empathized. I told her that I used to sketch fantasy characters for the same reason, and I tried to tell her that things got better. I don't know. I guess I was trying to build her confidence."

At her words, Bowie froze, his expression almost comical as he realized his screwup. A cocktail of emotions swirled in his gray eyes—dismay, contrition, and a touch of embarrassment. Back in high school, Katie had dreamed of eliciting just such an expression.

She couldn't help it. A smug smile tugged at her lips. After all he'd put her through in the past, the man deserved to squirm a little.

⁓

Bowie was a first-class a-hole. Again.

He shouldn't have flipped out. He knew it, but his protective instincts had surged into overdrive.

Abby had always been vulnerable about how her class-mates treated her. He had no idea how to help. Although he'd never been wildly popular until he'd hooked up with Sawyer, he'd also never been picked on. Yeah, sure, through the years, there'd been some boys who tried to talk trash, but his fists had always been able to take care of that. However, he didn't think that telling his daughter to slug the other girls in her class would resolve any-thing. So he just comforted her the best he could when she came home in tears. The last thing he needed was Abby learning that he'd been a bully himself.

"Uh, look, I'm sorry about that," he told Katie. "I shouldn't have jumped to conclusions."

"No, you shouldn't have," she said crisply as she petted the cougar cub in her arms. By the large splash of black between the cub's tiny ears, Bowie identified it as the male that his daughter had named Dobby.

"Abby has a hard time with the kids at school. I don't think it would help if she knew what a jerk-off I used to be. I don't want to see her hurt any more than she already is," Bowie confessed.

Katie's face softened as she watched him with a seri-ous expression. "Bowie, there is a lot of nasty history between the two of us, but I would never drag your child into it. She's off-limits. I get that."

"Thanks."

"You don't have to thank me. For whatever reason, you seem like a great dad, and your daughter clearly looks up to you. I wouldn't jeopardize that…for her sake."

Strong emotion clamped down on Bowie's heart with the force of one of Fluffy's bites. From the moment that he'd first held his daughter, he'd promised himself he

would turn his life around for her. Growing up shut-
tled between his messed-up parents and foster care,
he'd had no idea how to provide a stable home. Lou
and Gretchen had helped him, and loving Abby had
always just come naturally.

There were moments, though, when Bowie wondered if he was handling everything right.

Since Gretchen had died over six years ago,
Abby hadn't had any female influence. Other than
Lou, Bowie didn't have anyone to turn to for advice
on raising Abby. Although Lou was an incredible
man, he'd never been a father before either.

Katie Underwood didn't like Bowie. She might
even detest him. He had, unfortunately, given her
plenty of cause. She had no reason to praise him
and every incentive to criticize him.

When she called him a great dad, she meant it.

Those words counted. A lot. Even when Bowie
had teased Katie in high school, a part of him had
always admired her. No matter how mean the tricks
had become, she had never flinched—not once
that he'd seen anyway. He couldn't recall her ever
crying. She hadn't changed her personality either.
If anything, she'd become more unabashedly nerdy.
During the two weeks that he'd pretended to date
her, he recalled her being incredibly straightfor-
ward, not like most people in his life. She had also
graduated first in their class.

So, yeah, Katie's opinion mattered.

"Abby's a good kid," he heard himself say
gruffly. "She makes parenting easy."

Katie laughed, a bright sound that created

an odd ripple effect inside Bowie. It made him feel
strangely lighter.

"From what I hear, being a parent is never completely
easy. And speaking of taking care of babies, what am I
supposed to do with these cubs?"

Grateful for the change of subject, Bowie eagerly
switched into his zoo director role. Here, he felt more in
control, more balanced. He showed Katie where to find
the formula and the supplies for mixing more. Then he
demonstrated how to feed the cubs properly. Since the
little guys were only about a week old, it was important
that all four paws remained on the ground and that the
caregiver supported the kit's head and neck to prevent
milk from traveling down the windpipe. He also showed
Katie how to massage their bellies to encourage them to
go to the bathroom. In order to make sure the cubs were
staying healthy, he and Lou kept a detailed record of their
eating times, along with when they urinated and defecated.

"Sylvia is our capybara," Bowie told Katie. "When
you're done feeding the cubs, put them on her belly. She's
got an amazing maternal instinct and has been a foster mom
to a lot of the zoo's orphaned and abandoned young. We've
got a couple of coyotes who think they're capybaras. Sylvia
raised them from pups after a local rancher shot their mom
for stalking his sheep and killing his chickens."

"What is a capybara exactly?" Katie asked as she
walked over to scratch Sylvia on the forehead. The
animal gave a sigh of happiness as she twitched the tiny
ears situated on top of her large head.

"She's a hundred-pound rodent, but don't tell Sylvia.
She thinks she's a pet dog. In fact, other zoos typically
use rescue dogs to nurture abandoned babies. A few years

back, when orphaned coyote pups were dropped off at the zoo by the Fish and Wildlife Service, I went to the animal shelter to pick up a female Lab mix. It turned out the dog had been adopted, but Sylvia was there. Her owners had bought her as a pup. They hadn't realized how much she'd weigh as an adult or that she'd chew up their furniture to wear down her sharp teeth. I knew we could give her a better life, so I brought her back to the zoo. I'd heard that capybaras got along well with other species, so I introduced her to the coyote pups. Sylvia immediately trotted over and started nuzzling them. She's been helping take care of our zoo babies ever since."

When Bowie finished, he found Katie watching him with a penetrating expression. He really wished she'd stop doing that. In the last twenty-four hours, he'd been visually dissected more than a science experiment gone awry.

"Do you have any questions about taking care of the cougars?" he asked her, hoping that he didn't sound defensive.

She shook her head. "Not about taking care of the cubs. You were very thorough...surprisingly thorough. You really know your stuff, don't you?"

Bowie shrugged, once again feeling slightly uncomfortable with her praise. "I get by."

"How did you become a director of a zoo?" Katie asked. "It's not exactly how I pictured your life when we graduated from high school."

No, she'd probably imagined him behind bars. Everyone else had. Like father, like son.

Hell, like mother, like son.

Ironically—or maybe poetically—a criminal act had led him to working for Lou in the first place, but he didn't relish telling Katie that story. She had already witnessed enough of his bad side without delving into his juvenile-delinquent behavior. But Bowie had never hidden his past. He had realized long ago that if he ever wanted to truly leave it behind, he couldn't simply bury it. He had to confront it and hope like hell that he'd learned something.

"I got my start here after I tagged the place."

"Tagged?" Katie asked in momentary confusion, and then her expression cleared. "You mean spray-painted it with graffiti?"

He nodded. "I'd done stuff like that before. Been busted for it, but that was the first time as an adult." He'd actually been caught by her father, but he didn't think now was the time to reveal that. She might take it as a criticism that he didn't intend. He'd broken the law, vandalized people's property, including Lou's, and her dad had just done his job.

"Why'd you do it?" To his surprise, Katie didn't sound particularly accusatory, just honestly befuddled.

"Tag in general or the zoo in particular?"

She shrugged. "Both, I guess. I mean, I never understood graffiti myself. Some of it is pretty artistic, true, and I can see painting a mural on an abandoned building. What I don't get, though, is why anyone would want to vandalize someone else's property."

Because they were a lost kid who was desperate to leave a lasting mark, for someone to pay attention.

Bowie gave her the easiest, most direct answer. "I tagged the zoo the night after I found out Sawyer was pregnant."

Katie's eyes grew wide, and he thought he might even have detected a glimmer of understanding. No matter, he'd succeeded in silencing her.

"Sawyer broke up with me. Said I'd ruined her life."

It had been an ugly scene. Sawyer—a drama queen under normal circumstances—had vacillated between screaming and crying uncontrollably. She had wanted to abort the baby, but her parents had found the pregnancy test and threatened to cut her off if she terminated the pregnancy. At first, Bowie had just stood there, trying to absorb the fact that he was going to be a father. When Sawyer started hurling the contents of her purse at him, he'd finally snapped out of his stupor. He'd tried to comfort her, but his attempts had only escalated the situation.

When Bowie had told Sawyer that he'd be there for her and the baby, she'd laughed at him—not hysterically, but cruelly. He'd heard that laugh countless times when Sawyer made fun of yet another classmate, but she'd never directed it at him. Then Sawyer asked just how a piece of homeless white trash like him could ever provide for her and a child.

Since he'd been kicked out of his foster home only a week before on his eighteenth birthday, the words had stung. He had been camping out as he tried to find another job in addition to his part-time gig at a local burger joint.

But Bowie didn't want to reveal those particular details to Katie. Even all these years later, he couldn't shake the shame of it all. So he opted to tell her the CliffsNotes version.

"I lifted a can of spray paint from an open garage after Sawyer told me the news." His ex-foster family's, but he also wasn't getting into that. "I passed the zoo, saw all the buildings, and well…all that rage had to come out somewhere."

"Did you break any windows or trash the place?" Katie asked.

Bowie shook his head sharply, glad he could at least honestly deny that. "Naw, I never got into stuff like that. I always stopped at tagging."

It had been enough for him just to leave a mark.

"So what happened next?"

"I got caught. Hauled into the police station. For the first time, it freaked me out. I was eighteen, and I was going to be a father." He'd felt as useless as Sawyer had accused him of being.

"Did it scare you straight?" Katie asked.

"I don't know," Bowie answered honestly. "I don't know what I would have done if it hadn't been for Lou. He told the police that he wanted to talk to me before he pressed charges. He was well regarded in the community, so they let him. And do you know what he did?"

Katie shook her head.

"He looked me in the eye, and he asked me why I did it. Not rhetorically. Not as an accusation, but as an honest question. No adult had ever done that before… given me the benefit of the doubt. So I told him everything. I don't think I meant to, but once I started to explain, everything just sort of poured out.

"Afterward, Lou sat silent for a while. Then he looked at me and asked point-blank whether or not I wanted to be a father. I thought for a bit and told him the truth…that I wanted to be, but that I didn't know how. Then he gave me a choice. He'd said he'd drop the charges if I agreed to clean up the spray paint. If I did that well, he'd give me a full-time job."

"Lou sounds like a pretty amazing guy."

Bowie didn't even try to stop the fond smile that curved his lips. "Yeah, and his late wife, Gretchen, was one terrific lady. They ended up giving me much more than a second chance. Without them, I might not have Abby today. Sawyer's parents and Sawyer wanted to give Abby up for adoption in another state. Lou and Gretchen helped me find a lawyer, and they even footed the bill. They couldn't have kids of their own, so they took me in and then Abby."

"What about your parents?" Katie asked.

Obviously, she had never listened to school gossip. By the time he'd turned seventeen, Bowie had been a true orphan—not just a ward of the state. His mom had OD'd when he was fourteen, and his father was killed in a prison brawl at the state pen three years later. If Katie didn't know, he didn't feel like enlightening her. He'd always hated people's reactions. They looked at him with pity, horror, or disgust.

"Out of the picture," Bowie said. Katie appeared to be mulling whether she should pepper him with another question, so he quickly asked one of his own.

"So what about you, Underwood?" he asked. "What have you been up to these past ten years or so?"

"I went away to college, then got a job designing packaging for a mulch plant in Minnesota. It was literally located in the middle of a forest. The nearest city was Duluth, but Minneapolis was two hours away."

Bowie had never been farther east than the Rockies or west of the Sierra Nevadas. Except for an occasional trip to pick up an animal for the zoo, he generally didn't travel farther than fifty miles from Sagebrush Flats. He could tell from Katie's voice that she hadn't thought much of the location of her job, but he envied and admired her for leaving their dusty hometown behind for a while. Less than two hours outside a major city like Minneapolis didn't sound half bad to him.

"Why'd you come home?"

"My father was shot in the chest," Katie said as Bowie nodded sympathetically. Although she spoke the words easily enough, he could see the vestiges of fear and pain swimming in the brown depths of her eyes. Something turned and squeezed inside him. He didn't like seeing Red like this. Worried. Upset. He much preferred the woman who'd scaled the rock face to rescue cougar cubs, even if she'd been as mad as hell at him the whole time.

"I'm sorry." He had said those words to her before, but there really were no others.

For a moment, tears glistened in Katie's eyes, and Bowie had to fight the urge to gather her in his arms.

"I am too. It's been hard on all of us, but especially my mom. I think we'll all feel better when his attacker is caught."

"I heard about the manhunt."

"Yeah, the state police are doing their best, but he's still on the loose," Katie said, and Bowie heard the worry in her voice.

"You said yesterday that your dad was doing better?"

"Yes, his physical therapist is really pleased with his progress. He's also sleeping through the night now, and his bandages don't need to be changed quite as often."

Bowie studied Katie with concern. She didn't look exhausted, but maybe she hid it well. "Are you sure you're up to taking care of the cubs? I'll do the pig-kissing video if you'll still agree not to charge me your full fee until we get more revenue."

She shook her head. "No. Dad's doing well enough that Mom no longer needs me 24/7. I've never required much sleep, and I can do my design work while I'm here. It'll be good for me to take care of something cute and cuddly."

Bowie studied her. Not many daughters would give up their jobs and move home to help their mom take care of their invalid father. Katie was, he realized, just a generally good person. Not for the first time today, he wished he'd realized that in high school. He would have done much better if he'd dated a stabilizing person like her rather than destructive Sawyer. But then Abby wouldn't have been born, and he'd date a thousand Sawyers if it meant having his daughter in his life.

"Are you planning on sticking around Sagebrush Flats?" Bowie asked. To his surprise, he found that her answer mattered to him, which was asinine. After what he'd done to her, she'd never consider dating him, even if he wasn't on the brink of financial disaster.

Katie shook her head. "I'm not sure. Right now, I'm trying to get as much freelance work as I can. Hopefully, after I build up my portfolio this summer, I can get a job in a big city if I want. LA. New York. The Bay Area would be nice. Housing costs are insane in San Francisco, but one of my best friends from college lives out there and would let me crash at his place. It's a nice one, since he's done really well as an IT security consultant."

Unbidden jealousy seared through Bowie. Before he could think better of it, he blurted out, "He?"

He must have spoken more sharply than he'd intended, because Katie shot him a sidelong glance, not that he blamed her. He had absolutely no right or even reason to act jealous. He and Katie had just reconnected today, and they hadn't been exactly on the best of terms twelve years ago. Plus, Bowie was fairly certain that he was on the short list of men that she would never, ever date—even if stranded on a desert island or if the fate of humanity rested on them procreating. In fact, he knew he would hear one of those lines if he even hinted about them meeting each other for a casual lunch.

He decided the best way to fix his blunder was to change the subject. "Well, I'm glad you're in town for the moment. Your marketing plan for the zoo sounds great, and I really do appreciate your volunteering."

Katie gave him a smile. This one was easy, without a barbed edge in sight. "At least I get some long-overdue payback out of it."

"Glad to be of service."

"Yeah... Well, I did check the website. Thanks for posting the pig-kissing announcement."

"Red river hog," Bowie corrected with a grin of his

own. "Daisy might get insulted. She's very particular about these things."

Before he could say more, his mouth stretched open into a yawn. Although he tried to stop it, he didn't quite succeed.

"You look exhausted," Katie said.

Bowie started to shake his head, but another yawn caught him. Katie's expression softened, and she motioned to the air mattress he'd set up in the room. "Go to sleep. I'll wake you if I run into any trouble with the cubs."

Bowie didn't fight her. He hadn't operated on this little sleep since Abby's infancy. It didn't help that the honey badger kept escaping his enclosure. Luckily, Abby had been able to capture the animal relatively quickly, since the stubborn creature actually listened to her. But Abby wasn't always around to corral Fluffy, so even after barely sleeping for two nights in a row, Bowie had forced himself to finish digging the trench on the west side of the pen. He'd somehow managed to also find the energy to pour the concrete required to finish the project.

At least with this round of sleepless nights, Bowie didn't have the additional worry that Abby's nighttime crying would eventually cause Lou and Gretchen to kick them out. Of course, now he realized that Lou and Gretchen never would have ordered or even asked him to leave, but back then, he'd assumed they'd treat him like his parents and foster parents had. He'd memorized each creaky floorboard so he'd make the minimal amount of noise possible while nervously pacing to lull Abby

back to sleep. Eventually, he'd realized that Lou and
Gretchen saw Abby as their grandchild and would never
abandon her or—to his surprise—him.

Now, though, the zoo's precarious financial situation
gave Bowie a whole different set of stressors. This time,
he didn't just have Abby and himself to take care of, but
Lou and all the animals. He'd pull through for them. He
had to.

———~~~———

Katie watched out of the corner of her eyes as Bowie
finally crashed. She hadn't exaggerated. He looked
bone-weary. Between his drawn features and the presence of the air mattress in the room, she deduced he'd
spent the last forty-eight hours caring for the cubs. She
hadn't thought she could ever feel anything but loathing
for her high school nemesis, but she had to admit to a bit
of grudging respect and sympathy.

As much as she looked forward to repaying him for
his old pranks, she didn't want to torture the guy. The
stunts she was planning might mildly embarrass him,
but they wouldn't scar—not like his had. And Bowie
had always possessed a healthy self-confidence, even to
the point of arrogance. She doubted that even the cruelest prank would faze him, and she planned on keeping
hers lighthearted.

Smiling, Katie hunkered down for the night. Booting
up her computer and inserting her earbuds, she plunged
into overhauling the website. The current one was barely
navigable. There was no point in creating marketing
material if no one could find it.

The night passed quickly. She hooked up the cubs'

webcam just in time for their first feeding. Tonks woke up first, and Katie gently lifted the little girl from Sylvia. Bowie had built the cubs a den in the corner of the nursery. The handmade crate was raised slightly off the floor and had a mesh bottom that made cleaning easier and kept the cubs dry. Sylvia could get in and out as long as the door was open, and the whole contraption moved easily.

With Sylvia helping to calm Fleur and Dobby, Katie managed to stick the nipple in Tonks's mouth before she woke Bowie with her chirping. The cougar drank lustily, which Bowie had told her was a good sign. After Tonks had her fill, Katie carefully recorded the amount. It surprised her that Bowie and Lou still kept physical notes, but the zoo seemed behind on technology.

Katie picked up Fleur next, and the tiny cub snuggled in to her. Midway through the bottle, Fleur started to fall back asleep, but Katie stroked the kit's cheek with her finger, just as Bowie had instructed her. It worked, and Fleur began to suck greedily once more. Katie cuddled the cub against her shoulder for a little bit before placing her back on Sylvia and reaching for Dobby. The male cub ate happily. When she returned him to Sylvia, he yawned and fell promptly to sleep.

With the cougars slumbering peacefully, Katie headed back to her computer to work on the website. When her computer monitor showed that four o'clock was approaching, she glanced over at Bowie. The man appeared haggard even in slumber, and she couldn't bring herself to wake him.

With a sigh, she tried to return her concentration to the website, but she found her eyes drifting back to Bowie. For five long years starting in middle school, she had imagined herself in love with him. In her mind, she had created a character just as vivid and as unreal as her old sketches of fairy-tale princes. Then he had systematically obliterated any heroic attributes that she'd ever ascribed to him.

In the last two and a half years of high school, he'd become the cruel but beautiful villain. A modern Dracula. In the intervening years—when she'd thought of Bowie at all—she'd pictured him as a slick, womanizing con artist or a bookie. It wasn't any surprise that the antagonists she had drawn through the years had always possessed gray eyes, black hair, or both.

But Bowie wasn't the cartoonish bad guy either. He'd not only chosen to raise his daughter, but had fought for custody. Bowie had not shared details, but she sensed an underlying thread of emotion in his voice that hinted at unspoken difficulties. Then, of course, he talked fondly of the elderly couple who had supported him and Abby. And she couldn't deny the tender way that he handled the cubs.

So who was Bowie Wilson?

And what was with his reaction when she'd mentioned crashing at her friend Josh's house in the Bay Area? If she didn't know better, she would have thought Bowie was jealous. Years ago, she'd made the foolish miscalculation of thinking that he cared for her, and she'd suffered for it. Just as before, Katie was fabricating romantic signals that didn't exist. As tired as the man was, he'd probably just zoned out and lost track of the conversation. There was probably no meaning behind his questioning tone when she'd talked about living with Josh.

Whatever was occurring with Bowie, Katie knew one thing for certain.

She would be civil to the man. She *might* even become friends with him. But she would not—under any circumstances—give Bowie the opportunity to hurt her again.

———∿∿∿———

A giant paw swiped down in Fluffy's direction. Before the tip of the claw could sink into his fur, he quickly darted to the left. Frida roared in frustration, but Fluffy could see the glint of excitement in the old bruin's eyes. They'd been chasing each other for a good five minutes. Twice, Fluffy had let the bear think she'd cornered him, but at the last second, he'd scurried away. Fluffy noticed that Frida held back when she bore down—not that a honey badger needed such consideration. Fluffy was more than capable of escaping the elderly animal, whether or not the bear swung at full strength.

As soon as Frida began to lag, her breathing labored, Fluffy lost interest. What was the point of a chase when his opponent could barely keep up? With one last tail twitch in Frida's direction, the honey badger clambered down the moat and then over the wall. The bruin bellowed one last roar as if *she'd* chased Fluffy away. Fluffy let the bear have her delusions. He had more important business tonight than harrying Frida.

Fluffy headed straight toward the main zoo

facility and peeked into the room where the Black-Haired One currently slept with the cougar cubs. Despite the biped's recent efforts to keep Fluffy contained, he had escaped easily tonight by climbing up the cracks that had appeared in the newly applied concrete.

Fluffy twitched his black snout when he discovered that the Black-Haired One was not alone. The redheaded female sat on the opposite side of the room. She was bent over one of those thin, light boxes that had an uncanny ability to hold the attention of the humans for hours. Fluffy let out a whicker of frustration. Clearly, the Black-Haired One did not understand proper court-ship rituals.

The female lifted her head. Fluffy scuttled backward, not wanting her to spot him.

Leaving the facility, Fluffy chittered softly to himself. The Black-Haired One needed help in wooing the reluctant female. And Fluffy was quite happy to assist anything that led to more wee ones. When it came to treats, honey badgers were excellent at the long game.

Chapter 4

KATIE DIDN'T WAKE BOWIE, EVEN WHEN THE CUBS began to mew again for food. Sylvia raised her head, saw that Katie had things under control, and immediately snuggled back down. Katie made sure to give the kits plenty of attention before returning them to the capybara. Bowie had told her that female mountain lions spend a lot of time with their young and that the newborns required a lot of snuggles. Not that she minded. She was looking forward to playing mama cougar over the next month while the cubs needed round-the-clock feedings.

Around six in the morning, Katie heard the door open. She looked up to see Abby standing there with a thermos and a bagel. Katie placed a finger on her lips and jerked her head in Bowie's direction.

Abby nodded and tiptoed into the room. She sat down beside Katie and whispered, "You stayed the whole night?"

"Your dad looked tired, and I thought he needed a break. What time does the zoo open?"

"Ten o'clock."

"I think we should let him rest more."

Abby nodded solemnly. "Okay, but I know he doesn't like to sleep past seven. He's normally up way earlier."

"I'll make sure we wake him."

Abby pushed the breakfast in her direction. "Here. I can bring Dad some more later."

"Thanks," Katie said. She'd brought snacks and Red Bull but hadn't planned on pulling an all-nighter.

"What are you working on?"

Katie tilted the screen in Abby's direction. "A new website. Do you want to see what I've done so far?"

Abby nodded eagerly. As Katie flipped through the unfinished pages, the girl leaned close.

"That looks so awesome!" she said.

A smile spread across Katie's face. Sharing her work with a tween was completely different from showing her old, grouchy boss. Abby squealed constantly and even clapped her hands twice. She pointed at the screen, excitedly giving suggestions. Some, especially her personal stories about the animals, were great. Katie's fingers flew across the keyboard as she felt a rekindling of her old excitement for web design. In fact, she and Abby were so engrossed in the website that they didn't even notice when Bowie woke up.

"How long was I out?" he asked. Katie turned to see him sitting upright on the air mattress, rubbing the back of his head. The gesture caused his already disheveled shirt to hike up, revealing several inches of nicely toned abs. It also had the side effect of flexing his right bicep—his very nice, very muscular bicep.

Katie's stomach flip-flopped. The man was seriously attractive.

Even a model would have trouble pulling off sexy dishabille so effortlessly. Sleep had cured Bowie's drawn features and dark circles. The fact that he wasn't fully awake only added an element of intimacy, despite Abby's presence. His black hair stood up in uneven spikes, making Katie want to smooth it down...and not just because it looked messy.

Bowie wore the sexy look well—too well.

Katie didn't want to feel that slow, pleasurable tug again. It had muddled her mind in the past, and she didn't want to start gazing at him with puppylike adoration, especially now. She was having enough trouble trying to figure out her career path without adding distraction into the mix—especially distraction of the male variety.

She was an adult. She understood the pull of sexual attraction and knew how to prevent it from turning into infatuation. She certainly knew not to mistake it for love.

"It's six thirty," Abby chirped happily, bouncing up from the floor. "I gave your breakfast to Katie. I'll go grab another bagel."

She bounded from the room with the energy only someone under the age of thirteen could possess. Bowie yawned and stretched, showing even more of his stomach muscles. Halfway through, he must have realized that his shirt had slid up, because he stopped and yanked it down.

Pity. Although, really, wasn't that what Katie wanted?

"You should have woken me," he told her, standing up.

She shrugged. "You looked like you needed the rest, and I was on a roll with the website."

Bowie shifted uncomfortably and said gruffly,

"Thanks, but you didn't need to do that. I've run on little sleep before."

"No biggie. So have I. And I had plenty of fuel." Katie gestured to the two empty cans of Red Bull beside her.

"Did the cubs wake up for a feeding?"

She nodded. "They drank like champs."

"So what were you and Abby looking at when I woke up?"

Katie got up and handed him the laptop. "She was helping me put together information about the animals for the website. What do you think so far? I've kept it professional and user-friendly. We can add some flashier features, but I think the portal should be streamlined."

"This looks great," Bowie said, the enthusiasm in his voice sounding legitimate. "You accomplished all this last night?"

A part of her thrilled at his words. Even long after Katie should have known better, she'd yearned for his and Sawyer's respect. Suddenly, her dad's words from yesterday popped into her mind. Was a part of her still trying to prove herself? Is that why she wanted a flashy job so badly? To have something to brag about? To automatically impress people?

Before Katie could reply, the door opened, and Lou entered. He walked a little stiffly but was still steady on his feet. She wouldn't call him frail, but he didn't quite fit the category of robust either. Lou glanced back and forth between her and Bowie, and Katie didn't like his speculative look. Both the elderly zookeeper and her mother were a little too eager for them to work together. Thankfully, Lou didn't make any comment. Instead, he just greeted them cheerfully.

"So how are my charges this morning?" he asked.

"They're good," Bowie told him. "Katie said they took their bottles well last night."

Lou turned toward her. "So, you stayed the whole night. Couldn't tear yourself away from the little critters, could you?"

"Nope, especially when they were curled up in little balls next to Sylvia. Plus, Bowie looked like he was on his last legs, so I thought I'd give him a few extra hours of sleep."

Lou's eyes gleamed at her last comment, and Katie nearly winced at her blunder. She did *not* want to encourage the elderly vet's matchmaking.

"Would you like to help me weigh the cubs and check them over?" he asked.

Katie nodded eagerly. "I'd love that."

"I'll be out feeding the animals," Bowie said. "Let me know if you're too tired to drive home, Katie. Lou can watch the cubs, and I'll give you a lift."

"I'll be fine," she told him, surprised by his offer.

He gave her a close look. "Are you sure? It's not easy staying awake after an all-nighter."

"It's not my first," Katie said. "I'm wide awake."

Bowie nodded and was starting to leave when Katie thought of something. "This is most likely nothing, but I thought I heard an animal last night. It was probably just my imagination."

He immediately turned around, his voice resigned. "What did you hear?"

"A chittering sound," Katie said, and then, as best as she could, she mimicked it.

Bowie exchanged a look with Lou. Then both

men said simultaneously in the same exasperated tone:
"Fluffy!"

"Who's Fluffy?" she asked.

"The zoo's honey badger, but he isn't a true badger.
He's more closely related to a weasel or a marten,"
Bowie answered.

Katie had never heard of the creature, which surprised
her. "What part of the world are honey badgers from?"

"Africa," Lou answered before he turned to Bowie.
"You better get Abby before she leaves for school."

"Abby?" Katie asked in confusion.

Bowie nodded at Lou before turning to her. "Abby is
the only person who can catch Fluffy."

"Honey badgers are ornery critters," Lou said, "but
Fluffy has a real soft spot for our girl."

Bowie scowled. "It's those honey-covered larvae that
she sneaks him."

Lou chuckled. "I think it's more than that. I know
they're solitary creatures in the wild, but I swear Fluffy
bonded with Abby when he was dropped off by his
owner in a box when he was just a cub. She toddled over
to him before we could stop her, and instead of biting
her, Fluffy made something like a purr."

Bowie snorted, but Katie could still hear the underlying affection in his voice. "Fluffy wouldn't know how to
purr, even if I gave him a whole jar of treats."

Lou laughed again. "No matter what, you can't deny
that Abby is the only one who can get that animal to do
anything."

"True enough," Bowie agreed before he turned to
Katie again. "If you start feeling tired before you leave,
just let me know."

"Will do," she said.

Bowie gave both her and Lou a parting nod before he ducked out of the room. Katie turned to find Lou studying her thoughtfully. He didn't say anything at first. Instead, he turned his attention to the cougars. Switching into professor mode, he gave her the rundown on cougar cub care while he examined the kits.

Unhappy at having their slumber disturbed, the cubs squeaked their displeasure. Lou opened the door to their crate, and Sylvia slowly rose and then carefully stepped from the wire-mesh bottom to the floor. She stretched her round body before meandering over to Lou to bump her snout against his leg a couple of times. Evidently satisfied that she'd greeted him properly, she headed over to her food dish.

Despite the capybara's adorable morning routine, Katie had trouble looking away from the cubs. Since their eyes hadn't opened yet, the only flashes of color came from their little pink noses and tongues.

Like Bowie, Lou handled the kits with practiced gentleness. Tonks curled into his arms as he carried her over to a table to be weighed and measured. He lifted her onto a gently curved metal scale. As Lou started to record the cubs' weight, he said nonchalantly, "Since you're Helen and John Underwood's daughter, you must be a local girl. Where have you been keeping yourself these last few years?"

She had to hide a half-amused, half-exasperated smile. Thus, the grilling began.

"Minnesota," Katie said. "I moved there right after college for a job."

"It was very good of you to come home to help care for your father after he was shot. While you and Bowie were out rescuing the cubs, your mom told me how much help you've been. I'm glad to hear that his recovery is going well."

She nodded. "It's been a rough road, but Dad's definitely turned the corner for the better. I just hope they catch the guy soon. It's been weighing on my mom."

Lou nodded. "The whole town has been worried about your dad."

"Everybody's been driving out to the ranch to visit and drop off casseroles," Katie said. "That's one good thing about growing up in Sagebrush: neighbors stick together."

"I suppose you went to Sagebrush High then?"

She hoped her smile didn't look forced. "Yes. Bowie and I were in the same graduating class."

"Were the two of you friends?"

"Uh, not really," Katie said, trying to be as vague as possible. "We really didn't hang with the same crowd." She omitted the reason why.

Lou gave an understanding nod. "He's changed a great deal since I met him. He's a good man...an excellent father."

"I think that's pretty clear to anyone who spends more than five minutes with Abby."

Lou nodded approvingly. "Bowie's smart too. Has better business sense than I ever did. I don't know how he's held this place together, between the bad economy and Gretchen's medical bills. My wife and I transferred the zoo over to him, but he mortgaged it when we had trouble making ends meet."

Katie whipped her head around to stare at Lou. She

never would have expected Bowie to make such a sacrifice. Yes, he had chosen to raise his daughter instead of giving her up for adoption, but Abby was his child. Not many people would incur debt to help an elderly couple who weren't blood-related. Although it sounded as if Gretchen and Lou had helped Bowie out and given the property to him in the first place, the Bowie she thought she knew wouldn't have cared.

"He's got a natural affinity for taking care of animals," Lou said. "It's a darn shame that he never had a chance to go to college. He would have made a real good vet."

Katie made a noncommittal sound. She'd never doubted Bowie's intelligence. His pranks had been too well executed and diabolical. But she didn't want to chorus Lou's praise. He could definitely rival her mother in matchmaking.

"Do you have a special someone back in Minnesota?"

Katie shook her head. "Nope."

"Bowie's single."

You don't say, she thought. Instead, she responded with her trademark *hmph*.

Lou gave her a sidelong glance but thankfully returned the discussion to the cougar cubs. No matter how much Bowie might have changed, he still wasn't good for her, especially now with her life upended. She needed to find a direction, and Bowie Wilson wasn't it.

"So Katie seems like a very sweet young lady. Cute too," Lou pronounced while leaning against the fence as Bowie cleaned out the llama pen. The herd ignored both of them, but Lulubelle, the camel, immediately wandered over to the eighty-year-old.

Bowie groaned as he shoveled manure into a wheelbarrow. "Don't even go there."

Lou threw his hands up in mock innocence. "I don't know what you're talking about."

"*Sure* you don't," Bowie said.

"Scout's honor."

Bowie snorted. "I wasn't in the Boy Scouts, but somehow I think you have the definition screwed up. And I mean it, Lou. No matchmaking."

Lou reached over and scratched the camel on her head. "Why not? Katie's a bright young lady and attractive too."

"Not going to argue with you there."

"So why don't you ask the girl out to see a movie... or whatever you young folks do today? She's single."

Bowie leaned his shovel against the fence as an unpleasant suspicion formed. "How do you know she's single?"

"I asked." Lou didn't even try to appear contrite. In fact, he looked borderline smug. "Told her that you weren't in a relationship either."

This time, Bowie did groan. He loved Lou. He really did. Although Bowie had met the older man late in life, he still considered Lou his father. But that didn't mean he enjoyed Lou's latest mission to see him married or at least in a committed relationship. Luckily, there weren't too many single women in Sagebrush, so Lou rarely had a target for his matchmaking.

"Lou, why would you do that?"

Lou gave Bowie a piercing look. "Because you've locked yourself away in this damn zoo. You can't make this and Abby your whole life."

"Aw, Lou, you're part of my life too."

Lou ignored Bowie's weak attempt at humor. "I am an old man, Bowie. Abby's mature enough now that you can start dating. I can see why you don't want to introduce a woman into Abby's life unless things get serious, but—"

Bowie cut him off. "Lou, I'm happy. I really am. If someone comes along who interests me, I promise you that I will ask her to the movies...or whatever young kids are doing these days."

"Katie doesn't interest you?"

Damn. Lou would have to ask a direct question, and Bowie couldn't lie to him. Not even about this.

"Lou, she wouldn't go out with me if I asked."

Lou's expression turned defensive. "Now don't go start worrying again that you don't have any fancy degrees or that you've never left Sagebrush for longer than a four-day weekend. Any woman would be lucky to have you."

Lou's faith in him never failed to warm Bowie. This time, though, it was a tad misplaced.

"Lou, I was a complete and utter jackass to Katie in high school."

That didn't even faze the older man. "Show her that you've changed."

"That may not be as easy as you think."

"The good relationships are never simple." Lou leaned over the fence and laid his hand on Bowie's shoulder. "Don't be afraid to try. You're not the same punk who spray-painted the zoo, and you haven't been for some time. Let Katie see that."

Bowie didn't think she would ever forgive him for all of his pranks, and he didn't blame her. But he didn't want to keep rehashing his past with Lou, so he nodded noncommittally.

Thankfully, Lou focused his attention on Lulubelle. "Does she seem any better?"

Bowie shook his head. "Nope. I heard her crying again this morning when I went to feed Frida."

Ever since one of the llamas had given birth a few months ago, Lulubelle had been out of sorts. It didn't help that every time she had tried to mother the little cria, the mother had chased her away. Even the rest of the herd had become more standoffish. Poor Lulubelle had slipped in her ranking in the herd and had faced more than her share of llama spit recently. She had always been sensitive—even for a herd animal—and she felt her demotion keenly. Not only had she become more needy for human affection, but she'd taken to moaning.

Lou made a tsking sound. "She's lonely."

Bowie nodded as he walked over to scratch the old girl. In response, the gangly animal shifted her massive weight in his direction. Only practice kept him from being stepped on. Lulubelle had a tendency to try to act like a lapdog. For that reason, he never let Abby into the llama pen unless she was closely supervised.

"I think she wants a calf of her own," he said. "I'm looking into some breeding programs. I'm hoping I can convince another small zoo to loan us a bull this winter. I'll take a look through stud books."

"A baby would be a good start," Lou said, "but

Lulubelle needs a permanent mate. It will be good
for her to have more camels around."

"The budget isn't great, Lou, and I'd rather use
any extra cash to diversify the stock."

Lou responded with a meaningful look.
"Lulubelle needs companionship, Bowie. It's not
good for a body to be alone."

With one last hard stare, he left the llama enclosure. Bowie sighed as he patted Lulubelle's side.

"I don't think he was just talking about you,
Lulubelle. What do you say, girl?"

The camel emitted a raspberry sound before she
wandered back to join the herd. Bowie grinned, but
the smile didn't stay on his lips for long.

He had a thing for Katie Underwood. He
couldn't deny that. Oh, he suspected that his body
turned her on. He'd caught a glimpse of heat in her
eyes this morning when he'd accidentally flashed
his abs. In high school, she'd clearly found him
visually appealing, and it seemed that time hadn't
changed that. Which wasn't all that surprising, even
given Katie's initial animosity toward him. Most
women found his features attractive, even if they
knew nothing else about him.

Bowie had always possessed good looks—
something his dad and his drinking buddies used to
razz him about when he was younger. He'd never
had trouble picking up women at a bar. Half the
time, they didn't care what he did for a living. They
just saw his face and build and made up their own
romantic fantasies—not that he was complaining.
It worked for him, especially right after Abby was

born. Back then, he hadn't been looking for a serious relationship. Then, when his daughter grew older, Bowie had taken over full responsibility for the zoo, and he hadn't wanted the drama of dating.

Until now.

Even without their past history, Bowie doubted that Katie would accept a date with him. He wasn't college educated. He was a single dad. He had more debts than assets. The only thing he was good at was taking care of animals in a zoo that was on the brink of folding.

Yep. He was a catch.

Yet Bowie's mind kept replaying the image of Katie and Abby bent over the laptop. He hadn't been fully awake, and the sight of them had been the first thing his brain had registered. They'd looked so natural and at ease with each other. Abby always got along better with adults than children her own age, and she and Katie just seemed to click.

He sighed again. He'd ruined his chance with Katie a long, long time ago. And he didn't have time to dwell on past mistakes. He had a zoo to run. If his mind drifted occasionally to Katie as he worked, well, so be it.

"Are you going back to the zoo again tonight?" Katie's mother asked a few days later, her tone brimming with hopeful speculation.

Katie paused in unloading groceries. "Mom, no matchmaking. You promised."

Helen Underwood held up her hands in mock surrender. "I'm just trying to figure out your plans tonight, sweetheart. That's all."

Katie *hmph*ed before she swiveled to place the packages of frozen vegetables in the freezer. Since the attack on her father, she'd done most of the grocery shopping. At first, her mom didn't have time to run errands. Now, having Katie do them gave her a chance to get off her feet while her husband rested.

"Mom, you know that I'm committed to helping watch the cubs for at least a month," Katie said.

"I'm sure it doesn't hurt how cute their keeper is."

Katie groaned. She couldn't help it. Hoping to distract her mother, she handed her three cans of corn. Unfortunately, it didn't work.

"You two must be getting pretty close," her mother continued.

"Mom, this will only be the fourth night that I've slept over at the zoo."

"Yes, but you're also doing all that marketing," her mom said. "The updates you've done to the website are terrific."

Katie felt her annoyance drift away. Her mom was always her biggest fan. "Those are just the preliminary changes. Wait until we roll out the rest."

Her mother beamed. "See? I told you that you could find business here in Sagebrush!"

Suddenly, it struck Katie that her mother's desire to set her up with Bowie wasn't just part of her campaign for more grandbabies. Other than Katie's oldest brother, who'd joined the military, she'd been the only Underwood child to leave Sagebrush for any extended time. Even Alex now lived within a day's drive.

"Mom," Katie said quietly, "you know that I'm

still considering finding a job in a major city. I even called Josh a couple days ago to see if he could put in a good word for me in San Francisco."

"But Sagebrush has so much to offer!" her mom said brightly, although Katie could detect a flicker of hurt.

"Like attractive zookeepers?" she asked gently.

Her mother paused. "Well, yes."

Katie reached forward and rested her hand on her mother's. "Mom, do you really want me to stay in town just because of a cute guy?"

Even her mother had to smile at that. "All right, I see your point, but don't sell your hometown short."

"You know, Dad told me something similar when I drove him to physical therapy this week."

"He's a smart man. That's why I married him."

"And here I thought it was the uniform."

"Intelligent men know what attracts the ladies," her mom said crisply before she sobered. "Are you considering staying here?"

Katie sucked in her breath. She didn't want to get her mother's hopes up, only to crush them when she left. Helen Underwood always supported her children's decisions, but Katie knew that her mother had never liked her living so far away. Plus, her mom would worry if she lived in a large city.

"I'm not sure, Mom," Katie said slowly, but even that weak statement was enough to cause a light to shine in her mother's eyes.

Her mom clasped her hands together. "Oh, sweetheart, it would be wonderful if you moved back permanently. You could see your nieces and nephews so much more often."

"Mom, there are a lot of variables. First, I don't even know if that's what I want. And even if I did, I'm not sure my freelance work is going to be enough to pay the bills."

Her mom's excitement did not lessen. Helen Underwood was a perennially optimist. "Look at all the work you've found here already! And there's the national park too. Maybe you can do something for them. We've been getting more tourists, and there are so many new businesses starting up. Plus, you could get clients over the internet. And…"

Katie couldn't stop her fond smile. "Mom, as much as I appreciate your faith in my abilities, building a graphic design company from scratch is difficult, and it's not necessarily stable work."

"Your father and I will help you out during the thin times."

Katie didn't doubt that for a second. "I know, Mom, but I don't want to rely on you two. I'm almost thirty years old. I came home to help with Dad, but now that he's better, I need to restart my career. I've always dreamed of working for a big company. I'm not sure if I'm ready to give that up."

Her mom's joy dimmed, and Katie felt terrible. "I just don't want to disappoint you if I ultimately decide to leave."

"Sweetheart, you could never disappoint me."

But Katie could. She knew that with absolute certainty. And she needed to be careful not to give her mother any more false hope that she might make Sagebrush her permanent home again.

After Katie's discussion with her mom, she checked in on her dad. To her surprise, she didn't find him resting or watching TV. Instead, he was working on a model ship. Although building the intricate vessels was one of his hobbies, he hadn't felt up to the detailed work since he'd been shot.

"Someone must be feeling better," Katie said.

He looked up and smiled at her. "Well, I'm not ready to go for a run yet, but this I can do."

"Did you know Mom has it in her head that I'm going to move back to Sagebrush?"

"Honey, that thought has been swirling in your mother's mind since you first left for college," he said. "She's a mom. She's always going to want her babies around her, but that doesn't mean she wasn't happy when you were living in Minnesota."

"Could you talk to her? Let her know that I might not be staying? I don't want her getting more hurt than necessary."

Her dad nodded. "I can do that, kiddo."

Katie studied him carefully. His color looked good, and his old spirit seemed back. "I was thinking about heading over to the zoo early today. I'd like to see more of the animals so I can get pictures for the website. And I need inspiration for the new logo. Will you and Mom be good here?"

"Go." He waved her with his hand. "I'm not about to keel over anymore. We'll be fine."

"Don't tell Mom that I went to the zoo ahead of schedule. She's already imagining a grand love affair between the zookeeper and me."

Both her father's eyebrows shot up. "Lou Warrenton?"

Katie laughed. "No, even Mom isn't so desperate to keep me here that she'd set me up with an eighty-year-old. There's a younger guy in charge who's my age. Lou still lives on the property, though, and helps out with the animals."

"Your mother means well."

"I know," Katie said as she bent to kiss her dad goodbye. "But this is probably the last guy in town who could convince me to stay."

"Which animals would you like to see today?" Bowie asked when Katie arrived at the zoo. She'd called him before she left her parents' house to let him know she'd be dropping by early.

"None in particular," Katie said. "I just want to get to know more of the zoo's residents so I can write better bios. The photos on the website need an update too, so I brought my camera."

"The animal park isn't too big," Bowie told her as he led her from the zoo's office toward the bear exhibit. "A lot of the species are local, but it still gives kids a chance to see wildlife up close. We're too small and understaffed to be accredited, but we take in the animals that no other zoo wants. One thing we do have is space, and we make sure we follow all the recommended guidelines for the enclosures, even those that are stricter than what the law requires.

"Lou still has a lot of ties with licensed wildlife

rehabilitators. If they can't release an animal back into the wild, they call us. One of the park rangers at Rocky Ridge National Park interned with us years ago, and she sends abandoned young our way who won't survive on their own and who won't be able to be rehabilitated. Sometimes, law enforcement or even other zoos call Lou when they learn about an exotic pet that someone has been keeping illegally."

"How about you?"

Bowie shot her a quizzical look, so she continued. "Do you have connections to the conservation community?"

He glanced away quickly but not before Katie detected a glimmer of something. Regret? Frustration? Embarrassment? Maybe a combination of all three?

"I don't have the right letters after my name," Bowie said, his voice curiously neutral. "I'm hoping the cougar cubs will help make the zoo more credible as a sanctuary for confiscated exotic pets and animals that can't be rereleased. It would be great to eventually become an accredited zoo. That would take years, though. We'd require more volunteers and a bigger staff. Although Lou's done a better job at keeping up with medical equipment than he has with other technology, we'd need to update the animal hospital and other zoo facilities. I'd also have to get a degree myself."

"Oh," Katie said. She kept her tone light, realizing that she might have just prodded an open sore. Lou had told her that Bowie had never gone to college. That fact didn't surprise her. Bowie had never put any effort into school. Half the time, he'd either skipped class or he'd been serving an in-school suspension. That didn't necessarily mean Bowie didn't regret the lost opportunity. It had to be difficult to convince scientists that he was running a legitimate zoo when he didn't have any higher education.

"What other kinds of animals do you have?" Katie asked, steering the conversation away from him.

"Well, there's Frida here," he said, jerking his thumb in the direction of the grumpy grizzly. "She's about nineteen years old. You might remember her from when you were a kid. She was brought to Lou as a juvenile with a damaged foot. Poachers had set up a bear trap in Rocky Ridge National Park, and Frida had been caught in it for days before a ranger found her. She's walked with a pronounced limp ever since, so she couldn't be reintroduced into the wild."

"Poor girl." Katie leaned against the fence to get a better look at Frida. The bear lifted her head to emit a long-suffering sound halfway between a grunt and a roar.

Katie laughed. Bowie joined her by the rail, his T-shirt brushing against her bare arm. Unwanted desire flared within her. She almost succeeded in suppressing a tremble, but then he chuckled—the sound low, deep, and most of all warm. The husky timbre of it washed over her. Despite the wave of heat, she shivered.

Bowie's gray eyes darkened at her reaction. With the summer sun beating down on her back, Katie couldn't claim a chill to explain away her body's instinctual reaction to him. Instead, she changed the subject.

"I guess Frida doesn't like to be called 'poor,'" she said.

"Frida has her dignity," Bowie said. And then he grinned. Devastatingly.

Katie's heart squeezed. A rush of sweet fire swept through her again, threatening to burn through her shields of self-preservation. She straightened before she did something very foolish, like trying to capture Bowie's smile with a kiss.

"So, what's the name of your camel?" she asked as she pushed back from Frida's fence. "She always trots right over to me for a pet when I pass by on my way to watch the cougars."

"That would be Lulubelle," Bowie said as he led Katie around the corner. "She's always been a little needy, and she's been having a particularly hard time lately."

Katie knitted her brow in concern as they approached Lulubelle and the llamas. "How so?"

"She's lonely," he said. "Ever since one of the llamas had a baby, Lulubelle has seemed to be longing for one of her own. Lou thinks she wants a mate too."

"Awww," Katie said as they approached the llama pen. Lulubelle instantly raised her large head and raced toward them. She thrust her neck at Bowie in clear demand. Katie swore that the animal sighed as he scratched the thick patch of fluff on top of her head. After thoroughly nuzzling him, Lulubelle turned her attention on Katie. Finding her line of vision full of insistent camel, Katie laughed and petted the old girl. When she dropped her hand and both she and Bowie began to turn, Lulubelle emitted a plaintive rumble.

"My goodness," Katie said as she whirled back around. "It's okay, Lulubelle. I'll be back tomorrow."

The camel made a raspberry sound in response.

Bowie shook his head. "She'll keep you here all evening if you'll let her."

"But that cry was awful!"

"I know," he said as he ignored his own advice and rubbed the camel's neck. "I wish we had the funds to purchase and take care of another camel or two. I'm hoping another zoo will at least lend me a stud."

A thought struck Katie. She spun toward him, unable to stop her exuberance. "Bowie, I think I have a brilliant idea!"

He seemed to freeze. Too excited to pay much attention to his reaction, Katie spoke in a rush. "You can use Lulubelle as part of a fund drive."

It took Bowie a second to respond. He stared at her for a long moment, then blinked hard. "Lulubelle?"

"Who can resist a lovelorn camel?" Katie asked. "I mean, look at her liquid-brown eyes and those ridiculous lashes. We could really sell her story of wanting a partner and a baby. There are so many sites on the internet where anyone can set up a fundraiser. We could get people involved in the process of finding her a companion. Maybe you could pick a few candidates to be her mate, and the public could vote. We could even set jars outside the llama pen with pictures of potential boy camels, and visitors could cast their ballot by putting in cash!"

Bowie rubbed the back of his head, clearly considering her idea. "It could work, and it might bring in more foot traffic too."

Katie nodded enthusiastically. She hadn't been

this excited in years about work. Her old boss had slowly killed her enthusiasm as he'd rejected idea after idea. It felt good to unleash her creativity on a receptive audience.

"Come on," she said. "I want to see more of the zoo while I'm on a roll."

Then, without thinking, she grabbed Bowie's hand, tugging him forward. He chuckled—the sound once again low and this time even edged with surprising fondness. His fingers curled around the back of Katie's hand, his body heat searing her. Instantly, she released her hold and kept her focus forward.

"Hurry up," she said instead. "I don't want to lose momentum. What's next?"

"Well, there are the zoo's river otters, Larry, Curly, and Moe," he said.

Katie couldn't stop her exclamation of delight when she rounded the bend to discover what looked like a miniature water park. Several gently sloping concrete slides twisted into a shallow pool. Two sleek, brown animals shot down the chutes, chasing each other, while a third sunned himself on a rock.

"These guys are local like Frida. Remember I told you that we get some animals from a park ranger at Rocky Ridge? Actually, you might know her. Lacey Montgomery was a few years behind us in school, but her mom owns the Prairie Dog Café."

Katie nodded. "Yeah, she used to help out at the restaurant. Our families were close too. I think we're distantly related…third or fourth cousins."

"A tourist thought that the otter pups were abandoned, so he brought them back to the ranger station in his backpack. They needed so much medical care that it wouldn't have been possible to reintroduce them into the wild. Lacey contacted us, since we'd recently lost our otter to old age. Lou and I were able to nurse the pups back to health."

"They're so adorable! I'm glad you were able to save them."

"Otters are one of my favorite animals," Bowie said. "Abby's too. When she was little and wouldn't stop crying, I'd bring her over to this exhibit, and she'd always start giggling instead."

Katie tried to imagine Bowie cradling his infant daughter and carefully positioning her so that she could watch the animals play. At first, she had trouble bringing the image into focus. It jarred too much with her memories of him. Then, suddenly, the scene snapped into place, and she could clearly see Bowie holding baby Abby in the crook of his arm, his cheek pressed close to his daughter's as he pointed out the antics of the otters.

Surprisingly, the image worked. Too well.

Katie's heart squeezed, and she felt herself softening toward Bowie. More than she wanted. Much, much more.

Time to change the subject again. Not caring if the transition was abrupt, she blurted out, "Do you have any monkeys? I think there were some when we were kids."

"Charlie the Chimp died about seven years ago," Bowie said. "He's probably who you remember. A lot of people still ask about him. We've got two capuchins and a sloth."

"What's a capuchin?"

"Organ-grinder monkey."

Katie nodded. "Oh, one of those. They show up in movies a lot, don't they?"

"They're pretty trainable and inquisitive," Bowie said. "Bonnie and Clyde—our capuchins—actually can pickpocket, and no, before you ask, I didn't teach them. Their previous owner did before he was arrested and the animals confiscated. The bigger zoos didn't want them, but one of their directors was friends with Lou and called to see if our animal park would take them."

Katie stared at him. "People teach monkeys to pickpocket?"

"Yep. They'd been at the zoo for a couple of years before I started, and they had the meanest temperaments. Working with them was my first job after cleaning up the spray paint. I think Lou wanted to test my character and prepare me for fatherhood. It took a lot of patience— and even more treats—but I was able to retrain them. Eventually, I developed a show that we hold on Saturdays if we have a large enough crowd. It's one of our biggest hits, if you can call anything around here a hit."

"We should tape it for the website."

Bowie looked unconvinced. "It would be cute, but I don't know if I want to encourage them being seen as pets. They can be dangerous, especially when they get older. When we do the skit, Lou and I have hold of each monkey at all times."

Katie regarded him steadily. "You really do love the animals and this place, don't you?"

He shrugged and said simply, "It's home."

Did he have to sound like the perfect guy? His answer threatened to make Katie feel all gooey and melty again, a reaction that she definitely didn't want around Bowie Wilson. Lust...well, maybe that she could handle, but the softer feelings were most definitely unwelcome.

———∿∿∿———

When Bowie walked into the cubs' nursery, he stopped in his tracks at the sight that greeted him. Lou stood holding Fleur, and the little kit stared right back at Bowie with cobalt eyes. A wide smile slowly spread across Bowie's face. He turned back toward Katie. "I think there's something you're going to want to see." Then he stepped aside so his body no longer blocked her view.

Katie gasped as she spotted the kits. "Oh my goodness! Their eyes are open! They're so blue. They almost glow!"

The cougars' eyes weren't the only thing in the room practically shining. Katie's joy seemed to reach out and wrap straight around Bowie's heart. She swiveled in his direction. "I thought they couldn't get more precious, but they are just so darn cute!"

"Wait until they start exploring more," Bowie said.

Dobby mewled, his little whiskers framing his pink mouth. Katie immediately rushed forward. "Don't worry, buddy. Food is coming."

Lou chuckled. "Don't let the little tyke fool you. I fed them a bit ago. He's just trying out his voice. That's all."

Dobby's sisters moved awkwardly around the floor of the nursery. Lou must have taken them out of their den to allow them a chance to explore.

Bowie smiled as he crouched to get a better view of the kits. They lumbered around clumsily. Occasionally, their back legs wouldn't cooperate with their forelimbs, and their rears would plunk to the floor, their feet splayed out. It didn't take them long to scramble back into position. Undaunted, they stuck out their paws and pulled their slight bodies forward.

"They remind me of my niece and nephews when they were beginning to crawl," Katie said as she joined Bowie on the floor.

"Wait until they start getting into trouble," he warned as Fleur crawled in their direction.

Katie glanced down at the little cub, who was pushing against her leg. "You could never be trouble, now could you?"

At the sound of Katie's voice, Fleur squeaked happily. Katie's brown eyes looked exactly like melted chocolate as she ran her hand down the puma's spine. Fleur snuggled closer to Katie's knee, and Bowie felt another tug in the vicinity of his heart. There was something about Katie that drew him—even if the woman herself didn't appear to want his attention. He hadn't missed how quickly she'd dropped his hand earlier today after she'd grabbed it in her excitement. It was best if he didn't try pursuing anything with a woman who didn't want him. He didn't have time to chase Katie—not with the zoo and Abby.

At the thought of his daughter, Bowie checked his watch and then straightened. "I better head to the house now. Abby will be getting off the school bus soon. She'll want to know that the kits' eyes are open."

"We've got to announce it on the website too," Katie

said. "It's a shame that we didn't have enough time to generate a ton of interest about when their eyes would open, but at least we still have the count-down clock to when the cubs go on exhibit."

Bowie nodded, but for the first time in a long while, he didn't feel as worried about attracting visitors. He and Katie were coming up with a solid marketing plan, which was another reason he shouldn't push for a relationship. He didn't want to mess that up. But as he walked across the zoo to meet his daughter, he couldn't help but wonder what it would have been like if he and Katie hadn't had their past history.

From his vantage point near Frida's enclosure, Fluffy chittered to himself as he watched the Black-Haired One leave the zoo office and head to the big house where the human made his den. Alone. Without the red-haired female.

Fluffy grunted again for good measure. The biped should be staying in the female's burrow in order to produce more wee ones.

The biped had no instinct for proper mating ritu-als. None at all. He was worse than Lulubelle with her lonely whines.

Good thing Fluffy had decided to leave his enclosure early. He'd successfully surprised Frida, who'd grown too lax during the daylight hours. Now Fluffy had a chance to witness the Black-Haired One's failed courtship.

Perhaps the Black-Haired One was having trouble

picking up the red female's unique odor. How the biped could miss it, Fluffy did not know, but humans—the pathetic creatures—seemed to have weak senses. Honey badgers communicated by scent even if they preferred to live alone. A male could detect a female's smell in the dirt and follow her back to her burrow.

When Abby called him, Fluffy came immediately. He needed to plot. As soon as Abby released him back into his enclosure, Fluffy scurried to his den and laid his head down on his paws. How could he entice the Black-Haired One with the redheaded female's scent? Fluffy thought about the strange material that the humans wore. One time, the Black-Haired One had left a pair of work gloves in Fluffy's enclosure while he took a break from digging the trench. Fluffy's entire home had reeked of the biped.

Fluffy smiled, showing his teeth.

Since the Black-Haired One clearly lacked the vision necessary to produce more wee ones, Fluffy would need to lend him some honey-badger cleverness. And he had the perfect plan. He just needed the scraps of fabric the redheaded female wore.

Chapter 5

A DAY LATER, KATIE QUESTIONED HER INTELLIGENCE... and her sanity. Why had she volunteered to videotape her former crush? Didn't his mere smile already send her traitorous hormones cartwheeling? Surely, she should have realized that staring at the man through a camera lens would trigger an unwanted reaction.

Like accelerated heartbeat. Sweaty palms. A slightly euphoric feeling. Hot zings of attraction. Excited nerve endings.

Yep.

Katie had all the ingredients of an unhealthy cocktail of lust whirling inside her.

Luckily, Bowie appeared too busy staring into the camera to notice. He had, she had to admit, a good presence. He avoided any stiffness as he delivered his prepared script from memory. It didn't hurt that his smile would appeal to any woman between the ages of fifteen and one hundred and fifteen.

"Now, I would not suggest kissing a red river hog under normal circumstances," Bowie said. He was crouched next to Daisy, who was busily rooting around in the dirt. Bowie reached over and scratched the pig on her bristly back. "They are wild animals and very capable of defending themselves. Even females like Daisy have tusks.

Although Daisy was hand-raised and kept as a pet, it's not a good idea to try to force wild species into being companions for humans…even those who are cousins to our domesticated friends. Daisy ended up becoming too aggressive for her owner and was constantly rooting around, tearing up the lawn and the house. She's much happier here, where we're equipped to offer her more space and plenty of places to explore with her snout."

Bowie glanced away from the camera and back up to Katie. "How'd I sound?"

"Great," she said truthfully.

He scrambled to his feet. Daisy made a couple of snuffling sounds but otherwise appeared undisturbed. Bowie regarded the pig with an undisguised look of affection. The man truly did love the animals at the zoo—something that still surprised Katie.

"She's a sweet girl," he said.

The pig brushed its stout body against Bowie's leg, her beautiful, ruddy orange-red hide contrasting with his plain khaki slacks. With her long, bumpy snout, the pig didn't exactly qualify as cute, but there was something endearing about her. Happily snuffling in the dirt, Daisy wandered a few inches away from Bowie.

"She looks a little bit like a rusty warthog."

Bowie laughed as he bent down to give Daisy one last scratch before turning to leave the enclosure. "I think the coolest thing about them is their ears. They look just like tails, especially when the river hogs use them to chase away flies."

Katie studied Boris, who lay inside the wooden shed that served as the hogs' shelter from the hot sun. Bowie had drawn the gate closed when he'd lured Daisy out in the yard with an apple, but Boris didn't appear to have any interest in leaving the shade. He lolled on his side, his surprisingly slender legs jutting out from his large body. The boar remained perfectly still except for the occasional flick of his ears.

Bowie was right. Boris's ears did taper off into a taillike shape, complete with a long, white tuft at each tip. They were kind of adorable. Katie would have loved to scratch the big boar's belly, but she didn't think the animal would appreciate it. At all. Instead, she glanced at her watch to check the time.

"We still have forty minutes before the big smooch," she told Bowie.

"Would you like to see more of the animals while we wait?" he asked. "I doubt anyone is going to show until at least five minutes before."

"Of course," Katie said, lifting her camera. "It'll be a good opportunity to take more photos for the website."

"Do you have any shots you need to get?"

She shook her head. "I think I've gotten pictures of the most popular exhibits."

"Then how would you like to hold a chinchilla?"

Katie couldn't stop her squeal of delight. "I'd love to! They've always reminded me of adorably oversized cartoon mice with their huge ears and fluffy tails."

Bowie laughed. The sound had an unnerving warming effect on Katie. She really didn't appreciate this man's control over her hormones.

"Well, you're in luck, because we have a little fellow who loves to snuggle, although he can be shy at first," he said as he led her away from the red river hogs.

They'd just turned the bend when Katie heard a scurrying sound behind her. She jerked her head and caught sight of a little white-and-black head peeking out from underneath a native shrub planted along the path. She raised her camera and managed to take a shot before the creature fled, its thick tail low to the ground.

"Who was that?" she asked.

"The infamous Fluffy," Bowie said, his voice a mixture of exasperation and fondness as he reached for his cell phone. "I need to text Lou to have Abby coax Fluffy back to his den. He doesn't try to bite humans—which is unusual for the species—but it's not good having him running around, especially when we have an event today."

"Do you want to go after him?" Katie asked.

Bowie shook his head. "He won't listen to me. Abby's good at capturing him. She's had plenty of practice. The little rascal won't stay in his enclosure, no matter what I do to secure it. He's so good at climbing and digging that we never know where he'll show up next."

"Ooo, that gives me a great idea! We should post weekly pictures of where we spot Fluffy. It could be like *Where's Waldo?* or *Where in the World Is Carmen Sandiego?* I can even design it so visitors can upload their own shots."

"That's a great idea," Bowie said. "It might even bring in more visitors who are hoping to catch a glimpse of him."

"I'll get it set up once I finish the pig-kissing video."

They paused outside a narrow building. Bowie pulled open the door and held it for her. "Before we meet Ferdinand, what's your opinion of snakes?"

Katie wrinkled her nose as she stepped inside and spotted the rows of glass cages. Behind the closest one, a rattlesnake shifted its triangular head to stare at them. Its tail popped up, and a sound like maracas echoed through the room.

"Reserved," she admitted, remembering this hallway from childhood. "My brothers loved this exhibit, though."

"I didn't know that you have brothers."

"Four of them," Katie told him. "Two are older than me. The second oldest graduated right before our freshman year at Sagebrush High. The twins started the year after we left. My oldest brother, Alex, is in the air force, and the second, Luke, is a lawyer. Mike's a cop, and Matt is a mechanic."

"I guess I owe you another thank-you."

Katie shot him a confused look. "For what?"

He gave her a wry grin. "For not telling them about the pranks that I pulled on you in high school."

"How do you know that I didn't?"

"I'm still breathing, aren't I?"

She laughed. "True. Very true."

Bowie paused at a larger cage containing two grayish fur balls. He opened the door and murmured softly to the two chinchillas. Both fluffs swiveled in Bowie's direction, but only one moved toward his voice.

"Hey, Ferdinand. There's someone here who wants to meet you."

The braver chinchilla paused as if debating whether he wanted to receive visitors or not. After a moment, the little guy slowly did a hop-skip in

Bowie's direction. Bowie placed one hand palm up on the floor of the cage while he stroked Ferdinand with the other. The rodent made happy squeaks as it snuffled Bowie's fingers. Seemingly satisfied, it climbed onto Bowie's hand. Bowie placed his other palm around Ferdinand's furry tummy as he carefully lifted the little chinchilla. Immediately cuddling the animal close, he shifted so Katie could get a good look at the animal's wiggling little nose surrounded by black whiskers.

"Try petting Ferdinand first, so that he gets used to you," Bowie encouraged.

Katie nodded as she reached out to stroke the animal. When her hand accidentally brushed against Bowie's chest, she tried hard not to notice his firm pecs. Unfortunately, her body refused to cooperate, and an unmistakable thrill of attraction sizzled through her. Thankfully, when her hand came in contact with the chinchilla, her focus switched back to the animal. "His fur is so soft!"

"Chinchillas average sixty hairs per follicle," Bowie told her as he clearly switched back into zoo-director mode. "Unfortunately, that also made them valuable to furriers. One species is almost extinct."

"I suppose that's not the species sold in pet stores."

Bowie shook his head. "No. Scientists believe that the domesticated chinchilla came from the less vulnerable species. Ferdinand is the kind you can buy."

The little rodent began arching into Katie's hand, chittering contentedly. Bowie smiled fondly. "He seems to like you. Do you want to try holding him?"

She nodded eagerly. Bowie adjusted the animal to make the transfer easier. "Make sure to support his hind legs and rear end. Once you have a proper hold, cradle him against you like I'm doing. Chinchillas need to feel protected and secure."

Katie nodded again as she accepted the animal. Ferdinand curled his slight, soft body into hers. She couldn't stop the cooing sounds that escaped her throat as she carefully balanced the furry rodent in her hands. Bowie let her cuddle the chinchilla for a few minutes before he showed her how to place the little guy back in his cage.

As they turned from the chinchilla exhibit, Katie asked, "Do you have any other animals in here other than reptiles?"

"No other mammals, but this is also the home of Rosie the Rocker, our cockatoo. Her perch is right around the corner."

As they turned the bend, Katie caught sight of a white bird with a wild yellow mohawk. Spotting Bowie, the cockatoo squawked and began doing a little dance. Katie laughed at the sight. "Someone likes you."

Bowie gave a sheepish grin. "She knows who brings the birdseed."

Rosie chose that moment to let out another happy screech, her head bobbing frantically. Bowie unlatched her cage, and the bird immediately flew to his shoulder. She began to gently pluck at his short hair with her beak. Another chuckle escaped Katie.

"Oh, I think it's more than food," she said. "I think she might have a little crush on you."

Bowie's gray eyes latched on to hers. The unexpected heat in them seared Katie. Her heart—that weak, susceptible organ—squeezed. Heady pleasure shot through her. Firmly, she stifled the flames, but even the smoke left over from the conflagration seemed to intoxicate her.

Clearing her throat, she tried changing the subject. "Why did you name her Rosie the Rocker? Because of her yellow head feathers?"

"Not exactly." Bowie walked over to the utility closet and pulled out a towel and an old boom box. Slinging the cloth over his shoulder, he positioned Rosie on top of it and then carefully bent at the knees to select a song.

"Oh my gosh, is that a CD player?" Katie asked. "I haven't seen one of those in years. Does it even work?"

Bowie shrugged the shoulder without a bird perched on it. "It still gets the job done."

"Where do you even find CDs for it?"

"Rosie's tastes are old school," Bowie said as Quiet Riot's "Cum On Feel the Noize" started to blare through the speakers. To Katie's utter amazement, the cockatoo began to tap its gray foot in time with the beat. Then, with a primal squawk, the bird began to head-bang, keeping perfect tempo. Next, it scooted back and forth on Bowie's shoulder, its footwork absolutely flawless.

Katie clapped. "Now that is impressive. How did you teach her to do that?"

Bowie shook his head. "I didn't. Some species of birds are natural dancers. There have been a couple of studies about it. I read about it years ago in *National Geographic*. That's what gave me the idea to try it with Rosie."

Katie fell silent for a moment as she watched the bird strut its stuff on Bowie's shoulder. It was a mesmerizing performance. "We need to get this on video for the website."

Bowie nodded. "Sounds good. We can videotape Rosie after we finish with the pig-kissing scene."

Katie shook her head. "I don't want to add too many videos to the site at one time. We need to build anticipation. Besides, I think Rosie might be a perfect sidekick for you in one of my pranks."

"Are you going to make me kiss her too?"

Rosie squawked loudly as she stamped her foot high in the air. Katie howled and shook her head. "I don't think Rosie likes that idea. Maybe I was wrong about her flirting with you after all."

"Ha. Ha. Ha," Bowie said sarcastically and then sobered. "What is your plan then?"

Katie shrugged. "I'm not sure yet, but it'll be good. I promise you that."

Bowie feigned a groan, and she felt the slightest twinge of guilt. Maybe she was being too hard on the man. After all, it had been over a decade since high school. But it wasn't as if she was surprising him with mean tricks. Yes, she was sort of blackmailing him with her promise to volunteer, but she wasn't forcing him. He could back out if he wanted, and Katie had no doubt that the videos were going to make excellent advertisements for the zoo.

"Speaking of your stunts, we'd better head back to the red river hogs," she said. "People might be wandering in."

Bowie checked the time and gave a doubtful shrug. "I wish that would be the case. We don't draw big crowds—unless you count the occasional

school group—and unfortunately, there isn't one scheduled for today."

"Ah, yes, but there were flyers for this event."

Bowie wrinkled his brow. "Flyers?"

Katie nodded. "I came up with the idea last night
when I was watching the cubs, and I figured out the
rest of the details with June this morning. She's always
awake before dawn to start the baking for her tea shop,
so I popped by before I headed home. June agreed to
hand the flyers out to her customers. I also dropped some
off at the Prairie Dog Café on my way out of town."

She reached into her pocket to pull out a copy and
handed it to him. "Hopefully, these draw in more people."

Before Katie had left the zoo this morning, she'd
managed to capture a shot of Daisy that looked like
the pig was lifting her snout for a kiss. Since Katie had
already taken photos of Bowie for the website, it hadn't
been hard to find one where he looked like he was
posing for a magazine cover. Under the pictures, Katie
had written Bowie and Daisy's dating stats along with
details about the fund-raiser and its location.

Shoving his hand in his hair, Bowie studied the flyer.
He looked a little tense as he handed it back to her.
When he spoke, his voice sounded tight, maybe even
a little edgy. "It looks great, Katie. A lot more professional than anything I could've done."

"Nervous?" she asked.

"Weirdly, yes," he admitted, somewhat to her surprise. "I don't know why. We give talks all the time, but
we don't normally draw crowds. Do you think a lot of
people will show?"

Katie shrugged. "I don't know. Both June's tea shop

and the Prairie Dog Café typically have a bunch of customers on Saturday."

Bowie blew out his breath slowly. "At least the zoo will make money."

"Hey, you don't kiss pigs every day either. It's okay to be a little anxious."

"Red river hog," he corrected.

"Ah, yes, red river hog, so much more dignified."

Bowie laughed for real this time. "Well, I did promise to kiss Daisy in public for you."

Katie sobered, feeling another prick of conscience. "You are okay with this, right?"

He nodded. "It's just stage fright. This is actually fun. If it gets our numbers up, then I wish I would have tried stunts like this sooner."

Just then, Katie and Bowie rounded the corner. Although a mob hadn't descended upon the red river hogs' enclosure, a small crowd was milling about. Abby scampered over to them with a huge smile on her face. Lou followed at a more sedate pace.

"There are, like, three kids from my class here!" Abby squealed. "This is going to be so awesome!"

Other people started to drift over to ask Bowie questions about what the fund-raiser was for, how he was going to kiss the red river hog, and what was a red river hog exactly. Katie quietly slipped away to check that the video equipment was set up and working. When the scheduled time drew near, she wove through the small throng that had formed around Bowie.

"Time to pucker up, Romeo," she told him.

He promised the onlookers that he'd answer

more questions after the kiss, and then he headed into the enclosure. As Katie watched through the camera lens, she had to admit that he gave a great performance. He started with a couple of quick, interesting facts about porcines in general and red river hogs in particular. Then he had the audience laughing when he exaggeratedly demonstrated how male red river hogs protect their mates and litters of piglets, including pretending to fight another male for Daisy's affections. Unimpressed, Daisy munched her food. Each time Bowie tried a new stunt, she ignored him, causing him to lift his hands in mock frustration. The crowd loved it.

Then came the kiss.

Bowie hunkered down beside Daisy. Rubbing her side, he spoke to her softly, getting her comfortable with his presence. When he finally laid one on her snout, the sow emitted a loud and decidedly disgruntled oink. Bowie scrambled backward, landing on his backside. Daisy squealed again and took off at full speed toward the opening of her indoor pen.

"Well, I guess Boris—our male red river hog—has nothing to fear," Bowie quipped as he rose stiffly from the ground, making a show of rubbing his posterior. Katie debated about zooming in on his butt but decided it wouldn't fit with the family-friendly tone of the video. Plus, she didn't want to tempt fate. She already had enough trouble battling unwanted lust without studying Bowie's tight rear in close-up.

The crowd laughed good-naturedly at Bowie's antics and started peppering him with more questions. Katie busied herself with cleaning up the video equipment. By the time she finished, the number of people had thinned.

She only had to wait a couple more minutes until Bowie headed over to her.

He approached slowly, a broad grin on his face. Her traitorous heart flipped—just as it had when she was a teenager. What was it with Bowie and his effect on her hormones? They hadn't been this active in over a decade.

"I think that went well," he said. "There were definitely more people here than usual. The ticket sales will be a start toward climbing out of the hole we're in, but we'll need more."

She nodded. "Hopefully, the next event that we plan will draw an even bigger crowd. We can start advertising it sooner, and it'll help if we get a good response to this video. I'll edit it tonight and post it on the website."

His grin faded slightly as his expression turned serious. "Did you enjoy the show?"

Bowie's question was layered with meaning. Unfortunately, Katie couldn't determine exactly what that meaning was. She wasn't even sure if he knew what he was asking. Did he want absolution? Was he concerned that the pig kissing had brought back bad memories? Did he want to know if everything was in the past? Was he wondering if a part of her was upset that it had gone so well—that he hadn't made a fool of himself?

Even if Katie could figure out the actual unspoken question, she would have no idea how to answer. Bowie left her conflicted. She didn't understand the man. Every time she thought she did, he changed again. Before she could even begin to wade through her chaotic feelings, she needed to establish a clear read of Bowie.

She decided to dodge his question entirely. "Uh-uh, you're not going to get out of our deal that easily."

He didn't press her but responded just as lighthearted-ly. "You can't blame a guy for trying. So, what's next week's video going to be about?"

Katie gave him her most wicked grin. "How do you look in a poet shirt?"

"A what now?"

"White, billowy shirt. Lots of frills." Katie paused for effect. "Goes well with an eye patch."

Understanding dawned on Bowie's face. "You want me to dress as a pirate?"

Katie nodded. "Blame Rosie...or maybe thank her. She inspired me today. I was originally thinking about you reciting odes to the animals, but this idea is so much better."

"I'd have to order a pirate costume. I guess I can get one that's not too expensive, but I don't know if it would ship on time if you want to do a video by next Saturday."

She shook her head. "No need. One of my younger brothers dressed as a pirate last Halloween. You're of similar enough build that it should fit."

"I guess it could work," Bowie said slowly.

Katie grinned at him. "The idea is perfect! We could have Rosie dance on your shoulder during your video and announce that we're going to have a pirate-themed day at the zoo in a few weeks. We could even coordinate the event with the last day of school."

—◦◦◦—

Although Bowie wasn't crazy about playing dress-up, he had to admit that Katie's idea had potential. Kids would love Pirate Day, and so would their parents.

"We wouldn't have the funds for anything fancy," Bowie warned. "We brought in some money today, but most of that will go toward keeping this place running."

"My mom used to be an art teacher," Katie said. "I'm sure she can come up with a project the kids could do that wouldn't be too expensive. I'll talk to her tomorrow. And for the next video, June is going to up her sponsorship to $350. We can talk to some of the other local businesses about doing cross promotions. Maybe the Prairie Dog Café could have a fish-and-chips special on Pirate Day."

"Let me guess, part of the festivities will include me walking around dressed as a buccaneer?" he said.

She nodded eagerly. "That's right, matey!"

"Argh," Bowie responded without inflection.

Katie laughed and shook her head. "You're going to have to improve your pirate-speak, mister."

"So how gimmicky am I going to look?"

"Bowie, there is nothing sexier than a good-looking man in a poet shirt and breeches...*if* he wears them right."

"And you think I'll wear them right?"

Katie gave him a slow and deliberate once-over. Her intensity sparked a flash of heat that roared through him. It wasn't from embarrassment but from anticipation. Bowie's brain might recognize that the unabashed smolder was only for effect, but his body didn't. At all.

"Oh yeah," she said, her voice purposefully throaty. "You'll wear them right."

―〜―

"You want me to help at the zoo? Oh, this is wonderful!" Katie's mom beamed.

Katie exchanged a look with her father before she turned her attention back to the sink. Her dad had felt up to eating lunch in the kitchen, which was a good sign. Before, he'd been having meals in his recliner. Although Katie lived in the geodesic dome house behind the old homestead, she found it easier if she ate with them. Her mom cooked, and Katie did the cleanup.

"Mom, it's no big deal…" Katie began as she wondered if she'd made a mistake in involving her mom.

"It's such a great idea, sweetheart. I'm so glad to see you becoming invested in the Sagebrush community again!"

"Now, Helen," Katie's dad said. "Katie's just doing her job. I wouldn't read too much into this."

Her mother ignored him. "I have so many ideas. A pirate theme is perfect. We could make hats, treasure boxes, cardboard swords―"

"Mom," Katie said as she leaned over to put a bowl in the dishwasher, "we don't have a lot of funds or time. We want to tie the event to the last day of school, which is only three weeks away. We've got to keep the activities simple."

"Don't worry," her mom promised. "I won't get ahead of myself."

But Katie was very much afraid that her mom already had―and not just about the craft projects.

―〜―

The next evening, Katie had just finished designing the web page for Fluffy's misadventures when one of the cougar cubs began mewling for food. She carefully placed her laptop on a counter so that it was out of reach of curious paws before heading over to the pumas. Sylvia paused in nuzzling Dobby long enough to give Katie clear access to him. Katie patted Sylvia on her head before she lifted the small mountain lion into her arms.

"Hi, little guy," she said.

Cobalt eyes met hers. Three days on, and Katie still couldn't get enough of those baby blues. Watching the kits discover the world around them was fascinating. They were starting to explore so much more, although they always came back to Sylvia whenever they got tired and needed a snuggle. Or milk. Not that Sylvia could provide the latter.

"Hang on, little dude," Katie said as she cuddled the wiggling cub. "We'll get your bottle in a second."

Dobby, however, didn't seem convinced. His squeaks lengthened into long, demanding whines. As if to punctuate his displeasure, he writhed in Katie's arms. She could feel his strong paws push against her stomach as he struggled.

That's when she felt it. The warm spray of liquid spreading across the front of her shirt. She lifted the cub and stared into his innocent blue eyes. "You did that on purpose. Didn't you?"

The cub squealed louder, and Katie shook her head. "You're lucky you're so cute."

Nestling Dobby in her arms, she grabbed his formula. Sitting cross-legged on the floor, she placed the bottle against his lips. Now that the cubs were a little older, she was able to feed them in her lap. Dobby's pink mouth immediately closed around the rubber tip as he sucked greedily. His big paws reached up to wrap around the bottle, almost like a baby human's. Katie sighed as she stroked the puma's fur. "You are trouble."

Dobby ignored her and kept drinking. After he'd had his fill, he fell asleep. Katie gently laid him down against Sylvia. The capybara tiredly raised her head to check on her charge. Content that he was once again peacefully slumbering with his sisters, the rodent settled back down.

Katie smiled at the sweet scene. Satisfied that the animals would be fine without her for a few minutes, she tiptoed out of the room. Thankfully, she'd brought spare clothes, and Bowie had pointed out a utilitarian shower in the building.

Stripping down, she jumped quickly into the spray. As she reached for the soap, she thought she heard a sound. Glancing around, she didn't notice anything. Since it was two in the morning, she doubted anyone was awake. With a shrug, she turned back and focused on finishing as quickly as possible.

Fluffy chittered softly.

Tonight was already proving to be a success. He had broken out of his enclosure in record time, courtesy of the "enrichment" toys accidentally left in his pen. The Wee One had brought him a cardboard box earlier in the day and had forgotten to retrieve it. Fluffy wasn't quite sure how the empty cube was supposed to enrich him. It was not honey-covered larvae. But he hadn't minded pushing it around with his nose or tearing it with his teeth. It also made excellent building material for an escape.

He'd roughhoused with Frida before heading to the animal hospital. He'd been watching the redheaded female closely, and now his vigilance had paid off. The biped had left a mound of scent-covered fabric in a messy heap. Although the human was momentarily distracted, he would need to work quickly. Fluffy grabbed the pieces with the strongest odor. They also happened to be the smallest articles, which made transport easier.

First, he carried them to the bush outside the maintenance facility. At the moment, he didn't dare risk the time it would take to properly deposit them. The redheaded female could leave the water box very soon, and he did not want her to catch him.

He managed to steal four pieces in quick succession. When he scurried back for the last two, he found the biped standing in the middle of the room with a confused expression on her face as she swiveled her head back and forth. Fluffy backed away before she spied him. He had work to do.

Returning to his ill-gotten gains, he pulled one piece of fabric from the pile at a time. Working rapidly, he created a trail that even a weak-nosed biped couldn't miss that led straight to the redheaded female's burrow. As Fluffy ran through the zoo, dragging the woman's scent behind him, he was quite pleased with himself. If his mouth had not been full of fabric, he would have smiled.

Chapter 6

WHEN BOWIE STARTED DOWN THE STAIRS FROM HIS back porch, he stopped. A piece of nude-colored fabric lay on the bottom step. Curious, he picked it up. It was a lady's sock and too big to be Abby's.

Odd.

About a yard later, he discovered its mate. Then a pair of black bikini bottoms. On the bush outside the animal hospital, he discovered a woman's lacy black push-up bra hanging from the branches. *What the hell?*

Suddenly, realization struck him. Only one creature in the zoo would leave a trail like this—Fluffy. The furry devil!

Bowie glanced down at the clothing in his hands. Where would Fluffy have found them? Despite all the honey badger's nocturnal adventures, he never strayed from the confines of the zoo. The little rascal probably knew how good he had it.

A cold sensation slid through Bowie. It couldn't be. Could it?

But he *had* told Katie to bring an extra set of clothes. Working at a zoo, especially with baby animals, meant anything could happen. Animals made a variety of messes all the time. Or, he thought glumly, a honey badger could steal someone's undergarments and deposit them throughout the zoo.

Bowie groaned again. He was not looking forward to

returning the clothing to Katie. Although he supposed it was better that he'd found her stuff before
another staff member or volunteer did, she was
going to think he was either a perv or back to his
old prankster ways.

He had to bring Fluffy along. Katie would never
believe him otherwise. Even with the actual culprit
in tow, Bowie had no idea how he'd explain the situation. Luckily, Abby had not left for school. Putting
Katie's stuff into a plastic grocery bag, Bowie left
it in the maintenance facility and returned to the
house where his daughter was finishing breakfast
with Lou. It didn't take her much time to catch
Fluffy. The wild creature lay complacent in her
arms, but as soon as Abby handed Bowie the mus-
telid, the little devil began to twist and snarl.

Fortunately, Bowie knew how to dodge Fluffy's
sharp teeth and claws.

He quickly carried the irate honey badger
through the zoo and into the maintenance facility
where he'd left Katie's belongings. As he grabbed
the bag of clothes, he glanced down at the struggling animal.

"You wouldn't know anything about this, would
you?"

Bowie swore the little devil grinned. Broadly.

Katie yawned and checked the time on her computer monitor. Bowie was late in relieving her from
cub-watching duty, which was unusual for him. He
was generally very prompt.

She stretched, jerking her head from side to side to work out the kinks in her neck. Just as she was starting to debate whether she should call him, she heard his footsteps outside the room. She looked up to ask him if everything was okay, but the words got lost in her burst of laughter.

Bowie stood with a contrite expression on his face. In one hand, he held a bag with one sock peeking out. Hooked under his other arm was a squirming tube of enraged mammal. Fluffy certainly wasn't happy about getting caught.

"Ah," Katie said, "so that's what happened to my clothes."

Bowie's grin seemed a tad hesitant. "You're not upset?"

Katie shook her head as she reached for her camera. "Amused. A story of sock theft will be great for the website."

After she snapped a photo, Katie bent a little at the knees so that she was level with snarling Fluffy. She wanted to pet him, but she didn't want to lose a finger... or a hand. "Hey, little guy. You're still cute, even if you are kind of surly."

The honey badger did not appear to be impressed by her compliment. In fact, his upper lip curled more. Katie laughed. "I don't think he likes being called cute."

"He prefers to intimidate," Bowie said dryly.

"So where'd you take my clothing?" Katie addressed the honey badger. At her question, she swore she saw a gleam spark in Fluffy's dark eyes.

Bowie coughed and seemed to shift uncomfortably. Katie even thought she spotted the faintest trace of red creeping up his neck. Who would have guessed that the high-school prankster could blush?

"Well, where did you find it?" Katie asked him.

Bowie cleared his throat again. "There was a trail. It led from my house to the animal hospital."

Katie blinked, nonplussed by his answer. Then, when she finally wrapped her head around the image, she erupted into laughter.

"Oh my gosh," she said between unstoppable guffaws, "now even a honey badger is trying to set us up."

Heat flared in Bowie's gray eyes, threatening to sear Katie's heart. In fact, it might have burned to a crisp, if not for the firewalls she'd set up around it years ago. She swallowed. Hard.

It didn't help. So she tried again. Still nothing.

"Is that so bad?" Bowie asked, his voice sounding rich and thick. Like a milk shake made with Belgian chocolate. And she wanted what he was offering. Craved it even.

"What?" Katie feigned ignorance, hating how her voice seemed sharper and maybe…just maybe…a tad breathless.

"Us."

The word hung between them. Tempting. Intoxicating. Dangerous. Like a sweetly perfumed but deadly flower. And having experienced this particular poison's aftereffects before, she had no desire to partake again. No matter how alluring.

Ignoring his question, she broke their gaze and jerked her chin at the honey badger still squirming in Bowie's grasp. "Well, at least he's given us a great story to tell."

Katie thought she sensed a flicker of disappointment from Bowie's corner before he turned his attention back to Fluffy. "Yeah, well, we're not going to be short on those. Fluffy thinks he owns the zoo, and this won't be his last misadventure."

Katie laughed. She bent at her knees again to stare into the honey badger's surprisingly sweet face. "Is that true?"

The honey badger chose that moment to sniff and toss its head. Katie laughed. "Well, aren't you clever!"

Fluffy appeared to grin. Katie clasped her hands, impossibly charmed by the little guy. "He's adorable."

Bowie grunted. "Not the word I would choose, but I have to admit there's something about him that sucks you in. Lou says it's the bit of the devil in him. Abby claims it's because he's a big softy underneath all his snarls."

"What's your theory?"

Bowie lifted the animal to regard it thoughtfully. Fluffy hissed in protest at the undignified treatment. Lowering Fluffy, Bowie shrugged. "Everyone deserves a home. Even those with the nastiest of temperaments."

Something in his tone struck Katie. She sensed that she stood at the edge of an uncharted ocean. He wasn't just talking about animals, but she wasn't interested in diving into his waters. Not when the undertow could threaten to drown her. She'd survived the whirlpool of attraction once, and she wasn't about to attempt another exploration. At least not an emotional one. A physical one, though… The thought might be starting to appeal to her. As long as she didn't get attached, would an affair really make leaving Sagebrush that much harder?

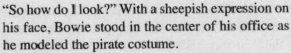

"So how do I look?" With a sheepish expression on his face, Bowie stood in the center of his office as he modeled the pirate costume.

Katie's twin brothers had always loved Halloween, and they spared no expense on their costumes. This one was no exception. It had everything—bandanna, eye patch, knee-high boots, and fake cutlass.

Not many men could pull off the ridiculous ensemble, but, oh, could Bowie. The cotton poet shirt clung to his broad shoulders, highlighting them, while the flowing sleeves provided a perfect foil for his muscles. The result was at once romantic and undeniably masculine. There was something alluring about a swashbuckling pirate, especially one with a face like Bowie's.

"You look like you're ready to sail the high seas."

Bowie tugged at the front of his shirt, causing the material to pull taut across his biceps. "Did I tie this right? I didn't want to leave too much of a gap."

Katie studied the placket. "I think you may have laced it a little tight. The ruffle isn't lying flat."

He groaned and started fiddling with it. She watched in interest as the sides of the collar fell away. Unfortunately, the V-neck opening wasn't that large. She had only the slightest glimpse of taut skin before Bowie pulled the fabric together. This time, he secured it too loosely.

"Why did men ever wear shirts like this?" he grumbled as he tried again.

"Buttons were more expensive and hard to come by?" Katie wagered a guess.

Bowie grunted, and she could hear his frustration. He yanked too hard, and the material puckered even worse than the first time. His bow hung lopsided, one side twice as long as the other.

"It would help if it wasn't surrounded by frills. The cuffs keep getting in my way."

Katie laughed. Bowie shot her a glare, and she sobered. "Would you like me to help?"

"Yes." He practically growled out the word, and she had to smother another chuckle.

"Here, let me." She stepped forward and reached for the lacing. Her fingers brushed against his, and awareness immediately sizzled through her nerve endings. Biting her lip hard, she tried to concentrate on the task, but she couldn't turn off her senses. Heat radiated from his body, and his unique scent—spicy and masculine— washed over her. Her breathing grew irregular, but she managed to tie the shirt properly. She stepped back and patted his chest.

"There," she said, her voice strained. "All done."

Then she made a critical mistake. She looked up.

Bowie's eyes had turned a molten gray. Katie hadn't realized the smoky color could burn, but his gaze practically seared her.

For a moment, they just stared. She didn't think she had ever experienced such a sexually charged moment. Never had a mere glance carried such impact. She could feel herself grow wet as his heart thudded beneath her hand.

She didn't know who shifted first. Maybe they both

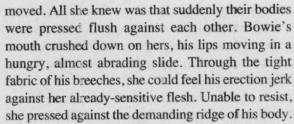

moved. All she knew was that suddenly their bodies were pressed flush against each other. Bowie's mouth crushed down on hers, his lips moving in a hungry, almost abrading slide. Through the tight fabric of his breeches, she could feel his erection jerk against her already-sensitive flesh. Unable to resist, she pressed against the demanding ridge of his body.

At the contact, Katie moaned into Bowie's mouth. He grabbed her bottom and pulled her even closer. When she gasped, he moved his mouth to trail hot kisses across the vulnerable skin near her jaw and down her throat. Just as she'd yearned to do for years, she dug her hands in the soft waves of his hair.

There was no finesse in their embrace—just blistering, wild, urgent need. She reveled in it. She wanted this, craved it even. Obviously, Bowie did too.

And why not? Why not indulge?

She wasn't sixteen and in puppy love. As long as she recognized this for what it was—two adults with a healthy attraction enjoying each other—she wouldn't get hurt. She would make sure she protected herself this time.

Sex with Bowie would be fun, explosive, and playful. The perfect summer fling. What it wouldn't be—and never could be—was serious. If she never lost sight of that, she was going to have a good time hooking up with him.

It was time to start the party.

Quirking her lips ever so slightly upward, she hooked her finger in the waistband of his breeches. Then she lifted one eyebrow in a silent question.

Bowie swallowed noticeably and gave a firm

nod. She grabbed the fabric with both hands and pulled down his pants and underwear in one smooth, flawless move. His erection bobbed free. Not satisfied, Katie undid the lacing she'd just tied moments before and removed the poet shirt.

Only then did she step back to admire. Oh, he looked good. All lean, athletic muscle to match his handsome face. The Greeks could have used him as a model for one of their famed statutes.

Yes, she had definitely made the right choice.

Bowie had lost all capacity to think coherently.

Even if he could cobble together more than a fleeting thought, he doubted he could unravel exactly how he ended up stark naked in front of Katie Underwood. Oh, he'd certainly fantasized about having sex with her over the past two weeks, but he'd never believed it would happen.

But it *was* happening, and the foreplay was already more erotically intense than his imagination. Even with Katie standing a few feet from him, his body hummed with energy. He could practically feel her gaze caress him as it swept slowly over his body. Maybe he should have felt objectified, but he didn't. Her blatant appreciation stirred something hot, deep, and primal.

He wanted to see her naked too.

"My turn." His words came out in a hoarse growl, but Katie didn't balk at his demand.

Instead, she stared him straight in the eye and, with unhurried deliberation, peeled off her T-shirt. His body tightened even more as he caught sight of her plump breasts clad in black lace demi cups. Then Katie slowly

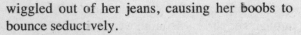

wiggled out of her jeans, causing her boobs to bounce seductively.

His cock jerked in response.

Damn, he wanted to be inside her.

A triumphantly sexy smile lit Katie's face as she unhooked the front of her bra. He felt her steady gaze as he hungrily watched the fabric drop away. She had the kind of breasts guys idealized. Full and heavy — and perfect for cupping in a man's hand. He itched to feel their weight against his palms.

A movement caught his eyes and dragged his gaze downward. A pair of silky black bikini bottoms slipped slowly down Katie's legs. She had soft, round hips to match her breasts. Katie probably saw her slightly extra padding as weight to battle. Bowie never could understand why women didn't realize that a man liked to sink into softness when he made love.

"So," Katie asked in a conversational tone that impressed the hell out of him, "where do you keep condoms around here?"

Condom. Right.

"Uh," Bowie floundered as tried to push through the lust filling his mind to find a coherent thought. It had been a while since he'd seen any action. He'd certainly never had any in his office. Maybe he had a condom in his wallet, but he didn't know how old it would be.

"I think I may have an emergency one in my purse," Katie said.

Sweet, nerdy Katie Underwood carried emergency condoms? Before his brain could fully register that tidbit, she turned around and bent over to dig through her purse. His mind went blank again.

She had a really, really great butt.

"Got one," Katie declared. "Found two actually."

She turned around and lobbed one in his direction. He reflexively caught it against his chest. He barely had time to rip open the packaging and slip on the condom before Katie crashed into him. She snaked one bare leg around him while pressing her mouth against his. He wrapped his arms about her, resting his hands on her bottom. It felt even better than it looked.

Hoping to elicit more sounds of pleasure, he trailed his lips down Katie's sensitive neck. Once again, she arched her back, thrusting her bare breasts practically into his face. He tentatively began to kiss in that direction. Katie slid her hands into his hair and guided him down to the valley between her breasts.

Oh yeah.

As Bowie explored with his mouth, he could hear Katie's short gasps of delight. Between the taste of her velvety skin and her sensual cries, he grew even harder.

Then she pressed against him.

He groaned against the onslaught of lust. His hands instinctively kneaded the soft flesh of Katie's bottom. She responded by moving her hips in a rhythmic circle.

Bowie felt as if he was going to explode. With a harsh intake of air, he managed to pull away just in time.

"Katie...sweetheart," he managed to force out between ragged breaths. "We've got to slow down, or I'm not going to last."

The right side of her lips quirked upward in a pure, sensual challenge. "Let's speed up instead. I'm ready for you."

Before Bowie's lust-hazed mind could fully process her statement, she pushed on his chest. He automatically took a couple of steps backward. When his calves hit the front of his desk, Katie gently shoved him. His legs buckled, and he plopped down.

She straddled him, placing one knee on either side of the desk. Then, she slowly lowered her body, one delicious centimeter at a time. As her warmth encased the length of him, he groaned helplessly. She began to move then—slow and steady. Need swelled inside, driving him to the brink of madness.

Bowie grabbed Katie's bottom and increased the speed as he thrust upward. She gave a cry of pleasure as she lifted her breasts in clear invitation. He circled one nipple with his tongue before taking it into his mouth.

She dug her fingers into his scalp as her inner muscles convulsed around him. Encouraged, he increased the tempo, their sweat-slicked skin rubbing against each other's.

Katie came first. Her muscles spasmed around him as she cried out. His body responded with a shattering climax of its own.

Bowie collapsed back on his desk, pulling Katie with him. She sprawled limply across his chest. As they lay sucking in air, he idly ran his fingers against the soft skin of her back.

His brain scrambled to understand what the hell had just happened. He knew one thing for certain. He had just experienced the single most erotic episode of his entire life.

In his office, of all places.

He was grateful they'd locked the door to film the video and that the blinds were pulled. Even though it was still early, since they were shooting right after Katie's shift with the cubs, he didn't want Lou or, especially, Abby walking in on them.

Katie lifted her head a couple of inches from his chest and shot him an impish look.

"So, I've got another condom. When do you think you'll be ready for round two?"

———— ⁓ ————

Round two, unfortunately, was postponed. Katie still wanted to film the video so they could upload it to the website on schedule, and Bowie didn't have much time before the zoo opened for the day.

Despite the fact that her nerve endings still sizzled, Katie managed to hold the camera steady as she taped Bowie and Rosie. The little cockatoo was a natural performer. As soon as Bowie placed the bird on his shoulder, she preened, running her gray foot through her yellow mohawk as she stared coquettishly into the lens. While Bowie gave facts about parrots, Rosie pulled affectionately at his hair. Right after he mentioned the natural curiosity of cockatoos, she explored the strap of his eye patch.

But when Katie flipped on the music, Rosie stood at attention and started tapping her foot to the initial notes of "Yo Ho (A Pirate's Life for Me)." She bobbed and weaved on Bowie's shoulder, keeping perfect time. When the song ended, Rosie squawked and ducked her head, shaking out her plume. The gesture looked exactly like a little bow. Luckily, Katie managed to keep from cooing and ruining the perfect take.

Bowie reached over and carefully lifted Rosie off his shoulder. He placed her in the cage they'd used to transport her from her exhibit. With the bird in one hand, he turned back to Katie.

"That went well," he said, resting his hand on the back of his head. It struck Katie that he was feeling a little nervous after their lovemaking and maybe even a tad unsure. And, darn, if she didn't find that sweet and flattering.

"Kids and parents will love the video," she told him. "Pirate Day is going to be a huge success. I just feel it."

Bowie nodded and cleared his throat. "Well, I guess this is goodbye then... For now, I mean."

At his quick clarification, Katie smiled. Who would have thought that Bowie Wilson could have an awkward side?

Unable to help herself, she stood on her tiptoes and brushed a kiss over his lips. As she stepped back, she gave him her sexiest smile. "See you tonight, Bowie." Then, with one last flirtatious grin, she pulled the office door shut behind her.

Despite having taken care of the cubs all night, Katie felt energized and maybe even a little giddy as she drove home. But by the time she'd stopped at the ranch house to say hello to her parents and then headed to her own place, the frenetic energy had ebbed, leaving her drained. She fell into a deep, sated sleep as soon as she climbed into bed and woke rejuvenated just before it was time to head to the zoo to care for the cubs.

As Katie walked into the nursery, she noticed that Bowie had moved the air mattress into the adjacent room. It was close enough that they could still hear the little guys if they cried for milk, but its location would give her and Bowie more privacy. Anticipation bubbled inside her.

Humming happily, she tinkered with the zoo's website while the cubs played. Fleur, the most affectionate of the trio, crawled over and bumped against Katie's leg. Katie smiled as she reached down to ruffle the cougar's head. After some snuggles, the little puma began her clumsy crawl to rejoin her siblings, who were playing with plush animals. Katie returned to her design work. She was so absorbed, she didn't notice that Bowie had entered the room until he nuzzled the side of her neck.

"Mmmm," she murmured as she leaned back against his strong chest. She smiled contentedly as his lips found all the right spots.

"Sorry it took me so long," he said between kisses. "I had to clean up the dishes and put Abby to bed."

"No problem," Katie said as she turned to kiss him full on the mouth. She welcomed the warm waves of pleasure that rolled through her.

Although the embrace lacked the urgency of this morning's encounter, it was every bit as potent. Instead of igniting Katie's passion, it drugged her with languid sensuality.

Just then, Dobby began to mewl plaintively. Bowie grabbed a prepared bottle and expertly fed the little guy. Knowing that once one started complaining, so did the others, Katie took charge of one of the sisters.

When the cubs had had their fill, they lumbered over

to Sylvia. Bowie and Katie lifted the little guys into the crate. The capybara had fallen asleep, but she patiently tolerated the invasion. The trio climbed over her until they all found comfortable positions. It didn't take long until all four animals were slumbering together in the most adorable heap of fur.

Bowie turned back to Katie, his expression downright wolfish. He crossed over to her in two masterful strides.

"Now where were we?" he murmured as he dipped his lips to meet hers. Then, to her surprise, he grabbed her by her butt and effortlessly hoisted her into the air. She instinctively wrapped her legs around him. Without breaking the kiss, Bowie carried her to the adjacent room where he'd moved the air mattress. He bent over and gently deposited her on the makeshift bed before kneeling down beside her.

The show of masculine strength sent a thrill through Katie. Sitting half-reclined, she reached up to brush her hand over his bicep, relishing the feel of his hard muscles.

When she pulled at his T-shirt, he obligingly shucked it aside. Leaning forward, she licked his chest while he undid the buttons on her shirt. Although he fumbled slightly, it didn't take him long to push back the fabric. With adorable concentration, he unhooked the front of her bra as she sat up to give him access. He didn't even give her time to slip out of her loosened clothes before his mouth closed over one of her breasts. His warm hand kneaded the other until he had her gasping and writhing with pleasure.

Desperate to have him inside her again, she undid the fly on his jeans. He eased back just long enough to pull down his pants. While he put on a condom, she fully removed her shirt. She started to pull down her jean shorts, but Bowie gently laid his hand on her wrist.

"Let me," he said, his voice husky and honey-smooth. She stopped and allowed him to peel back the denim fabric two inches at a time. She watched, fascinated, as he paused to kiss each swath of her body as he revealed it. When he reached the sensitive areas of her inner thigh, he sucked slightly, his gray eyes steady on hers. She wiggled against the absolute pleasure building inside her.

When she thought she could no longer withstand the unfulfilled sparks he ignited, Bowie finally finished removing her shorts. Then, he slipped her dampened panties from her body and placed his mouth against her. Her body arched at the feel of his tongue. With his calloused thumbs, he rhythmically stroked the seams of her inner thighs.

As wave after wave of intense, brilliant pleasure coursed through her, Katie helplessly gripped the sides of the air mattress. Her whimpers grew into cries as she shattered. By the time she finished, she was panting heavily. When some semblance of sanity returned, she found Bowie watching her with pure male satisfaction.

"You liked that, didn't you?" he asked.

She managed a breathless *uh-huh*, which only made his grin broaden.

"Would you like some more?"

She nodded emphatically, and he chuckled. He lowered his body onto hers, then sank slowly inside her, the friction further stimulating the already-sensitized nerve endings. Their lips met, pressing together in a frenzied dance.

Bowie started to move, slowly and deeply inside her. Katie made a sound in the back of her throat as she thrust her hips upward, urging him to increase the speed. He needed no further prompting. Soon, they moved at a frenetic pace. His lips found a sensitive spot between her shoulder and neck, expertly heightening her pleasure.

Katie came first, and then she felt Bowie's muscles stiffen. He gave a cry of his own and partially collapsed against her. With a groan, he flipped their bodies so that she lay draped over him. Tracing lazy circles over his chest with her finger, she regarded him. His eyelids had drifted half-closed, and he had a blissfully satisfied expression on his face.

She lay there for a few minutes, enjoying the feel of his strong body under hers. So far, he was one of the best lovers she'd ever had—maybe even the best. There was something raw and primal about their couplings. Maybe it was because she had decided ahead of time that their relationship wasn't going to progress beyond the physical. She knew better than to be romantic about Bowie. Maybe even to be romantic about anyone. He'd taught her that lesson early on, and it had stuck with her. Sure, she'd done some dating and had even had some relationships that lasted for a while, but she had never invested her heart fully, and she'd never been particularly devastated when those relationships came to a natural end. It was safer that way.

Bowie's breathing grew heavy as he drifted off

to sleep. Quietly, Katie tried to climb off the air mattress without disturbing him. His eyes flew open just as she stood up. She could see his appreciation as his gaze fell on her nude body. It was nice having a man as attractive as Bowie Wilson study her with such undisguised lust. Although Katie didn't obsess over her body image, she knew she wasn't perfect. She carried too much flab around her thighs, hips, and butt, but when he looked at her like that, she felt like a goddess.

"Sorry." Bowie stifled a yawn. "Didn't mean to fall asleep right away."

Katie gave him a smile to show he hadn't offended her. "That's okay. You've had a long day."

He raked his hand through his hair as he stared at her. "You're sure you're not upset?"

She shook her head. "Bowie, it's okay if we keep things casual."

His eyebrows pulled downward. "Ah, just so there is no misinterpretation, and I don't accidentally end up being an insensitive jerk, what exactly does 'keep things casual' mean?"

"Friends with benefits."

Bowie frowned. "So, you and me? It's just sex? Nothing more?"

She nodded. "Yeah. Just no-strings-attached sex."

<center>~~~</center>

Katie confused the hell out of Bowie. Of course, it didn't help that his mind was currently fried from a second round of mind-blowing sex in less than twenty-four hours. Through the years, he'd had his share of one-night stands, but even those women demanded a semblance of affection after tearing up the sheets. Hell, he didn't blame them. It wasn't asking much for a guy to stay the night instead of hightailing away as soon as the action stopped.

He didn't know if Katie really meant no-strings-attached sex. Hell, he didn't think such a thing existed outside of porn. Sex had consequences unless the couple never encountered each other again, and Katie was fairly intertwined in his life at the moment. Even if she quit volunteering and helping him with marketing, Sagebrush wasn't a big town. They'd run into each other eventually.

Plus, Bowie was fairly certain that Katie planned to continue having sex with him, something he would very much like to encourage. He didn't want to screw things up by acting like a jerk. He also didn't want her to bail on helping out at the zoo.

He rubbed the back of his head. "I don't want to be dense, but I want to make sure that we're on the same page. You would be okay if I walked out of here right now and went home to bed?"

Katie nodded.

"Then what? We hook up when we're in the mood, and other than that, we continue as though nothing else has changed?"

"Yes. I was being honest when I said we could just be friends with benefits. I appreciate you trying to make sure I know what I'm getting into, but this works for me, especially right now. I'm not sure how long I'll stick around Sagebrush, and I wouldn't want to complicate things by starting something serious."

Bowie wondered if he knew what *he* was getting into. He'd never done anything like this before. It wasn't as if Sagebrush was a hotbed of sexual activity. The dating scene basically sucked for a single dad.

Sagebrush had some skiing—nothing impressive like in Aspen, but it brought in college students and young professionals looking for a cheaper alternative to an expensive ski weekend. In the summer, nearby Rocky Ridge National Park attracted backpackers and outdoor enthusiasts. When he was younger and before Gretchen got sick, Bowie would hit up the local bar every now and again. He'd had a pretty good success rate at meeting solo out-of-towners who'd invite him back to their lodgings. When Gretchen was first diagnosed with cancer, Bowie hadn't wanted to bother her or Lou with babysitting Abby. Then he'd found himself taking care of both the household and the zoo. Now he was so busy that when he had downtime, he wanted to spend it with Abby, not a random woman. And since he'd just turned thirty at the beginning of the summer, he was way too old for picking up coeds.

Hell if he knew anything about real relationships. The only long-term commitment he'd experienced had been the two and a half years he'd spent with Sawyer. It had been a clichéd high-school romance—high drama, multiple breakups, unchecked hormones, the whole gambit.

"This is what you want?" Bowie asked.

Katie bobbed her head again and then paused as if considering something for the first time. "Are you okay with it?"

Was he okay with it? He was a guy. This was

supposed to be his nirvana, right? "Sure." he said. "I'm good. So, um, I guess this is good night then."

"Get your rest, cowboy," Katie said, as she wiggled her eyebrows suggestively. "You might need some extra energy tomorrow…if you're lucky."

Despite its recent workout, his body tensed in anticipation. With an awkward half smile, Bowie ducked out of the room and headed across the zoo to his house.

Friends with benefits. It sounded like a great setup, especially for a busy single father. Steady sex with little effort. No theatrics. No fuss. Just pure physical pleasure.

So why was he feeling a little like the lovelorn Lulubelle?

———

Fluffy grinned. Broadly. His plans had come to fruition. The Black-Haired One was staying in the redheaded female's burrow. Soon, there would be more wee ones.

Satisfied with his handiwork, he shuffled away from the animal hospital. He had other adventures tonight. Frida needed more excitement and exercise than she got from playing with the ball the bipeds had given her. The Black-Haired One could carry on now without Fluffy's manipulations. Natural instincts were engaged, so nothing could go wrong. Fluffy was certain that even the bipeds couldn't mess this up. Well, almost certain. They were human after all.

Chapter 7

BOWIE RECOGNIZED KATIE'S OFFICIOUS KNOCK BEFORE she burst into his office. Over the last two weeks, he'd never known what to expect when she dropped by the zoo at times other than the routine hours she spent with the cubs each night. For some reason that escaped Bowie, she'd taken an honest interest in the place. Even better, she possessed excellent instincts for marketing and fund-raising. He never would have thought of half her ideas for using social media.

And then there was the sex. The incredible, rock-your-world, explosive sex.

Given the way they'd been going after each other as if it was the seasonal rut, Bowie thought the white-hot, frenzied passion would have mellowed.

It hadn't.

If anything, the intensity had increased. The creativity certainly had. They had found a use for just about every surface in his office. When Bowie discovered that any move requiring strength provoked an enthusiastic response from Katie, he used that knowledge to his full advantage. He'd lost count of how many times he'd taken her against the wall, her amazing legs wrapped around him.

"Great news," Katie told him brightly. "Website traffic is way up, and we've gotten over a hundred new followers on Twitter just this week alone."

"Ah, that's good," Bowie managed. His mind hadn't completely switched its focus away from images of Katie crying out as he moved inside her.

"I posted a story about Lulubelle's love troubles on Facebook last night. It's already gotten tons of likes and a decent number of shares, and the page views are the best they've been except when we posted the pirate video."

Thoughts of sex gone, Bowie straightened in his chair. "Really? That's great."

"I talked to the Prairie Dog Café. They recently hired me to redesign their menu, and I suggested that they name some of their dishes after the animals in the zoo and include pictures of each critter. Karen Montgomery loves the idea, as long as you include a link to their restaurant on your website."

"That's awesome! Every time I go to the Prairie Dog, I see a bunch of tourists from Rocky Ridge National Park. How do you keep wrangling so much support for the zoo?"

Katie shot him a cheese-eating grin. "I can be pretty persuasive when I want to be."

A warmth—gentler and calmer than the molten lust she generally inspired—spread through him. Her smile had a tendency to do that.

"Thank you." Even to his own ears, Bowie's voice sounded husky. Katie's brown eyes softened, but just for a fleeting moment. Almost instantly, she turned all business again. Not for the first time, a sense of foreboding slipped through Bowie like a cougar stalking its prey. The physical part of his relationship with her was terrific, but every time he attempted to be remotely affectionate, she pulled back.

"Speaking of publicity," Katie said, "we're getting a lot of comments on the zoo's social media outlets. The most popular inquiry is the topic of your next video."

Unfortunately, that no longer surprised Bowie. Within days after posting the pirate video, the zoo had received countless emails and even a few calls. Over the last couple of days, they'd experienced a spike in visitors. The only drawback was that people, especially women, kept coming up to talk to him. Before the marketing campaign, he'd occasionally received questions about the animals, but visitors had never asked him anything personal. Now, adults wanted to know all about *him*, especially if he was single or in a relationship.

At first, he hadn't known how to respond. Part of him felt flattered, but mostly his recent celebrity discomforted him. For the past decade, he'd led a very quiet life. Even before that, he'd always lived on the periphery with the sole exception of when he'd hung out with Sawyer.

But Bowie couldn't deny that his newfound fame helped the zoo. The local news planned to come next week to do a story on the cougar cubs and on Pirate Day. He just needed to figure out how to translate his internet notoriety into cash, especially since he doubted the buzz would last much longer.

"I've been thinking of ways that we could use my stunts to get people more engaged with the zoo itself," he said. "I know our deal is that you come up with the ideas, but would you be okay if we posted two options for the next video and people voted on their favorite?"

"I think that's a great idea. I was actually going to tell you that you're off the hook…at least as far as I'm concerned. I think you should do more zany stuff to keep interest up, but it's your call. I'll volunteer regardless."

Bowie straightened in his chair as he watched Katie carefully. Something shifted inside him, relieving a pressure he'd tried to ignore. "I'm forgiven then?"

She shrugged. "That was high school. This is now. Besides, I think we'll have more fun if we come up with the fund-raising ideas together."

It didn't escape his notice that Katie had dodged his actual question. Some of the heaviness returned. At least she seemed willing to move beyond his juvenile stupidity.

Bowie genuinely enjoyed Katie's company, even when they did nothing but brainstorm about zoo promotions. Although Lou had a wealth of veterinary knowledge, even he freely admitted he didn't have a head for business. Gretchen had balanced the books, and the zoo had limped along. After her death, Bowie had figured out the finances and managed to keep the whole damn thing from folding. Now, he actually had a chance to raise capital for improvements. It helped having someone like Katie whose brain just seemed hardwired for marketing.

"I actually have a plan in mind," he said. "What if we filmed one of the videos live at an event even bigger than what we're planning for Pirate Day? It might take more coordination, but I think if it's done right, the zoo could bring in a lot of money. We could even coordinate it with the cubs' public debut."

"Ooo, I *like* that idea. Maybe we could throw a little festival. We could ask local vendors to set up booths."

"I drew up some ideas and did preliminary budgeting," Bowie said as he went to pull up the file on his computer. He'd been reading through grant criteria before Katie's entrance, which reminded him of the other thing he wanted to discuss with her.

"I was wondering if you wouldn't mind helping me brainstorm for another project," he said.

"Sure," Katie said, brightening. "What is it?"

"There's a foundation that puts small zoos in contact with environmental groups looking to place abandoned animals. Their main focus is on polar bears. But the best thing about them is that they give the money before the animal arrives to help pay for the proper equipment and enclosures. This could really help rejuvenate our rescue program."

"I'm sensing a 'but,'" Katie said.

"They want community involvement, including pledges to volunteer and to contribute 25 percent of the cost. I'm putting together a proposal for an exhibit design, which is supposed to be state of the art. You need to include water features that the bears can play in and that can even be stocked with fish for them to catch. I was wondering if you could help me come up with a strategy to get support from our town."

"Of course," Katie said. "I can start with the website, and we can definitely do something during Pirate's Day and the festival—"

Just then, without warning, the door burst open. Abby flew into the office, tears streaming down her face. Her little shoulders shook with suppressed sobs.

Bowie sprang to his feet as his heart slammed into his chest. Abby didn't cry often, and she was never prone to the dramatic.

"What's wrong, honey?" Bowie asked as he crossed over to her. Abby only shook her head helplessly as sobs choked her.

Frantic with worry, he crouched beside her to check for injuries. He didn't observe any. She launched herself at him, burying her face against his chest.

"Are you hurt?" he asked, cradling her. Abby shook her head, her wet cheeks soaking his shirt. Running his hand gently down her hair, Bowie tried to soothe her. Right now, she seemed as vulnerable as a frightened chinchilla.

"What happened, Abby Bear?" he asked, using his nickname for her.

"They." *Sob*. "Clarissa." *Sob*. "So mean." *Sob*. "Laughed at me." *Sob*. "Awful."

Okay, that didn't help Bowie. At least, he could rule out catastrophic injury. He'd heard Clarissa's name before. She was in Abby's class and led a group of girls who picked on his daughter.

He knew from experience that when Abby became this distraught, it was best just to let her cry it out. Now that he knew she wasn't in danger, he could wait to ask questions. All he could do was hold his daughter, even if every sob tore at him. He hated when his kid hurt, especially when he couldn't do a damn thing about it.

Remembering Katie's presence in the room, he turned his head. Since he and Abby blocked the only exit, she'd moved to the farthest corner. Katie was studying the blank wall with great interest, but she must have felt his gaze. When she turned, their eyes locked, and she sent him a concerned, questioning look. He gave a slight shake of his head to indicate that he didn't fully understand the source of Abby's tears.

Finally, after a few minutes, Abby's sobs subsided enough to allow her to speak coherently. Bowie pulled back and wiped away some of his daughter's tears.

"Tell me what's wrong, Abby Bear," he said, keeping his voice soft and comforting. Abby swiped at her nose, and Bowie dug into the pocket of his jeans for a tissue. Life as a single dad had taught him to always keep a few handy. Abby took it and blew noisily.

"Clarissa, Monica, and Gabby were talking about me during recess today," Abby got out before her face crumpled again.

"Did they say something to hurt you?" Bowie asked.

Abby sucked in her bottom lip in an attempt not to cry. She nodded solemnly. Bowie waited patiently until she gathered herself.

"They pretended not to see me. They said I was so ugly that I couldn't be your daughter, 'cause everyone says you're so handsome." Abby's words came out in a jumbled rush before she pierced him with a pained look in her gray eyes. "Is it true? You aren't my real dad?"

Anger, disgust, and a little disbelief warred inside Bowie. He ached for his daughter and wished he could do something, anything, to stop Clarissa's bullying. But what could he do? At least the end of the school year was only a little over a week away.

"None of what they said is true," Bowie said. "I am definitely your father." He had the DNA results to prove

it. He'd needed them during his custody case, not
that he would reveal that to Abby. Even without the
genetic proof, Abby looked like a blend of him and
Sawyer. True, she had more of Sawyer's delicate
features, but she had his coloring, smile, and laugh.

"But I'm ugly!" Abby wailed.

"Abby Bear, you're not ugly. You're very pretty,
and you're going to grow up to be a beautiful young
woman."

To Bowie's surprise, Abby struggled out of his
embrace. "That's not true! You're lying. Are you
lying about everything?"

Bowie's heart broke at the raw anguish in his
daughter's voice. He reached out to touch her, but
she darted away. He wished like hell he knew what
to say to her. He hated that these girls made her
doubt herself to the point that she questioned her
relationship with him. Worse, he had no idea how
to break through the irrational wall of pain surrounding his kid.

Suddenly, he felt Katie kneel beside him. She
grabbed Abby gently by the shoulders.

"Abby," she said in a soft but no-nonsense voice,
"look at me."

Watery-eyed, Abby complied.

"Do you think I'm ugly?" Katie asked.

Abby shook her head.

"I used to think I was ugly," Katie said.

That appeared to shock Abby out of her crying
as she stared transfixed at Katie. Bowie, however,
felt worse. He hoped like hell that Katie didn't tear
up too.

"Do you know why I used to think I was ugly?"

Abby shook her head again, her gray eyes wide.

"Because kids at school told me that. They told me over and over and over again until I believed it. And you know what? I let them convince me of that for years."

Bowie now felt like complete and utter shit. Although he didn't know if he'd ever directly called Katie ugly, his pranks certainly would have made her feel that way. Hell, one Halloween, he, Sawyer, and her friends all wore Ronald McDonald or Little Orphan Annie wigs. Since Katie was the only curly-haired redhead in the school, everyone knew who they were mocking. Although that particular idea had been Sawyer's, Bowie had put on the damn wig.

Intellectually, Bowie had always known that he'd hurt Katie. He'd regretted his actions for a long time. But it was one thing to think about it in the abstract and another to hear it from a woman he cared about. Worse, just as with Abby, he couldn't fix the problem. Not only had it happened years ago, but he couldn't very well kick his own ass.

"But...but you're pretty," Abby protested. "Why would they make fun of you?"

"Because kids can be mean," Katie said simply. "Some of them do it because they're not happy with themselves. Others may be jealous. And sometimes, people are just cruel."

"But I'm weird," Abby said. "I'm not like everyone else."

Katie gave her a kind smile. "Thank goodness for that. We're all a little unique. Even the girls who make fun of you are different. The trick isn't to hide it or be embarrassed by it. You need to make it work for you."

Abby cocked her head and watched Katie intently. "Were you really unpopular?"

"I was called Katie Underwear since first grade. When I went on a high-school ski trip, someone sneaked into my room and changed the wake-up alarm so that I got left at the lodge. A couple of popular kids once marked their cheeks with the school letters in face paint and asked me if I wanted one on mine too. They drew a pig's face instead with permanent marker. When I tried out for a school play, they switched the name in the script with the nickname of the high school mascot to trick me into confessing true love to a horned toad."

Abby's mouth formed an O, and Bowie's gut clenched with guilt. Other than the Underwear appellation and the redheaded wigs, he'd engineered every one of those pranks. Sawyer had loved his ideas. He remembered her clapping her hands in delight when he came up with a scheme. Guys in their group would slap him on the back while the girls laughed. For once in his life, he'd belonged somewhere. Yet, he knew, as soon as he stepped entertaining them, he'd go back to being the white-trash nobody. That didn't make what he did right. Hell, it probably made everything more despicable, because he'd known it was wrong.

"I won't sugarcoat it, Abby," Katie continued. "School can be hard. What Clarissa and her friends said was horrible, but don't let them define you.

Your dad loves you, and there's no doubt that you're his daughter. You have his eyes."

"I do?" Abby asked.

Katie nodded. "And he's also right about your looks. You have very pretty features."

"But I don't *feel* pretty," Abby protested.

"Have you ever tried?" Katie asked.

Abby frowned and pondered this for a moment. Then, slowly, she shook her head. "You can't *be* pretty by just *feeling* pretty."

"I'm not talking about physical appearance. There have been plenty of women throughout history who led people because they were amazing, not because of how they looked or how they dressed."

"Really?" Abby sounded skeptical.

"Eleanor Roosevelt, for one. Harriet Tubman, Justices Sandra Day O'Connor and Ruth Bader Ginsburg. I could give you a whole list."

"Are you saying if I'm confident, I'll be popular?"

"Not necessarily…at least not right away," Katie said. "But if you have strength of character, you *will* draw people to you."

"Do you think I could grow up to be like you?"

Katie smiled fondly at Abby. "I think you will grow up to be a wonderful woman and completely your own person."

Abby launched herself at Katie. Nearly caught off-balance, Katie reflexively caught her. At first, Katie seemed unsure, but then she relaxed into the embrace. A tremulous smile stretched across Abby's face, and in the curl of her lips, Bowie detected a glint of belief in herself.

A band formed around Bowie's throat. Abby had

always been on the fringes at school, but this past year had been incredibly tough. More than once, she'd cried herself to sleep after Bowie had failed to console her. He hadn't known what to say to convince her that things would be okay. He certainly didn't have any advice on how to deal with a mean-girl clique. He'd read a few articles online for single dads, but they hadn't helped.

Katie's words had. With middle school and high school looming, Bowie knew there would be other cruel words and disappointments. But he also had no doubt that Katie's words had resonated with Abby…and they'd impacted him too.

Even in high school, Bowie had respected Katie's inner strength when she hadn't broken under their pranks. But tonight, after watching Katie comfort Abby, his admiration soared. It took self-assurance and a kind heart to share past humiliations, especially in front of the guy who'd masterminded them. Katie was an amazing woman.

Abby sniffed and beamed up at Katie. "Would you like to come to dinner? Dad doesn't mind, do you?"

No, he didn't, but from the nonplussed look on Katie's face, she very well might. And, damn, if that didn't cause an unwelcome twinge of hurt. Did she seriously have that deep an aversion to a committed relationship, or did her refusal have more to do with him?

"Katie is definitely welcome, but she might already have plans," Bowie said, giving her an out. He wasn't going to coerce the woman into having dinner with him.

Abby's face fell, and Katie visibly caved. "Dinner sounds nice."

"Good!" Abby gave Katie a quick hug before she spun from the room. "I'll tell Lou."

Abby vanished as quickly as she'd come, and Bowie and Katie got to their feet. They stood there awkwardly. Bowie rubbed the back of his head.

"Uh, thanks for that. You were really great with Abby."

Katie shrugged. "She's a good kid. I'm glad I could help."

Bowie cleared his throat as guilt swirled inside him. "What you said. About high school. I just wanted to let you know that I'm sor—"

Katie's expression turned studiously blank. "I don't want to talk about it. Not now. Not ever."

Bowie swallowed and gave her a nod. "Fair enough." He wouldn't force his apologies on her, even if it would make him feel a damn sight better. This was about her, not him. Still, he wished he could explain that he understood that he'd acted horribly. He didn't want to excuse his behavior; he wanted to acknowledge it. But he wasn't entitled to what he wanted. He'd hurt Katie, and the least he could do was respect her desire not to discuss the past.

───✧───

Clutching cupcakes she had purchased at June's tea shop, Katie walked up the neatly painted wooden stairs to the Victorian house. Even though the old home was adjacent to the zoo, she'd never considered that Bowie lived here. With its cupola and gingerbread woodwork, it looked too

cute and fussy. There was also the paint job—the
very pastel and very intricate paint job. Frilly lace
curtains hung in the windows. Somehow, though,
the house didn't look over the top, just tastefully
period. But it certainly wasn't a place where she'd
expect two bachelors to live, especially one who'd
just turned thirty.

Katie knocked on the door and heard the clatter of
feet. The door swung open to reveal an excited Abby.

"You're here!" The girl grabbed Katie's hand
and unceremoniously pulled her into the house.
Abby didn't let go of Katie as she continued to
chatter excitedly. "Dad's cooking chicken enchila-
das. They're my favorite."

Katie found herself dragged down the hallway
to an unusually spacious kitchen for a Victorian.
Bowie stood chopping vegetables at the counter. He looked surprisingly and most deliciously
domestic. He smiled broadly. "Sorry. I'm a little
behind schedule. Fluffy got into the storeroom
again. I took a picture of him for the website before
he scampered off, but it took a while to get the mess
cleaned up. Lou was going to start the food preparation, but he's having an off day."

Katie frowned. She really liked the older man.
"Is he okay?"

"Yeah. He just has days when he's more tired
than usual," Bowie said. "He's resting now, but
he'll be down for dinner."

"Is he up for company?"

Bowie nodded and glanced down at Abby. "I
think he's about as excited as Abby. Since Gretchen

died, we haven't had many visitors. She enjoyed entertaining."

"Ah," Katie said as the exterior of the house suddenly made more sense. "Am I safe to assume she's responsible for the lace curtains?"

Bowie laughed. "Gretchen loved this house and its history. She wanted to keep the Victorian as historic as possible, except for the kitchen. She remodeled one of the larger sitting rooms and turned the old kitchen into a mudroom."

"Isn't it hard maintaining the exterior?" Katie asked. "Paint doesn't last that long on old wood, does it?"

"Unfortunately, no. It's a constant project, but Lou doesn't have the heart to change it. He says it's like having a bit of Gretchen still here."

Katie had a pretty good idea that Bowie felt the same. After all, she doubted that eighty-year-old Lou would be climbing a ladder to apply the paint.

And maybe, just maybe, Katie's heart squeezed. Only a little. Because she didn't want to experience tender feelings that could make her vulnerable. Today, while comforting Abby, it had gotten too personal. She hadn't wanted to discuss the past, especially around Bowie. She never talked about being bullied. Her mother didn't know what had transpired, nor did June. Katie's other friend from college, Josh, knew a little, but only because he and Katie had gotten drunk together one night and had swapped high-school horror stories. Even he didn't know most of the details.

But Katie hadn't been able to watch Abby suffer— not when she could try to help. So no matter how much Katie's brain had screamed at her to protect herself, she'd knelt down and opened up to Abby. But that didn't mean she wanted to make herself vulnerable around Abby's father.

A tug on Katie's hand pulled her from her reverie. Evidently, the preteen had had enough of adult conversation.

"Do you want to see my room?" Abby asked her eagerly. "It's in the turret. Well, it's not *really* a turret, but I like to pretend it is. Like the one in *Tangled*."

Katie barely had time to nod before Abby pulled her from the kitchen. Katie glanced back at Bowie, who gave her a brief salute with a wooden spoon.

Considering that Abby dressed like a tomboy, her bedroom was surprisingly frilly and pink. It looked like a girl's room in a movie, at least the bits of it that would have predated Abby's embellishments. The girl had definitely left her own stamp on the space with the animal posters covering the walls and the gerbil and guinea pig cages in the corner. Even if the place wasn't a pristine showplace, it was a room for a princess—at least Daddy's little princess.

Even years later, Katie could still see the love that had gone into applying the pink-and-white-striped wallpaper and hand painting the toy box to look like a treasure chest. The window seat's alcove had also been decorated to look like it was ivy covered. Katie supposed Gretchen could have been responsible, but she didn't think so. She pictured eighteen-year-old Bowie, nervous papa-to-be, preparing this room for his baby girl. A smile drifted across Katie's lips as she thought about how excited—and anxious—Bowie must have been when he first brought newborn Abby here.

Before Katie's mind could drift for too long, Abby decided to expand the tour to the rest of the house. Although clean and neat, the Victorian had a distinctly outdated and little-old-lady feel. More than one room had pretty but decidedly old-fashioned floral wallpaper. Nothing was masculine, except the study, which featured two serviceable La-Z-Boys, an older-model TV, and a fossil of a computer. Of course, Abby's tour didn't include Bowie's bedroom, so Katie supposed it could be a bastion of maleness. But really, all the place was missing were lace doilies. And Katie had a sneaking suspicion that doily removal was the one alteration Bowie and Lou had made after Gretchen's death.

Abby was just finishing showing Katie the downstairs when Bowie called that dinner was ready. When Katie followed Abby into the dining room, Lou winked at Katie.

"I heard we were going to have a special guest this evening," he said.

"I don't know about special," Katie hedged as Bowie came into the room with a steaming baking dish.

"Nonsense. This is a treat for all of us," Lou said, his eyes twinkling. "It's been a long while since we've had a guest."

"My friends come over," Abby piped up.

"I think Lou meant adult guests," Bowie said as he shot Lou a warning look. The man seemed on the verge of matchmaking, which didn't surprise Katie. Every time she bumped into him, he slyly slid in as many compliments about Bowie as he could. Katie was worried that when her mom came to help with Pirate Day, the two would start scheming together. The last thing her mother needed was encouragement. Despite Katie's and her father's best efforts, her mom was convinced that Katie was going to stay in Sagebrush, even though she knew Katie was getting ready to submit her résumé to a couple of advertising firms.

Unfortunately, Lou disregarded Bowie's unspoken order not to matchmake. He gestured toward the bubbling dish in the center of the table. "Try some. Cooking is one of Bowie's many talents."

Bowie grunted. "It's passable. Keeps us from starving."

Katie bit into the enchilada and was pleasantly surprised by the burst of creamy flavor. It wasn't a traditional enchilada but an Americanized version. It tasted delicious and reminded her of homemade macaroni and cheese.

"This is really good," Katie said between mouthfuls.

"You should try his Thai Lemon Ginger Chicken," Lou said. "That's the best recipe he's gotten off the internet."

"Or his crepes," Abby chimed in.

Lou glanced over at Bowie. "Abby has a good point. Weren't you planning on making crepes this Friday?" Then, before Bowie could answer, Lou swiveled toward Katie. "Would you like to join us?"

Seizing the opportunity, Katie said, "On one condition."

"What's that?"

"No more matchmaking." She tempered her words with a smile.

Abby perked up, and Katie realized that she

might have made a tactical error. Her eyes huge, Abby surveyed Katie and Bowie with undisguised speculation. Bowie shot Katie a sidelong look that screamed *Help!* She was scrambling for something to say when Lou unexpectedly came to their rescue.

"Now, Katie, you know I'm just teasing," he said, although she realized the words were for Abby's benefit only. "I like seeing you and Bowie flustered, but we all enjoy your company."

Katie smiled gratefully. "Then I suppose I'd better accept your invitation. I haven't had crepes since I was in Paris."

Abby stared at her. "You've been to Paris?"

Katie nodded. "Back in college, June, Josh, and I spent a month backpacking across Europe."

"You did?" Abby said, the awe clear in her voice. As Katie launched into a couple of highlights from the trip, she felt herself relax. Eventually, the conversation turned to the animals Lou and Bowie had cared for over the years and the search for a mate for Lulubelle. Katie couldn't stop laughing when Abby, Bowie, and Lou shared stories about Fluffy's various methods of escape. When Katie left that evening, she realized she had thoroughly enjoyed herself. It felt good to be with friends—even friends who included an octogenarian, a preteen, and a former enemy turned lover.

"Oh my goodness, they are adorable!" Katie's mother clasped her hands together as she watched Fleur, Tonks, and Dobby scramble around the floor. "They are even cuter in person than on the animal cam."

"Do you want to feed them solid food?" Bowie asked. He still wore the pirate costume, even though the festivities had ended twenty minutes ago. Although they hadn't done a final tally, Katie knew the zoo had made money. The idea to coordinate the day with the end of school had been brilliant. Tons of kids and their parents had attended. They'd almost run out of construction paper to make pirate hats, but Katie had been able to run to the store and back. Her mother, who'd led the art projects, had been in her glory. They'd even gotten a few pledges to donate money if Bowie could secure the grant to care for orphaned polar bears.

"Oh, I'd be delighted!" her mom said as Bowie handed her a small plastic container. She peered inside and wrinkled her nose. "It looks like baby food."

Bowie laughed. "It's strained chicken, so you called it right."

"Do they eat only meat now?" her mom asked.

He shook his head. "No, they still drink a lot of milk. We just introduced solids to them about a week ago. We'll wean them gradually."

Katie's mom placed the bowl of chicken on the floor. The cubs immediately scrambled over to it, their tails swishing in excitement. Over the past couple of weeks, they'd lost their clumsy crawl and begun to tussle with each other more. Katie found their little pounces adorable. Fleur, though, still liked her cuddles.

"When are you planning to introduce them to the public?" her mother asked.

"In a little over a month," Bowie said. "I'm building a temporary exhibit off the nursery."

"It's going to be adorable," Katie said. "I've seen his plans for it. There'll be plenty of structures for them to crawl on."

"Katie's agreed to paint the walls so it will look like the cubs' natural habitat," Bowie added.

Her mother shot Katie a knowing look. "Did you, sweetheart?"

Before her mom read too much into that tidbit of information, Katie quickly added, "But this won't be the kits' permanent home."

Bowie nodded. "Once I finish with this small one, I'll work on a larger outdoor enclosure. I need to complete it soon, so Fleur and Tonks can slowly get used to it before we move them there full time."

"What about Dobby?" Katie's mom asked with concern.

Katie reached over and patted her mom's hand. "He'll be transferred to another zoo."

A protective look instantly flashed over Helen Underwood's face. Katie's mother watched the cubs every day on the webcam, and she'd clearly taken a personal interest in them. The idea of one of the babies leaving must have triggered her maternal instincts. "But why? Why would you do that?"

"Mom, they're siblings. Bowie can't keep him with the girls when they get older. Bowie will find him a good home, one with a female he's not related to."

"There are plenty of networks out there to rehome animals," Bowie added. "They help make sure the captive gene pool stays healthy."

Her mother appeared mollified but still crest-fallen. "It's such a shame you have to send him away."

"Dobby'll be fine, Mom."

Her mother looked at Katie. "You know how I hate it when my babies leave."

Yes, which was one of the many reasons why Katie was not letting her mom know about how physically close she'd become with Bowie. Her mom would imagine a fairy tale that ended with Katie staying in Sagebrush forever.

Before she could further reassure her mother about Dobby's fate, Fleur pranced over and nudged Katie's leg with her paw. At the demand, Katie sat on the floor, and the little puma crawled into her lap. Her mom clasped her hands together and cooed.

Bowie chuckled. "Fleur's really bonded with Katie."

As if on cue, Fleur jumped up on Katie as if to embrace her. Katie caught the little puma in her arms and held her close. "She's my girl."

Her mother beamed and then turned to Bowie. "Katie always was a natural nurturer."

Katie felt her face flame. A matchmaking Helen Underwood knew no boundaries. Gently placing Fleur next to Sylvia, Katie stood up. "Mom, we'd better head home. It's getting close to dinner, and Dad is probably wondering where we are."

Her mother immediately checked her watch. "Oh, you're right, dear. We'd better hurry."

Katie glanced at Bowie. "This is the first time my dad's been on his own since the shooting."

"I wanted one of the boys to stay with him, but your father is a stubborn man."

"Mom, Dad was happy for the alone time. He needs this, and you heard what the doctor said. Dad's on the mend."

"I can't help but worry."

"I know, Mom." Katie happened to look over at Bowie. He was watching her exchange with her mother with the oddest expression on his face. Longing, maybe, but that wasn't quite right. Curiosity? But that didn't seem to fit either. Before Katie could identify it, his expression smoothed as he gave her mother one of his brilliant smiles.

"Thank you for coming and helping us today. I know you made the day special for the kids."

"Any time," her mother said, clearly pleased with his compliment. "I miss working with children. I enjoyed it."

"Maybe you could come back for one of our other events."

Excitement practically radiated from her mother as she turned to Katie. "You didn't tell me you were planning more."

"Just a festival this summer," Katie said quickly. "I don't know if I'll be here for much of autumn, since that's when I'll start my job search in earnest. Hopefully, it won't take too long to get an offer."

Her mother's joy immediately dimmed, and Bowie said, "We're very grateful for any help that Katie can give us. She's really improving the zoo's visibility."

Her mom smiled again. "See, Katie, your talents are put to good use here in Sagebrush."

"Time to go," Katie said, shepherding her mother from the nursery.

"I don't know why you're so bent on finding a job in a big city," her mother said as they shut the door to the animal hospital behind them. "There are plenty of opportunities in Sagebrush."

"Mom, I love you very much, but we've had this conversation."

Her mother fell silent as they walked through the zoo and climbed into the car. As soon as Katie started the engine, though, her mother turned and cheerfully said, "So Bowie seems like such a nice man."

Katie shot her mother a sidelong glance. "Not going to dispute that, but I'm not starting a serious relationship right now, Mom."

"His daughter is adorable."

"Yes, she is."

"She seems very comfortable with you."

Katie focused on the road. "We spend a lot of time together when I'm helping out with the cubs. I've promised to keep in touch with Abby when I leave."

"Maybe we should invite them to your birthday party. Lou as well."

"Mom, my birthday is still over a month away, and I told you I didn't want a big blowout…just family."

"But it's your thirtieth! Your friend Josh is even coming. June will be there too."

Katie sighed in frustration. "I've known June and Josh since college. We're very close."

"But—"

"So what did you think of the cougar cubs?" Katie asked, hoping to steer the conversation away from Bowie. Although her mom allowed the subject change, Katie recognized the resolute set to her shoulders. Helen Underwood was determined to see Katie resettled in Sagebrush, and she'd just found a ready-made family. Now her mom wasn't just imagining having Katie home for good. She was picturing a brand-new granddaughter and son-in-law. Katie needed to be very careful about how much she talked about the zoo and Bowie.

Bowie reclined in his office chair, his breaths coming in quick, hard pants. With an energy that surprised him, Katie climbed off his lap. Sure, she'd only walked into his office ten minutes ago—but the way they'd just spent those ten minutes…

Yeah, he didn't think he'd be getting up for a while. Maybe he'd just fall asleep in his chair.

Katie yanked down her shirt. Nonchalantly, she walked over to the door and gathered the rest of her clothes, which she'd discarded the moment she'd entered and locked the door. Bowie probably should arrange himself and zip up his fly, but it honestly felt like too much effort.

"So I was thinking," Katie said as she pulled her hair back into a ponytail.

"Yeah?" he asked as he tried to get his muddled mind to focus. She had that effect, especially when she burst into his office unexpectedly and jumped him. Considering how often that had happened lately, he should have acquired the ability to keep at least a few brain cells fully charged.

"June and I would like to take Abby on a shopping spree. Our treat."

That caused Bowie to straighten up and fix his pants. He was not about to discuss his daughter with his junk hanging free.

"So, what do you think?" Katie asked.

Bowie paused. Since Katie had first eaten dinner with them, she had been spending more and more time with Abby. Although he appreciated how Katie managed to pull Abby from her shell, he couldn't help but worry. Abby talked about Katie constantly. He knew his daughter had begun to idolize her and was even starting to regard Katie as a mother figure. Hell, she'd made a habit of telling Bowie that Katie was nice and pretty and questioning why didn't he ask her out.

When Katie left—and she would eventually leave—Abby would be crushed. Katie might live in the backwoods town of Sagebrush now, but Bowie doubted she'd stick around. Oh, she'd still drop by to visit her folks, but she wasn't planning on moving back permanently. Just the other day, she'd mentioned she was adding the zoo advertisements to her portfolio. She definitely was using the summer to beef up her credentials before embarking on a serious job hunt in the fall.

There was another thing Bowie knew for certain, though. Once Katie left Sagebrush, whatever she and he shared would end as suddenly as a mountain lion's deadly pounce.

Although Bowie knew Katie's relationship with his daughter had little to do with him, she wouldn't be around much, especially if she ended up in New York. He hoped she would make time for Abby when she visited her family. Even if things ended badly between Katie and him, he didn't think she would just abandon his daughter. But Abby would still feel her absence.

"Uh, Bowie, it's really a simple question."

He rubbed the back of his head and regarded Katie steadily. "Actually, it isn't."

She frowned. "Why? Are you worried about what June and I will help her pick out? We know she's a preteen."

Bowie shook his head. "No, not that, but I don't want her getting too attached to you. You're still planning to leave town, aren't you?"

Katie paused, considering. When she finally spoke, she did so very slowly, as if working through the problem as she talked. "True, but I've been up front with her about it. I'll make sure I keep in touch. Abby and I have even made plans to write each other letters. She liked the old-fashioned idea."

Bowie relaxed slightly, helplessly charmed that Katie had already thought about how her eventual departure would impact Abby. He hadn't known the two of them had discussed it. He shouldn't have been surprised that Katie had thought to prepare his daughter.

"Abby's growing really close to you," he said. "I guess you've already figured that out."

Katie nodded, her face solemn. "Yeah. I like her too. She's a good kid."

"When things with us…" He paused, not sure how to say the words. He really didn't want to think about their…well, whatever this was…ending.

"My relationship with Abby is separate," Katie said.

"No matter what happens with us or where I move, I'll still be her friend as long as she needs me. I see it as an unofficial Big Sister–Little Sister thing."

"Yeah, I figured that's how you viewed it, but—"

"You want to protect your daughter. I get it. No offense taken."

Bowie nodded sharply, glad Katie understood. "Since you've already talked to Abby about your plans to leave town eventually, I guess there isn't any harm in you and June taking her shopping. It will be on my dime, though."

"June and I would like to buy her one outfit, if that's okay."

"I guess, as long as it's just one." It felt odd, letting someone else take his kid to the store. Gretchen had before her death, but for years, it had just been him.

"Oh, and June may want to take Abby for a haircut. You okay with that?"

Bowie frowned. "What's wrong with her hair?"

Katie shrugged. "June has an eye for these things, and she's normally right. I'm hoping that a day out might give Abby more confidence. Don't worry, I won't let anyone put makeup on her. She's only eleven. Besides, this isn't about giving Abby a makeover. It's about having some girl fun."

"I guess so," Bowie said, but it felt even weirder for someone else to take his kid for a haircut. Even Gretchen hadn't done that. "But I'll want to pay for that too."

"No problem." Katie turned to leave, and he sucked in a breath. Abby's relationship with her wasn't the only thing that had started to bug him. Over the past couple of weeks, Katie had joined his family for dinner several times. He enjoyed her company. A lot. He wanted to spend more time with her beyond talking about the zoo or even just having sex.

"Speaking of Abby," Bowie said, "she's sleeping over at a friend's house tomorrow. The cougars are old enough now to be left alone at night, and I thought it might be nice if the two of us drove to the Rocky Ridge lodge for dinner. I've never eaten there, but Lou says the view is great, and the food is decent."

Katie swiveled in his direction, her face unreadable. "I appreciate the offer, Bowie, but like you said, I'll be leaving town soon. I want to keep things casual. Besides, I finally convinced my mom to take a break and go to her sister's house in Boulder for a few days. Dad doesn't need to be babysat, but it would make my mother nervous if I went all the way to Rocky Ridge."

Yeah, but maybe Bowie wanted something more than a casual fling. Not that he would admit it aloud.

"Okay." Bowie shrugged. "Suit yourself."

A speculative grin suddenly curled Katie's lips. "But you know, it might be nice to actually use a bed for once. Why don't you swing by my place after you drop Abby off at her friend's? I can order a pizza."

"Yeah, that sounds great," Bowie said, glad that his voice didn't betray his disappointment. He was the guy. He should be ecstatic that Katie wanted pizza and nooky instead of an expensive dinner he could barely afford. For the first time, he had a steady sex life. Maybe Katie was right. Why screw with that?

Still, the feeling of glumness lingered like a grizzly's

bad breath. Bowie couldn't even shake his funk when he distributed feed for the animals' evening meal, which was generally his favorite part of the workday. He told himself his bad mood was partially because he'd spotted Fluffy leaving Frida's enclosure again. But deep down, he knew that didn't make sense. The honey badger roamed the zoo all the time, and his antics kept the old gal active. Plus, with Abby home from school, she could catch the little trickster quickly enough.

As Bowie heaved a bale of hay off the back of his pickup into the llama enclosure, Lulubelle sauntered over, her woolly head at a dejected angle. He climbed down and reached over to give her a scratch.

"Sorry, girl. We're working on finding you a mate. I promise."

Lulubelle curled back her lip and let out a mournful, rumbling wail. Bowie leaned his forehead against the camel's massive one. Staring into her liquid-brown eyes, he said, "I know how you feel, girl. I know how you feel."

Pathetic. Fluffy didn't know who was more pitiful. The pining camel or the lovelorn biped. Fluffy had arranged everything for the Black-Haired One. It should have been easier than invading an unguarded beehive.

But no. The Black-Haired One had apparently managed to make a jumble out of his own mating ritual. Fluffy had experienced such high hopes. Both the Black-Haired One and the red-haired female had appeared happy and pleased with themselves. A good sign indeed.

However, successful males did not share soulful heart-to-hearts with lovesick camels. Something had gone awry with Fluffy's plan, and he intended to fix it. The Black-Haired One clearly wasn't capable of wooing his own species without assistance.

Chapter 8

WHEN BOWIE HEARD THE DOOR TO HIS OFFICE open, he grinned broadly. He was ready for a break. He'd been staring too long at the paperwork required to keep the zoo's licenses up to date. The animal park had quite a few variances, including those that allowed them to keep the cougars and Frida. Although they always passed inspections—Bowie made sure that they exceeded all regulations—keeping up with the requirements was still a headache. He'd specifically chosen today to focus on legal mumbo jumbo, since he was looking forward to tonight.

It would be his first time making love to Katie in an actual bed. The whole day, he'd plotted how he would take full advantage of a mattress and box spring. Needless to say, despite all the administrative crap, he was in a pretty terrific mood.

"Couldn't wait until this evening?" he asked as he swung his chair around from the computer where he'd been working.

"Ooo, does somebody have a hot date?"

Bowie froze when he caught sight of Sawyer Johnson standing in the doorframe. As he sat dumbfounded, she sashayed into his office and plopped uninvited into one of the chairs.

He hadn't talked to Sawyer in almost twelve

years. Due to the size of Sagebrush, he'd spotted her from a distance a few times at the supermarket or in town. Either he or she promptly went in a different direction. He hadn't even spoken with her during her pregnancy—at least not without both their attorneys and her parents present. Bowie had heard that her family had lost big in a pyramid investment scheme that had hit their community hard. Afterward, she'd married a rich, local rancher about twice her age. Bowie didn't recall the man's name. It honestly hadn't mattered to him.

As Bowie sat in stunned silence, Sawyer scanned his office with patent disgust. "So this is where you've been keeping yourself," she said in a tone that indicated she wasn't impressed.

"What are you doing here, Sawyer?" Bowie asked sharply. He was glad that he'd already dropped Abby off at her friend's home. Abby knew that her mother was alive, but she wasn't aware that the woman still lived in the same town.

"Rodger and I can't have children," Sawyer said.

Rage and disbelief slammed into Bowie. Surely, this woman hadn't breezed into his life after twelve years just to announce her inability to conceive a baby. Hell, the last thing she had said in his presence was how much she wished her parents would let her have an abortion. Her words had been a cruel echo of his parents' taunts that they should have gotten rid of him when his mom got knocked up in high school.

"I don't see how that is any concern of mine," Bowie said evenly.

Sawyer ignored him. "I had my tubes tied. I didn't want to risk another pregnancy. Unfortunately, there were complications after I tried to get the procedure reversed."

Bowie barely bit back a sarcastic comment. Although Sawyer didn't seem too broken up by her infertility, he wouldn't stoop so low as to make light of it. Sawyer had always hidden any sign of vulnerability beneath layers of smug superiority. Even when they'd dated, she hadn't opened up to him, but he hadn't been stupid either. He'd known her parents had always paid more attention to her older brother. Whenever her parents had caught Sawyer and Bowie together, her father had called her a stupid girl. Instead of showing any hurt, Sawyer had doubled down on her rebellious attitude. So even if Sawyer was heartbroken over her inability to conceive, Bowie doubted she would reveal any pain.

"Rodger really wants to have kids. When he didn't understand why I'd get my tubes tied in the first place, I told him about the teen pregnancy. He was really understanding."

"That's nice," Bowie said. "Kind of him really."

Sawyer shot him an annoyed look before continuing. "So, anyway, I am here for my daughter."

For a moment, Bowie didn't react. He couldn't. Finally, his shell-shocked mind managed to succeed in processing that, yes, he had indeed heard correctly. Absolute fury unfurled inside him, burning through any sympathy for Sawyer. For a moment, he could do nothing but focus on keeping that rage under control.

This woman had abandoned his baby girl. Hell,

she hadn't even wanted to bring Abby to full term. And, now, after twelve fucking years, she thought she could waltz back into his daughter's life.

"Is this her?" Sawyer asked as she idly reached for the photo of Abby that he displayed on his desk. Sawyer clicked her tongue off the roof of her mouth in disapproval. "Well, obviously, she's going to need a makeover. Luckily, she has my facial features—"

"You don't fucking have a daughter." Bowie tore the picture from Sawyer's grasp.

Clearly surprised by the move, Sawyer stood momentarily stunned. It only took a second, though, before indignation replaced her shock.

She straightened and glared at him. "Excuse me?"

"You aren't Abby's parent," Bowie said. "I am."

"I most certainly am her mother."

"You may have given birth to her, but you have no right to call yourself her mother. I have the legal documents to prove it. You can't just announce after twelve years of no communication that you're here for your daughter, whatever the hell that means."

Sawyer stiffened while her eyes narrowed. He remembered that mannerism all too well from high school. She always held herself like that before she attacked.

"I. Am. Her. Mother." Sawyer hissed each word as she leaned over his desk. "I have the stretch marks to prove it."

Bowie laughed but not at all humorously. Clearly, Sawyer's vanity hadn't diminished any more than her inflated sense of self.

"You have stretch marks," he repeated, his voice laced with sarcasm. "You think that fucking stretch marks make you a mother?"

"I sacrificed my figure, my body, to bring that child into the world," Sawyer said, stabbing at her chest.

"You." Bowie could barely force the words out through his ire. "You sacrificed. Where the hell were you when Abby had colic and she needed to be rocked to sleep every night? You were at college. Where were you when it was time to read Abby bedtime stories? You were out clubbing. Where were you when she needed help with homework? Oh yeah, taking a fancy trip with your husband."

"Oh, like you would have gone to college anyway," Sawyer snapped.

"That…that's what you got out of all of that?" Bowie roared.

Something in Sawyer's brain must have finally realized that badgering him was counterproductive. Her waspish expression vanished, leaving in its place a contrite pout. At seventeen, it had appeared sexy. At thirty, not so much.

"Okay, yes, you put in your time, but Rodger and I would like to be a part of Abby's life too," Sawyer said in a wheedling voice. "Don't you think she deserves time with her mother?"

Bowie stared hard at Sawyer. "Why do you want Abby in your life? You said Rodger really wants to have kids. What about you?"

Sawyer stiffened defensively, and Bowie forced himself to think rationally. Maybe if he ferreted out her motivation, he could squelch this ridiculousness before it could hurt Abby. "So what is it, Sawyer? Trouble in paradise, so you need a kid to patch things up?"

She shook back her hair in a careless gesture that Bowie remembered. The haughtier Sawyer acted, the more she wished to cover something up. Maybe her husband was pressuring her for kids. He was an older man, and she'd said he loved children. Maybe he'd married a younger woman because he wanted more offspring.

"Rodger and I are just fine," she said airily.

Bowie skimmed his eyes over her. Sawyer was still as beautiful as she'd been in high school. She'd put on weight, but it had been in the right places. Of course, her husband might have a roving eye, but Sawyer probably wouldn't care as long as she had disposable income and the freedom to engage in her own affairs.

Then it struck Bowie. This was about money.

"Signed a prenup, didn't you?" he said.

Sawyer stared down her nose. She had a singular talent for that. "I hardly see how that is any of your business."

Bowie leaned back in his chair, plastering on his face the smuggest grin he could manage. "So what is it, Sawyer? Did you cheat on him? What do you want? A kid to fix the problem or to get you sympathy cash if things sour?"

Sawyer glared but didn't respond. Bowie felt some of his anger slide away. Although he still wanted to throttle the woman, at least he didn't feel so unbalanced. He knew Sawyer's angle now.

"Let me tell you why that's not going to work, *sweetheart*," Bowie said. "First, you don't have any legal right to Abby. Second, there's no way in hell that I am going to let your hubby adopt *my* daughter. Third, if you pursue this, whatever sob story you told Rodger is going to unravel."

She crossed her arms over her chest and stared him down. "Rodger and I can afford the best lawyers."

"Sawyer, it's been twelve years. You signed away all rights. Hell, I was so desperate to get custody of my own kid that I signed every paper that your parents wanted saying that I'd never go after any money from you or them. I agreed to never contact any of you. I don't care how good your lawyers are. They can't undo that."

"It was statutory rape!" Sawyer cried.

Bowie blinked. He had no better response. "I was seventeen when Abby was conceived. Hell, you would've probably just turned eighteen since your birthday is before mine."

Sawyer's brow furrowed. "No, you weren't that young. You were held back at least a year or two."

"No. No, I wasn't," Bowie countered. "Hell, Sawyer, don't you remember I was kicked out of my foster home on my eighteenth birthday? It was right before you found out you were pregnant."

Sawyer pursed her lips in displeasure. Obviously, she hadn't remembered. And really, why would she? He had never meant more to her than a good time and a way to rebel. She had found him attractive, but he doubted she had ever cared for him.

Her gaze swept around his office. Then she stood up. Resting her hands on his desk, she leaned over it. "Your dinky zoo is all that you have. I might not win a legal battle, but I can make it long and protracted. I can bleed this little place for all it's worth."

Bowie focused his efforts on concealing the fact that her barb had struck him. Although the zoo's cash flow had increased, he didn't have the resources to pay for a lawyer and court costs. He might not have footed the bill the last time, but he knew how long Sawyer's attorneys had dragged out the custody fight.

"What do you think that will do to your precious daughter?" Sawyer asked. "Do you think she'd be happy that you kept her from me?"

"You don't care about Abby."

"What if I do?" Sawyer asked. "I am selfish. I will never deny that, but she is still my daughter, and I am still her mother. Doesn't she deserve a chance to know me?"

Abby deserved a better mother than Sawyer. Unfortunately, Sawyer was the woman who had given birth to her.

"Think about this, Bowie," Sawyer said. "If you let Rodger and me into Abby's life, we can introduce her to things that you can't. Rodger is good with children. He will set up a college fund for her like he has for his boys with his first wife."

"Sawyer, I'm not letting you take my daughter."

"If you'd stop arguing, you'd realize that I'm only asking for partial custody. Rodger and I want a chance to spend time with her, but if you deny us that, we will fight you. And I *will* let Abby know that I am her mother."

Bowie couldn't prevent that. He couldn't get a restraining order. Sawyer might be a pain, but she hadn't done anything illegal or threatening. Even if Bowie tried to keep her away from Abby, all it would take was one unpreventable meeting in town or even at the zoo.

"Look, you can give me what I want, and Abby will get to know me and Rodger," Sawyer continued. "We

can take her on trips…expose her to culture. Or
you can play hardball and make it more difficult
on her."

She straightened and walked to the door. She
paused at the threshold. "Rodger and I are going on a
two-month trip. He thought it would be best if Abby
had some time to adjust to the idea. When we get
back, I expect that we will be able to see her. If not,
we will begin legal proceedings."

With that, Sawyer flounced out of Bowie's
office. He dropped his head into his hands and
rubbed his eyes. What the hell was he going to do?

One thing, he wouldn't allow Sawyer to regain
any degree of legal custody. Granted their first
interaction in twelve years had lasted less than an
hour, but she'd acted just like the girl he'd dated
in high school. With a couple of cutting words,
Sawyer could slice through any of the new self-
confidence he and Katie had painstakingly instilled
in Abby.

But Bowie couldn't completely reject everything Sawyer said either. Abby had asked about
her mother over the years. How would she feel if
he hid this meeting? He had no doubt that Sawyer
would carry through with her threat to talk to Abby
directly.

Maybe Abby could benefit from small doses of
Sawyer. Although he wouldn't risk his daughter's
emotional well-being for any college fund, he
realized that student loans could cripple a person.
College was more expensive every year.

Not for the first time, Bowie wished he could just

perform a search on the internet and download the perfect course of action. It didn't exist, though. And that was what sucked about being a single parent. The decision was all on him. Sure, he could discuss this with Lou, but at the end of the day, Bowie was the parent.

His phone rang. The sound almost caused him to jump in his chair. Glancing down, he recognized Katie's number. On autopilot, he picked it up.

"Hey," he said.

"It's Katie," she said, her voice sounding wonderfully normal to his ears. "Do you mind picking up a pizza on your way over? I can't find anyone who will deliver out here."

Pizza. Her house. Right. He was supposed to spend the night with her.

"Uh, yeah," he said dully. "Sure. Do you want to order, or should I?"

"I'll call since you're busy at the zoo. Does Tony's work for you?"

"That's fine."

"Any preferences?"

"Yeah, um, no anchovies, not a big fan of Hawaiian. Other than that, I'm good."

"Okay," Katie said. "See you in a bit."

When Bowie hung up, he sucked in a deep breath, trying to calm his rioting thoughts. A night of hot sex. That's what he needed. It would help release his edginess. Then tomorrow after he left Katie's, he could more rationally figure out how to deal with Sawyer's threats and revelations.

⁓

Fluffy's nose twitched at the scent of the blond female's perfume. He did not like it. It overpowered his senses, and he liked being alert.

He was glad he had escaped his enclosure earlier today. He'd rested his food dish on top of his den and grabbed onto an overhead tree branch. He liked climbing the best and hadn't been able to wait until nightfall for his escape.

He did not want other female humans visiting the Black-Haired One. It interfered with his plans, even if this woman did smell slightly like the Wee One. No, the blond female needed to go.

Immediately.

Fluffy did not have time to develop a cunning scheme. Instead, he went for the crudest but most effective method for getting rid of pesky bipeds. The surprise attack.

As the woman's high heels clipped past him, Fluffy darted from his hiding place under a bush, snarling fiercely. The woman yelped. Fluffy showed his teeth. Shrieking now, the female human darted around him. He followed. She screamed and walked faster. He easily closed the distance. She began to run. He growled and picked up his speed. When she reached the parking lot, he stopped and watched as she scrambled into her conveyance.

Fluffy smiled. That had been fun. Now it was time to let Frida chase him instead.

When Katie's doorbell rang, it took a moment for the sound to register. She'd always had delayed reactions when deep in design work. After saving her artwork for a new menu for the Prairie Dog Café, she stretched. Cracking her neck, Katie padded downstairs to the front door.

She checked the peephole and ascertained that, yes, Bowie stood on her porch. Although she lived directly behind her parents' house, the family was still on edge, since the police hadn't yet found Eddie Driver, the ex-con who'd shot Katie's father. There'd been some unconfirmed sightings of him in the area, so her little brother, the police officer, had insisted on installing security systems in both the old homestead and the geodesic dome where Katie lived.

She pulled open the door. "Hey. How was your da…"

Her words trailed off as she caught sight of Bowie's face. She couldn't miss the odd set to his jaw. His body seemed tense, coiled for action.

Quickly, she stepped back to let him into the house. He entered automatically and awkwardly thrust the pizza box in her direction. She took it and studied him closely.

"What's wrong?" she asked.

Bowie shoved his hand in his hair and started to pace. "Sorry about this, Katie, but I don't think I'll be good company tonight. We should probably do a rain check."

Okay, now she was worried. Bowie never acted oddly. In fact, he always seemed in control of the situation, whether kissing red river hogs or shooting YouTube videos in a poet shirt and an eye patch.

"Bowie, I'm okay if you need to cancel tonight, but can you tell me what's bothering you? Is everything okay? Abby and Lou are fine, right? There are no problems at the zoo?"

He blew out a long, frustrated breath. He stared at her for a moment and must have noticed her concern. Dropping his hand from his head, he turned to face her squarely.

"Sawyer showed up at the zoo office today," he said.

Okay, Katie hadn't expected that answer.

Bowie gave a short, bitter laugh. "Yeah, you look as stunned as I feel. The woman abandons her daughter for twelve years, and she thinks she can blithely announce that she's ready for motherhood and step right in."

"She wants custody?" Katie asked in surprise. Sawyer didn't seem like the maternal type, but heck, Katie hadn't talked to the woman for twelve years.

"I don't know exactly what she wants," Bowie snapped, but Katie realized his ire wasn't directed at her. "She's not dumb, so she knows she can't just take my kid away from me, but she wants a relationship with Abby."

"I'm pretty sure she couldn't legally force you to do that," Katie said.

Bowie grimaced. "Yeah, but she can drag it out and bury me with attorney fees. Plus, she's going to tell Abby who she is. I can't stop that. Then there's her husband. The guy would set up a college fund for Abby. Do I have a right to keep this from my daughter?"

His conflicted expression tugged at Katie's heart. He clearly loved his kid and wanted to make the right decision. Unfortunately, given the situation,

Katie doubted that the perfect solution would present itself. If she had a child of her own, she would want to wrestle with the options. Either way, Abby could end up hurt.

"Do you want to come in and talk about it?" Katie asked.

"Yes. No. Maybe. Ah, hell." He jammed his hand in his hair again. "I know Sawyer was never your favorite person. Are you sure you want to hear about this?"

Katie closed the front door and gestured to her living room. "At least you know my prejudices. Besides, you look like you need someone to unload on, and I'm actually pretty good at listening."

Bowie regarded her for a moment, his gray eyes suddenly warm. "Thanks, Katie. You don't know how much I need this right now."

Katie shrugged, suddenly feeling uncomfortable with the intimacy that threatened all her dating rules. "No problem."

She turned and led him to the wide-open main room. Although she laid the pizza box on the counter that separated the kitchen area from the living space, Bowie didn't touch it.

"So what happened?" she asked as she settled down beside him on the IKEA couch that she'd brought from her apartment in Minnesota.

When Bowie recapped Sawyer's unexpected visit, disgust filled Katie. She couldn't comprehend how Sawyer thought she could appear unannounced in Bowie's office after twelve years and demand time with her daughter. Then again, Sawyer had always possessed a singular talent for viewing the world through the microscope of her needs. If reality didn't suit Sawyer, she just ignored it and fabricated her own.

"Why do you think she's reappeared?" Katie asked after Bowie had finished. "Is she serious about having a relationship with Abby, or is she after something?"

"There's definitely something in it for her," he said. "Sawyer's not the self-sacrificing type. I think her marriage is on the rocks, and she believes this will help patch things up. It sounds like her husband has a soft spot for kids. But I also can't say for certain that she doesn't have some desire to be a mother. You knew Sawyer in high school. Do you think she would want to be a mom?"

Katie blew out a long breath, wishing he hadn't asked her opinion. "Bowie, you know my history with Sawyer. Honestly, I never saw any redeeming qualities, but I'm biased, and I haven't seen her for over a decade. I wouldn't have guessed you'd be a good father, but you're a really great one."

He rewarded her with a hesitant smile. As if of its own volition, her hand reached out and rested on his jean-clad leg. "Trust your judgment, Bowie."

"What if…" He hesitated, then plunged forward. "What if I *want* Sawyer to be undeserving of my daughter? What if deep down, I don't want to share Abby, and that's coloring my perspective?"

Katie could feel her expression soften. Her whole body might have just melted. "Bowie, the fact that you would even think to ask that question proves it isn't the case. You're not thinking of yourself. You're thinking of Abby. If I were in your position,

I'd be ripping Sawyer apart, but you're not. You're focused on protecting your daughter."

Bowie laid his hand over Katie's and laced their fingers together. Then he turned to gaze at her, his look earnest. "You really think that?"

Katie nodded, an odd tightness banded around her throat. "Yeah, I do. And you're going to figure out the right way to handle this."

He turned her hand over in his, then stared down for a moment, drawing his thumb over the back of her knuckles. Pleasant energy rippled through Katie's nerve endings, but she kept her focus on Bowie.

"I wish I knew how to keep Abby from getting hurt, but I don't know if that is possible."

Katie frowned. "Do you think Sawyer would hurt her?"

Bowie shrugged. "Not intentionally. I don't think she's cruel enough to purposely belittle her daughter, but she might accidentally. You know what she said when she saw Abby's picture on my desk? That Abby obviously needed a makeover. Her tone indicated she'd be embarrassed to call Abby her daughter until she 'fixed' her looks."

"I think I might have physically attacked her."

Bowie gave a half smile. "Unfortunately, that wasn't an option for me." The grin fled. "What if she says something like that in front of Abby?"

"Then we'll be there to tell her how wrong Sawyer is."

Bowie's gaze jerked toward hers. "We?"

Feeling slightly uncomfortable, Katie nodded. "I care about your daughter, Bowie. You know that. I don't want Sawyer ever making another little girl feel...well, like she made me feel."

"I'm sorry I was a part of that, Katie."

She gave a quick shake of her head as she fought an unexpected wave of tears. Thankfully, Bowie didn't appear to notice.

"This isn't about me," she said. "It's just that I'll be there. I can help Abby get through it. Heck, it's not like I can't commiserate. Maybe it won't come to that. Maybe Sawyer will be a halfway decent mom, or maybe you'll decide not to have them meet."

"Unfortunately, deciding they shouldn't meet isn't an option. Sawyer will corner Abby. I don't have any choice but to tell her what's going on."

"Has she ever asked about her birth mom?"

"A couple times. I told her that her mother loved her very much but was just a girl herself and wasn't ready to be a mom."

Bowie had been just a kid too, but Abby wouldn't realize that yet. To her, an eighteen-year-old probably epitomized the peak of sophistication.

"Do you think she'll want to meet Sawyer?" Katie asked.

"Honestly, I don't know. She's never expressed any longing for a mother, just curiosity about why she didn't have one. But all kids want their parents to love them…even if they have crappy ones."

"Are you going to let Sawyer meet Abby?"

Bowie paused, clearly thinking it over. His haunted look started to fade as he took a breath. "I think I am…as long as Abby wants to meet her. That way, I can control it. My time. My turf. Not Sawyer's. If it goes well, I can consider if I'll let Sawyer and her husband spend more time with

Abby. If I think it won't be healthy for Abby, or if she doesn't want anything more to do with them, then Sawyer can sue me. Literally. I'll figure out a way to find the money to fight her."

"You know," Katie said slowly, "my brother Luke is one of the best family law attorneys in town."

Bowie gave a lopsided grin. "Then he's probably out of my price range."

"I could get him to do it pro bono."

Bowie's jaw hardened. "I don't want charity, Katie."

"It's not charity," she said, "and it would be for Abby. It's not fair to either of you that Sawyer is putting you through this again. My brother can help level the playing field."

"I'm not sure."

Katie resettled on the couch so that she could fully face Bowie. "He occasionally takes pro bono cases, and he'll do this as a favor for me. He owes me big. I quit my job to help out Mom and Dad after the shooting since he and my other brothers couldn't handle the drama. Besides, if I tell him what Sawyer did to me in school, it will be his pleasure to eviscerate her case."

"If you don't tell him my part," Bowie grumbled, but she could sense his resistance disintegrating.

"Luke's very good at his job, and he's got a great reputation. There's a good chance he can get this case squelched right at the beginning."

"Do you really think he'll do it?" Bowie asked.

"Yes, I do," Katie told him truthfully. "He's a father himself. He went to law school to litigate cases like yours. He'd probably represent you pro bono even if you didn't know me."

"Okay," Bowie relented.

"Okay as in you'll think about it, or okay as in you want me to call him? There's a good chance Sawyer might try to hire him herself."

"Give him a call," Bowie said gruffly.

Katie checked her watch. "His family should be done with dinner, so I can do it now."

"Might as well get it over with."

Katie called Luke and provided him with a quick rundown. Luckily, Sawyer and her husband hadn't already contacted him. As Katie suspected, he readily accepted the case.

"So," she said as she hung up the phone, "you have a lawyer if you need one."

"Thanks." Bowie stood up. "For everything."

"No problem."

He stood there uncomfortably before he took a deep breath. "I know you and I planned for this evening to go completely differently. It's not late, but I don't think I'm up for a night of sex."

Katie gave him an understanding smile. "Don't you know that's the girl's line?"

Bowie rubbed the back of his head and grinned, but his smile didn't quite reach his eyes. Although he didn't seem as raw as when he'd first walked in, she could tell that the Sawyer situation still bugged him. And she didn't blame him.

"Uh, so I guess I should be leaving," Bowie said awkwardly. He turned to leave, but Katie found that she couldn't let him. He needed company. Abby wasn't home, and Katie knew Lou went to bed early.

"Bowie."

He turned and waited for her to speak.

"Would you like to stay? To watch a movie? I can reheat the pizza and make some popcorn."

A slow smile spread across his face. "I'd like that. A lot."

—◦◦◦—

Bowie found himself alone in Katie's living room, staring at her video collection. She was in the kitchen gathering snacks for them to eat. Although her odd geodesic dome house had an open floor plan, she'd put enough distance between them to give him a semblance of privacy. She must have sensed that he needed space, and he was glad for the few minutes to pull himself together. He still felt as unbalanced as a newborn giraffe. Although he hadn't come here to unload on Katie, he was glad she'd let him.

She'd helped him sort through his tumbled thoughts and emotions. Her pointed questions had focused him, allowing him to push aside the emotional clutter and realize the best action for Abby.

Then there was Katie's steadfast belief in his parenting skills.

With Katie, tonight, he felt different. More intimate and connected. For the first time, he didn't feel alone in a crisis, which was asinine. He and Katie weren't even officially a couple. In fact, he wasn't completely sure what they were. Only she seemed to have that answer. But whatever this thing was between them, it had helped him tonight.

Sighing, he tried to focus on a movie. Finally, he grabbed an action flick. He'd always preferred the genre, and given the number that Katie had, so did she. Unfortunately, since Abby had been born, his movie watching had skewed more toward Disney princesses than elite strike teams.

"You okay with a war movie?" he called to Katie.

"Sounds good," she said as the microwave chimed.

Bowie headed over to the TV to get the DVD cued up while she dumped popcorn into a bowl. It was oddly domestic, and he liked it. He'd never hung out with a woman like this before. For once, his life felt normal…well, as normal as you could get with an ex demanding custody of your child.

Katie laid the pizza and the popcorn on the coffee table in front of the couch before snuggling against him. Bowie felt his entire body relax. Smiling, he pulled her close as she rested her head on his chest. He didn't know why, but when he held this woman, everything seemed to slide into place.

The stress of the day ebbed away as a sense of calm washed over him. He didn't know when he'd enjoyed a movie so much. For an action flick, it had decent dialogue and an interesting plot. Of course, it didn't hurt that he managed to steal a few kisses from Katie. After the film ended, they picked another.

Bowie didn't want to cut the evening short, but when midnight rolled around, he couldn't hide his yawns anymore. He typically hit the sack around eleven o'clock so he could rise early to feed the animals.

"Sorry," he said before the third yawn in a row hit.

"No problem," she said. "You've had a long day."

He stood. "I guess I'd better get going before I'm too tired to drive."

Katie didn't speak for a moment. She seemed to be having an internal debate before she finally said, "You can stay the night if you want."

"Are you sure?" Bowie asked and then immediately had to smother another yawn. He'd like to stay, but her invitation had felt hesitant.

Katie's face softened. Rising from the couch, she gently tugged on his hand. "Let's get you to bed before you fall asleep on your feet. You're too big for me to carry."

Bowie let her lead him upstairs and into her bedroom loft. As she headed off to take a shower, he stripped down to his boxers and collapsed onto the huge bed. It was a shame he didn't have the oomph to take advantage of it tonight. Unfortunately, he needed all his energy just to stay awake until Katie returned.

When she crawled into bed, he immediately reached out and pulled her toward him. Katie complied, rolling her body in his direction. When she nestled against his bare chest like one of the cougar cubs, he couldn't help the sigh of contentment that rumbled through him.

It was nice sleeping with Katie. Although he'd dozed off in a woman's bed before, he'd never simply slept with one. He liked it. His eyes drifted closed, and deep sleep claimed him.

When Bowie woke in the morning, he found Katie still wrapped in his arms. He lay there for a moment, relishing the scent and feel of her. The blinds surrounding her room didn't let in much light, but there was enough glow for him to study her. She wasn't traditionally beautiful, not like June or Sawyer, but every time

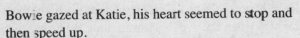

Bowie gazed at Katie, his heart seemed to stop and then speed up.

Slowly, gently, so as not to wake her, he brushed away one of the red tendrils of hair that had fallen across her face. She looked so sweet in repose that it made him ache inside. He'd never felt like this before when he woke up with a woman. Normally, he just wanted the morning to end with the least amount of awkwardness.

If he could, he'd spend the entire day with Katie. Preferably in her bed. Naked.

Unfortunately, he had to pick up Abby around noon. Plus, he needed to get back to the animals, even though the zoo wasn't open to the public today. He had arranged for one of the employees to take the early shift, so at least he didn't have to rush back immediately.

Typically, he didn't have the luxury of lingering in bed. Right now, he could afford a few moments to savor the languid feeling washing over him. Gazing down at Katie, he planned the morning. He knew he had at least an hour or two before she woke. First, he'd grab a shower. Then, he'd scope out what she had in her kitchen and whip them up something to eat. Maybe there'd be enough time for a quick bout of sex.

Bowie shifted slightly as he tried to figure out the best way of untangling their limbs without waking Katie. As he started to withdraw, she emitted an unhappy sound somewhere between a squeak and grunt. It reminded him a bit of Daisy, the red river hog, although he knew Katie definitely wouldn't appreciate the comparison.

He'd almost succeeded in extricating his body from under hers when she wiggled toward him. When her face brushed against his chest, she nuzzled his skin before settling back down with a contented sigh. Bowie's heart swelled. He knew no other way to describe the feeling burgeoning inside him. He'd never felt so much affection for another human being, except for his daughter.

He wanted this, he realized. He wanted the sweetness and the tender moments, along with the mad, hot, passionate sex. It wasn't enough for him to be friends with benefits with Katie. He wanted a real relationship.

Bowie just needed to convince her. She had made it clear that she didn't want anything more than to be sex buddies. Hell, she'd flatly refused his dinner invitation, and she'd certainly hesitated before inviting him to spend the night. If he pushed too quickly for an actual date, she might not only shut down his offer, but also end their affair.

He would need to proceed slowly. When they'd first started sleeping together, Bowie hadn't been sure if Katie completely liked him. Now, they had become friends. If he remained patient and persistent, he could transform that friendship into something more. After all, he thought as he bent to brush a light kiss on Katie's forehead, he had a feeling that this particular woman was worth the extra effort.

～～～

Katie woke to the aroma of food. For a few moments, she thought she'd fallen asleep on her family's couch again. Stretching, she opened her eyes to find herself in her own bedroom. The night before came flooding back. Glancing to the side of the bed where Bowie had slept, she found the covers tossed to the side.

He hadn't left—not with the great smells emanating from downstairs. Occasionally, she could hear the clang of a pot or running water. The man was cooking breakfast in her kitchen.

For her.

The realization sparked an odd, off-kilter feeling. Katie wouldn't exactly classify it as bad or good—just different. She felt strangely vulnerable, as if she had just stripped naked in front of Bowie for the first time.

Unable to shake the peculiar sensations enveloping her, she stopped struggling against them and climbed out of bed. Throwing on her bathrobe and some slippers, she padded downstairs. She found Bowie softly humming to himself as he whipped batter in a bowl.

"Good morning," he told her cheerfully.

She blinked at him with what she was fairly certain were bleary eyes. "Mornin'." Then she immediately shuffled over to the trusty Keurig that Josh had bought her for Christmas two years ago. Selecting the lightest roast, she pressed the button and turned back to Bowie. She needed plenty of caffeine to meet his energy level.

"Pancakes okay?" he asked as he flipped one of the hotcakes with a spatula.

"Sounds good," she said, the statement ending on a large yawn. Bowie smiled at her. She paused in lifting the coffee cup to her lips. The warmth in his gray eyes caught her off guard. Although she'd had guys give her appreciative glances before, this felt different, deeper.

Heady, sweet emotion swelled inside her. She hadn't felt this way in years. Not since high school when her secret crush had smiled at her and asked her out on a date.

But that was then, and this was now. She wouldn't permit those giddy feelings to scramble her logic this time around. As an adult, she recognized the intoxicating sensations for what they were—lust wrapped up in a fantasy of romantic love that didn't exist.

Chapter 9

"WHAT IS THAT?" BOWIE EYED THE WIG SUSPICIOUSLY. A garish fluorescent-yellow mohawk sprouted from a flesh-colored cap. It looked like part of a costume from a low-budget slasher film. The fact that one end of the wig was sopping wet didn't help.

Bowie should have expected trouble when Katie had shown up with June in tow. He'd gotten to know the other woman over the past few weeks while she'd been helping Katie and him put together the zoo's big festival. He couldn't help but like June. But underneath her undeniable Southern charm lay cleverness that rivaled Fluffy's.

"Isn't this just the sexiest little wig on God's green earth?" June asked as she turned it slowly in her hands like she was a damn shopping-channel host.

"No," Bowie said dryly.

"Bowie, it's perfect!" Katie said, and he couldn't help but smile at her enthusiasm. Her brown eyes sparkled as they did when she had a particularly good marketing idea. "It looks just like Rosie's plume."

Cocking his head at an angle, Bowie studied the hideous hairpiece. Katie did have a point. With a little effort, the yellow mohawk could be spiked to look like the cockatoo's yellow feathers.

"I see that now," Bowie conceded slowly, not knowing what else he was tacitly agreeing to.

"You have just got to model it for us, darling," June said.

Before Bowie could swerve to avoid her, June had plunked the wig on his head. She stood back, made a "tsking" sound at the back of her throat, and reached up to adjust it. Seemingly satisfied, she smiled. "Now can you be a dear and bob your head like Rosie?"

Bowie glanced helplessly at Katie. She just grinned and nodded. He crossed his arms. "Uh-uh. I'm not doing anything else until one of you tells me what's going on."

"You know how you want to do a skit with Rosie at the festival?" Katie asked.

"Yes," Bowie said slowly. Although the festival headliner was going to be the cubs' first public appearance, other events were scheduled throughout the day. Bowie wasn't thrilled that he'd be wearing a Tarzan costume to introduce the cougars, but that's what the public had voted for. Luckily, Katie had found a tasteful costume that only bared one shoulder, although Bowie would still essentially be wearing a dress. Katie referred to it as a tunic, but from Bowie's perspective, the bottom part was a skirt—no matter what anyone called it.

He had no idea how he'd let Katie talk him into playing the King of the Jungle, but he couldn't complain about the money the event had already raised. Between the voting campaign and presales for the festival tickets, he'd already made enough to buy a male camel for Lulubelle.

The stud was due to arrive a couple of days before the big day. Although it would have been good publicity for the two to meet during the festival, Bowie hadn't wanted to put more stress on the animals, especially on the male, Hank. Even though Hank had been owned by a roadside zoo and regularly gave rides to tourists, Bowie wanted to ease him into his new home. The camel and Lulubelle needed time to bond before Bowie introduced the new couple to the public. Katie planned on filming the *meet-cute*, as she called it, for the website.

"You can put on this wig before we bring Rosie out," Katie said excitedly. "Then, you could head-bang simultaneously. The crowd will love it."

They would, and so would the internet. For that reason alone, Bowie would wear the ridiculous mohawk. Plus, it made Katie happy, and he loved her smile.

"I thought we could include clips of the other animals bobbing their heads," she said. "I can use my video editing software to put a yellow mohawk above them, but June and I actually tried the wig on Lulubelle. It worked out well...except for the end."

Katie handed him her smartphone. Lulubelle looked sillier than ever with the ill-fitting wig perched on top of her massive head. Tinny strains of a pop song played in the background as the camel morosely bobbed her head. When the hair-piece finally slipped off, Lulubelle caught it in her mouth. She looked decidedly happier as she began to chew on the yellow hair.

"That explains why it's wet," Bowie said.

"We wrestled it back before Lulubelle could do much damage," June drawled.

"I think we can end the video with Lulubelle gumming the wig," Katie said. "I think this could be our best yet."

It could. Although Bowie didn't have Katie's knack for visuals, even he could picture it. Both kids and adults would eat it up.

"All right." Bowie relented. "I'll wear it."

"Perfect," Katie said. "Speaking of the festival, I found someone willing to pay for the tents we need."

"Who?" Bowie asked.

"Our friend Josh from college," June drawled. "He's richer than Croesus from his computer security work, but I swear he squeezes a quarter so tight that the eagle screams."

Bowie barked out a laugh at her imagery. "If he's so cheap, why is he donating money?"

"Katie sweet-talked him like she always does. Josh is as ornery as a mule with two lame feet, except around her."

"That's not true," Katie protested. "He's close to you too."

"Ahh," June said, "but I don't share an artistic connection."

An unbidden bolt of jealousy shot through Bowie. He tried to squelch it, but he didn't quite manage it. "Artistic connection, huh?"

Luckily, Katie didn't pick up on the slight sharpness in his voice. June, though, shot him a suspicious look. Over the past couple of weeks, he'd been getting quite a few of those from her. It bugged Bowie that Katie clearly hadn't told her best friend about their relationship. But he was pretty certain June suspected that he and Katie were sleeping together.

Katie waved a dismissive hand. "Josh and I coauthored a comic strip for our university's newspaper."

"Whatever happened to your collection of them?" June said.

"Josh has it," Katie said.

"You and Josh are pretty close then?" Bowie asked, hoping his voice sounded neutral. It really shouldn't bug him that Katie shared her love of art with another man. But it did. Probably since she was still pushing him away. Not once had she accepted any of his offers for a real date since their night at her house a couple of weeks ago.

It was June who answered Bowie's question. As she did, she studied him closely, obviously gauging his reaction. "She and Josh used to date."

Katie groaned. "For a nanosecond during our freshman year at State. Then we decided we were better off as friends. June took both of us under her wing."

"That is true," June agreed, still watching Bowie. "The three of us are like siblings."

Bowie nodded, but he couldn't help the uneasy feeling that slithered through him like a rattler. Katie was so open and generous, but she still kept an invisible wall between them. He wanted more than ever to tear it down, but he felt like he hadn't even put a chip in it.

"Josh is going to be coming to town for the festival," Katie said.

"Oh," Bowie said.

"He wants to check out the zoo. He's been following all of our marketing."

"That's nice," Bowie said. He really didn't want the guy on his property, which was crazy. There was no reason to act territorial, and he hadn't even met Josh. He was being ridiculous. He knew that, but he couldn't stop himself.

"In fact," Katie added, her face brightening, "he's even shown some of my recent work to his clients."

"Which is a very big deal," June interjected. "Josh consults for all kinds of tech firms on the West Coast."

"A couple companies even asked for my résumé."

"That's great!" Bowie almost winced at the sound of his own voice. He sounded too enthusiastic, too eager. Even Katie picked up on his odd tone as she shot him a questioning look.

But, hell, he didn't want her to leave their hometown again. Not that he'd try to stop her. She'd made it clear that she wanted out of Sagebrush, and he wouldn't want to persuade her to give up her dream job. He should be happy that her friend was willing to network on Katie's behalf. Part of Bowie, though, couldn't help but want to punch the bastard.

"Josh said I could room with him if I got a job in the Bay Area. There's no way I could afford living there otherwise."

"And Josh's place is just drop-dead gorgeous," June drawled. "It's an absolutely darling Victorian…a lot like yours but on a sea cliff."

Of course, Josh would have a home that overlooked the ocean in one of the priciest real estate markets in the world. Bowie was beginning to really dislike this faceless Josh. He had it all. The house. The career. Money. Katie's trust.

And that. That last thing. *That* was why Bowie really resented the man.

"Josh says he can't wait to meet you," Katie said.

"I can't wait to meet him either," Bowie lied.

"Not to be as nosy as a blue tick after a coon," June drawled as she and Katie sat on the floor with the cougar kits, "but what is that air mattress still doing in the room next door? I thought the cubs no longer required watching during the night."

Sometimes June's attention to detail could be a nuisance. Katie shrugged in response. "Your point being?"

June shot her a significant look as Fleur playfully batted her knee. "Makes things a mite more comfortable, doesn't it?"

"I don't know what you're talking about."

June's lips curved into a smug, knowing smile. "And a bee doesn't know how to sting."

Katie sighed. Heavily. "Okay. Fine. We're sleeping together. Have been since filming the pirate video."

"I knew he was the right guy for you." Pure delight flashed in June's green eyes.

Katie did not share her enthusiasm. "We're just friends with benefits, June. That's all. I didn't want to start something serious when I could be leaving any time."

"Katie, I swear you have a bigger commitment phobia than any guy."

"I'm choosy." Katie crossed her arms over her chest. She knew she was acting defensive, but she couldn't help herself.

June lifted both eyebrows in patent disbelief. "Honey, I have known you for over ten years, and not once have you had a real relationship."

"Not true. I dated Steven for almost a year."

June delivered her most withering look. "He was a pilot, lived two hours away in Saint Paul, and was gone half the time."

"It worked for us," Katie said stubbornly.

"Katie, honey, you need to open yourself up to the possibility of romance. I'm afraid that you're going to let a good thing go just because you're too stubborn to be vulnerable."

"When I meet the right guy, I'll settle down."

June arched one perfectly tweezed blond eyebrow. "Says the woman who just wants to be sex buddies with a deliciously attractive man who cooks, loves animals, and dotes on his adorable daughter."

Katie started to stand up in agitation, but Dobby chose that exact moment to pounce on her lap. He wiggled between her crossed legs, trying to use her body as a shield to crouch behind as he spied on his sisters.

"June, he is not my Mr. Right. Can we drop this?"

"Just give me one good reason, Katie, and cross my heart, I swear I'll leave it be."

Katie lifted Dobby from her lap and gently set him on the floor. "Because Bowie's the reason that I keep myself shut off. Okay, June?"

That succeeded in silencing her. For half a second.

"Why?" June asked. "Did y'all date before?"

"I don't want to talk about it," Katie said stubbornly as she turned her attention to Tonks, who was brushing her back against Katie's leg while Dobby wrestled with Fleur. "You said to give you one good reason. Well, I did, so the subject is closed."

"Katieee," June said, drawing out the *eee*.

Realizing that her friend wouldn't let this go, Katie blurted out, "Fine. He pretended to date me in high school. Not only did he trick me into kissing a pig like I told you before, but his real girlfriend sneaked a video of it into the morning announcements."

June snickered. Actually snickered. Katie shot her a death glare.

"What?" June said. "You have to admit it's kind of funny, especially after he kissed that red river hog for you."

"June, he crushed my heart and made me the laughingstock of the school for two and a half years. Even my friends didn't want to be around me because they thought they'd be targeted next."

The laughter left June's face. "I had no idea it was that bad, Katie."

"It was, and he's the last guy I would ever want to open my heart to," Katie said. "I won't deny that I am attracted to him or that he's changed since high school, but he's not dating material. At least not for me."

"Okay, I'll let it go," June said, "but you've got to start taking risks with your heart sometime, honey."

"Not today. Not with him," Katie said as she turned her attention back to the tussling cubs.

Two weeks later, a copper-haired man with a welcoming grin on his annoyingly handsome face climbed from the sporty car in the zoo parking lot. Instead of the casual attire that sane people wore to zoos, Josh Calhoun sported a tailored suit that even

Bowie could tell reeked of money. He embraced June and then Katie. Bowie tried not to glower. He wished like hell that Katie and June hadn't decided to meet Josh at the zoo. At least they were on Bowie's turf.

Katie tugged on one of Josh's lapels. "So why are you so spiffy today?"

"I had a meeting near the airport. I'm thinking of expanding my consulting services beyond the West Coast," Josh said.

"Do you *ever* not think of business?" June asked.

"Nope." Josh grinned boyishly, reminding Bowie of a damn movie star. One of those Cary Grant debonair types.

Then Josh turned in Bowie's direction, and the man's mouth flattened. When Josh extended his hand, the offer felt more like a challenge than a welcoming gesture. Sure enough, Josh practically ground Bowie's fingers together. Bowie returned the bruising grip threefold. Josh may have a couple of inches of height on him, but Bowie was more muscular, and he didn't sit in front of a computer all day.

"Wilson," Josh said Bowie's last name, his voice flat and unyielding.

"Calhoun," Bowie returned in the same tone.

Katie looked curiously at them. "Uh, did I miss something?"

Josh dropped Bowie's hand, the smile back on his face. "No. Why?"

"For a moment there, I thought you were one of my brothers or my father meeting my date for the evening," she said.

"Anyone ever tell you that you can be paranoid sometimes, Underwood?" Josh asked.

"Hmm," Katie said suspiciously, glancing back and forth between the two of them.

Josh slung his arm over Katie's shoulder. "So let's see this zoo you've been texting me about."

Katie studied her friend's face closely and finally nodded. "What do you want to see first?"

"The lovelorn camel," Josh said. "And that dancing bird. Do you think it will head-bang to 'The Imperial March'?"

Katie laughed as she linked her arm through her friend's. "Darth Vader's theme really doesn't have the driving beat that Rosie likes."

"Damn. I was hoping I could buy her a specially made black helmet. That would be fucking awesome."

June shook her head. "You are such a nerd, Josh Calhoun."

"Yep. And damn proud of it."

Bowie trailed after the trio. As much as he fought against it, that foster-kid feeling kicked in. He was the interloper. The kid on the outside, always looking for a way in and not quite finding it.

Despite feeling like a stranger on his own property, Bowie still enjoyed watching Katie show off the zoo. Her face lit up every time she introduced an animal. And the zoo residents clearly loved her. Even Lulubelle perked up and came gleefully stomping toward Katie. When they visited the cubs, the cougars made a beeline in her direction, while Sylvia eagerly nudged Katie with her big snout, demanding and receiving pets.

Later, they spied Fluffy lurking near the concession stand as he polished off an ice cream cone a child must have dropped. Katie snapped a picture with her phone. Fluffy, being Fluffy, remained standoffish, but Bowie couldn't shake the feeling that even the disgruntled honey badger had developed a soft spot for Katie.

As they walked past Frida's enclosure, the bear looked up from the ice block Bowie had given her. Normally, the old gal focused all her attention on gnawing the frozen fruit and vegetables embedded in the treat, but she sniffed in Katie's direction before returning to eating.

When Rosie caught sight of them, she squawked a greeting from her perch, her head bobbing happily. Bowie pulled her from her cage and placed the bird on his shoulder so she could show off her dance moves. She bopped along to "Sheila," and Bowie swore that she purposely bowed in Katie's direction when the song ended.

When they'd finished the tour of the zoo, Katie and June started debating where they should take Josh next. They finally decided to stop at the Prairie Dog Café for drinks before heading out to Katie's family's ranch. Evidently, Josh was crashing with Katie in the geodesic dome while he was in town.

"Why don't the two of you head over to the Prairie Dog first," Josh said, his attention fixed on Bowie. "There's something I want to talk to Wilson about."

Katie frowned. She didn't seem convinced, but Bowie didn't mind some time alone with the jerk. Obviously, Josh didn't trust him any more than Bowie did him. For Katie's sake, they needed to resolve whatever dislike brewed between them.

"Go on," Bowie told her. "We'll be fine."

Katie hesitated and then finally nodded. "If you say so. Just try not to kill each other."

Josh gave her a reassuring smile, which had the opposite effect on Bowie. "Don't worry, Katie. I don't want to get blood on my suit."

"How very comforting," she said dryly.

June tugged on Katie's arm. "Let's leave the boys to their caveman ways." Then, looking over her shoulder, she gave Bowie and Josh a classic June smile. "Y'all play nice, you hear?"

As soon as June and Katie disappeared from view, any vestige of geniality fled from Josh's face, leaving it stone cold. Bowie swore the man's golden-brown eyes even turned an icy greenish blue. Bowie had no idea why Josh apparently hated him, unless the man still had romantic feelings for Katie. Frigid silence descended. Bowie didn't attempt to break it.

When Josh finally spoke, the frost in his voice matched the chilliness in his eyes. "You may have June fooled, but I know exactly who and what you are."

Bowie stiffened at the damning words as a sense of unease trickled through him. "Yeah, and what is that?"

"A bully," Josh said succinctly.

The disquiet in Bowie grew. Hell, maybe the guy had a legitimate reason to hate him. Bowie supposed he should have been prepared for this, but Katie had kept their past a secret from June and the rest of her family. It bothered him that she would have confided in this man when she hadn't done so with anyone else.

Josh watched Bowie for a moment. Then the man

smiled. Smirked, actually. "What? Did you think you humiliated her so much that she wouldn't tell anyone? Well, she did, and I'm not letting you hurt her again."

Guilt flashed through Bowie, hot and searing. He'd expected to be on the offensive, not the defensive. "How I acted toward Katie was wrong. I know that, and I've told her the same. I've changed since high school."

Josh pierced him with a flat, unyielding look. "You may have started to convince Katie, but you aren't going to be able to trick me. Like I said, I know who and what you are."

Bowie crossed his arms. "You met me ten minutes ago. You couldn't possibly know me."

"Oh, I know you," Josh returned with another sneer. "You're the same guy who shoved me in a locker, who forced my head into a toilet, and who duct-taped me to a urinal."

"I never did any of that. Ever," Bowie growled.

"So you're just the type who picks on girls. Who humiliates them in front of the entire school with pig-kissing videos, by stealing and publicizing their diaries, or tying underwear to their car."

A part of Bowie recognized that Josh had a point. Bowie knew how he'd react if some jackass did that to Abby and then tried to date her years later. He probably wouldn't let the man live. But he was Abby's father. This guy wasn't even related to Katie. Bowie would grovel to her brothers or father, but he wasn't about to let this man judge him or his relationship. His past with Katie was something he and Katie needed to work through without this man's interference.

"Yeah, I was a douche bag. I won't deny that," Bowie

said. "But I don't need to explain myself to you. This is between Katie and me."

"There are very few people in this world who I care about," Josh said. "Katie is one of them. I'm making this my business."

"So what, you're jealous of our relationship?"

Genuine surprise flickered in Josh's otherwise glacial eyes. "Katie and June are the closest thing to family that I have, and I won't let either of them get hurt, especially by someone like you."

"Someone like me," Bowie repeated. "You keep coming back to that, but you don't know me. All you know are some stupid, idiotic things I did years ago. You don't even know why I did them."

"Oh, I know why," Josh said. "I know your type. Golden boy. Jock. The most popular guy in school."

Yeah right, none of those things had ever described Bowie. "Golden boy?"

"The apple of Mommy and Daddy's eyes. A precious little tyrant who can't do anything wrong, who the teachers love. When you caused trouble, people either laughed or used the excuse that 'boys will be boys.'"

It was Bowie's turn to smirk. "Katie might have told you a little about high school, but she mustn't have told you much. None of what you said is accurate."

Although Katie didn't know about his parents or foster care, she certainly wouldn't describe him as a golden boy. He'd never played a sport or participated in any extracurricular activities—unless detention counted. Some days, he'd spent more time in the principal's office than in the classroom.

Josh's expression didn't change. His eyes bored into Bowie. Finally, the man relaxed a fraction—just a fraction.

"Come. I have something I want to show you."

Oh goody.

Still, Bowie didn't protest. He'd gained some ground with Katie lately, and he didn't want to lose it. If he wanted to forge a real relationship with her, he couldn't afford to alienate one of her closest friends and the guy helping her find a new job. As much as Bowie wanted to punch Josh's smug face, he needed to remain civil.

"Lead the way."

Less than a minute later, Bowie found himself back at the man's showy rental. Josh popped open the trunk and pulled out a briefcase. "You got a private place where we can talk uninterrupted?"

"My office," Bowie said, unable to stop a wave of curiosity. What the hell was the man up to? Bowie led the guy back through the zoo. For once, the sight of the animals didn't give Bowie the peace it generally did. Guilt, anger, and a trepidation that he couldn't shake mixed inside him like a Molotov cocktail ready to explode. He just hoped Josh wouldn't light the wick.

———

Fluffy was not sure how to feel about the copper-haired male. He did not like him as well as he did the tall, blond female. This biped was too full of himself.

Fluffy scurried across the parking lot to explore the man's vehicle. It was clean. Much cleaner than the Black-Haired One's truck. Even in the twilight, it shone. The sparkly quality annoyed Fluffy.

He tried to get into the car but could not. He settled on placing tracks all over the surface. Very wet, very muddy tracks.

<hr />

When Josh and Bowie entered the zoo's office, Josh shut the door firmly behind him. As he flipped the lock, Bowie raised an amused eyebrow. He hoped the guy didn't want to fight him. He could probably take down the lanky desk jockey with one well-aimed punch. It might have been years since Bowie had last exchanged blows with someone, but he'd spent his middle school and high school years getting into one fight after another.

Instead, Josh walked over to Bowie's desk and started spreading out newspaper and magazine clippings, along with a few computer printouts. He nodded his head toward the pieces of paper. "When we were in college, Katie and I coauthored and drew a comic for our student newspaper. It made fun of things around the school. Later, I asked her to draw some comic book–style advertisements for my business. A lot of my clients are geeks and loved the concept, so she does a monthly comic for my web page."

Suddenly interested, Bowie focused on the artwork. He vaguely remembered Katie showing him some sketches when he'd pretended to date her in high school, but time had fogged his memories.

"Which ones are Katie's?"

A look of challenge crossed Josh's face. "Can't you recognize her work? She has a very distinctive style."

Crap. He'd walked right into that one.

"I'm not an artist. I don't know how to pick up on subtle details," Bowie said, not willing to admit that he hadn't seen any of Katie's drawings except those for the zoo and her other local clients.

Josh studied him with interest. "How much of her work have you looked at? Surely, Katie would've shared her recent comics from my website. If you care for her, you'd realize how important her drawings are to her."

Bowie had no good answer. Katie hadn't opened up to him like that. At least not yet. And he didn't want to explain their relationship to Josh. So he deflected. "What is your problem with me anyway? Do you really think I'll start pulling juvenile pranks again?"

Josh glanced at him almost dismissively. "You do seem like the type who peaked in high school and might try to relive the glory days, but no, that's not my main concern."

"Then what is it?"

"You might not pull humiliating pranks anymore, but I think this is a power play for you. Prove that you've still got it. That you can make Katie fall for you twice, even with her knowing how you treated her in the past."

"And you don't think she's smart enough to figure out if I'm just manipulating her?" Bowie demanded.

"You succeeded last time, and you've got enough pull on Katie that she's overlooking what you did to her before."

Not completely, but Bowie didn't want to reveal that. "Maybe it's because she realizes that ten years have passed, and I'm not the same immature dickwad I once was."

Josh regarded him carefully. "You know, I do think Katie is intelligent enough not to let you get too close. After all, she hasn't shown you the work she does for my website. So I'm thinking that she's holding herself apart."

Yeah, she was, and Bowie didn't need another reminder.

"So that should make you happy," Bowie snapped.

"It does somewhat," Josh admitted.

Bowie clenched his hand so hard that his fingers actually hurt. He didn't make a move to swing his arm, but he was close.

"You hurt her last time. Deeply. Maybe you actually do care about her, but you damn well don't deserve her. I honestly don't think you could ever make her happy," Josh continued.

"That's where you're wrong. I might not have a college education or a job that brings home a lot of money. Hell, you're probably even right that I might not fully deserve Katie, but I can bring her happiness, and I can be the man she needs."

The tension suddenly left Josh's face. The man didn't exactly smile, but he didn't seem ready to shoot beams of deadly frost from his eyes either. Bowie's own body uncoiled a fraction. It felt a little anticlimactic, but perhaps he'd convinced Josh of the sincerity of his interest in Katie.

Josh swept his hand over Bowie's desk. "All of these drawings are Katie's."

Bowie wasn't sure if the man was extending an olive branch, but he wasted no time in studying the pictures. He wanted to see Katie's work. Although he didn't know much about any form of art, Katie's drawings possessed a compelling vibrancy. With deft strokes of her pen, she managed to make the characters seem as if they could leap from the page.

"She's really talented," Bowie said with a smile.

Josh didn't return it, but he didn't scowl either. "Yes. Yes, she is."

Bowie returned his attention to the artwork. Josh walked over beside him.

"I purposely picked these clippings because they all show the villains that Katie has drawn over the years." Josh pointed with his index finger as he continued speaking. "This is the mascot of our main school rival. Here's the professor who was basically a caricature. He would grade papers by throwing them down the stairs, stuff like that. Next, Katie created this little guy to represent a computer virus in the ads for my company. Then there's the computer hacker."

"They're really good," Bowie said.

"Do you recognize anything about the drawings?"

Something about Josh's tone caused Bowie's sense of foreboding to return. Cautiously, he turned his attention back to Josh.

"No." Bowie chose his words carefully. "Should I?"

Josh grabbed one of the pictures and handed it to Bowie. "This one might help. He was a recurring character in our comic series. He personifies a college student's insecurities. Katie named him 'Self Doubt.' He's like the devil who appears on someone's shoulder, but instead of persuading them to do something bad, he goads them into acting awkward."

Josh fell silent as Bowie studied the character. The villain was a young, surprisingly good-looking twentysomething. He hovered above a young woman's shoulder—a young woman with curly hair who looked a lot like Katie had back in high school. Self Doubt wore a black cape that billowed about him to reveal a toned body clad in leather. Bowie was so caught up in the artistry that he almost missed the man's facial features.

Was that...? Naw, it couldn't be. Could it?

"Katie told me that she came up with the idea for Self Doubt in high school." Josh confirmed Bowie's suspicions.

Ah, hell, it was him. The guy who caused the Katie look-alike to lose faith in herself was modeled after him. The realization slammed like a serrated knife into Bowie's gut, then twisted mercilessly.

"Now look around again," Josh said, the smugness back in his voice. "See the familiarities now?"

As Bowie surveyed the clippings strewn on his desk, the gnawing ache in his stomach turned even more vicious. Every damn villain shared some feature with him. Even the evil computer virus had gray eyes.

Stricken, Bowie glanced back at Josh. The guy grinned. Evilly.

"You see, you may be right. I may not know all the details about who you were and who you are now, but I do know who you are to Katie."

Josh paused, probably for dramatic effect. Not that Bowie needed it. He already felt clobbered.

"You are Katie's villain."

Chapter 10

As THE TRUCK CONTAINING THE NEW MALE CAMEL pulled into the zoo parking lot, Katie glanced over at Bowie with concern...and not for the first time. Ever since Katie had left him with Josh yesterday, Bowie had seemed strangely subdued. Last night, she'd grilled Josh about it, but her friend had remained mum.

Katie sensed there was something off, and it bothered her. She wanted Bowie to enjoy the upcoming zoo festival after all his hard work. With the Sawyer mess hanging over his head, the man needed a break. If Josh had said anything to ruin the celebration, Katie would personally wring his neck.

"Are you sure everything is okay?" Katie asked Bowie again. "You seem quiet."

Bowie nodded. "Yeah. Just under a lot of pressure with the festival coming up."

Josh strode up to them, effectively ending the conversation. Bowie stiffened almost imperceptibly, but Katie caught the slight movement. For his part, Josh appeared relaxed...too relaxed. She still had no idea what had transpired between the two men, but she didn't like it. Since Josh seemed borderline smug, Katie instinctively sided with Bowie. She might not have decided to trust him completely, but she didn't want Josh making him feel uncomfortable.

She brushed her hand against Bowie's bicep. Josh's

eyes narrowed slightly, but Bowie's muscles relaxed under her fingertips. She rested her hand against his skin long enough to send both men a clear message. She wanted Bowie by her side, regardless of Josh's overprotectiveness.

Bowie smiled down at her, some of the normal warmth returning to his grin. "I better go help the truck driver unload Hank. Camels can be ornery, especially after being cooped up in a trailer."

Sure enough, a loud, guttural bray echoed through the quiet parking lot. The truck driver had already lowered the ramp and was pulling on the camel's lead. But there was no sign of Hank, who stubbornly remained inside. Bowie joined the handler and added his strength to the rope.

Hank's nose and lips appeared first. His large nostrils flared with indignation, his mouth open in a gaping bray. He snorted as the rest of his fuzzy head emerged. Glowering the whole time, Hank used all his strength to resist. Inch by inch, more of his long neck became visible. The rest of the camel remained hidden in the trailer. Not even one foot had made an appearance.

"Glory be, how long is that poor creature's neck?" June asked. "He looks like candy at a taffy pull."

"An angry piece of candy," Josh observed.

"Well, would you be happy about being stretched like that?" June asked.

Just then, the first hoof materialized, then the next. Hank kept his neck low and fully extended. With gravity now helping the men, the camel had no choice but to scramble down the ramp. He did not appear pleased by the process. When his feet reached the ground, he began to twist his head like a writhing serpent ready to strike.

"Oh my, Lulubelle will have a devil of a time charming that one," June said, laughing.

"She's up to the task," Katie said, completely confident about the feminine wiles of the cheerful camel.

Just then Hank decided to spit. Quite profusely and quite accurately. Right into Bowie's face.

Instead of getting angry, Bowie just wiped off the liquid with his shirtsleeve and grinned up at the bull. "Welcome to Sagebrush, Hank."

Hank did not appear impressed. He brayed, but it did not sound like a greeting. More like a protest.

"I know." Bowie reached up and rubbed the camel's neck. "You had a rough trip. But it's over now, and we have someone here who you're going to want to meet."

Hank stared mulishly, clearly unconvinced. Still, the steady ground beneath his feet must have provided the animal with reassurance, because he at least stopped thrashing wildly. Bowie kept stroking the animal until the camel's breathing calmed.

"That's it, boy. You're home now." Hank snorted, and Bowie grinned. "I mean it."

"I'll give Katie's new guy credit for one thing," Josh observed quietly so only Katie and June could hear. "He does seem to genuinely care for his animals."

June punched Josh's arm. "You play nice now, you hear? Bowie's been treating our girl very well. I approve."

Josh looked as disgruntled as Hank. "The jury's still out."

Katie shook her head. "I think you two are forgetting

that it's my opinion that counts, but June's right, Josh. You play nice."

Before Josh had a chance to respond, Hank had settled enough to allow Bowie to lead him away from the parking lot. June grabbed Katie's arm excitedly. "I am just dying to see the camels meet. Do you think it will be love at first sight?"

"I don't think it works that way," Josh said dryly. "Lust at first sight, maybe. Love? Not a chance in hell."

June glared at Josh. "I swear, Josh Calhoun, you lack any romantic bone in your entire body."

Josh grinned as the three of them followed after Bowie and Hank. "Thanks for the compliment."

"It wasn't one."

"Would you two be quiet?" Katie hissed as they got closer to the new camel enclosure. "I'm supposed to be filming this meeting, remember? I don't need you two bickering in the background."

"What mood music are you going to play?" Josh asked.

"Shhh," June hissed. "You'll disrupt the camel love."

Thankfully, the two fell silent as they rounded the corner where Abby and Lou were waiting for them at the camel enclosure. At the sight of Hank, Abby immediately began bouncing up and down. A wide smile spread across Lou's weathered face. As Bowie led Hank into the pen, Katie stood far enough away that she could capture all the action without picking up any sound.

Lulubelle's head perked up. So did Hank's. In

fact, the formerly reluctant camel picked up speed. A lot of it. Instead of Bowie having to tug the bull forward, he now had to restrain the beast.

"Looks like he's in rut," Lou observed.

When Bowie answered, his voice was strained from the effort of trying to contain the now-enthusiastic male. "It's too early for that. Doesn't the rut normally start in November?"

Lou shook his head as he leaned against the fence. "Not necessarily for dromedary camels. Hank here isn't a young'un, and he can be ready any time of the year. Lulubelle knows. See how she's flicking her tail? Why do you think Hank's giving you so much trouble?"

"Maybe you should stop filming," June whispered.

Katie kept her camera trained on the animals. "I'll edit the video before I post it."

Bowie released Hank. The camel dashed into the enclosure, his head held high in a clear bid to impress Lulubelle. It seemed to work as her tail swished even faster.

"June, can you take Abby back to the house?"

"I'll go with Abby," Josh volunteered.

"Squeamish much, Josh?" June drawled.

"Yes," he agreed quickly. "Come on, Abby. Why don't you show me some of the other animals?"

Abby looked a little reluctant but perked up at Josh's suggestion. She loved showing off the zoo.

As soon as the two left, Hank began to rub his neck and head all over the fence posts. Lulubelle's tail picked up an even greater tempo.

"Once again, Lou, you're right," Bowie said as Hank began—literally—to drool over Lulubelle.

"Good to know they'll get along," Lou said, glancing at Bowie and then Katie meaningfully. "'Bout time we had a successful pairing."

"I think that's it," Katie said as she stepped back from the wall she'd been painting in the cubs' temporary exhibit. She had a smudge of red paint on her cheek from the sandstone formations she'd been painting. Two days ago, Bowie would have immediately wiped it off, but he still couldn't shake the awkward feeling that had formed since he'd discovered that he'd been the inspiration for all Katie's villains. Katie, though, didn't pick up on his tension. Instead, she surveyed the new enclosure with a wide smile. "This place looks great."

"Thanks to your artwork," Bowie said.

"I'm not the one who lugged all the logs and built the climbing platforms," she pointed out. "Or who added the addition onto the nursery."

"Yes, but it's the backdrop that pulls it all together."

"When do you think we can let the cubs into the exhibit?" Katie asked. Bowie planned on introducing the pumas to their new play area before the festival so the little guys wouldn't be so overwhelmed.

"How soon will the paint dry?"

"Most of what I did today was touch-up work, so not too long. About an hour or so."

Bowie checked his watch. That would take them to about seven o'clock. "Abby's going to be dropped off by her friend's mom around seven thirty. Let's wait an additional half hour. She'll be over the moon."

"You know," Katie said suggestively. "I have an idea of how we can spend the time."

"You do, huh?" Bowie said, although his enthusiasm felt a little flat. He wanted her. No doubt about that. But he couldn't stop yearning for more.

"You bet, Tarzan."

Bowie nearly groaned at the reminder of the costume he'd be wearing to introduce the cubs. Katie winked and headed to the small door that connected the new exhibit to the nursery. With one smoldering look over her shoulder, she crawled through the opening. As she did so, she gave her butt a wiggle, and Bowie couldn't help but smile despite his glumness.

He should be happy. A sexy woman wanted him. They always had a great time together. He'd told himself previously that he'd take it slow and give Katie the chance to start thinking of them as a couple. Maybe it was time he talked to her directly. But not today. Not with the festival coming up. Afterward, when things settled down, he'd explain how he was feeling.

Until then, he might as well enjoy himself. Bowie followed after Katie. As soon as he maneuvered his large frame through the exit, she grabbed his hand, a sultry smile on her face. He let her lead him through the nursery to the adjacent room with the air mattress. She started to unbutton her jean shorts, but he stopped her.

"Can we take this one slow?"

She smiled wickedly. "Slow sounds good for a change."

Bowie dipped his chin and just kissed her. Nothing more, nothing less. He let his lips glide against hers, soft

and slow. As though it was their first kiss. When
Katie sighed, he licked the corner of her mouth with
tiny, gentle flicks of his tongue.

She giggled, the sound bright and happy. It was
lighter than the gasps she normally made, and he
loved it.

He cupped the back of her head with his hand
and felt the silky slide of her auburn locks. For a
moment, he just reveled in the sensation of her hair
slipping through his fingers as he opened his senses
to her. To *all* of her.

This. This was about savoring, and he planned
to get his full taste.

Bowie tilted Katie's head so he could more fully
access her mouth. Only then did he begin to kiss in
earnest. He poured all his tenderness into the embrace.
Inch by inch, her body grew pliant as his hardened.

Placing his arm around her back, he steadied her,
sharing his strength. But he did not lessen his demand.

She tore her mouth from his. Gasping for breath,
she buried her face against his shoulder. When she
spoke, her voice was shaky. "Bowie, I think you're
going to kill me with a kiss."

He tipped up her chin with one finger. "I haven't
even gotten started." And he let his lips descend
once more.

⁓

Bowie's kiss was like a Long Island iced tea. It had
started out with honeyed innocence until it grew into
something dangerous to Katie's sanity. Although
she wouldn't deny its sweetness, it swirled through

her like a potent cocktail, weakening her better judgment. Her limbs felt deliciously loose and languid. If Bowie hadn't held her, she would have collapsed.

But the most perilous part was that it slid past her defenses. Her need went beyond the physical. She wanted him close. Against her. Inside her. Surrounding her.

Without breaking the maddening kiss, Bowie lifted her into his arms—and not how he normally did. Every other time, he'd grabbed her by the thighs so her legs wrapped around him. It was elemental and sexy, and it drove her crazy. This time, he cradled her like a princess...or a bride. This was romance, and it threatened to melt her.

Bowie gently laid her on the air mattress, their lips still pressed together. His body covered her, enveloping her with warm heat. As he ran his hands down her sides, his touch lingered at her breasts. The feather-soft caress triggered a longing deep inside her.

She reached up and stroked his back—not out of lust but out of affection. He hadn't removed his T-shirt, but she could feel his muscles bunch beneath the material. He shifted, drawing kisses down her jaw and throat. Liquid need spread through her. He slowly unbuttoned her shirt, his fingers brushing against the exposed skin. She shivered at the contact, and his mouth closed over one of her breasts.

Her eyelids fluttered down. Before her brain went mindless with need, she tugged at Bowie's shirt. He only raised his head long enough for her to pull the fabric from his body. His tongue darted out, circling her nipple, and then she was lost under a sea of churning desire.

Time faded away as Bowie licked and caressed Katie. His hands danced across her soft skin. Sensations flooded him as he massaged and tasted. He lingered on each breast before dipping his head to tease her between her thighs. Gently, he licked each juncture of her legs and hips. She whimpered, but he did not give in to their desire. Not yet.

Gently, he stroked the delicate skin behind her knees before returning his attention to her neck. Again and again, he explored her body, seeking the closeness she denied them. By the time he entered her, they were both shaking. Still, he kept his pace slow. He almost withdrew completely before he sank deep. Her hips arched toward his. Both of them moaned. Yet somehow, he forced himself not to rush. Not to give in to the pounding of his heart and the rush of blood. He called instead upon the affection pooling inside him. The emotion steadied him, even as it weakened his limbs.

She came first, clutching his shoulders, her body beautifully taut below his. His eyes half-lidded, he still managed to watch her. This woman had become so vital to him, so necessary.

Bowie's own climax came with a shuddering intensity. The power of it thundered through him, leaving him helpless. He threw his head back, straining against the fiery glory. When it ended, he collapsed against Katie, burying his face in her soft hair. He lay still for a moment, breathing in the scent of her.

When he lifted his head to smile down at Katie, he froze. On her face, for just a moment, Bowie thought he witnessed pure panic.

―⁓―

What had just happened?

The vulnerability snaking around Katie's heart had nothing to do with her nakedness and everything to do with the emotions Bowie had just unleashed. The sex had been good. More than good. But it always was with Bowie.

This was different.

He'd opened something inside her. Something she'd wanted closed. She'd started to feel for him again, and not just as friends. There was tenderness…and joy. Feelings that could get a girl hurt if she wasn't careful.

―⁓―

Bowie glanced over at Katie as she held Fleur to her chest. They were about to introduce the cubs to the temporary exhibit, and Abby radiated excitement beside Katie. If his daughter hadn't been holding Dobby, Bowie knew the girl would be bouncing right now. He wished he could share his daughter's enthusiasm, but he couldn't shake the memory of Katie's expression after they'd finished making love.

Had he imagined it? It had vanished so fast that he couldn't be sure. He'd been so focused on being the inspiration for the Self Doubt cartoon that he could easily have projected an emotion Katie didn't feel.

But what if she did? What if the idea of intimacy with him frightened her?

And that…that was like getting kicked in the sternum by an angry camel.

But Katie didn't seem bothered now. She was

laughing as she and Abby headed to the opening that connected the nursery to the cubs' exhibit. She seemed fine. Normal.

Trying to act the same, Bowie followed them. Holding Tonks, he climbed in last and deposited the kit on the floor with her siblings. The cougars sat still for a moment, their little tails twitching as they surveyed their surroundings. Then Tonks jumped on one of the platforms. Dobby came by to sniff at it, and Tonks batted him with her paw. He jumped back and scrambled up a nearby log to assume a better attack position. Fleur explored more cautiously, but soon, she joined the fun. It wasn't long until all three were jumping on each other, chirping happily.

"I think they approve of their new home," Katie said.

Bowie nodded. "Yeah. Seems like it."

"They're so cute!" Abby said. "I just want to snuggle with them."

"I know, Abby, but we've got to let them grow up and be cougars, which means less handling," Bowie told her.

"I know. I know," Abby said a little glumly. "I remember when I had to stop playing with the coyotes."

"How does Sylvia handle it when the orphans no longer need her?" Katie asked.

"Pretty well," Bowie says. "Capybaras are social animals, so I make sure she has plenty of interaction with the other animals at the zoo. She and Rosie get along pretty well."

"Really?" she asked.

"Yep," he said. "Rosie likes to ride on Sylvia's back. So do Bonnie and Clyde, our monkeys."

"I've got to get a video of that," Katie said.

"And she likes hanging out with the prairie dogs," Abby added.

"It's a wonder they don't think she's some sort of god. She looks like a giant one of them."

Bowie laughed, but it didn't come as easily as it normally did. "I don't think they knew what to do with her at first, but they've come to accept her."

"I'm glad she won't be lonely when the cubs grow up."

No, Sylvia would be fine, but the question that truly bothered Bowie was how he and Abby would deal with Katie's departure from Sagebrush.

The day of the festival arrived bright and cloudless, but even that didn't calm Bowie's nerves. At least his schedule didn't leave much time for worry. He'd risen before dawn to check on the tents he'd pitched the night before. Then he'd had to make sure everything was in order when the vendors arrived to set up their stands. He honestly didn't know how he would have managed to pull off the event without Katie and June buzzing about. Those two women could organize a colony of prairie dogs into military precision.

And as much as Bowie hated to admit it, Josh had also helped. He'd shown a couple of the older vendors how to manually accept credit cards using their smartphones without the need for extra hardware. The computer whiz had even downloaded the proper app and explained the fees involved. Bowie was fairly certain that seventy-year-old Mabel Gregory, who was selling handmade quilts, had developed a crush on the Californian.

Josh had also pitched in when Bowie set up the tent for the craft activities Katie's mom was overseeing. Although Helen had planned the details at home, she'd arrived at the zoo early in the morning to organize the volunteers Katie had drummed up. Although Bowie had sunk quite a bit into art supplies, they'd already recouped the loss and then some with the presale tickets.

And the moment Bowie had seen Lou's face light up at the sight of the huge crowd, he had known all the preparation had been worth it, even if they hadn't been raking in money. The older man's eyes had filled with tears. He hadn't said anything, but he'd squeezed Bowie's shoulder, silently thanking him. Although Bowie could never repay Lou, the fact that he had finally managed to fill the zoo triggered a sense of accomplishment.

When Bowie stepped inside the cubs' temporary new home and gave a jungle cry, he didn't feel as ridiculous as he'd thought he would. The Tarzan costume seemed fitting, festive even. Through the large picture window, he could see people waving. He raised his hand in greeting before he launched into his opening statement. Katie and Josh had set up speakers so the crowd could hear, and in the corner of the exhibit, Katie crouched out of view as she live-streamed the event. Bowie kept his initial comments brief as he warned everyone not to tap on the glass and frighten the little guys.

Lou opened the gate that connected the back nursery to the front room. Dobby's nose appeared first, his little head swiveling back and forth as he surveyed his surroundings. Bowie had let the cubs explore their new home the last couple of nights, but the place was still new to them. Tentatively, Dobby put one paw forward and then another. Suddenly, he scampered into the area. Fleur entered even more cautiously, but Tonks bounded right inside, ready to attack her siblings. As the cubs explored the branches, rocks, and ropes, Bowie talked about the need to protect the cats and a little about the trio's personal history. Fleur scampered over to him and batted him with her paw. Even with the glass separating them, Bowie knew the crowd had just broken into one long *awwww*.

He was trying to cut back on the cubs' interactions with humans, so he didn't pick up the little girl, but he did bend down to stroke her fur. As he did so, the other two surrounded him. As they took turns pouncing on his knees, he explained how play allowed baby animals to learn important survival skills.

By the time he concluded his talk, the cubs had completely charmed the visitors. With one last jungle cry—this one modulated a little softer to avoid startling the cougars—Bowie exited the exhibit. Katie ducked out behind him. They'd leave the kits to play for a while longer before returning them to the main nursery.

"I think that went even better than your performance with Rosie this morning," Katie told Bowie.

Lou, who'd walked over to join them, nodded at her comments. "I haven't seen crowds like this in years. And everybody seems to be having a good time."

"I've overheard more than one parent say they need to bring their children more often," Katie added.

"Let's hope they do," Bowie said.

Beside him. Lou nodded. "It's a darn shame how kids these days don't get enough exposure to real animals. They'll watch that video of the panda sneezing over and over, but you can't get 'em excited about seeing animals in person."

Katie shook her head. "Lou, I never should have introduced you to viral videos."

"It seems like a lot of the crowd is from out of state. Your ad campaign must have worked pretty well," Bowie told her.

She nodded. "Hopefully, they'll review us positively on TripAdvisor. I included a spot in the festival program asking them to rate us."

Lou patted her on the shoulder. "You've been a lot of help this summer, young lady. And it's been a pleasure working with you."

Katie smiled. "Thanks."

"So have we convinced you to stick around Sagebrush?" Lou asked.

Bowie tensed at the question. He'd wanted to ask it himself. Many times. But he hadn't. Not when it could push Katie away. He still couldn't shove from his mind the panic he thought he'd seen in her expression when they'd slept together after finishing the cubs' exhibit.

Katie gave a noncommittal laugh. "We'll see."

"Now what's that supposed to mean?" Lou asked.

"Honestly, I'm not sure. My parents want me to stay, obviously, even though Dad's doing much better now. I've drummed up more work than I thought I could in Sagebrush, but there's only so much I can do here. I'd have to build up a customer base outside the town."

"Have you received any interest from people who liked your video campaign for the zoo?" Bowie asked.

"A little," Katie said. "I guess I'd need to be more proactive about marketing myself as a business. I'm not sure it's worth the effort if I'm going to get another job. Josh will be keeping his ear out for open positions this fall in San Francisco."

Josh again. It took all Bowie's efforts not to snarl like Fluffy. "Have you considered using his connections in the tech world as an opportunity to promote your freelance services instead?"

The words flew out of his mouth before he considered them. Luckily, Katie didn't appear taken aback. Unfortunately, she wasn't ecstatic either.

"I guess that's a possibility," she said slowly. "I hadn't really considered it."

"Well, you should." Lou patted Katie on the shoulder again. "We like having you around."

She nodded. "I'll think about it, but we'd better get a move on. There's a performance with the capuchins scheduled in about thirty minutes."

As Bowie left Katie and Lou to collect Bonnie and Clyde, he forced himself not to dwell on the conversation or the fact that Katie still seemed set on leaving. Thankfully, he had plenty to distract himself. Still, he couldn't help but notice that some of the brightness had faded from the day.

———

June and Katie had just left June's booth at the zoo
festival when Katie heard it: the high-pitched, mocking laughter of a group of mean girls. She'd recognize the sound anywhere. An uneasy feeling snaked
around her heart and squeezed. Grabbing June's arm,
she steered her in the direction of the sound. Sure
enough, she spied poor Abby cornered by three girls.
Two eleven-year-old boys stood off to the side.

"Oh look," the female ringleader—most likely
the infamous Clarissa—sneered, "*it's* trying to look
pretty."

To her credit, Abby stuck out her chin and tried
to sidestep around the group of preteens. But Katie
couldn't miss Abby's sheen of tears. And she
knew the eagle-eyed girls wouldn't either. Clarissa
shifted so that she blocked Abby's path.

"Are you sure you're not a monkey that your
father found and put in a dress?" Clarissa asked. The
girls laughed in unison, and even the boys snickered.

"I'm going in," June hissed.

Katie grabbed her arm. "June, you're an adult. If
you say anything, you'll make it worse."

June shook her head. "Katie, I'm well acquainted
with these girls. Why, I've given talks at their Girl
Scout troop for years. I'm like a cool big sister."

Before Katie could stop her, June freed herself
and strode over to the group of children. With a
groan, Katie followed—although she didn't know
what damage control she could manage short of
pulling June away.

When Clarissa and company caught sight of June, they froze. Pretty smiles replaced the snide grins. June greeted all of them, but she was especially warm to Abby. Clarissa shifted her chin to an even haughtier angle as if she sensed a threat to her power.

"Abby, I'm glad I caught up with you," June said. "I wanted to tell you how cute you look in that outfit. I like it even better than when you tried it on in the store."

"Thanks," Abby said, a grateful smile on her face.

Clarissa shifted and crossed her arms, looking decidedly bored at the interchange. Obviously, she didn't appreciate the attention being taken away from her. She reminded Katie keenly of Sawyer at that age. Now, it was Sawyer's daughter who needed help fending off the mean girl.

June must have also noticed Clarissa's bid to bring the focus back to herself. "Katie and I should get going. Abby, we'll have to go shopping again soon. I just love your fashion sense."

"You like *her* fashion sense?" Clarissa blurted out, her surprise clearly outweighing her strategic politeness around adults.

"Yes, why wouldn't I?" June asked, her confusion sounding real. "She has a natural ability to pick what looks best on her, the way Parisian girls do. And nobody dresses better than the Parisians. It's refreshing that she's not a slave to fashion magazines like a lot of kids her age."

Clarissa colored, and one of the other girls laughed. Clarissa shot her friend a dirty look. Although the preteen sobered, she couldn't completely remove her smug, satisfied smile. Obviously, at least one of Clarissa's minions would like to see her dethroned.

"Abby, have you told your friends about helping to raise the cougar cubs or feeding the bear?" June asked.

The boys perked up. One asked excitedly, "You've fed a bear?"

Abby nodded. "I help take care of all the animals."

"Isn't it scary? Especially for a girl?" the other boy asked.

"Not for me."

"Do you throw the bear raw meat?" one of the girls asked. "Isn't that gross?"

"I get to give them their treats. Frida—that's our bear—loves ice blocks with fruit or vegetables in them. Would you like to see her eat one?"

"Yes!" all the kids chorused, except for Clarissa.

As the group started to follow Abby, Katie heard one girl ask, "What about the cougar cubs? Do you get to hold them?"

"Well, they were cuddlier when they were real small, but yeah, I still play with them all the time."

"What other animals do you get to touch?" another child asked.

"There's Fluffy, the honey badger. I'm the only one he'll let near."

"Is he the animal who keeps escaping? The one who gets his picture posted every week?"

"Yes, that's him," Abby said.

"What is a honey badger?"

As Abby kept answering questions, June grabbed Katie's arm and whispered in her ear, "I think our work here is done."

Katie waved to the group and allowed her friend

to drag her away. Only June could make the nerdy girl seem cool rather than pathetic when an adult came to her aid.

Behind them, she heard the kids clamoring for more information. What did honey badgers eat? Did cougar cubs take bottles like real babies? Did any of the animals ever try to bite her?

Clarissa's voice was curiously absent as Abby fielded the questions. She didn't babble or trip over her words the way Katie would have at that age. A smile spread across Katie's face. Maybe Abby would never be the most popular girl, but it didn't sound as if she'd be relegated to the lowest rung on the social ladder either.

A few minutes later, Katie and June found Bowie helping the vendors pack up for the day. The main festivities had ended, and the zoo was beginning to clear out. Bowie paused in lifting a crate of warming trays to wave at them. He'd changed out of his Tarzan costume and the cowboy one he'd worn for the Bonnie and Clyde skit. The man could make anything look sexy—even the ugly mohawk wig—but Katie preferred him like this. In jeans. Working hard to keep the zoo running.

"The turnout has been great, Katie. I still can't believe you managed to get this many people to come," he said as she and June approached. "We've reached our pledge goals to apply for the polar bear grant!"

"That's great!" Katie said. The deadline for the application was drawing near, and Bowie had been nervous that they wouldn't be able to meet it. With all the work he'd put into drawing plans for an exhibit and writing a proposal, she was glad he'd at least have a chance to submit them.

"Clarissa and her minions even made an appearance," June said dryly. "Abby just ran into them."

Bowie's mouth flattened. "How'd that go?"

Katie exchanged a look with her friend. "Not well at first. June stepped in and turned things around. When we left, the kids were asking Abby all sorts of questions about the zoo, the boys especially."

"Boys?" Bowie echoed.

"Umm-hmm," June teased. "Two cute ones."

Bowie shook his head. "Abby's too young for boys. She's only eleven."

"She's going to middle school next year." Katie pointed out.

"Pluh-eese, I had my first boyfriend in fifth grade," June said and then dropped her voice dramatically. "We *held hands.*"

"Not funny," Bowie said stiffly.

"I'm not joking. Not entirely. His name was Billy Gregson, and he had the most beautiful brown eyes," June said.

Bowie looked at Katie. "Help me out here."

She shrugged. "Hey, my first crush was the summer between fifth and sixth grade." It had actually been him, but she wasn't about to reveal that tidbit.

"Abby's too down-to-earth to be interested in boys already," Bowie said stubbornly.

Katie couldn't help it. She exchanged a look with June, and the two of them broke into laughter.

Before Bowie could respond, Abby dashed up to

them, a broad smile on her face. "That was the best day ever! Thank you. Thank you. Thank you!"

Without warning, Abby launched herself at Katie. Before Katie knew what was happening, she found herself wrapped in a tight hug. Just as with the last unexpected embrace, Katie's arms reflexively circled around the young girl.

Abby beamed up at her, and Katie's heart melted. She remembered Bowie's words about how important she was becoming to Abby. She hadn't realized how much until just this moment. As for herself, well, she was really starting to care for the kid. What would happen to their relationship when she moved to the West Coast? Sure, she'd keep in touch, but it wouldn't be the same.

And Abby wasn't the only reason that Katie was beginning to wonder if she should stay in Sagebrush and focus on establishing her own business. The girl's father was playing a major role in her reconsideration of her career plan. And that concerned Katie.

A lot.

"You're awfully quiet, sweetheart," Katie's mom said as Katie drove them home from the festival.

"I'm just thinking about something, Mom," Katie said as she turned onto the long drive that led to the ranch.

A pleased smile stretched across Helen Underwood's face. "Or someone."

She was right, but Katie wasn't about to divulge that. She was having enough trouble sorting through her feelings without her mother's perpetual optimism. If Katie tried talking this over with her, she knew her mom couldn't help but steer her toward dating Bowie and staying in Sagebrush Flats.

"It's the potential job openings in the Bay Area."

"Oh," her mom said, and Katie couldn't miss the disappointment in her voice. Katie turned to look at her.

"Mom, you know even if I go, it doesn't mean I haven't enjoyed my time here this spring and summer. I love being close to you and Dad, but I can't give up on my dreams either."

If they still were her dreams.

Her mother's smile had a tinge of sadness. "I just wish they wouldn't take you away from Sagebrush."

"I know, Mom. I know," Katie said as she pulled up to the ranch and parked her car. When she and her mom entered the house, they found Katie's father reading a book on naval ships as he reclined in his armchair.

"Dad?"

"What, kiddo?"

"Do you feel up for a walk…just a little one?" Katie asked. Her dad's physical therapist allowed him light exercise. Although Chief Underwood wasn't ready to scale the rock formations surrounding the ranch, he could handle a short stroll.

"Sure, Katie," her dad said, giving her a penetrating look before he placed his book on the end table. He rose a little stiffly, but he no longer needed any assistance.

"Be careful, John," her mother warned. "There've been reports of Eddie Driver in the area."

"I'll take my old service revolver, Helen. We'll

be fine. I'm not going to let the man get a jump on me a second time."

As they headed outside, Katie let her father set the pace. When they were beyond hearing distance from the old homestead, Katie turned in his direction.

"I've been thinking lately about what you said. About how you didn't want to be a big-city cop, you just wanted to say you were."

Her father nodded solemnly to show that he remembered, and Katie continued. "You know how Josh will be helping me line up interviews on the West Coast?"

"Are you thinking about not going now?"

"Someone mentioned to me that maybe I could use that opportunity to drum up freelance work instead."

"Your mother?"

Katie shook her head. "No. Someone else."

"Ah," her father said meaningfully. "I see. And what do you think of the idea?"

Katie sighed and kicked at a piece of tumbleweed that had blown in her direction. "I don't know. I think...I think I might like the idea, but I'm not sure if I like it for the right reasons."

"And what would those be?"

Katie shoved her hands in her pockets as she stared at a distant rock formation. "It's safe here, familiar."

"There's nothing wrong with that, kiddo, if that's what makes you happy. Some people work their whole lives to find a bit of peace. It's fine to hold on to it once you find it."

"And there's this guy."

"Ah," her father said in the same tone he'd used before. "The someone else?"

Katie bobbed her head. "I'm not sure if it's serious…or if I even want it to be. But there's something there, and I don't want to be the girl who makes a major life choice because of a boy."

She thought about the night she'd had sex with Bowie right after they finished the cougar exhibit. She'd felt a connection. And it had scared her. But as much as she didn't wish to make a bad decision chasing after love, she didn't want to base her career on running away from it either.

Her dad puffed out another breath of air that had nothing to do with exerting himself. "You always did ask the tough ones, Katie."

She managed a half smile. "Sorry, Dad."

He was silent for a while, his gaze trailing over the landscape as he thought. His great-grandparents had helped settle Sagebrush Flats, along with his wife's relatives. The land was in his blood, her blood too. Katie felt its draw and wondered if she should leave it again.

"What would this freelance business of yours be like?"

"If I could land a big customer or two, it could be pretty awesome," Katie said. "Josh said his clients have enjoyed the cartoons that I do for his website, so there's a chance they might hire me. I'd be cheaper—a lot cheaper—than the big advertising firms."

"Would you like the work?"

Katie debated. "I think. It's hard to say what I would get."

"How about compared to working for a big company?"

"Well, for starters, as a freelancer, I'd be in charge. I wouldn't be subject to a project manager or supervisor, just the client."

Her dad smiled. "You always did like being in control, kiddo."

"That's true," Katie agreed.

"I know you've always wanted the big-city life, but what do you like about Sagebrush? Is it just that you've got roots here, or is there something more? Besides that 'someone else'?"

Katie chuckled before she turned sober and mulled over her father's words. When she was ready, she answered slowly. "I enjoy living in Sagebrush. It's nice being able to talk with June in her kitchen instead of texting her, and there's something special about walking into the Prairie Dog Café and knowing everyone there. And as much as they annoy me, I like being closer to my brothers. Then there are Luke's children and you and Mom."

"Seems like you might have some reasons to stay that have nothing to do with a man," her dad said. "But you don't need to make a decision now. You aren't planning on starting to interview until the end of summer. Take time and think about it, and if you need to talk to someone, I'm here."

Katie snaked her arm around her father's waist, and he pulled her close, just like he'd done when she was a little girl.

"Thanks, Dad. You're a good sounding board."

"Any time, kiddo. Any time."

Fluffy was not happy. At all.

Scores of loud, noisy, boisterous bipeds had invaded the zoo during his prime sleeping time. True, a couple of boys had thrown empty popcorn cartons into his enclosure. Not only had he enjoyed licking the buttery residue, but the Black-Haired One had not noticed the debris. The empty containers had made excellent building material. But even the salty yumminess of the leftovers didn't make up for the extreme annoyance of the day. Children had continually stood at his fence, yelling for him to come out of his den.

Fluffy had not capitulated but the shouting had disrupted his sleep. This, he did not appreciate. At all.

He had escaped his enclosure once during the festival, but too many people had spotted him. They had raised odd devices and pointed them in his direction like the redheaded female did. The Black-Haired One had not needed to call the Wee One to coax Fluffy back to his den. He'd returned on his own.

Now that the interlopers had left, Fluffy could reemerge. Finally. After he harried Frida, he planned on paying the Black-Haired One back by tipping over the garbage cans. All of them.

But before Fluffy reached the grizzly's home, he heard it. Stealthy footsteps. In his zoo. At night.

Irritated at this new interloper, Fluffy scurried to investigate. Sure enough, another biped lurked in the darkness. He did not belong to the zoo. He smelled different—and quite pungent for a human. There was also something about him that Fluffy did not like. Something off. Something mean. Something cruel.

He reminded Fluffy of a poisonous snake. And Fluffy knew what to do with serpents. You bit them. Hard.

So Fluffy crouched in the shadows, waiting for his opportunity. It came when the man had his back turned to peer into the windows of the zoo office. Fluffy moved fast, sinking his teeth into the fleshy part of the man's calf. The human tasted awful, but there was something satisfying about chomping down on a biped.

The man howled in pain. Fluffy would have smiled, but that would have meant releasing his hold.

The man made strained grunting noises, and Fluffy realized the human was trying to hold back screams. Interesting. Why was the snake being so stealthy?

The man shook his leg. Fluffy didn't care. He held on fast. This was the most excitement he'd experienced in years. He could get used to this.

Then, the snake struck Fluffy with something solid. It hurt, quite a bit, but Fluffy still didn't care. The pain just made him angrier and more determined. He sank his teeth deeper into the man's flesh.

Another blow came. Then another. The third knocked Fluffy off. That, Fluffy did *not* appreciate. However, he remained undeterred. He lurched toward the man again. The snake yelped and dashed away. Fluffy gave chase.

The man tore from the zoo and jumped into a van that belched smoke almost as badly as the Black-Haired One's truck. As Fluffy watched the red taillights disappear, he smirked. He had successfully chased two unwanted visitors from the zoo. As Fluffy limped back to his den, he felt particularly smug. This latest invader had been very dangerous indeed.

Chapter 11

GLANCING DOWN AT BOWIE ASLEEP ON THE AIR mattress, Katie debated waking him. The festival had ended three days ago, and Bowie was still exhausted. He'd spent the last thirty-six hours cleaning up and then getting started on the cubs' permanent exhibit. He'd been hauling rocks and digging fence posts. Katie had pitched in to help his staff feed the animals, and she'd stayed late. Then she and Bowie had crashed together on the old air mattress after a round of hot sex.

Katie didn't know if it was because he was bone-weary from all the physical labor he'd been doing, but she'd sensed something different tonight. He seemed to hold back a little in their lovemaking. Oh, he'd made sure to send them both crashing into oblivion, but there was an element missing. She wouldn't quite say the spark, because tonight had been as intensely hot as always. But before she'd drifted to sleep in his arms, she'd felt a subtle shift that left her feeling a little bereft.

She considered staying until morning to talk to Bowie, but she typically left well before dawn. Now that the cougar cubs didn't require round-the-clock care, she didn't have an excuse for spending the night, and Bowie didn't want Abby knowing about their nighttime activities.

Katie stretched and checked the time. It was after midnight, and she knew Bowie would want to walk her to her car. A few days ago, her father's attacker had been spotted in the area again. It had been all over the local news channels, and Bowie had insisted on making sure she got home safely when she stayed late.

He grunted in his sleep and burrowed deeper under the covers. Katie hated to disturb him. Making her decision, she quietly slipped from the bed. Katie doubted Eddie Driver would be hanging out at the Sagebrush Zoo parking lot in the middle of the night. He was after her father, not her. In fact, he probably didn't even know she existed.

Pulling on her clothes, Katie gave Bowie one last glance before leaving the room. She pulled the door shut softly behind her and headed to her car. As she started to cross the parking lot, she thought she heard a sound. Glancing around, she saw nothing.

Katie shook her head. Bowie's concern was affecting her imagination.

Then she heard more. Footsteps. From behind. She started to whirl around, but something hard and heavy cracked into the side of her skull. White light seared her vision. Katie managed one bloodcurdling scream before her legs collapsed. Her body slammed painfully into the pavement. She cried out once more before darkness descended.

Katie's scream jarred Bowie from a deep sleep. He bolted upright, his heart pounding as he scanned the room. He saw no sign of her as he scrambled to his feet. Had he dreamed the sound?

Then he heard it. The second terrified cry. If he wasn't mistaken, it had come from the direction of the parking lot.

He tore from the room, glad that he always pulled on a pair of pants before falling asleep beside Katie. Between his daughter and the zoo animals, he never knew when he might need to dash off to an emergency. He couldn't very well do so in his boxers or nothing at all.

When Bowie reached the parking lot, a sharp blade of pure fear sliced his gut. The security lights illuminated a terrifying tableau. Like a crumpled doll, Katie's motionless body lay on the asphalt. Her red curls spilled onto the blacktop. A hooded figure stood at her side, dragging her body to an open van half-hidden in the shadows.

A hoarse cry must have erupted from Bowie. The figure turned and faced him. The barrel of a gun glinted. A bullet whizzed past Bowie. A warning shot, he realized dimly.

"Fuck off. This isn't about you. But make another move, and I'll blow your head right off your fucking shoulders."

Bowie couldn't make out the man's features—not with the hood covering his face—but it didn't take much deductive reasoning to figure out that this was Eddie Driver, the man who'd attacked Katie's father.

"This isn't about Katie either. She's an innocent in all this," Bowie said, forcing his voice to remain calm and steady despite the fear pulsing through him.

"Her father needs to pay," the man said, sneering. "He destroyed my fucking family. Convinced my whore of a wife to leave me. Threw me in a fucking jail cell. Now I'm going to return the favor and destroy his happy little life, starting with his daughter."

Bowie's mind scrambled for a solution. He didn't know how Eddie had immobilized Katie or what harm the man was causing by dragging her over the blacktop. Lou—or at least Abby—would have heard the screams and the gunfire. Abby would have woken Lou, who would have called the police. If Bowie could stall Eddie for a few minutes, help would likely arrive, but then what?

Who knew how Eddie would react to the sirens? The news reports had called him volatile and dangerous with a history of mental-health issues. Plus, there was no telling if the police would arrive before Eddie managed to get Katie into the van. The vehicle wasn't parked far from where Eddie stood, making a quick kidnapping still possible. Just as troubling, she could have a neck injury that could be aggravated by Eddie's rough treatment.

Bowie wet his lips and tried once more to reason with the man. "She has nothing to do with what happened to you."

Eddie ignored him. Instead, he began to drag Katie toward the van. Fear stabbed Bowie as he watched helplessly. Eddie would kill her, Bowie realized with grim certainty. The man was as unpredictable as a rabid coyote, and he had a history of violence toward women. He'd beaten his wife, and the media had reported that he'd been arrested for assaulting his former girlfriends too.

The van was less than a foot away, and Bowie still didn't hear even the faintest sound of sirens. He made a snap decision. While Eddie's attention was focused on hauling Katie into the back of the vehicle, Bowie charged. Eddie glanced up, dropped Katie's body, and scrambled to aim the gun.

Bowie felt something hot sear into his bicep, but he ignored the burning pain.

———

Danger. Attack. Defend.

Pure instinct had overtaken Fluffy. The snake had returned to the zoo, and he threatened Fluffy's territory. If the Black-Haired One or the redheaded female died, that would disrupt all of Fluffy's carefully laid plans for more wee ones. And no one threatened Fluffy's bipeds and got away with it. No one.

Just as the snake pointed an object at the Black-Haired One, Fluffy sank his teeth into the man's calf—right where he'd bitten the interloper before. A horrid sound cracked through the air. Then, before Fluffy could react, the man collapsed. Fluffy barely had a chance to scramble away before the biped's full weight landed on him. His hind leg got caught, but he managed to squirm free. He watched as Bowie wrestled the snake.

Fluffy smiled. The Black-Haired One had more honey badger in him than Fluffy would have expected.

———

Bowie knocked into Eddie at full speed, sending both of them crashing to the hard ground. Eddie absorbed most of the impact as Bowie used his bulk to pin the slighter man. For a moment, Eddie lay stunned, probably from the shock of having the air knocked out of him. Out of the corner of Bowie's eye, he spotted Fluffy limping away.

He realized then why Eddie's shot had only grazed him. The honey badger must have bitten the man. Bowie hoped the little critter wasn't hurt too badly, but he couldn't afford to check on Fluffy. First, he had to subdue Eddie and take care of Katie.

Bowie reached for Eddie's pistol but realized the other man must have dropped it during their collision. It had skittered several feet away. Bowie debated whether to scramble for it, but he wasn't that experienced with guns, except for tranqs. And he didn't want to risk Eddie snatching it instead.

Eddie began to screech and struggle beneath him. Bowie struck the man hard in the temple with his fist. Eddie went limp again. Bowie sat up and shook Eddie to make sure he truly was incapacitated. The man's head lolled uselessly, but he was still breathing. Bowie dropped Eddie to the ground and quickly collected the gun. He put on the safety and shoved the weapon into the front of his waistband as he bent to check on Katie.

Bowie's heart squeezed at the sight of blood near her temple. It looked like the creep had coldcocked her. Bowie gently ran his fingers down the uninjured side of Katie's face. She moaned slightly, and her brown eyes flittered open. Bleary and unfocused, they gazed up at him in confusion.

"What...what happened?" Katie asked, her voice wobbly.

A wave of hot ire rose inside Bowie, momentarily threatening to drown him before he shoved it down. As much as he wanted to beat Eddie for harming Katie,

Bowie knew she needed him more. Right now, Eddie was sufficiently subdued.

"The man who shot your father attacked you," Bowie said stiffly.

"What!" Katie said as she started to scramble into a sitting position. She groaned and began to sway. Bowie gently grabbed her before she crashed to the ground. He cradled her against his chest, thankful to feel her warm and safe in his arms. She sighed and nestled into his embrace.

"Holy crap, my head hurts," she said.

"He knocked you out," Bowie said stiffly.

Katie tried to raise her head and then moaned again. "Okay, moving isn't a good idea."

"No, I don't think it is," Bowie said.

"Where is he?" Katie asked. "My father's shooter?"

"Right beside us. He's unconscious," Bowie explained.

Katie rubbed her forehead. "How did that happen?"

"My fist," he said succinctly.

Finally, Bowie heard sirens. Two cop cars squealed into the parking lot, their lights flashing. Bowie glanced up at the dramatic entrance he would have appreciated three minutes ago. The police probably would be disappointed that he'd already subdued Eddie. The guy had shot one of their own, and they didn't get to see much action in sleepy Sagebrush.

Four cops emerged, their guns drawn. Since Bowie was currently holding Katie, all weapons were pointed at him. Unfortunately, it wasn't the first time he'd had a cop train a gun on him. The last time had been Katie's father, and one of the policemen even reminded Bowie of the man.

"It's fine," Katie said without lifting her head from Bowie's shoulder. "The perp is the one on the ground."

"Katie?" the cop who reminded Bowie of Katie's father asked, his voice a mixture of surprise and concern.

"Mike?" Katie gingerly turned her head in the direction of the policeman.

"What the hell?" Mike holstered his gun as he strode quickly toward them.

"Let me guess," Bowie said dryly for Katie's ears only. "The cop brother?"

"The one and only," Katie whispered back. "I'd better sit upright before he goes all protective male on me."

Bowie held her firmly. Although he would have preferred not meeting Katie's brother shirtless with Katie curled on his lap, he wasn't letting her go until the ambulance arrived. She needed to remain still, and he wasn't ready to release her. Not yet. He'd almost lost her tonight, and his body wanted the reassurance that she was safe.

"It'll just be worse if you sway again or black out," Bowie told her.

She sighed and relaxed against him. "I suppose you're right. I guess he'll figure out we're sleeping together anyway."

Bowie stiffened at her last comment, but before he could question her, Mike reached them. Bowie tightened his hold on Katie. He couldn't help it. After watching Eddie drag her limp body almost into his van, Bowie had every right to feel protective. Right now, Katie *was* sleeping with him, and he was going to protect her and take care of her—whether she or her cop brother liked it or not.

———— ⁓ ————

"Katie," Mike said as he rushed to her side. "What's going on? The police scanner said there'd been shots fired. What in the hell are you doing at the zoo at this hour?"

She felt like she was attempting to think through gelatin. Her fuzzy brain refused to focus on the blast of questions Mike fired at her.

Bowie spoke instead. "I believe the man on the ground is Eddie Driver."

At the name of the man who'd shot their father, Mike swore sharply. "So that's the bastard." He reached down and pulled back Eddie's hoodie to reveal the unconscious man's face.

"I think he coldcocked Katie with his gun," Bowie said. He shifted her slightly but carefully in his arms. He withdrew a pistol from his waistband and handed the weapon to Mike. "I heard Katie scream twice, and by the time I got to the parking lot, she was unconscious. Eddie was dragging her to the van."

With her brain sloshing like the sea during a tempest, Katie just stared dumbly at the weapon. Her attacker had a gun? She hadn't known that. How had Bowie disarmed him? Her mind swam again, and a wave of nausea washed over her. She did not want to be sick in front of Mike. Her brothers would never let her hear the end of it.

Gosh, why wouldn't her mind focus?

"Shit," Mike said, glancing over at Eddie, who was being cuffed by his partner. Mike's jaw clenched—a sure sign that he was holding back his rage. Katie started to stand to reassure him but only managed to half sit up. The world dipped dangerously, and she plunked back down with a moan.

Mike's attention immediately returned to her, and he dropped to his knees. He scanned her, his gaze lingering on her temple. He looked over at one of the other cops.

"See how far out that ambulance is," he barked.

"I don't want one," Katie quickly protested.

"You're getting one," her brother said at the same time Bowie said, "You need a doctor, Katie."

Mike's eyes locked on Bowie's and narrowed. "And who are you?"

"Bowie Wilson," he said. "I own this zoo, and I'm sleeping with your sister."

"Bowieee," Katie hissed. Her brother's protective instincts were already on high alert. She'd never convince Mike not to tell her other brothers about Bowie. Then one of them would tell her mom. The boys would tease her endlessly, and her mom would escalate her matchmaking tenfold. Worse, her mom would be convinced Katie was going to stay in Sagebrush, and Katie didn't need any additional pressure.

"Katie, you're at my place after midnight, and I'm only half-dressed. Your brother already knows."

"What the hell were you doing letting my sister walk alone in a parking lot in the middle of the night? Everyone in town knew that the guy who shot our dad was still on the loose."

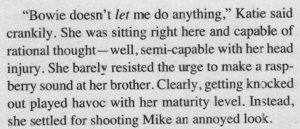

"Bowie doesn't *let* me do anything," Katie said crankily. She was sitting right here and capable of rational thought—well, semi-capable with her head injury. She barely resisted the urge to make a raspberry sound at her brother. Clearly, getting knocked out played havoc with her maturity level. Instead, she settled for shooting Mike an annoyed look.

"I was asleep. It shouldn't have happened," Bowie said.

Katie groaned in annoyance. "Bowie wanted to walk me to my car, but I let him sleep. He works longer shifts than you do, Mike."

Just then, the ambulance whirled into the parking lot, siren blaring. Katie attempted to glare at it in disgust, but the flashing lights triggered a searing pain deep inside her skull. The noise didn't help either. "I'm not going to the hospital, you know."

"Katie, you can't move without groaning," Bowie said.

"You're also covered in blood," Mike pointed out.

She was? Her shirt did look wet and sticky. She reached up and gingerly felt her temple. Wincing, she quickly withdrew her fingers, which were slick with blood.

"Head wounds bleed a lot. I'll be fine," she said. She didn't want to fuss with a hospital. Her mother would be beside herself if she found out Katie had been taken away in an ambulance.

"The police scanner said there were shots fired," Mike said.

Katie straightened and then closed her eyes at the onslaught of more dizziness. "I didn't hear shots."

"There were two," Bowie said. "Eddie fired a warning shot at me when I first reached the parking lot. He didn't want me coming closer."

Katie's eyes flew open as she stared at Bowie in concern. Eddie had shot at him? A sick feeling twisted inside her. Until then, she hadn't really thought of the danger Bowie had faced. He was so physically imposing compared to her attacker's slight frame. But Eddie had carried a gun, and he'd nearly killed her father.

Katie should have realized. She probably would have if her head weren't currently useless.

Mike's mouth flattened into a hard line. "When was the second fired? Did you have a gun too?"

Bowie shook his head. "Eddie shot at me when I charged him."

"What!" Katie said. She sat up this time, ignoring the uncomfortable sloshing in her stomach and the suddenly searing pain in her head. She scanned his body. She saw red, wet patches on his skin.

"Is that my blood or yours?" Katie demanded.

"Uh, mostly yours, I think," Bowie said, his tone suspiciously casual with a twinge of sheepishness.

Mike slapped his notebook against his thigh as he stared at both of them in annoyed disbelief. "Are you telling me, after five minutes of interviewing you, that you've been shot?"

"Grazed a bit maybe."

"You're the one who needs to go to the hospital," Katie said.

"You both need to go to the hospital," Mike said with exasperation.

"He just winged me. It barely hurts," Bowie said.

Mike waved a paramedic in their direction. "Adrenaline could be sustaining you. You just charged an armed assailant to save my sister. You need a professional to check your wound."

Bowie glanced down at Katie. "I'll go to the hospital if she goes."

"Fine," she huffed. "I will, but only if you do too."

Mike shook his head. "Hell, Katie, I think you might have found your perfect match. He's even more stubborn than you."

Several hours later, Bowie found himself with his arm in a sling, sitting in Katie's ER room next to her brother. Although the bullet hadn't hit a bone or anything major, it had caused more damage than he'd thought. Still, they'd had him patched up before they were done running tests on Katie. He'd even had time to check in with Lou and Abby again. Everyone at the zoo was fine—including Fluffy, who was back in his enclosure, thanks to Abby.

Before Bowie and Katie had left for the hospital, Mike had sent a policeman to the Victorian to let Lou and Abby know the situation was under control. They had managed to make it to the parking lot just as Bowie was being loaded into the second ambulance. Poor Lou had blamed himself for not coming sooner when Abby heard the shots, but Bowie had pointed out that someone needed to make sure Abby stayed safe. Bowie knew the two of them would be awake and worrying, so he had called as soon as he'd had something concrete to report. Unfortunately, he still didn't know much about Katie's condition. He could only sit and wait.

Mike had been openly studying him since Bowie had entered Katie's ER room. Bowie didn't know how to respond to Mike's scrutiny. He'd never met a brother of a girl he'd dated. Sawyer's had been away at college, and her parents hadn't exactly invited Bowie to family dinners even before the pregnancy.

But Katie's injuries and Mike's penetrating stare weren't the only reasons Bowie felt edgier than an impala being stalked by a lion. He realized that Katie had just suffered a head injury, but her reluctance to reveal their relationship bugged him. Sure, he could understand that she didn't want to announce that they were sleeping together, but she didn't seem to want to acknowledge any connection to him. And that burned.

"You're not like the men my sister normally dates," Mike said without preamble.

Bowie decided he wasn't in the mood to be baited. He turned and fixed Mike with a frank, unimpressed look. "You met me less than two hours ago. I doubt that you know me."

Mike gave a one-shouldered shrug. "I'm a cop. I'm trained to observe."

Bowie leaned back in his chair. "Impress me."

Mike started to count off points on his fingers. "First, you're a hometown boy. Katie always dated big-city guys from Duluth or Minneapolis. Second, you own a zoo. Katie's last boyfriends would have panicked if you asked them to keep a plant alive for a week. Third, you live with your daughter and an elderly man. Fourth, you're not trying to smooth talk me, and you certainly aren't attempting to impress me. Fifth, you also don't secretly think you're better than the rest of Katie's hick family."

Mike paused and looked Bowie straight in the eye. "And finally, none of Katie's previous boyfriends would have rushed an armed man to save her."

Bowie had no idea how to react. He'd been steeling himself for an attack like Josh's. He hadn't expected Mike to like him.

"You better watch it," Bowie said, "or I might start to think that you approve of me dating your sister."

Mike's face broke into a wide grin. He didn't share many features with his sister, but he did have Katie's brown eyes. And her smile.

"I don't approve of any guy dating my sister, but you're not half bad."

"Thanks," Bowie said dryly, but he felt some of the tension ebb.

Just then, Katie was wheeled back into her room in the ER. Her white, drawn face concerned Bowie. He noticed stitches by her temple, and the sight made him wish he'd been rougher with Eddie.

Katie's gaze found his, and he didn't like how bleary it appeared. He rose to gently stroke the side of her face with his good hand. He didn't care if she didn't want her brother to witness affection between them.

"Are you okay?" he asked as she lifted her hand to brush her fingers over his knuckles.

"Concussion," Katie said. "What about you?"

"I'm all patched up now," Bowie said, pressing a kiss against her forehead. "Don't worry about me, but make sure you get rest. I've had concussions before, and you'll need plenty of sleep."

"I hate rest," Katie grumbled. She sounded so much like a child that Bowie couldn't help but smile.

"You know"—Mike stood on her other side—"you're going to need to tell Mom and Dad now. The doctor said you shouldn't be alone tonight."

Katie frowned, and her eyes looked a little glassy. When she spoke, she did so slowly, as if she had to concentrate on each word. "I told you that I don't want them knowing until tomorrow. Mom will panic, and Dad still needs his rest even if he is doing better. And I don't want you going into detail about how you found me with Bowie. Mom is looking for any excuse to convince herself I'm not moving away again."

Bowie tried not to take it personally, but it sliced at him that Katie still wanted to keep their relationship a secret. He understood a general need for privacy, but surely she didn't hide all her boyfriends from her parents with such unyielding diligence. Was she embarrassed by him, or did she just care so little that she didn't want the aggravation of introducing him to her parents?

"Katie, you need to be woken up every two hours. I've got to take the next shift when I get back, so someone else in the family needs to know tonight."

"She can stay at my house," Bowie said.

Katie started to shake her head but then winced painfully. "No need. I'm fine. You don't need to fuss."

Bowie's temper snapped. He was tired of her shoving him away, tired of her telling him he shouldn't care. He did. He cared that she'd almost been abducted. He cared that a deranged man had knocked her out and had planned to kill her. He cared that she lay pale and dizzy in a hospital.

"You're coming home with me."

———◇———

Katie's head still ached and swam, and her stomach hadn't stopped sloshing. The bright hospital lights hurt. A lot. She couldn't think, at least not easily. She wanted to curl up in her own bed in a dark, dark room. She did not want to deal with Mike, her parents, or any of her siblings. She just wanted to go home.

Bowie sounded angry, but she didn't understand why. He'd been shot. He needed to sleep too. Otherwise, she would ask him to hold her. Right now, she craved his touch.

"Your arm," she said weakly.

"What about it?" he asked tersely.

Katie glanced at Mike for assistance. "He was shot."

Mike looked over her at Bowie. "I think she's worried about you. She's probably right. You need to heal as much as she does."

Bowie's hard expression softened slightly. He brushed his hand over the uninjured side of her face, and she reveled in the sensation. "Lou and Abby can make sure you wake up every couple of hours. I doubt either of them are sleeping after all this excitement."

"The animals," Katie said as the thought crept into her muddled mind. "Who will take care of them?"

"I'll manage."

Katie might have trouble processing, but she

knew that Bowie shouldn't be hauling feed. Most of his volunteers and staff were female, and he always performed the bulk of the physically demanding tasks. Once again, Katie looked to her brother for help. "Mike, he can't take care of the zoo. Not with his arm in a sling."

"I'll call Matt tomorrow," Mike said. "It's his day off, and by then, we'll have to tell Mom and Dad anyway. This is going to be all over the news."

"I'll be fine, really," Bowie protested.

Mike fixed him with a hard look. "You may have just saved our sister's life. The least Matt and I can do is help out. We'll both pitch in until your arm is healed."

—⁓—

Katie didn't pad down to Bowie's kitchen until six o'clock in the evening. They hadn't arrived back at his house until around four in the morning. Luckily, Lou had convinced Bowie to let him check on Katie every few hours while Bowie slept. As soon as Bowie relented, she had climbed the stairs to the guest bedroom and promptly fallen asleep. Aside from Lou waking her periodically, she'd slept solidly.

It wasn't until Katie heard Matt's and Mike's voices and smelled McDonald's food that she'd risen. Yawning, she found Bowie's kitchen full of men. Matt, fresh from the shower, was digging into one of the bags of food. Mike, who'd probably just finished his shift, wore his uniform. Lou sat in one of the chairs, while Bowie was pulling dishes out of the cabinets.

Abby spotted Katie first and immediately ran over to her. "Are you okay? I wanted to see you today, but Dad and Lou said you needed to rest. Does your head feel okay? Were you scared last night? Wasn't Dad brave?"

Although Katie felt marginally better than she had last night, her head still whirled uncomfortably at Abby's barrage of high-pitched questions. Luckily, Bowie noticed and appeared at her side.

"Let's give Katie a second to sit down," he said. "She was hit in the head pretty hard."

Grateful for the interruption, Katie allowed Bowie to guide her to a stool. She ran her eyes over him. He looked drawn, and his mouth was pinched slightly.

"How's your arm?" she asked in concern.

Bowie shrugged. It was telling that he only lifted his right shoulder. Katie still couldn't believe that he'd literally taken a bullet for her. She knew the reality of that hadn't fully hit her. It felt too surreal…and maybe a little intimidating. Bowie had risked his life to save hers, and she hadn't completely come to terms with what that meant

She had just taken a bite of hamburger when her phone buzzed. Glancing down at it, she frowned at the text message from June that Josh had arrived early. Her sluggish brain slowly resolved the mystery. Her thirtieth birthday party was tomorrow. With the attempted kidnapping, the event had completely slipped her mind. Her mother had planned it, despite Katie's repeated protests. In addition to the immediate family, her mother had invited Josh and June.

Katie stole a look at Bowie. She hadn't told him about the party or the fact that her thirtieth was looming. Bringing him to an Underwood function would cause all sorts of complications with her mother. And although it sounded silly, Katie wasn't ready to open up like that. Meeting the family was a big step, and she and Bowie weren't even officially dating. And with the chaos of planning the festival, she hadn't given much thought to her birthday.

Now, with her head simultaneously throbbing and swimming, it was hard to process anything. Her brain still felt scrambled. She knew one thing, though. She didn't want to flaunt the fact that she hadn't invited Bowie to her party. She hadn't meant to slight him, but he might feel that way. She wouldn't have thought so before, but something had changed last night. Something she hadn't fully deciphered yet. He'd gambled with his life to save hers. That meant something.

"Who's that?" Matt asked.

"It's just June."

Mike grabbed a fry from her container, since he'd already finished his. Her brothers inhaled rather than ate food. "Is she checking up on you, or has Josh arrived already for your birthday party tomorrow?"

Well, so much for keeping that under wraps.

"The latter," Katie said as she texted June that she was still at Bowie's house. She'd already talked to June on the way back from the hospital. She'd wanted her friend to break the news to her parents before they heard about the attack on the radio or from one of her brothers, who'd make a mess out of the delivery and cause their mom to panic even more.

She was just typing to June that Mike and Matt were with her as well when Bowie asked in a decidedly neutral tone, "Your birthday's tomorrow?"

Katie glanced up at him and saw that his expression

was carefully blank. She tried for equal nonchalance. "Yeah. My thirtieth. I didn't want to make a big deal about it, but my mother had other plans."

"I see," Bowie said slowly.

An awkward silence descended. Even Abby remained quiet as she glanced from one adult to another. Katie's brothers exchanged a look—one of those annoying, silent twin-speaks. Lou looked disappointed in her.

A horn sounded in the driveway. Grateful for the interruption, Katie placed her napkin on the counter and announced brightly, "That must be June and Josh. I'll go greet them."

Bowie forced himself to remain calm. So, Katie hadn't told him about her birthday. No big deal, right? She wasn't under any obligation. She'd made it clear that their relationship was just about sex. Who was he to think that he merited enough to know about her thirtieth birthday?

Heaven forbid if he did something like buy her a damn gift.

Katie bounced up from the table, all smiles. He noticed that she swayed slightly at the sudden motion. Part of him wanted to get up and help her as he had when Abby's stream of questions overwhelmed her. He didn't. He remained rooted to his chair.

She left the kitchen, and Bowie concentrated on his food. He didn't want to see any of the expressions in the room again. He'd seen her brothers' looks of consternation and then dawning understanding, but it was Lou's crestfallen face that had torn at Bowie. Luckily, Abby hadn't seemed to pick up on anything except the sudden tension.

"Oh my gosh!" Katie's excited voice drifted in from the hallway. "Josh, you didn't!"

June's voice followed hers. "Guys, you have to come out and see what Josh bought Katie."

The twins exchanged another glance and then simultaneously sprang to their feet and headed to the door. Abby jumped up excitedly. "Can I go see?"

Bowie nodded, and she scampered away. He rose slowly and looked over at Lou. "I guess I might as well go see what it is."

Lou gave him an encouraging smile that only made Bowie feel worse. "Katie probably meant nothing by it, Bowie. You know how women can get about their birthdays, especially their thirtieth."

The sad part was that Lou was likely right. Katie had meant nothing by it. And that's what killed him. Bowie had been fooling himself into thinking that he'd manage to convince her to have a real relationship with him. He should have known better. He was just a small-town guy she'd had the hots for in high school. He was good for a fantasy-fulfilling fuck but nothing more.

Bowie headed out to his back porch to find Josh smiling from ear to ear. The fact that the jackass was standing in Bowie's yard and that Bowie had to play nice only fueled his growing irritation. He wanted to punch that self-satisfied grin from the douche's mouth.

That's when Bowie spotted it. The expensive camera. With a big bow on it. The perfect gift for a woman like Katie. It was her hobby and her career wrapped into one.

And Bowie had a feeling that Josh had bought a professional camera that probably cost at least four thousand bucks. Bowie would be lucky to scrape together enough money for a small piece of jewelry. Hell, he didn't know what he would have bought Katie if she'd given him the chance, but it wouldn't have been a professional camera. Not on his budget.

"Bowie?" Katie's voice was soft, tentative.

He couldn't bring himself to look at her. He needed to rein in his emotions. "Not now, Katie," he answered quietly, his voice sounding gravelly even to his own ears. "Not here."

Josh sauntered up to Bowie. The smile had morphed into an even smugger grin. Bowie's temper spiked. He tried to turn and head into the house to avoid the confrontation, but Josh was faster.

"Nice house. It reminds me a little of mine that overlooks the Pacific," Josh said, sounding friendly.

Bowie only grunted. He wouldn't let Josh lull him into a trap this time.

"Sorry June and I descended on you, but I couldn't wait to show Katie the camera. She's had her eye on one of these for years. Did you know that?"

"No," Bowie said stiffly.

"I'm looking forward to seeing what you give her tomorrow," Josh said congenially, but Bowie recognized the underlying challenge. Unfortunately, so did everyone else, except for Abby.

Bowie's last shred of patience disintegrated. He was fed up with trying to prove to Katie and Josh that he'd changed. Sure, he'd treated her horribly in high school, but he'd tried to apologize, tried to make amends. He couldn't go back and change the past, and he was tired of waiting for Katie to trust him. She never would, and he deserved better.

Bowie stared Josh down and said in a matter-of-fact tone, "I wasn't invited to the party, so I guess you're going to miss seeing what gift I would have given her."

Josh's face was a picture of innocence. "Oh, I'm sorry. I thought you'd be there, with how close you and Katie are."

The man's nonchalant tone burned through Bowie's restraint. He lurched forward, clenching his hand into a fist. At the enraged advance, Josh moved back and stumbled down the front porch steps. The guy didn't fall on his ass, but it was close. Bowie almost took a swing at him, but he stopped. He wasn't about to let this douche bag or Katie turn him back into the angry, bitter kid he'd been. But he couldn't stop his next words from exploding from him without any regard for their audience.

"Why act so surprised, Josh?" Bowie said before turning his hot gaze on Katie. "We all know the villain doesn't get invited to the celebration."

With that, he stalked into the house. Behind him, he heard a chorus of voices, but he didn't care.

"Josh!" both Katie and June said in unison.

Then there was Matt's voice: "What the hell is wrong with you, man? You're rich, we all get that, but you don't need to be an asshole."

Mike added, "You know that he just took a bullet for her, right?"

Then Bowie heard Abby's voice. "Why did Dad call himself a villain? Why didn't you invite him to your party, Katie? I think you hurt him."

He squeezed his eyes shut at the last statement. He opened them to see Lou watching him in concern. "Bowie…"

He shook his head and just kept walking. He passed through the house and headed straight for the indoor llama pen. It was due for a cleaning, and he needed to work off his anger before it exploded. He hadn't felt this out of control since the night Sawyer had told him about the pregnancy.

As he marched by the llamas and the camels in their outdoor enclosure, the entire herd came to attention. The llamas had accepted the addition of Hank with relatively little spitting. Being one of two camels had improved Lulubelle's social standing. Between that and Hank's presence, her glumness had vanished. At the sight of Bowie, Lulubelle gave a rumbling greeting and ambled in his direction, followed closely by Hank, who'd become her shadow. Bowie ignored the two lovebirds and stomped into the barnlike shelter. Ripping off his sling in frustration, he grabbed a shovel.

When he heard the fall of footsteps behind him, he didn't need to turn to know the identity of their owner.

"Not now," Bowie told Katie.

"I didn't mean to hurt you."

White-hot rage coursed through him as he whirled to face her. "Like hell you didn't."

Then he turned. Ready to walk away. Not just for the moment. But forever.

Chapter 12

FLUFFY NEEDED TO ACT QUICKLY. ALL HIS CAREFULLY laid plans were about to die like a beehive sprayed with poison. If this human courtship ended without wee ones, Fluffy suspected it would be years before more tiny humans ran through the zoo to distribute treats.

Biting the Black-Haired One would not work. He did not want to chase the biped away, but to keep him in the llama shed.

Fluffy grinned his toothy grin as he spied a pile of feed sitting on a dolly right outside the door to the stall where the bipeds were arguing. Knocking over the wheeled cart would be child's play.

Katie watched with growing concern as Bowie started to stalk away from her. Just when she thought he'd leave without ever looking back, there was a huge crash. A dolly and a large bag of llama food pitched forward, blocking the stall door. Bowie swore and tried to shove it open with one hand. The door budged, but only a scant inch. He cussed again and started to push with both hands. Worried that he would reinjure his wounded arm, Katie laid her hand on his shoulder.

Bowie whirled around, his face a mask of pent-up rage. She almost stepped backward from the force of his anger. She had upset him. Even with her dulled senses, she registered his raw pain.

She'd meant her words, though. She hadn't wanted to wound him. She honestly hadn't thought herself capable of doing so. Bowie had always seemed indomitable. Even now that she knew him better, he remained a partial fantasy. The hot bad boy to her nerdy, geeky self.

"Bowie—" she started to say, but he cut her off.

"Katie, you won, okay? Don't try to justify it. Be happy with your victory, and leave me the hell alone."

"I won what?" she asked, hopelessly confused.

Bowie's face twisted into a grimace. "You paid me back for what I did to you in high school. You made me fall for you when clearly you couldn't care less about me. I guess I can understand why you wanted payback. Rejection feels like shit."

Katie's heart squeezed painfully. She truly hadn't meant to hurt him. Had she?

Maybe a little, she supposed. There was poetic justice in reversing the scales of unrequited love, especially given how Bowie had misused her affection.

But once she had gotten to know him, she'd let go of the anger. If she hadn't, she wouldn't have stopped blackmailing him into performing embarrassing stunts. She didn't want to punish the man he'd become—the man who'd become such an integral part of her.

What she hadn't done, though, was let go of the old pain.

She'd been holding herself apart, using all kinds of excuses. It hadn't been just her mother who

Katie had been worried about protecting if she'd started a serious relationship in Sagebrush. It had been herself.

"Bowie, I didn't want to let you into my heart," she confessed. "I couldn't afford to. I didn't want to get hurt again."

He shoved his hand roughly into his hair. "Katie, I don't know what else I can do to show you that I've changed. You won't let me take you on dates or do anything that shows I care. You wouldn't even give me a chance to buy you a birthday gift."

A sick feeling spread through her as she suddenly realized how callously she'd treated him. She'd been so worried, so focused on protecting herself that she hadn't given much consideration to his feelings. When she had, she assumed that he liked casual relationships. Most guys as attractive as him preferred to play the field.

Bowie exhaled and shook his head. "I've been trying like hell to prove to you that I won't hurt you, that I'll treat you like something precious to me, but it's no use. Josh is right. I'll always be your villain."

Katie knitted her eyebrows. "Why do you keep referring to yourself as a villain?"

"Josh showed me the comic you guys drew for your college newspaper," Bowie said flatly.

"What does my college newspaper have to do with us?" she asked in confusion. Her head was still hurting, and she couldn't follow the connections Bowie was making.

"Josh was kind enough to point out that I'm the spitting image of your personification of Self Doubt. Hell, Katie, all your villains look like me, even the computer virus."

Horror, understanding, and rage boiled inside her.

Josh had no right to attack Bowie like that. It was cruel and mean. Katie could see Bowie's buried pain. She couldn't imagine how she'd feel to be the inspiration for a battalion of bad guys.

"I'm sorry," she said. "I came up with those characters years ago, if that helps."

"No, Katie, it doesn't," Bowie said. "It doesn't explain why you constantly push me away. It doesn't fix the fact that you think so little of me that you wouldn't even tell me about your birthday."

"Bowie—"

"Katie, I charged a man holding a gun to save you, and all you could talk about in the hospital was how Mike shouldn't tell your mother about us."

"Bowie, I thought you'd want to be in a casual relationship…one that didn't involve meeting the parents or anything serious," she protested.

"Why the hell do you think I asked you to that fancy restaurant at the national park? I've introduced you to my family. You have dinner with us on a regular basis. Did you ever stop to think that maybe I'd like to get to know your folks? That I wouldn't like to be treated like some dirty little secret? Like something to be ashamed of?"

"I didn't think it would matter to you."

That brought Bowie up short. He blinked and stared at her in disgusted confusion. "Why would you think that?"

"I guess I never thought I'd mean that much to you. I certainly didn't think you'd believe that I was embarrassed about our relationship. You never seemed to care about other people's opinions, and you've always been so confident. You just didn't seem capable of being hurt."

"Everyone is capable of being hurt, Katie. Why wouldn't I be?"

She realized she was making a mess out of her explanation, but her head hurt. The more upset Bowie became, the more her brain seemed to buzz. "You're the hot, good-looking guy. You were the popular one. You could have had any girl you want...and you still can. Kids laughed at your jokes. You were the escort of the homecoming queen. The internet currently loves you. You had such a charmed life. I didn't think—"

"What do you think has been so charmed about my past that it wouldn't bother me to be treated as inconsequential by a woman who I've made part of my life? Who I've made part of my daughter's life?" Bowie demanded, his voice full of fury.

Katie opened her mouth, although she didn't quite know how to respond. Bowie barreled ahead, saving her from answering.

"Let's see. Could my amazing ironclad self-confidence come from the fact that neither of my parents wanted me? It's such a great confidence builder when your parents constantly argue over who is going to take little Shithead this weekend. I know firsthand that teenage pregnancies aren't easy, but you don't tell your kid you wish he'd been aborted and how much he screwed up your life. You certainly don't nickname him 'Shithead.'"

Bowie's words struck Katie's heart with an almost palpable force. She had never realized that he had been the result of a teenage pregnancy too or that his parents had made it clear they hadn't wanted him. Katie couldn't imagine growing up that way. No matter how awful school had been, her home had always been her refuge. Her family was loud and boisterous, and they loved her.

"Bowie..." she began, but he plowed ahead.

"What did you say about my looks? That they're the reason for this amazing charmed life of mine? Do you have any idea how much grief my father and his friends gave me for being a pretty boy? Making fun of me was their favorite pastime when they were drunk or high, which was pretty much all the time. They made a drinking game out of pelting me with bottle caps or beer-can tabs. I used to retrieve the caps because, hell, at least they were paying attention to me. Mom was always too strung out or in the bedroom with a john.

"Maybe my self-confidence came from helping Dad with the family business when I got a little older. His merchandise happened to be drugs, so I don't know if that fits into the character-building category. At least when Dad realized that the cops didn't check the backpacks of seven-year-olds, he didn't mind having me around as much. 'Course that only lasted until he went to jail."

The images of Bowie as a lonely, neglected child pelted Katie. She wanted to reach out and soothe not just the man before her, but also the boy that he'd been. When she tried to touch him, he jerked angrily away.

"Then my mother ended up in jail over solicitation and possession. I became a ward of the state, and foster kids really have a charmed life. I bounced around a lot. I did stay with a rancher for a couple of years. I lived like the hired hands…only they got paid. I broke my leg with a spiral fracture while baling hay and was told I'd be in a cast for months. The rancher called me a troublemaker, and Child Services collected me.

"But there was always my popularity. Sure, nobody messed with me…or at least they didn't after I punched out two guys in first grade. Still, parents don't want their precious darlings going to the home of a known prostitute or drug dealer. My foster parents didn't want a kid around unless there was a check involved, so that put the kibosh on having friends over. None of my guardians ever drove me to school functions or friends' houses. Sort of hell on the social life."

"Bowie—" Katie began, not knowing how much more she could process. Each word slayed her.

"I'm not finished. Women…they're the other reason for my charmed life, right? Sure, I'm a pretty boy. We've established that. I can get laid. No problem. But a relationship? I've had two… Well, at least until today, I thought I'd had two."

Bowie's gray eyes sharpened even further as they pinned Katie with accusation. She took an involuntary step backward at his anger. She had hurt him. Deeply.

"The first relationship was with Sawyer, a girl who told me to my face that the main reason she dated me was because I was hot and I pissed off her parents. I amused her with my pranks. You know why I teased you, Katie?"

She wordlessly shook her head, ignoring how the action made the world tilt and spin.

"Because it gave me an in with her crowd. For the first time in my damn life, I belonged. I knew, though, that the moment I stopped pranking you, the moment I stopped entertaining them, I'd be the foster kid nobody wanted with his con dad killed in prison and his hooker mom dead from an overdose.

"Do you know how my relationship with Sawyer ended? I had just turned eighteen the week before. Since there wasn't a check coming in, I got kicked to the curb. Literally. I was living on the streets. Sawyer came to me in a rage. Blamed the pregnancy all on me. Said she wanted to abort my baby…just like my parents wanted to do to me. Just like with them, her parents stopped it. I said I'd take care of her and the baby. You know what Sawyer said to me? That I was a worthless, homeless piece of white trash who couldn't even take care of himself. She and her parents harped on that theme for months while I fought for custody of my baby…a baby none of them wanted.

"Then there's you, Katie. My first relationship in years that wasn't a one-night stand after a bar pickup. And all you want from me is a series of meaningless hookups. So tell me, Katie, what about my life has been charmed—other than my daughter, Lou, Gretchen, and the zoo? My confidence has been hard won, and it doesn't make me impervious to pain. And you purposely excluding me from your birthday brought a lot of crap back up."

Bowie finally paused, his chest heaving. His anger fled as if he'd expended it to fuel his tirade. Horror replaced his righteous ire before he banked that too, making his expression unusually flat and devoid of emotion.

Sifting through the pain and guilt his words had evoked, Katie realized two important things. First, Bowie had not intended to reveal his painful past. She'd already made him feel vulnerable, and anger had propelled him to expose old, unhealed wounds. He didn't trust her with his secrets, and right now, she didn't blame him.

Second, Bowie's eyes had looked like that in high school—studiously blank. The seemingly confident, sexy bad boy had been just as lost as her, probably more. Much more.

She'd never considered that he'd made fun of her to preserve his own precarious social standing. It didn't excuse what he'd done, but it explained the mystery of how the cruelest guy in school became a loving father and good man.

Bowie was that. A good, decent man who deserved more than life had given him and certainly more than Katie had. She had messed up, maybe even worse than he had in high school. He'd been a kid; she was an adult.

Katie's mind scrambled for the right words. Her concussion made that difficult. She had obviously hurt Bowie, hurt him badly. Saying the wrong thing could cause irreparable harm to their relationship—if she hadn't done so already.

She sensed that he didn't want to talk about his past with her. Not right now, at least.

"I was wrong, Bowie," Katie told him honestly. "I should have gone on those dates with you. I don't see you as inconsequential or just a bed partner. I can't go back in time, but I can start now, and I'd like to begin by asking you, Abby, and Lou to my birthday party.

My mom always makes tons of food, and she'll be thrilled."

Bowie just stared at her. "Why?"

His question confused her. "Why what?"

"Why are you inviting me? Is it because of what I said? Because you feel sorry for me?"

"Bowie, I'm feeling a lot of things for you right now, but sorry isn't one of them. I want you to come because I want to try to start a relationship with you...an honest, heartfelt one."

He scrubbed his hand over the lower part of his face. "Katie, last night—hell, two hours ago—that would have been enough explanation for me, but I need more. I can't let you into my life—or Abby's life—any further until I know that this isn't some fling for you. I think I've already proven that it isn't for me. That it never was."

Bowie's words both warmed and terrified Katie. She'd never had a real adult relationship, never really wanted one before. But deep down, she did now. With this man. It was time to trust. Bowie might have triggered her commitment phobia years ago, but he also might be the one to cure it. After all, he'd faced down an unhinged man armed with a pistol to save her.

She sucked in her breath. "I might not say this well. My head isn't quite right yet."

Bowie's expression softened. "I'm not trying to judge your answer. I just need to understand where we stand. You can't suddenly switch from excluding me from your private life to inviting me to a family function."

"You hurt me last time," Katie blurted out. "Badly, and it didn't stop. You kept doing it for two and a half years."

Bowie's eyes clouded. "I know, Katie. I've beaten myself up about it. I want to protect you, but I am the guy who hurt you the most. That kills me."

She reached out and cupped his cheek, trying to get him to understand. "I didn't want to feel that pain again, so when I started to fall for you, I did everything to pretend it wasn't happening. I thought I was protecting myself."

"I won't hurt you," Bowie promised. "Not this time."

"You won't hurt me like last time," Katie agreed, "but there will be hurt. It comes with the territory of love. When you open yourself up to someone, you invite in a whole slew of emotions. Most of them are good, but there's also pain. That's how I know I've already made room for you in my heart. Because despite everything, despite all my efforts, nothing—nothing—has hurt me like hearing about your childhood."

—•—

Bowie's throat tightened at Katie's words. He hadn't meant to reveal his history. He'd never told anyone those details. Even Lou and Gretchen only knew snatches. He didn't like to think about his past. It resurrected an ugliness that he didn't want touching his life or, especially, Abby's. He'd finally found his family and had defied statistics by becoming a decent father.

That didn't mean there weren't times when the blackness reared out of the depths and clobbered him. He'd buried it, not vanquished it. In the darkness lay hurt, unresolved anger, and the constant expectation of rejection. Bowie never told his story because he didn't want to expose his vulnerability, and he'd always believed deep down that people would either turn from him or pity him.

Katie had done neither.

She cared…and that meant everything. He hadn't known it, but he'd waited years for someone to say exactly what she just had.

"I hate that I hurt you," she said. "You deserve better than how I treated you, and if you're still willing, I'd like to start over right now."

"I'm willing," he said, his voice rough with emotion. He couldn't manage more words, not with all the messy feelings slopping inside him. He felt both euphoric and strangely brittle, as though he might crack with exhilaration.

"Good." Katie beamed at him, her own joy and relief apparent. "I think we should start with the party."

Bowie pulled her against him with his good arm. "That's a good second step. The first should be this."

His lips captured hers. Her mouth immediately opened. The heat was there, as always, but something else slipped between their tangled tongues and sliding lips—a sweetness Bowie hadn't tasted before. It flooded his senses, sweeping him along in a torrent of pure magic.

Aside from the day that Bowie had ridden with Lou and Gretchen to bring Abby home from the hospital, he had never been this nervous. This time, instead of Lou behind the wheel, Bowie was driving the pickup. Abby bounced happily in the center of the bench seat, oblivious to his tension. Lou, though, was not. He kept sending Bowie supportive looks over Abby's head.

Bowie had never met "the parents" before. Oh, Sawyer had paraded him in front of hers a couple of times, but he'd felt no need to impress them. If he had, Sawyer probably would have dumped him. He hadn't even attempted to chat with them. They'd glare, he'd slouch, and Sawyer would toss her head defiantly as they headed out the door.

This time, this meeting mattered. Although Katie's mother had initially set them up, she didn't know Bowie's whole history, and she might not like what she learned. Then there was Katie's father. The man had arrested Bowie twice for vandalism. Chief Underwood had also hauled away his father and his mother. Even given his own past, Bowie knew he'd be uncomfortable if a guy with those credentials started dating Abby.

Following Katie's directions, Bowie turned into a street lined with mowed lawns and tidy postwar houses. Instead of hosting Katie's party at the ranch, her mom had decided to hold it in Katie's childhood home where her lawyer brother, Luke, lived with his wife and children. It was a nice middle-class part of Sagebrush. After Bowie's father had bought him a beat-up bicycle for delivering drugs, Bowie used to ride around this neighborhood. He'd see the kids out playing, sometimes with their parents, and he had wondered what it would be like to live here. As he'd pedaled, he'd imagined coming home to a house that didn't smell vile, that was bright and clean instead of dark and dingy. A home where parents were glad to see you and asked about your day, instead of cussing you out for waking them up.

Even as a foster kid, he hadn't lived in places like this. Most of his guardians had been local ranchers or farmers, happy for another set of hands and a little extra cash. The few foster parents who had lived in town had places that were only marginally better than his parents'. Sawyer had lived in a big, fancy McMansion with a manicured lawn. Even Lou's Victorian, although extremely well-kept, wasn't a typical suburban home.

Pulling into the driveway, Bowie sucked in his breath. Cheerful flowers lined the walk and spilled out of window boxes. A hanging basket decorated the lamppost.

Everything was orderly and unexceptionally average.

Bowie would almost have preferred it if Luke had lived in an impressive McMansion like Sawyer's. Then they would have expected first-time visitors to be slightly daunted. People with normal upbringings didn't find middle-class Cape Cod homes intimidating.

Bowie did. Especially this one. He'd been inside a few suburban homes when picking Abby up from her friends, but he'd never been a guest himself. Then, he was just a parent. Sure, most were surprised by his young age, but other than that, he was unremarkable. The parents of Abby's classmates were too old to have heard the gossip about his family. The chief of police would remember, though, and Bowie would be spending enough time inside the house that the rest of Katie's family might detect his awkwardness and wonder about it.

As Abby skipped up the sidewalk, he followed at a more sedate pace, his grip tight on the container of corn salad he'd brought. He felt Lou's hand grip his shoulder.

"You'll do fine," Lou said quietly.

"Am I that obvious?" Bowie asked in an undertone.

Lou shook his head. "I know you, Bowie. You held yourself like you are now for almost a full year when you first came to live with Gretchen and me. We're all just people. You're a good man. Katie is lucky to have you, and I'm glad she's finally realized that."

Although Lou's words didn't completely remove the queasiness in Bowie's stomach, they did make him feel marginally better. He wasn't the kid no one wanted. He ran a zoo. He had a daughter who loved him and a father figure in Lou. Sure, Bowie might need to work a little harder to prove to Chief Underwood that he was worthy of dating his daughter, but he could do that.

When Bowie knocked on the door, Katie opened it. The warm smile on her face curled around his heart. She'd never looked at him like that before—as though he belonged and just his presence made her happy. He could grow accustomed to expressions like that.

Katie looked great. She had on reddish-orange shorts and a summery top. She probably wouldn't find the outfit particularly special or sexy, but he did. It was down-to-earth and yet bright and cheery, just like the woman herself.

She stood on her tiptoes and planted a brief kiss on his lips. The public acknowledgment of their relationship warmed him. Abby emitted a happy little squeak that caused Bowie to smile. His daughter had been campaigning for this development for some time now.

Katie greeted Lou and Abby. "My parents are in the living room, and the rest of my family and June and Josh are in the backyard," she informed them. "I thought it would be less overwhelming if we did this in stages."

"Thanks," Bowie said.

"Just to warn you, my mother is ecstatic," Katie said. "Visions of grandbabies are already dancing in her head. Don't let that scare you."

Bowie grinned as he followed her. Abby piped up, "I wouldn't mind a brother or sister."

Katie groaned. "Not you too. I'll need to keep you and my mother apart."

Of course, that didn't happen. When they entered the living room, Katie's mother instantly zeroed in on Abby. That was the easy part for Bowie. He was proud of his kid, and he'd raised her to feel comfortable in any home. Abby was wearing one of the outfits from her shopping trip with Katie and June. She twirled about, showing her dress to Katie's mom as she happily chattered about the fun she had buying it. Katie's mom shot a pleased expression at her daughter over Abby's head.

The conversation soon turned to the zoo. Although Katie's dad didn't say much, he asked Lou a couple of questions. The two apparently knew each other, which didn't surprise Bowie. Up until Gretchen's death, Lou had been active in the community and had even served on the town council.

After about ten minutes, Katie's mom brought

her hands together. "I think it's time we adjourn to the backyard. The boys are grilling hot dogs and burgers. The grandchildren will be playing some sort of game. The oldest are about your age, Abby."

As everyone started to file out of the room, Katie's father remained where he stood.

"Bowie, if you don't mind, I'd like to have a quick chat."

Katie groaned. "Really, Dad, I'm not sixteen. You don't have to grill my boyfriend."

"It's okay, Katie," Bowie told her before he addressed her father. "I'd be more than happy to talk to you, sir."

Katie still lingered in the doorway, but Bowie sent her a look. He understood that she didn't want her dad giving him the third degree, but the man wouldn't be satisfied until he did so.

Besides, Bowie didn't blame him.

Katie still didn't know his history with her father. He needed to tell her soon, but he'd blurted out enough yesterday without going through his teenage rap sheet. Besides, she already knew that he'd been arrested for vandalism—just not by whom.

Katie turned toward her dad. "I like this one, so go easy, okay?"

Her dad only grunted, but her words pleased Bowie. Once she had resolved to be in a real relationship, she'd approached it like she did everything—with full commitment.

With one final glance at Bowie, Katie left the room. Her father gestured sharply toward one of the armchairs. Bowie sat as Chief Underwood slowly lowered himself into a recliner. Although Katie had said his injuries from

Eddie's attack were almost healed, the man still moved stiffly. He didn't fully sink into his chair but stayed on the edge of his seat, his posture unyielding. For a long moment, neither spoke.

Katie's father studied Bowie. It took all of Bowie's self-control not to fidget. Chief Underwood couldn't have been more intimidating if he'd taken out his old service revolver and cleaned it. Still, Bowie managed to meet his gaze. He wasn't a boy. Although he wasn't proud of everything in his past, he'd turned into a decent man.

Katie's father finally spoke. "Didn't I arrest you? Twice."

Bowie answered, "Yes, sir. For vandalism and trespassing."

Chief Underwood's mouth pursed slightly. Bowie couldn't tell if the man was displeased or simply mulling something over. Bowie waited in silence and didn't rush to excuse his past actions. He'd committed the crimes.

"Lou Warrenton seems to think pretty highly of you," Chief Underwood said.

Bowie didn't know how to respond without seeming like an ingrate or a pompous ass. He settled for a brusque nod.

"Lou Warrenton is a good man," Katie's father continued.

That, Bowie had no trouble seconding. "Yes. Yes, he is."

"I've generally found him to be a good judge of character."

Once again, Bowie gave a quick bob of his head,

keeping his back ramrod straight. Chief Underwood hadn't relaxed his posture either, and Bowie knew he hadn't passed the test yet.

"I was behind the two-way mirror that night, you know," Chief Underwood said.

Bowie started at the unexpected statement before studying the other man's face. It remained completely impassive. Katie's father continued, his casual tone belying his words. "The night you spray-painted the zoo."

Bowie held himself very still.

"Before Lou pressed charges, he wanted to speak with you," Chief Underwood said. "Since you were a repeat offender and an adult, I wasn't so keen on the idea."

Bowie wet his lips. He'd only talked about his childhood in detail twice—the night of his arrest for spray-painting the zoo and yesterday with Katie. Although he hadn't told Lou much, it wouldn't have been hard for the police chief to fill in the blanks. "So you heard my conversation with Lou?"

Chief Underwood nodded. He was silent for a second. "Your daughter seems like a fine young lady."

Under normal circumstances, Bowie would have grinned proudly. His mouth, however, felt frozen into an emotionless flat line. He jerked his head in agreement instead. "She's a great kid."

"Lou told me that he wanted to drop the charges, to give you a fighting chance to be a good father," Chief Underwood said. "Given what I knew about your parents and your own record, I had my doubts. I was wrong."

"I never did drugs," Bowie said. He wanted to make that clear. Even when Sawyer and her friends had done E, he'd made some excuse. He'd watched how it made people so desperate that they'd do anything for their next fix. As a kid, he'd had little control over his life as it was without making himself a slave to a dealer like his dad.

Chief Underwood nodded. "Lou was right. You're nothing like your parents, but what I want to know is that you're also not that angry kid I arrested. Twice."

"No, sir," Bowie said. "I haven't been since I first held my daughter."

Katie's father considered that for a moment. Then, he leaned forward again and asked Bowie, "Why did you charge Eddie when you knew he had a gun?"

"There wasn't an option. I didn't have another way to stop him."

Chief Underwood's mouth twisted. "There's always an option. You could have stood down. Most people would've."

"I couldn't let him take Katie into that van," Bowie said simply.

"I owe you for that. All of us do."

Bowie shifted uncomfortably. Even stated in a matter-of-fact fashion, praise still rested uneasily on him. Chief Underwood didn't miss his slight movement, but to Bowie's surprise, he thought he saw the man's expression soften.

Chief Underwood finally settled into the recliner. "So how much does my girl know about your past?"

"Some," Bowie said. "She knows I was arrested for vandalism. She doesn't know that you're the officer who arrested me. I'm planning to tell her everything when the timing's right, which will be soon."

"Fair enough," Chief Underwood said. "Just make sure you're open with Katie. If you hurt her…" His voice trailed off meaningfully.

Bowie finished for him, "I know. Mike made the same threat."

This time, Chief Underwood grinned broadly. "My other sons will do the same."

"I know," Bowie repeated dryly.

Katie's father rose and gestured for Bowie to follow suit. "We'd better head outside, or Helen will have my head for monopolizing you."

As soon as Bowie stepped out the door, Katie was at his side. She twined her arm through his uninjured one and shifted her body so it was flush against his. He smiled down at her. He could get used to this.

"You survived?" she asked.

Bowie grinned. "He wasn't that bad. Don't forget that I'm a father too."

Katie groaned. "Oh, poor Abby. I hope you didn't take notes, or her dates will be running from the house."

"You have to weed out the bad ones." Bowie shrugged his good shoulder.

"Are you ready to meet the rest of the family?" Katie jerked her head in the direction of two couples sitting in lawn chairs and talking to Lou. Bowie assumed they were her older brothers and their wives. Although Luke had agreed to represent him if Sawyer attempted to gain custody, Bowie hadn't met the lawyer in person.

"Are they going to threaten to kill me if I hurt you?" Bowie asked.

Katie laughed. "Only my brothers. The wives will be nice."

After the introductions were over, Bowie found himself nursing a beer as Katie and her siblings—along with her sisters-in-law and June—played an intense game of badminton. Evidently, it was a family tradition. The kids were engaged in a squirt-gun battle, and Abby was holding her own. Lou was talking with Katie's parents. Bowie was pretending to watch the game, but he couldn't stop the awkward feeling creeping through him. It should feel normal, natural, but instead, it was like watching an old seventies sitcom.

"It's weird, isn't it?" Josh asked, causing Bowie to start. He hadn't heard the man coming up beside him. In his hand, Josh held one of the fancy beers he'd brought to the party.

"What's weird?" Bowie asked. He didn't particularly want to talk to the jerk, but he was one of Katie's best friends.

"Being at a family picnic." Josh gestured with his beer bottle. "The old-fashioned games, the inside jokes, the backyard barbecue. It's supposed to be so damn normal."

Shock pierced Bowie. How was this asshole echoing his thoughts?

Josh must have sensed his consternation, because he added, "I'm a former foster kid too."

Bowie froze. "Katie told you."

"Not much," Josh said. "Nothing at all, really. She tore me a new one for the whole villain thing. I might have accused you of being a golden boy, but she set me straight. All she said is that you were in the system. That's it. She didn't say why you were in foster care or what it was like for you. My own experience was pretty fucked up."

Bowie relaxed. He didn't mind that Katie had told Josh that he'd been a ward of the state. It was common knowledge. The private details—the stories of how his parents and guardians had bullied, ignored, or used him for cheap labor—were the parts he wanted kept private.

"It gets better," Josh said.

"What does?" Bowie asked.

"Going to Underwood family functions," Josh told him. "I almost freaked out during my first one freshman year. Then, when Katie and her mom found out that I didn't have a place to go in the summer, I ended up staying here."

Suddenly, Josh's overprotectiveness made sense. He'd spoken the truth when he said June and Katie were the closest thing he had to family. Like Bowie, he'd created his own de facto family unit. Josh wasn't jealous. He'd truly been worried about Katie.

"This is my first backyard party," Bowie admitted. "Lou and his wife used to entertain, but nothing like this."

Josh nodded understandingly and then asked, "Why'd you do it? Pick on Katie back then."

"To fit in," Bowie said honestly as he took a swig of his beer. "The girl I liked was popular. I was finally part of something. I never enjoyed pulling pranks on Katie. I knew it was wrong, even back then."

Josh sipped his own drink as he stared at the badminton game. Then he shrugged. "Hell, I might have done something like that too."

"Katie wouldn't have," Bowie pointed out.

Josh sighed. "She's an amazing person, but she's always had family. We didn't. At least, not while growing up."

"Does that mean we're good now?" Bowie asked.

Josh contemplated that for a moment. Then he turned toward Bowie. "Katie says you've changed and that she wants a relationship with you. Even I can tell you're a decent father, and it's not like you had role models growing up. There's also the little fact that you took a bullet for her. I'm willing to give you a chance, but if you hurt Katie again—"

"You'll kill me," Bowie finished for him. "You'll have to get in line. Every male in Katie's family has threatened me with that. My money is on her dad reaching me first. I don't think there'd be much left of me by the time you arrived from San Francisco."

Josh chuckled. "I drive fast."

"Great," Bowie pretended to mumble before he turned serious. "I'm not going to hurt her, Josh. Katie means a great deal to me. I don't generally let people get close, and when I do, they have my loyalty."

Josh held Bowie's gaze for a long moment and then nodded.

Just then, the badminton game ended, and Katie crossed the yard to join them. She immediately zeroed in on Josh. "Do you remember what I said last night?"

"Relax, Katie," he said. "I was making nice. You're right. He isn't half bad."

Clearly unimpressed, she turned toward Bowie. "Is he bothering you?"

Bowie shook his head. "Nope. We just cleared things up. We should be good now."

Katie exhaled, and a bright smile replaced her frown. "Good, because you happen to be two of my favorite guys."

Bowie smiled at her as he allowed her to tug him over to where Mike and Matt stood with June. The twins greeted him warmly—although they threatened to cream him in badminton when his arm wasn't in a sling. Slowly, Bowie felt himself relax. This wasn't all that different from family dinners at Lou's. He could do this. He could belong. He just hoped Katie stuck around long enough to make this real.

Chapter 13

"Do you think Sawyer will like me?" Abby asked for the third time as she fidgeted on the couch.

Bowie ruffled her hair affectionately. "You're pretty hard not to like, Abby Bear."

Abby turned to Katie, her face scrunched with worry. "What do you think?"

Katie suppressed a groan and wondered, not for the first time, what she was doing here.

The last thing she wanted was to meet Sawyer again, especially under these circumstances, but Abby had asked her. Plus, even if Bowie hadn't said anything, Katie knew he wanted her by his side too. This wasn't easy for either of them, and they needed her more than she needed to avoid her high-school nemesis. Personally, Katie didn't know if her presence would improve the situation, since Sawyer had never liked her. Still, if Sawyer decided to go on the attack, at least Katie could draw her attention away from Bowie and, even more important, from Abby.

"I think your father is right." Lou saved Katie from answering Abby's question. "Anyone who meets you will love you."

Abby frowned. "But she already did meet me, and she gave me away."

"She was young and probably scared," Katie

said, refraining from adding that Sawyer was also horribly self-centered. For Abby's sake, Katie wouldn't judge Sawyer based on high school. Abby had a chance at a relationship with her mother, and Katie certainly wouldn't taint it. As long as Sawyer didn't hurt Abby and Abby wanted to continue to meet her mother, Katie would not say anything against her in Abby's presence.

The doorbell rang, and Abby slid across the couch like a magnet to her father's side. She pressed against Bowie as she gnawed her lip. Lou stood up.

"I'll get the door," he said.

"Thanks," Bowie said as he squeezed Abby close with a one-armed hug. "It'll be okay. No matter what happens, you'll always have me. I'm not going anywhere."

Katie's heart gave a pang. Not only were his words incredibly sweet, but they reminded her of how often Bowie had been alone during his childhood. No one had held him when he'd met his next set of foster parents for the first time. Careful not to touch his healing gunshot wound, Katie reached over and gently rested her hand on his arm. At the contact, he gave her a grateful smile.

Sawyer burst into the room with her husband in tow. Katie almost started in surprise. Sawyer looked… unimpressive. Oh, she was still attractive, beautiful even in her fashionable clothes, her hair and makeup all the latest style. But even with her pricey grooming, Sawyer wasn't stunning beyond belief. And best of all, Katie no longer felt like a frump beside her. She straightened as she realized she could hold her own against Sawyer.

Her husband was an athletic-looking sixtysomething with silver hair and striking blue eyes. As Sawyer sashayed into the room, the rancher hung back, quietly observing. The man exuded a quiet authority, tinged with sternness. He reminded Katie of a no-nonsense school principal.

Bowie got to his feet with Abby still clinging to him. Katie rose more slowly, not wanting to attract notice. Just as she had prayed vainly for in high school, she wanted Sawyer to overlook her— although for entirely different reasons. For once, she succeeded. Sawyer's entire focus was on Bowie and Abby.

"My baby girl," Sawyer practically crowed as she spread out her arms and bent slightly at her knees. Abby glanced up at her dad in confusion. Sawyer frowned, clearly expecting a more excited welcome.

"You don't have to get Bowie's permission," Sawyer said. "You can hug me. I'm your mother."

Reluctantly, Abby let go of Bowie's hand and stepped into Sawyer's waiting embrace. Katie watched Bowie closely and didn't miss his clenched jaw. Anyone could tell that Sawyer was playacting. She oozed fake, sugary-sweet emotion, and she certainly didn't show any consideration for her daughter's feelings. If Sawyer stopped casting herself in the starring role of this emotional drama, she'd notice Abby's trepidation. The girl needed gentle assurances instead of an overwrought reunion. Plus, Sawyer's protestations of motherhood had to sting Bowie.

"Let me look at you." Sawyer took Abby by the shoulders and held her at arm's length. Abby stood stiffly like a wooden doll as Sawyer studied her. Bowie reached out and placed a comforting hand on Abby's shoulder. Katie could feel the tension rolling off him. She knew he wanted to snatch up his daughter and take her far away.

"Your dress is cute," Sawyer said.

The sides of Abby's mouth quirked up, and she looked at Katie. "Thanks. Katie helped me pick it out."

Sawyer's gaze flew toward her, noticing her for the first time. Although Sawyer's eyes narrowed competitively, Katie didn't detect any glint of recognition. As Bowie had in the beginning, Sawyer simply did not place her.

"I can see introductions are in order," she said. "I'm Sawyer Johnson Carlton." She reached back and touched her husband's arm possessively. "This is Rodger Carlton, my husband."

Bowie stepped forward, positioning his body slightly between Sawyer and Abby. He gestured first to Lou. "You met Lou Warrenton already. He and his wife took me in after high school. Abby and I both consider him her grandfather."

Rodger Carlton extended his hand to Lou. "Lou and I go way back. He's helped me out with a few troublesome births with my mares and cows when the vet was busy."

"Rodger." Lou returned the handshake.

Rodger turned his attention to Bowie. "You must be Bowie Wilson."

Bowie nodded and shook the man's hand as well. Rodger and Sawyer both focused next on Katie.

"You must be Bowie's girlfriend," Sawyer said, her tone a tad frosty yet not out of the bounds of politeness.

Bowie cleared his throat. "Sawyer, you might remember Katie Underwood from high school."

Sawyer whirled toward Bowie. "Katie Underwood?"

Then she laughed. Not pleasantly. It was her high-school mean-girl laugh. "You're dating Katie Underwear? You and Katie Underwear?"

Bowie's face darkened. Lou and Rodger shifted. But Abby was faster than all of them.

"That's not nice."

Katie stepped forward. Her time of going undetected was over. "It's okay, Abby. That's just an old nickname from high school. Your mother is just shocked to see me. That's all."

"It's still mean," Abby said, not convinced.

Sawyer, however, didn't appear to notice her daughter's reaction. Instead, she'd turned toward her husband. "Katie was the oddest girl. She was always doodling."

Bowie rested his hand protectively on Katie's back. "Katie's an amazing artist and a brilliant marketer. She's really helped bring visitors back to the zoo, and our pool of volunteers is growing. We're in the running for a grant because of her efforts."

Rodger regarded Katie with a genial—if slightly paternal—smile. "That's interesting work for a lady."

Katie felt her grin become forced. Luckily, Rodger didn't seem to notice. She didn't think the man intended to be patronizing. He just seemed out of touch.

"I've heard that marketing has changed a lot," Rodger continued. "All that social media stuff. You'd be wise if you learned about Facebook and all that."

"Thank you for that tip," Katie managed to get out without her voice frosting over.

"Katie's really good with social media," Bowie interjected. "She's brought the zoo into the twenty-first century."

"Well, this is all fun," Sawyer said abruptly in a decidedly bored tone, "but I'd like to get to know my daughter." She turned to Abby and said in a voice normally reserved for toddlers, "Would you like to take me on a tour of the house?"

Abby glanced helplessly at Bowie. Clearly, she didn't know how to handle Sawyer's sudden intense bursts of interest. Katie didn't blame her.

"Why don't we start with the kitchen?" Bowie said as he shepherded Abby from the room. Lou and Sawyer followed, but Rodger hung back.

He turned to Katie. "Would you mind if I asked a few questions before we catch up with the others?"

Lovely. Katie didn't particularly want to field any inquiries, especially from the man who had treated her like a five-year-old and was married to her worst enemy. Still, she had no idea what he wanted, and she could potentially help Bowie.

"What do you want to know?"

"I would like to speak to you privately about the man you are dating."

"Oh," Katie said noncommittally, not particularly liking the turn of the conversation.

Rodger waited a few minutes until Sawyer's voice had faded away. As they stood in silence for a moment, he regarded Katie kindly. He reminded her of a concerned father.

"Pardon my intrusiveness, but I feel that it is my duty to warn you about Bowie Wilson's past."

Katie stiffened. "What past are you talking about?"

"From what I hear, he is not a good man. In high school, he used to mercilessly tease a young woman..."

Katie barely stifled her snort of laughter. Either Sawyer had bamboozled this man entirely, or he took mansplaining to a whole new level.

"I am well aware of that," Katie said dryly, unable to keep the sarcasm from her voice, "since I was the target of Bowie and Sawyer's pranks."

Rodger blinked. "Sawyer was involved?"

"Involved?" Katie said. "She's the reason Bowie pulled them in the first place..." Katie's voice trailed off as her mind stumbled across Sawyer's twisted game. "Oh, I get it. Sawyer wanted to make Bowie look bad. She just conveniently left out her role."

Rodger made a disapproving sound in the back of his throat. He sounded exactly like a disappointed father. "I'm afraid Sawyer is a bit highstrung. I thought she'd calm down as she matured, but she hasn't."

Katie's discomfort increased. She'd never liked Sawyer. At times, she'd actively hated her. But for the first time, Katie felt a twinge of pity for her old nemesis. No woman should be married to a man who talked about his wife as though she were a horse to be tamed. That cliché should have died in the Civil War.

"I wouldn't know," Katie said. "I haven't seen Sawyer in over twelve years." An awkward silence descended. Katie tried to smile, but it felt weak. "Maybe we should rejoin the others."

"I'm worried about that little girl," Rodger said stubbornly. Katie believed him. The man had his faults, but he thought he was doing the right thing. Even if he was going about it entirely the wrong way, he really did seem to want to help Abby.

"So am I," Katie said earnestly. "I love Abby, and I don't want to see her caught up in any scheme of Sawyer's. Whatever Sawyer told you about Bowie's relationship with his daughter is wrong. She's never had any contact with Abby until today. But Bowie has been there constantly. His daughter is the most important thing in his life, followed closely by Lou and then the zoo animals. He is a good, caring man, and his daughter is a very well-adjusted little girl."

When Katie finally finished her impassioned defense, she was breathing heavily. As she stood there, watching for Rodger's reaction, she realized something with utter clarity. She trusted Bowie. Fully and entirely. She'd finally divorced her high-school memories from the real, remarkable man. It was more than mere forgiveness. Her lingering feelings of resentment had vanished, and she found herself on the brink of tumbling into love.

Rodger was silent. When he spoke, his voice was pensive. "You really do care for Abby. You have a strong mothering instinct. I wish Sawyer had the same."

It struck Katie that although Rodger generally viewed her as incompetent, he just might trust any observation that sounded maternal. "Abby is a very special, sweet girl. She's dear to me, and Bowie loves her with all his heart.

All he wants is for his daughter to be happy and loved and given the advantages that he never had."

Rodger nodded. "I admit that Bowie seems very protective of his daughter, and the girl clearly loves him. I hadn't expected that. I'm not here to disrupt their lives. I just want to make sure Sawyer's daughter has what is best for her."

Katie regarded the man earnestly. He was patriarchal, but he clearly lived by a strong ethical code. If she could convince him that his and Sawyer's interference was hurting and not helping Abby, she was pretty sure he wouldn't push for custody. "I believe you, but is that Sawyer's motivation?"

Rodger sighed heavily. "When I married Sawyer, I wanted more children. I'd wished for a little girl. When I found out about Sawyer's infertility, I was disappointed. Then I learned about Abby, and I'd hoped I could still have a daughter."

"You could always adopt," Katie suggested gently, thinking of Bowie's childhood. "There are so many children who need love."

Rodger's expression darkened. "As I said, Sawyer lacks any maternal softness. I'd hoped with her own child, it would come naturally. Today was also to test that."

The sympathy Katie felt for Sawyer surprised her. To her shock, she found herself defending the woman. "Not all women want to be mothers. There's nothing wrong with that."

Rodger's expression indicated he felt otherwise. "When I married Sawyer, I made it clear I was hoping for a big family. I love my boys from my first marriage, and I wanted more kids. It was part of the deal."

-----◆-----

"Your house is so quaint," Sawyer said for the fourth time, condescension saturating her voice as they climbed down the back steps and headed into the zoo. Abby had wanted to show Sawyer the animals, but Bowie doubted the woman had any interest in them.

He gave a noncommittal sound at Sawyer's observation about the old Victorian. He didn't know how else to respond. For Abby's sake, he had to ignore Sawyer's constant digs. The woman was Abby's mother, and as long as Sawyer treated Abby well, he would stay silent.

Sawyer turned to Abby. "You'll have to visit my house. It is much bigger and very modern."

Not for the first time, Abby pressed close to Bowie, hugging his arm against her. The gesture tugged at his heart. His daughter clearly wasn't comfortable, but Sawyer didn't seem to register the fact.

"I like my house," Abby said in a quiet voice.

"We have a pool and horses."

"We have a zebra," Abby said.

Sawyer frowned, and Bowie barely suppressed a groan. She hated when anyone upstaged her. He doubted she'd even make an exception for her daughter.

"We don't have a pool, though," he said quickly.

Sawyer laughed, the sound high and superior. "Why would you have a pool? You don't know how to swim."

Even when they'd dated, Sawyer had lorded that over Bowie. Despite all her pool parties, she'd never offered to teach him. Since he hadn't wanted to make a fool of himself splashing around, he'd just hung out in a lounge chair.

Abby stared up in surprise. "You don't, Dad?"

Bowie shook his head. He'd taken Abby to swim lessons at the local Y for years. He'd wanted her to have that, even when money was tight.

"Of course, he doesn't, sweetheart," Sawyer said. "Your daddy is pure white tr—"

"Hi, guys!" Katie's overly bright voice broke into Sawyer's insult. Bowie shot her a grateful look as she rounded the corner of Frida's pen. Sawyer's husband did not look pleased. Bowie didn't know if he wasn't happy with his conversation with Katie or with his wife's aborted comment.

"We ran into Lou in the kitchen," Katie continued, her voice cheerful. "He said you'd gone outside."

"Yes," Bowie said. "Abby wanted to introduce Sawyer to the animals."

"Aren't they adorable?" Katie asked, her voice still a tad too cheerful as she turned to Sawyer. "Did you meet Lulubelle yet? She's one of the zoo's stars."

Sawyer looked decidedly bored. "No."

"She was a lovelorn camel until she met her mate, Hank!" Abby said excitedly. "The local news did a story on them. Lou says Hank is sweet on Lulubelle 'cause he's constantly following her wherever she goes."

"How cute," Sawyer said, although she clearly wasn't interested.

"Come here, Lulubelle," Abby called as they reached the enclosure. The camel looked up from a bale of hay. At the sight of Abby, Lulubelle gave an excited grunt. She ambled over, still happily chewing as her jaw worked from side to side. Hank, as always, trailed behind. Sawyer took a step back.

Abby stood on a rung of the fence in order to hug the female camel's neck. Still clutching Lulubelle, she gave Sawyer a shy smile. "Would you like to pet her? Hank too. They're very friendly. Hank's even been trained to carry riders. Lulubelle can't do that, but she can follow a lead rope. And she loves when you scratch her."

Sawyer's face collapsed into a look of pure disgusted horror. "Why would I want to touch them? They smell worse than cows. Ugh!"

At Sawyer's sound of disgust, Lulubelle curled her lip, and Hank snorted his displeasure. At the sound, Sawyer teetered back another foot. Hurt flashed across Abby's face before she focused her attention on Lulubelle.

Rodger nudged his wife. "Why don't you try it, sweetheart?"

Sawyer swung to look at him, aghast. "Rodger, you know how I feel about animals!"

"But it is important to Abby," he chided.

Sawyer's entire body stiffened, and Rodger sent her a look that Bowie would use on Abby. An uncomfortable silence fell over all of them. Poor Abby practically had her face buried in Lulubelle's woolly neck, and Katie was discreetly trying to back away from the group. Bowie scrambled for a way to defuse the situation. He was about to suggest they return to the house for dinner when he spotted a white-and-black streak out of the corner of his eye.

Fluffy.

Before Bowie could bend over and grab the little

bugger, Sawyer screamed. Loudly. Piercingly. She leapt into the air and started to scramble up the fence of the camel enclosure.

"Get that overgrown rat away from me!"

Fluffy, being Fluffy, stood on his hind legs and hissed. Sawyer shrieked again and moved up another rung. If she kept trying to escape over the fence, she'd be perched on Lulubelle's back... if the camel would allow her. Lulubelle didn't appear too happy about the invader to her domain. Beside her, a clearly agitated Hank shifted his massive weight. The llamas had paused in their chewing and were just staring at the scene before them.

"It's okay," Abby said. "That's just Fluffy, our honey badger. He only wants to say hello. He's got a curious nature."

"That *thing* tried to bite me last time I was here!"

"Now, darling," said Rodger, the soul of patience. "I won't let it hurt you." To Bowie's horror, the man started bending to pick up Fluffy. The honey badger whirled on the rancher, snarling fiercely. The man jerked back, lost his balance, and tumbled onto his ass. Bowie tried to snatch Fluffy but missed. The little devil scurried straight in Sawyer's direction. Bowie swore he saw an evil grin on the animal's face as it streaked past.

Sawyer began to wail hysterically as Fluffy advanced. As if in slow motion, Bowie watched as she pulled back to deliver a punishing kick to the honey badger's long midsection. Bowie lurched forward to intercept the blow, but Abby was closer and faster. Leaping from her own perch on the fence, she darted between Sawyer and Fluffy. Sawyer's high heel contacted with Abby's shin. Abby howled, grabbing her leg and jumping on one foot. Fluffy, of course, fled the scene.

"Sawyer!" The admonishment came from Rodger, because Bowie was too busy sweeping his daughter into his arms.

"Are you okay, Abby Bear?"

Abby bit her lip and shook her head. Tears had started to stream down her face. Katie rushed to their side, bending at her knees to be closer to Abby's level. Brushing the girl's hair from her face, Katie asked, "Why don't you let me look at your leg?"

"I didn't kick her that hard," Sawyer protested. "It was barely a tap."

Katie glared up at Sawyer. "You pierced her skin, and an angry red welt is starting to form."

"Sawyer, that was uncalled for," Rodger said.

"That—that *thing* was trying to attack me. I was protecting myself. I can't help it if Abby was stupid enough to stand between us."

White-hot anger snaked through Bowie. He scrambled to his feet, ready to defend his daughter, but once again, Abby was quicker.

"I don't like you," she blurted out. "You are a mean, horrible person."

"I am your mother," Sawyer snapped. "You don't talk to me like that. You show me respect."

"Abby," Bowie said, fighting to keep his voice under control, "why don't you go back in the house and find Lou? He can patch you up."

With a sniffle, Abby nodded and hobbled away.

"Little drama queen," Sawyer huffed, not quite under her breath.

Bowie ignored her. For now. But as soon as he heard the distant sound of the back door closing, he pivoted toward his former high-school sweetheart. This time, he didn't hide his rage.

"You. Do. *Not*. Talk. To. *My*. Daughter. Like. That," he said, punctuating each word.

"I'll talk to her any way I want." Sawyer crossed her arms. "I'm her parent."

"No, you are not," Bowie countered. "I am."

"I gave birth to her," Sawyer shrieked. "She owes me respect."

"Not when you belittle her," Bowie said. "She was only defending herself the best that any eleven-year-old can."

"As if someone like you would know anything about how to be polite," Sawyer scoffed. "You were a good fuck back in high school, Bowie Wilson, but that's all you are and all you ever will be."

"He's a successful businessman and an amazing single dad," Katie countered.

Although part of Bowie warmed at her ready defense, he winced. He didn't want her deflecting Sawyer's ire away from him. Sawyer's words didn't hurt as much as they used to burn. He had a family, a career, and a great relationship. He'd stopped being defined by his childhood a long time ago.

"Shut up, Katie Underwear," Sawyer said. "Do you really think a makeover improves your looks? You're still the girl with ugly hair. Remember in high school when you were too timid to look at me? Go back to that, you little—"

"Get out," Bowie said quietly.

"What?" Sawyer swung toward him again.

"Get off my property," he said. "You can attack me as much as you want as long as it isn't in my daughter's presence. Katie and Abby are off-limits. You treat them with respect and politeness, or you leave my home."

"If you kick me out, I'll fight you for custody," Sawyer screamed.

"Fine," Bowie said. "Take me to court, but you are never seeing Abby again."

Sawyer laughed. "Do you really think you can fight me?"

It was then that Lulubelle chose to spit. Directly into Sawyer's hair. She screamed, batting at her perfect blond coiffure that was now coated in camel saliva. Luckily, Bowie's ire kept him from laughing.

Sawyer glared at them. "I'll bury you for this. All of you. The camel and the rat-thing too."

"That's enough, Sawyer," Rodger said, his drawl hardening into steel. "We're not going to be burying anyone. We're going home. Now."

Sawyer whirled on her husband. "No. We can't. She's my daughter. I am a mother. I have a kid. She can be our kid. I promise."

"I'm not letting you use that girl to make up for your lies to me." Rodger snapped. "It's clear that you're not capable of being a mother. We're leaving now. Apologize to these people."

"But, Rodger…" Sawyer said in a wheedling tone.

Rodger ignored her and focused on Bowie. "We will not be suing you, and there will be no further contact from us. This meeting did not go well, to say the least. I apologize for my wife's behavior."

"Rodger!" Sawyer tried again.

When Rodger looked at his wife, his blue eyes were cold and unyielding. "It's over, Sawyer."

She paled in a way that left Bowie wondering if Rodger meant more than the custody claim. As much as Sawyer enraged Bowie, he couldn't stop a slight twinge of pity. Rodger treated her like a child—a spoiled one. The man acted just as Sawyer's father had. Arrogant and unintentionally belittling. It was a shame Sawyer had left her parents' household only to end up stifled by her own husband. No wonder she hadn't matured. She'd never been given a chance.

"Well, that was unpleasant," Katie said as Sawyer and Rodger walked around one of the animal exhibits and out of earshot.

Bowie turned to her. He studied her carefully, hoping Sawyer's toxic words hadn't wounded her. "How are you doing?"

Katie reached out and cupped his cheek. "She didn't say anything I didn't expect. How about you? She attacked you more than anyone."

Bowie shrugged. "I've heard it all before. I've come a long way in realizing that my parents have nothing to do with me or my life now."

Katie smiled and stood on tiptoes to press her lips against his. He sank into the tender embrace. As their mouths slid against each other, he marveled at how easily she could wash away ugliness with the sweetness of her kiss.

When they broke apart, Katie stared up at him with a worried expression. "Do you think Abby is going to be okay?"

Bowie nodded. "I think she recognized Sawyer for what she was—a mean girl. You and June gave her the confidence to stand up for herself. Sawyer's words stung, but I don't think they'll have a lasting effect."

"Good," Katie said. "That means I can forget about Sawyer, but personally, I think Lulubelle handled her the best."

Bowie laughed and pulled Katie close for another kiss. Life looked pretty sweet right now. He wasn't in danger of fighting a protracted custody battle, and Sawyer Johnson was no longer a problem. And he was dating an amazing woman who had his back no matter what. For once, it felt as if everything was going his way.

Fluffy silently slunk along Frida's enclosure as he made sure the mean blond female and the blue-eyed man left. He did not trust them, especially the woman. She had tried to injure him and had hurt the Wee One in the process. That, Fluffy could not forgive.

He was glad Lulubelle had spat on her. For once, the camel had shown intelligence. Not as much as a honey badger, of course, but Fluffy had to give the silly creature some begrudging respect.

The bipeds were talking in hushed tones. Fluffy followed closely as their chatter drifted in his direction. The mean blond female spoke the most. She seemed angry.

He heard her mention the red-haired female's name. Each time she did, her voice rose higher.

Frida lifted her head at the sound and growled. The blond female did not notice. She was too intent on arguing and pleading. The blue-eyed man did glance nervously in the grizzly's direction, despite the fencing and ditch surrounding the bear's home. Fluffy smiled. He knew how to make the bipeds leave faster.

He darted into Frida's enclosure. The humans did not spy him, but Frida did. She roared and dashed in the direction of the fence. The blond shrieked again—like a wounded rat, which would probably be tastier than the biped. Frida swiveled her massive head in their direction. The bear could not see well, so Fluffy helped her by darting along the ground. The bruin gave chase, and the silly bipeds thought the enormous beast was after them. They began to walk quickly. Very quickly.

Fluffy smiled, but he was not quite satisfied. The blond female should be watched carefully. She reminded him of a frustrated bee, ready to sting. Although bee stings never deterred him, Fluffy did not trust the buzzing insects. He did not trust the mean blond female either.

Chapter 14

"SO THESE ARE THE LITTLE COUGARS I'VE BEEN HEARING SO much about," Katie's dad said.

"Yep," Katie said. At the sound of her voice, Fleur's ears perked up. Although the cubs had grown more independent, Fleur still had an attachment to Katie. The girl bounded over in Katie's direction and rubbed her head against the chain-link fence separating them.

Bowie wasn't done with the cubs' permanent exhibit, but it was complete enough that the trio could explore the area. Although Dobby would eventually be relocated to another zoo, he would spend some time here before moving on.

Katie thought the exhibit was coming along nicely. Using concrete, Bowie had created a "rock formation" for the cougars to play on, and he planned on adding more boulders. An ash already grew at the site. Even though the tree required Bowie to add overhead fencing, it would provide shade and exercise for the pumas. Katie had helped him pick out other vegetation. They'd wanted local plants hardy enough to handle Sagebrush's arid climate, so they'd settled on the town's namesake and some junipers.

Bowie was going to build an observation deck because of the height of the fencing. Although the zoo wasn't accredited, he made sure the enclosure met all recommended guidelines.

"They seem to like their new home," Katie's mom said.

"Bowie did a good job," Katie agreed as she watched Dobby experimentally climb the fake rock edifice. Tonks was close behind. Fleur hung back, content to stalk a lizard that had wandered into the exhibit.

"They've certainly grown," her mom said.

"I know. I miss their baby chub. They're so lanky now."

Bowie laughed. "Almost all animals go through an awkward stage. They'll be very graceful when they're full-grown."

"How long do they keep their spots?" Katie's dad asked.

"They're starting to fade," Bowie said, "but they'll keep them for another month or so."

"Do you see the vertical markings by their eyes?" Katie pointed them out to her parents. "I think they've become more pronounced."

"Those they'll keep," Bowie explained.

"The cubs certainly are active," Katie's mom said.

Her father snorted. "They remind me of the twins. Those two never stopped."

"They still haven't," Katie added.

"They were a big help with this exhibit, though," Bowie said. "They pitched in when my arm was useless."

Both of Katie's parents turned in his direction. When her father spoke, his voice had a slightly deeper timbre than normal. "The Underwoods won't forget what you did for our family."

"I'm glad Eddie Driver is finally where he can't hurt us," her mother said. "Ever since the judge denied bail, I swear I'm getting fourteen more hours of sleep a week."

Katie noticed then that her dad looked a little pale. It had been a twenty-minute car ride into town, followed by a long walk through the zoo to reach the cougar pen. And they'd stopped to see the other animals, including Hank and Lulubelle. Although they hadn't found Fluffy in his pen, they'd spied the honey badger inside Frida's enclosure. Rosie had even danced to Katie's dad's favorite Rolling Stones song. Although Chief Underwood was almost fully recovered, this was still a big outing for him.

Katie quickly made an excuse for her family to leave, and Bowie shot her an understanding look. A burst of warmth exploded through her. A month ago, she would have panicked at the idea of developing silent communication with her boyfriend. Now, the thought had the opposite effect.

Bowie walked her folks to the car. Katie stood on her tiptoes and gave him a brief kiss. At the gesture, she could practically feel the excitement radiating from her mom. Although her mother didn't say anything then, Katie had barely pulled out of the parking lot when she heard, "I do like that Bowie Wilson."

Katie laughed. "So do I, Mom."

Her mother beamed, a self-satisfied expression on her face. She reached over and patted Katie's leg. "See, sometimes, your old mom knows what's best."

Katie chuckled again and asked, "What does good old dad think?"

Her father hadn't said much about Katie's

relationship, and Bowie had told Katie that Chief Underwood had arrested him twice for vandalism.

"I think he's a good 'someone,'" her dad said, and Katie had to smile at the reference to their conversation about whether she should stay in Sagebrush. Her mother, however, frowned at what she clearly deemed to be a less-than-effusive response.

"I think he's wonderful," her mother said. "And his daughter is such a sweet girl."

"Thanks for saying you'll watch her so Bowie and I can have dinner up at the lodge," Katie said.

"It will be my delight," her mom said. She was silent for a minute and then added, "Have you given any more thought to staying here permanently?"

Katie paused, thinking through her answer. Although she'd stopped using her mother as an excuse to avoid a relationship with Bowie, she still didn't want to give her mother false hope. But if she'd learned anything from the mistakes she'd made with Bowie, it was to stop avoiding emotional truths with the people she cared about.

"Don't get too excited, Mom, but it is a possibility."

Her mother squealed and clapped her hands. Katie sought her dad's gaze in the rearview mirror as she spoke next. "I'm starting to think that building my own business here in Sagebrush would be just as meaningful as living in the big city. Maybe more."

Katie's next words were for her mom rather than for her dad. "But it still isn't a sure thing. I've been marketing on the internet, but I need to see how the meetings in California go. And there's still some soul-searching left."

The warning did not dim her mother's enthusiasm. Katie bit back a smile. Her mom would never change, but Katie's understanding of her had. Helen Underwood felt emotions keenly, and she never shied from expressing them, but that didn't make her weak. Instead of Katie trying to protect her mother, it was time that she learned from her, including how to love completely without fear.

***

"I think you should ask Katie to marry you," Abby said without preamble at breakfast.

Bowie choked on his swig of orange juice. As the liquid burned the back of his throat, he pounded his fist against his chest a few times. Unperturbed, Lou passed him a couple of napkins.

When Bowie finally got his coughing fit under control, he found Abby and Lou staring at him expectantly. Although he and Katie had been practically inseparable in the month and a half since the showdown with Sawyer, Bowie hadn't expected his daughter to ambush him about his matrimonial plans over Cap'n Crunch cereal. It wasn't even as if Abby had been dropping hints about it.

"Abby," Bowie finally said, "Katie and I haven't even been dating that long."

His logic did not impress Abby. "So?"

Bowie glanced at Lou for assistance, but Lou merely shrugged. "Gretchen and I were married three months after we met."

"Do you love Katie?" Abby asked.

"I…" Bowie began before he paused and shut his mouth. He honestly didn't know. Beyond wanting a real relationship with her, he'd never tried to name his feelings for Katie, and she hadn't pressed him. He only knew that the past couple of months had been amazing and that he'd missed Katie like hell since she'd left Sagebrush a few days ago for the West Coast. Worse, he didn't know if the trip would turn into a permanent move. When Katie left, he hadn't wanted to grill her about their future. Their relationship was still in its infancy, and he didn't think it was his place to push her into giving up her dream of living in the big city. She'd said she was going to explore the freelance angle, but he knew that several of her interviews were for full-time positions.

Bowie knew he wasn't missing Katie just because they were in the "honeymoon phase." She grounded him and made him content in a way he hadn't known was possible. It wasn't as though he'd been dissatisfied before Katie burst back into his life, but everything was just better with her around.

"You love her." Abby said, her tone definitive, "and she loves you."

Bowie's heart squeezed and then sped up at Abby's last words. Annoyed, he reminded himself to calm down. An eleven-year-old was not an expert on love.

"Why do you say that?" he asked, careful to keep his tone neutral.

Abby flopped back in her chair and sighed dreamily. "It's how you look at her and she looks at you. It's like in the movies."

"Help me out here, Lou."

The older man held up his hands in mock surrender. "The girl's right. Katie stares at you the way I used to catch my Gretchen watching me. You look even more calf-eyed. I think even the zoo animals know you're in love."

"Except the snakes," Abby piped up. "They're not too intuitive."

Bowie groaned as he jammed his spoon into his cereal. He could not believe he was having this conversation with his daughter. "Katie and I haven't talked about love yet."

Abby shrugged, the gesture reminiscent of Katie's. "Tell her you love her and ask her to marry you."

"It's not that simple," Bowie said. This time, he didn't even try to look in Lou's direction. Clearly, he wasn't getting any assistance from that quarter.

"Why not?" Abby demanded.

Bowie sighed. Although things were currently great between Katie and him, he didn't know if she trusted him enough for a rush engagement or if she wanted to be tied down to Sagebrush permanently. Even if she established a freelance business, she could still live anywhere in the world as long as she had a good internet connection. He, on the other hand, couldn't very well uproot Abby, Lou, and their entire menagerie and transplant them to another city. Even long vacations were out of the question.

He had no idea how to explain his concerns to Abby. She would feel betrayed that he'd been a bully, and she'd probably feel guilty over tying down Katie.

"It's complicated," Bowie said.

"No, it's not. Adults just make simple things difficult." Abby crossed her arms.

Bowie laughed. He rose from the table, ruffling her hair as he walked past. "We'd all better get moving. The school bus will be here, and the animals need their food."

Abby grumbled, but she still listened. Lou got up to clean the dishes, and Bowie headed to the zoo. As he helped his staff distribute the feed, vitamins, and medicine, he couldn't chase Abby's words from his mind.

When he headed into the house for a late lunch, Bowie found himself powering up the ancient computer in the dusty home office he and Lou rarely used. Gnawing on his sandwich, he typed in a search for engagement rings. The prices depressed him.

He sighed heavily. He shouldn't take the advice of an eleven-year-old girl in figuring out when to propose. He was nowhere close to being able to convince Katie to marry him. He couldn't even scrape together enough money for a decent ring. So much for grand gestures. He'd have to win her over slowly and not rush this.

Just then, Bowie heard a sound. Lou must have woken up from his midday nap. Bowie quickly pulled up another page on the computer. Turning, he saw Lou enter the room. The man looked groggy, and Bowie hoped he'd changed the screen fast enough. He didn't need any more helpful hints. Lou was a born romantic, and times had been completely different when he'd asked Gretchen to marry him.

"Hey, Lou," Bowie said.

"I was about to go check on Tansy," Lou said, referring to their pregnant zebra.

"It shouldn't be too long now," Bowie said. "I noticed some milk discharge when I checked on her before lunch."

Lou nodded before he turned to leave. Bowie collapsed back into his seat and exhaled.

Lou hadn't asked him any questions, so maybe he hadn't seen Bowie's search. Powering down the ancient computer, Bowie pushed back his chair and headed outside. A news channel from the closest major city was coming to do a human-interest story on them tomorrow, and he wanted the place looking its best.

He spent the rest of the day cleaning out pens and completing the finishing touches on the cougar exhibit. He worked through dinner so that he didn't lose any light now that it was autumn. He stopped back at the house just long enough to put Abby to bed. Then he forced himself to head out to the office. With all the attention the zoo was receiving and the increase in visitors and volunteers, he wanted to submit more grant applications. Maybe this time, the zoo would actually be awarded one.

Yawning, Bowie sat down at his desk. He was concentrating so hard on filling out the application form and not falling asleep that he started when a knock sounded. Lou entered, surprising Bowie, since the older man was normally heading to bed at this time. And unless there was an extremely sick animal, he rarely came to the zoo at night anymore.

Lou shuffled forward, his steps even more faltering than normal. His arthritis acted up at night. Bowie

waited patiently until Lou had settled in the chair
across from him. The older man didn't say a word
as he reached into his pocket and placed a dusty
ring box on the desk.

Bowie's throat felt thick with emotion as he
reached for the worn, velvet-covered box. He
flipped it open to find Gretchen's engagement ring
nestled in the yellowed satin. The main diamond
sparkled even in the harsh glare of the overhead
fluorescent lights. It was a traditional, elegant setting. Katie would love its simplicity and history.

The sight of Gretchen's ring triggered a wallop
of emotion in Bowie. He had a flashback to the day
he'd given Abby her first bath. He'd been terrified
of her slipping from his grasp despite the fact that
she was in an infant bathtub. Gretchen had helped
him, and he remembered how steadily and compe-
tently her gnarled hands had held his daughter.

"It's Gretchen's engagement ring." Bowie lifted
his gaze to meet Lou's.

Lou nodded solemnly. "We both wanted you to
have it. She asked me to save it for you until you
met the right girl."

Emotion swamped Bowie as his hand fisted over
the box. Lou and Gretchen had given him so much.
He owed them his daughter and likely his life.
Without them, he probably would have ended up
dead in a prison brawl like his father. They'd given
him and Abby a family and unconditional love.

"Thank you," Bowie said, his voice sounding
rough to his own ears.

"Gretchen would have liked Katie," Lou said.

"She always said you needed to meet a smart girl with a good heart. And you know I've been rooting for Katie from the beginning."

Bowie swallowed. "This means a lot to me. That you'd give this to me. That Gretchen wanted me to have it."

"We always saw you as a son," Lou said. He'd told Bowie that before, and so had Gretchen. It still awed Bowie that they'd signed the zoo over to him.

"You and Gretchen were the only real parental figures I ever had," Bowie said. "My only role models too."

Lou leaned back in his chair. "I remember the day I first met you in that police station. I didn't know what to expect. I knew from the first moment that you weren't just some punk kid looking for a night of mischief. You were terrified about becoming a father, but it wasn't because you didn't want the responsibility. You were afraid that you couldn't provide for your baby and that your kid would end up with your life. Not a lot of teens would have that initial reaction...worried first about the child and not about themselves. I knew right then and there that you'd grow into a good man, a good father, and eventually, a good husband."

Bowie glanced up at Lou's last statement. Was that part of what held him back from proposing to Katie? The old fear of rejection? The sting of never being part of a family? The isolation of growing up without a single adult who truly cared about him? Did he still, deep down, see himself as not worthy, not deserving?

Ah, hell.

"Katie's an intelligent woman," Lou said, "although it took her longer than I would have liked to recognize the kind of man you are. You might not believe this, but that girl cares deeply for you. Sawyer's husband talked to me after our meeting. Katie defended you quite strongly to him, and I can see the way she looks at you when you walk into a room. It doesn't matter that you're not as rich as you'd like to be or that you've never left Sagebrush for more than a long weekend."

Bowie swallowed at Lou's words. The man knew him—and his nagging insecurities—so well. "I don't want to push her away, Lou, by asking too soon. We struggled to get this far."

"You just keep that ring with you," Lou said with a fond smile. "When the timing is right, you'll know. No sense in rushing these things unnecessarily, but at least now you're prepared."

Bowie's fingers tightened reflexively on the velvet box. "Thanks, Lou."

Lou nodded in response before creakily rising to his feet. "I'd better head back to the house. And don't stay up too late. A body's got to rest."

"I know," Bowie said, although he still had at least a couple of hours of work ahead of him.

Lou ambled out of the office. When the door shut, Bowie didn't turn back to the computer immediately. Instead, he stared at the ring. He wanted it. Marriage. Another kid or two. And he wanted it with Katie.

He loved her. Her intelligence. Her depth of generosity. Her humor. Her wild hair. She made him feel more contented, more complete, than he ever had in his life. He already felt like she was a part of him.

Resolve filled Bowie. He was ready, and he needed to find out if Katie felt the same—could ever feel the same. Snapping the box closed, Bowie placed it in his pocket. She wouldn't be back for a few days yet, which gave him plenty of time to plan.

"Hey." Bowie's deep voice sounded on the other end of the line, and Katie couldn't help the wide smile stretching across her face. She missed him, and talking to him eased the edge of that longing.

With her schedule, it had been hard for them to chat during her business trip. "Hey, yourself," Katie said as she unceremoniously kicked off her high heels and settled onto the bed.

"You're in San Diego, right?" Bowie asked.

"Yup, I took the train here from LA yesterday. I got to see so much of the coast."

"Abby's going to squeal when she hears that," Bowie said.

"Maybe the three of us can come out to California next summer if you have enough help to sneak away. Josh said we're welcome to crash at his place in the Bay Area. Maybe Lou could join us," Katie said. She meant it. Whenever she had a couple of stolen moments to sightsee, she kept imagining what Bowie would think and how Abby would react. She already had a bunch of gifts for the girl stashed away in her suitcase.

"It sounds nice," Bowie said, his tone deliberately casual. "But if we're going to hit the beach, I might need to take those swimming lessons after all."

"I miss you," Katie blurted out. She hadn't said it

yet. She didn't quite know why. It was probably a holdover from trying to maintain some degree of distance in relationships.

Bowie's voice softened. "I miss you like hell. I didn't know a week and a half could feel this long."

"I know," Katie said, warmed by his tone. "Just two more days."

She'd been counting each one.

"How's it going over there?" Bowie asked.

"Josh really came through for me with his contacts. A lot of the businesses I've visited seem really impressed with my work at the zoo and my designs for June and the Prairie Dog."

Bowie paused, his voice serious when he asked the next question. "Did you get any job offers?"

Katie paused, knowing that she and Bowie needed to have this conversation. She'd been doing a lot of thinking lately. "Yeah. A good one with a great company. The pay would be decent, even for the Bay Area."

"Oh," Bowie said, his voice suspiciously neutral. "Do you think you'll take it?"

Katie nervously played with the duvet cover on the hotel bed. It was hard, knowing if she was making the right decision. Her dream was within reach, but she didn't think it was what she wanted. Not anymore. Not with Bowie in her life. Did that make her weak? Naive?

"I-I actually don't think so. It's an amazing opportunity, but I'm not sure it's the right fit for me. I've gotten a lot of potential freelance work. And it's kind of nice being my own boss. I know that starting your own business is a risk, but in the end, I could make more money if it takes off."

"It'll take off," Bowie said immediately.

Katie laughed at the utter conviction in his voice. "I don't think it's a sure thing, Bowie."

"With your brains, talent, and drive, it is," he said without any doubt in his voice. "Just look what you've accomplished with the zoo. In Sagebrush."

Giddy excitement rushed through Katie. Maybe Bowie was right. Maybe she should start her own business. Heck, hadn't she done it already? If she could manage to drum up work in sleepy Sagebrush Flats, couldn't she bring in more, especially with the jump start Josh's connections had given her? She took a deep breath. She didn't need to decide her future now. She had a few days to respond to the job offer and the plane ride back home to think over her choices.

"Speaking of the zoo, how did your TV interview go?" she asked.

"The segment looked really good, and the news station posted a video online," Bowie said, the enthusiasm in his voice apparent. "They got perfect shots of the animals. There was even another spike in attendance. Lou said it felt like when he and Gretchen first opened the zoo in the seventies."

"I have to watch it right now," Katie said as she pulled out her laptop. "Do you have the link on the website already?"

"Of course. My PR consultant would kill me if I didn't." The teasing warmth in Bowie's voice washed over Katie, making her ache for him even more. Luckily, the video downloaded quickly, so she didn't have too

long to wallow. Bowie appeared on the screen next
to Lulubelle and Hank. Although they hadn't made
a public announcement yet, the pair were expecting a little calf. Since camels had a gestation period
of well over a year, Lulubelle was nowhere near
visibly pregnant yet. She batted her lashes at the
camera before she nuzzled Bowie on the shoulder.
There was a quick shot of Frida playing with a
pumpkin, her favorite fall treat, before the segment
switched to Rosie and Sylvia. The cockatoo was
bobbing her head as she danced on the capybara's
back while the rodent lay patiently on the ground.
The clip finished with the cougar cubs exploring
their outdoor exhibit.

"Bowie, that's great!"

"And I haven't told you the best news yet...
We're finalists for the polar bear grant!"

Katie straightened in the bed. She knew how
much it had bothered Bowie that he hadn't been
able to secure a grant. He blamed himself for not
having the right credentials. "That's awesome,
Bowie. Congratulations! I know how hard you've
been working at that. You and the zoo deserve it."

"They were impressed with the work Lou and I
did with the cougars and our fund-raising efforts.
The traffic on our website probably sold them, plus
I think the number of new volunteers helped."

He paused, the silence humming with his excitement even over the phone. "I still can't believe we're
going to be on a list to receive polar bear cubs!
Abby's over the moon. She's always loved them."

"Oh, Bowie, that's unbelievable," Katie said.

"You'll do such a good job with them. You and Lou have been so successful with your other orphans."

"And it'll be great for Frida! She can help show the cubs how to be proper bears."

"It doesn't matter that they're different species?"

"No. Polar bears are actually a subspecies of grizzlies, and they interact and even breed in the wild. Having cubs will be great for the zoo, and there's more…" He waited a beat.

Katie laughed. "Not nice. Don't leave me in suspense."

"The pig-kissing video went viral," he said. "Then the rest of the videos did."

Katie squealed. "How viral?"

"All of them hit news stations, and national newspapers have a link to the videos on their web pages."

"Oh my gosh!" Katie said. "That's terrific."

"*Good Morning America* called."

"You're kidding me!"

"Nope. They want me to come on the show with Daisy, Rosie, and a couple of other animals."

"Bowie, that's incredible."

He hesitated for a moment and then said, "Would you come with me? To New York? They'll give me some extra tickets."

"Of course, I'll be there," she said. "I wouldn't miss it for the world. I'm so proud of you. I love you."

There was a pause as her last words hung in the air. Katie froze. Had she just said that she loved Bowie? Oh goodness, she had, and she'd meant it. She loved Bowie Wilson. Not the puppy love of a teenager but the honest-to-goodness, death-do-us-part kind of love. And she'd just blurted it out over the phone.

Bowie was the first to break the silence. When he did, his voice was rough with emotion.

"I love you too, Katie," he said. "I have for a while now."

Katie's heart melted. The thirteen-year-old inside her did cartwheels. Bowie Wilson loved her too. The serious kind of love.

She realized she was laughing and crying at the same time. "I can't believe we've just declared our love to each other when we're miles apart."

"Me neither," Bowie said and then groaned. "I want to hold you so badly."

"Hold me?" Katie laughed. "I want to take you to bed."

He chuckled. "Well, that too."

"Two days," she said. "Two days, and I'll be back in Sagebrush with you."

"I'm picking you up from the airport," he said.

"Are you sure? Can you be away from the zoo for that long on such short notice? My mom and dad are fine picking me up like we'd planned."

"I'm picking you up from the airport," Bowie said, his voice brooking no argument.

"Two days," Katie said.

"Two days," he repeated.

The worst day of Bowie's life started innocuously. Katie was due to arrive the next day, and he'd be away from the zoo for at least six hours, so he needed to prepare. He spent the entire morning mucking out the enclosures and doing odd jobs.

Unfortunately, the food shipment was short, so he had to swing by the local feed store. He thought he noticed whispering, but he didn't pay it much mind. Since the videos had gone viral, the whole town had started to regard him as a local celebrity. It made Bowie uneasy, so he ignored the fuss.

Bowie loaded the pickup and climbed in. He hadn't gone far when he heard sirens. Glancing in his rearview mirror, he noticed a police cruiser behind him with its lights on. A look down at the speedometer showed he was only going four miles over the speed limit.

Confused, he pulled over. He didn't think his taillight was out.

He relaxed when he spotted Mike walking toward him. Maybe Katie's brother wanted to talk.

Bowie had gotten fairly close to the twins. Both of them had pitched in at the zoo while his arm healed, and Katie's parents had invited him to a couple of family dinners after her birthday party. Mike and Matt, who rented a house with a couple of other guys, had also asked him over to watch football a few times.

Mike, though, didn't look pleased to see Bowie. He wore a cop's expression. Cold. Remote. Disapproving. He looked exactly like his father had when he'd arrested Bowie. Bewilderment returned. Bowie didn't think Mike was joking. He was serious. Too serious.

For a long, pregnant moment, Mike stared down at Bowie without speaking, his jaw set in an unyielding line. Bowie fought the urge to shift under the unyielding scrutiny. He didn't say anything. He didn't want to piss the guy off any more, especially when he had no idea what the hell he'd done in the first place.

"License and registration," Mike barked. Bowie dug out his wallet and handed over the documentation. Mike scanned it and handed it back, his movements sharp.

"You've got decals on your back window and something hanging from the mirror," Mike said stiffly as he pulled out his pad.

Yeah, that shed a lot of light on Mike's bad mood.

"Sorry, sir," Bowie said. "I'll remove them."

"You're still getting a fine."

Bowie nodded. There was no other response. He racked his brain for what could have angered Mike.

"You know what," Mike said, "I think I smell pot."

"What?" Bowie said in confusion.

"Out of the truck," Mike said.

"Mike—"

"Out of the truck." Mike's voice was hard and unyielding. Bowie complied.

"Turn around and put your hands on the side of the vehicle."

Bowie did as he was told, the position unfortunately not unfamiliar. After all, he'd been arrested before. Mike patted him down—none too gently. Then he made Bowie stand like that while he searched the pickup. Thoroughly. Bowie's back even started to hurt. When Mike finished his agonizing investigation of Bowie's truck, he made him perform a series of humiliating balance tests. Finally, Mike finished with his power play and wordlessly handed over the ticket.

Bowie skimmed it and glanced at Mike in confusion. "My taillight isn't broken."

Mike turned, pulled out his nightstick, and shattered the left light. "Now it is."

"Shit, Mike, what the hell did I do?" Bowie asked.

Mike turned stiffly, his eyes deadly. "I suggest you check your email when you get home."

"My email?"

"Stay the hell away from my sister."

With that, Mike climbed into his Ford Explorer and peeled away. Bowie stood in the center of the road, ticket clutched in one hand. What the hell had just happened?

Slowly, Bowie returned to his truck and headed home. He only took enough time to unpack the feed before he made a beeline for his office. It felt like forever before the computer booted up. Opening his email, he saw two from Sawyer. A sense of unease filled him as he opened her latest.

> My husband kicked me out because of your lies! You took my child away from me! I get nothing, NOTHING, due to the prenup! You ruined my life for the second time! Now I've ruined yours! The world will know what kind of a horrible, stupid ass you are!

The unease turned to dread as Bowie scrolled to the email below. The addresses of a couple of Katie's family members and June's business accounts were listed in the email. So was Katie's.

> Everyone thinks the pig-kissing video is cute. Here's the real truth.

There was a link to a YouTube video. Bowie's stomach churned as he clicked on it. The filming quality was grainy, shaky, and poorly shot, but he recognized it at once. It was the high school prank. The high school prank that had started it all.

Bowie had never watched the entire video. Sawyer had only sneaked a brief clip into the morning announcements and edited it so that no one could see the culprits. The old version had begun with Katie in close-up. Her eyes were closed, and she was saying Bowie's name. Her lips puckered, and then she kissed the pig, held by unseen hands, square on the snout. The pig had squealed indignantly, and then the embarrassing clip had ended.

The complete video started the moment Katie stepped into the janitor's closet. Both Katie and Bowie were clearly visible and recognizable despite the bad quality. Katie was shy and hesitant, her hair a firestorm of color about her face. She looked so eager, so hopeful, that Bowie's heart cracked. How could he have done it? How could he have looked at her face and destroyed her?

His younger self stood there, cocky and arrogant. Bowie wanted to yell at the screen, to stop what was coming. Each frame cut a fresh slice in his heart.

This version of the video didn't end with the kiss. Katie opened her eyes, their brown depths filled with horror, confusion, and betrayal.

"What happened?" Katie asked, bewildered and hurt.

Sawyer chose that moment to emerge from behind the shelves, her face gleeful and triumphant. *"Did you really think that a hot guy like Bowie Wilson would be interested in a little geeky nobody? He's been my boyfriend all along."*

Katie swung toward Bowie. He just shrugged insolently.

Bowie wanted to punch his younger self. In the face. Or, hell, the balls. He deserved it.

"Come on, Bowie." Sawyer tugged on his arm. *"We've got better things to do."*

Sawyer flounced, and he sauntered out of the room. He didn't even look back. Not once.

When the door shut, Katie slumped against it and slid to the floor. She sat there, clearly fighting back tears. Her shoulders heaved with the effort.

Then she lost the battle. She cried. She cried as if her heart was breaking. It probably was. And she didn't stop.

Bowie prayed that it would end, but he didn't speed up the video. He deserved to see this, to hear this, to suffer through this, even if it seemed that the salt of every tear fell directly onto his already abraded heart.

He'd put her through hell. He'd hurt the woman he loved over and over and over.

He'd never witnessed Katie's tears. Not once. Bowie knew Sawyer had purposely kept the whole video from him years ago. He would have called off the prank after seeing Katie's devastation. Even then, he couldn't have withstood her tears. Now? Now, it decimated him. Sawyer still knew how to take down her enemies.

Bowie reached up to rub his face and found it wet. The phone rang. Numbly, without thinking, he picked it up.

"This is Alex," the clipped voice on the other end said. "Katie's brother. The one in the air force."

"Yes," Bowie said, bracing himself for his next round of punishment. On some level, he welcomed it. He couldn't very well defend Katie against himself. He might as well let her brothers do it by proxy.

"Do you hear anything?" Alex asked.

"No."

"Listen harder."

That's when Bowie detected the faint rumble of a jet engine. The sound grew louder and louder until it became deafening. The concrete-block walls even shook. His pen jiggled off his desk and fell to the floor. Then the sound slowly faded, and Bowie could hear the upset brays from the animals outside.

"I hear you got my message." Alex sounded smug.

"How many times am I going to get this message?" Bowie asked wearily.

"Depends," Alex said. "A new training route was just created. We'll see how it plays out."

"I guess we will," Bowie said.

"Oh, and, Wilson, stay the hell away from my sister."

The phone line clicked, and Bowie slumped back in his chair. He rather thought the warnings from Mike and Alex were unnecessary. He honestly didn't know if his relationship with Katie could survive this. It would dredge up everything they had just dug through and cast aside. His only hope was that Katie wouldn't catch wind of the video until he had the chance to prepare her.

A fist pounded on Bowie's office door. With a sigh, he rose from his desk as he wondered which brother was here now. He opened it to reveal both Matt and Luke. Luke punched him square in the eye. Bowie stumbled backward. For a lawyer, the guy could really hit.

"Ah, hell," Matt said. "That was my move. I'm the mechanic. That's what I've got. Brute force. You were supposed to threaten him with legal action."

"You can punch me too," Bowie said honestly. "I have another eye."

Matt threw up his hands in disgust. "I really can't hit you if you offer to take a punch."

"Knock out my other taillight then," Bowie suggested.

"Shit, Mike knocked out your taillight?" Matt turned to Luke in annoyance. "What is wrong with you guys? You've got to leave me something."

Luke shrugged. "I needed to punch Bowie."

Since Bowie wanted to hit himself, he could sympathize.

"Idiots," Matt said.

"Stay the hell away from my sister," Luke said.

"Hey, I was going to say that!" Matt protested.

"You might as well," Bowie said. "The rest of your brothers did."

"They even took that line from me," Matt complained.

"Sorry," Bowie said, hoping that he managed to hide his slight amusement. Although his eye and heart ached, Matt was pretty hilarious.

"You hurt her," Matt said. "You made her cry. She used to cry every night after school, starting her sophomore year. She didn't think anyone heard, but Mike and I shared a wall with her. We never knew why. Until now."

Any sense of humor fled. Bowie nodded stiffly. This time, he felt as if a knife had just scraped through all the other wounds on his heart.

"You might not believe this," Bowie said, "but what you just said... It was about the best way you could have punished me."

"Ah, shit," Matt said. "Now you had to go and say a thing like that. You even look all hangdoggy. I almost feel sorry for you."

"Don't," Bowie said. "I deserve whatever you dish out."

Luke clasped his hand on Matt's shoulder. "Let's go, Matt. I think the worst thing anyone can do to him right now is to leave him alone with his guilt."

Luke was wrong.

Later that afternoon, the door flew open, and Abby burst into Bowie's office. Her eyes were red and swollen, and Bowie could detect dried tracks of tears on her face. He instantly sprang to his feet.

"I *hate* you!" Abby hurled the words at him with a force and vehemence that only a preteen could muster.

"Abby Bear, what's wrong?"

"Don't call me that!" Abby shrieked, her voice full of betrayal. Bowie faltered. Her saying she hated him wasn't pleasant, but children said it occasionally. For Abby to tell him not to use his pet name for her—the one he used when he wanted to comfort her—killed something inside him.

"Sweetheart..."

"You're one of them. You're one of the bullies."

Bowie's legs felt weak. Abby had watched the video. He should have known, should have prepared.

"Abby—"

"You were the one." Abby stabbed a finger in his direction. "You were the one who was so mean to Katie. You made her feel ugly. You and Sawyer. You're just like them. All the mean kids at school."

"Abby, I..."

But really, what could he say? He had been a bully. What words could he use to explain to his daughter why he'd pranked Katie? *Sorry, kid, your father was an asshole because he, and therefore you, descend from a family of assholes. Did you know that your granddaddy died in prison and sold drugs? Oh, and Grandma? She died of an overdose. Feel better, sweetheart?*

"That's why Katie won't marry you," Abby said. "I don't blame her. I wouldn't marry you either."

"Abby—"

"I *hate* you! I never want to see you again." With that declaration, Abby whirled from his office. Bowie chased after her, but evidently, his little girl could run when given the proper motivation. She tore into the house and bounded up the stairs. Bowie raced past a startled Lou and made it to his daughter's door just before he heard the lock slide decisively into place.

He stared at the closed door as he heard his daughter weeping inside. Her heartrending sobs were a painful echo of Katie's from the video. Abby wasn't that much younger than Katie had been at the time of the prank. Two, three years. That was it. If some boy did to Abby what Bowie had done to Katie...

He turned away from his daughter's door, defeated.

He didn't know what to say to her. Somehow, he'd find the words. They'd get past this. But not now. Not when his heart was shredded. Not today.

He quietly walked down the steps to discover Lou at the bottom, looking concerned. "What was that about? What happened to your eye?"

"I take it you didn't watch the video."

"What video?" Lou asked in confusion.

"Come with me," Bowie said. Knowing the old house computer couldn't handle YouTube, he led Lou to the zoo's office. He gestured for the older man to sit down as he loaded the video.

"I'll be in the Victorian," Bowie told Lou wearily. "I can't watch it again."

Bowie found himself in the kitchen. He climbed up on one of the stools and rested his head on the cool countertop of the island. He should have stayed and watched the video. The damn thing just replayed in his head anyway.

It felt like an eternity before Lou returned. Bowie lifted his head, fully expecting to see condemnation. He didn't. Just compassion.

"You were a scared, lonely kid, Bowie," Lou said.

"I shouldn't have done it."

"No, you shouldn't have," Lou said. "You know that. I know that. We all know that. But you did, you've owned up to it with Katie, and you've both moved on."

"Have we, Lou?" Bowie asked. "Has she? What is that video going to do to our relationship? Her whole family hates me. Katie will watch it, and... Well, I

don't know what's going to happen, but I can't help but
feel that I've lost the love of my life. This could be what
pushes her into taking that job in California."

Just then, Bowie's phone beeped. He glanced down
to see a text message from Katie.

> At home. Wrapped early. Took early flight and
> rented car since you couldn't leave the zoo
> today. Will stop by after Abby goes to bed.
> Going to take a quick nap myself. Love you.

Katie hadn't seen the video—not with that message.
Relief warred with worry. He hoped she would crash
right away, but what if she checked her email?

"Lou, I have to go," Bowie said. "Katie came home
early. I need to speak to her."

Lou inclined his head in understanding. "Go. Good
luck."

"Thanks," Bowie said, grabbing his keys. "I'll need it."

He tore out of the zoo's parking lot, tires squealing,
taillight broken, and decals still on the back window.
He ripped off the car scent hanging from the mirror,
but that was the only concession he made to Mike's
complaints. Let Mike pull him over again. The guy had
purposely damaged his truck, and Bowie wasn't about to
let anyone or anything prevent him from seeing Katie—
even if all four brothers barricaded her door.

───※───

Fluffy smelled trouble. He'd watched the Wee One
run past his enclosure on the way home from school.
He did not like the tears streaming down her face. The

Wee One was always happy. Her displeasure could mean fewer treats, and the Black-Haired One and the redheaded female were taking too long to produce more small humans.

Something had gone wrong with his plan. Very wrong.

———

Luckily, Bowie didn't pass any police cars on his way to Katie's, and her brothers weren't guarding her house. He jumped out of the truck and dashed up her steps, taking them two at a time. He rang the doorbell and barely refrained from pressing it repeatedly until she opened the door.

He waited a couple of beats, couldn't stop himself, and rang it again.

Bleary-eyed, Katie opened the door. She was in the middle of a yawn, but when she caught sight of him, her mouth snapped shut. Concern washed over her features. "Bowie, what's wrong? Is everything okay? What happened to your eye?"

"Did you see the video?" he blurted out.

"The video?" she asked in confusion as she yawned. Then comprehension lit her face. "Oh, you mean that ridiculous one that Sawyer sent."

"You saw it?" Bowie asked. It was his turn to be bewildered. Why wasn't Katie angry? Emotional? Something? She just looked tired from her business trip.

"Yeah," she said, stifling another yawn. "June saw it and called me because she didn't want me to be blindsided. I'm not sure why everyone's making such a big deal out of it. It's not like I didn't live through it. I mean, if it had been posted to the internet when I was a kid, I would have been horrified. Now, I just can't figure out what Sawyer thought she'd gain by releasing it."

"You're not mad at me?" Bowie asked in disbelief.

"No, why?" Katie said. "You didn't do anything. I mean, you did, years ago, but there wasn't anything in that video that I didn't know or that I haven't forgiven you for."

Bowie grabbed her close, pulling her tightly against his chest. He breathed in her scent, relieved to his very core. When he spoke, his voice was rough, and it cracked slightly in the middle of his sentence. "I'd thought I'd lost you, Katie, just when I'd finally found you."

Chapter 15

THE RAW EMOTION ROILING FROM BOWIE SWEPT OVER Katie as he held her in an almost bruising grip. Her heart aching at his visible pain, she rubbed her hands gently against his back to soothe him. His strong shoulders heaved once, and she swore his body practically vibrated against hers.

"It's okay," she told him. "You haven't lost me. I'm here, and I still love you."

Bowie's shoulders jerked, and he squeezed her again. "How can you? After what I did? What I put you through? How do you move beyond that?"

"I did," Katie said simply. She would have brushed a kiss against his cheek or lips, but he was holding her too tightly. "It wasn't easy or simple. You know that. But I did. Fully and completely. You were a kid, Bowie. A kid who had no one to guide him, who just wanted to belong. Sure, you went about it the wrong way, but you're not naturally malicious. You're an innately kind and loving person. Given how you were raised, it's amazing that you are. That shows the strength of your compassion."

Bowie pulled back. His face still looked white and haggard, making a sharp contrast to his nasty-looking black eye. "I love you so much."

With that, Katie's heart thrilled. She smiled at

him warmly. "Yes, and we need to get down to celebrating that."

He grinned boyishly, but the smile didn't completely reach his eyes. He was still hurting. Badly. The video had shaken him. As a teenager, Katie had dreamed of him feeling her pain. She wanted him to steep in guilt and remorse until it tortured him. It appeared that she'd gotten her wish, and it slayed her.

She pulled him over to her couch. "Come on. Let's sit down and talk."

Bowie plopped down and dropped his head into his hands, his elbows resting on his knees. "I hadn't watched the video before, Katie. I mean, I obviously saw what Sawyer slipped into the morning announcements, but I never saw you cry." He looked up, his tormented gaze locking onto hers. "I never saw you cry."

Katie grasped the significance of his repeated words immediately. She'd never allowed anyone to witness her tears—or at least she thought she hadn't. Evidently, one of Sawyer's goons was still filming that day in the janitor's closet.

Katie patted Bowie's shoulder. There wasn't anything to say. He had made her cry. Quite often, in fact.

"I can't get the sound out of my head," he said as he stared at the floor. Then he swallowed. Audibly. "Matt said you cried yourself to sleep. Every night."

Something clicked in her mind. The black eye. Matt speaking to Bowie. Her brothers. She should have realized. The video was public knowledge. The stupid thing had gone viral since it was linked to Bowie's pig-kissing video. Of course, her brothers had seen it, and she had a feeling they'd reacted as all idiot brothers would. Her

siblings could be every bit as devious and as cruel
as Bowie had been.

"Bowie," Katie said slowly, "where did you get
that black eye?"

"It's not important," he said. "I deserved it."

"Bowie," she repeated, even more deliberately
this time, "what did my brothers do to you?"

He glanced in her direction. "Nothing I wouldn't
have done to a guy who treated my daughter like shit."

"Exactly," she said. "That's what I'm concerned
about."

"Katie, I made your life hell for two and a half
years," Bowie said. "They're guys, and they love
you. It's what guys do."

She ran her hand through his soft hair. "Yes, but
you're my guy, and they hit you when you were
down."

Bowie shrugged. "I was sort of glad they did. It
was better for them to beat on me than for me to do
it myself."

Katie's heart fractured just a little at that statement. "Oh, Bowie."

"I can't help but think about what Josh said to
me. I am your villain, Katie."

She knew then what she had to do. If she wanted
any chance of a future with Bowie, she needed to open
herself up completely to him, and that started with
her art. There was risk, sure, but the reward could be
great. It was time to stop letting doubt hold her back.

"Bowie, there's something I need to show you."

Katie gave Bowie an uncharacteristically shy smile when she returned to the room a few minutes later, and he had another flashback to high school. She used to look at him like that back then. A strong memory of her standing by her locker as he came down the hall popped into his mind. They'd been fake-dating back then—or, at least, he had. He'd remembered thinking that no one had ever looked that happy to see him, not even Sawyer.

It hadn't been too long afterward that Sawyer had decided to move to the pig-kissing phase of their prank. In retrospect, Bowie wondered if Sawyer hadn't recognized that he'd begun to soften toward Katie, maybe even fall slightly for her. But Sawyer had been pretty and popular, and being with her meant that the whole school respected him. If he'd chosen Katie, he would have been relegated back to the drug addicts' son dating that weird redhead.

"Gosh, I'm nervous," Katie confessed as she dropped a spiral notebook onto Bowie's lap.

On the front cover, she had scrawled in thick marker, "Property of Katie Underwood." Bowie reached for it and then paused. "Is this from high school?"

She bit her lip and nodded. "I used to draw fantasy characters…princes and princesses. I had whole stories in my head. Some of the drawings are even from middle school. I'd doodle in my class notebooks, and when I came up with something really good, I redrew it here in ink."

"Did you show this to me in high school?" Bowie hoped that she hadn't, not after the dick way he'd treated her.

Katie shook her head and settled next to him. "Not this. It would have been too personal."

She reached over and flipped open a page. The first picture was of a girl with wild, red hair dressed in leather. Bowie stared at it, transfixed.

"I know." Katie sighed. "She looks like the girl from the Pixar movie."

"No, she doesn't," Bowie said. "She looks like you did back in high school."

"Probably because she is me," Katie said. "At least the fantasy version of me."

She flipped to the next page. Bowie found a mirror image of himself. Unlike Self Doubt from Katie's college newspaper, this version of him had a teenage boy's thinner body with some muscles, but not fully ripped. His jet-black hair obscured one gray eye. The smile on his face was warm and welcoming, unlike the sinister smirk of Self Doubt.

That wasn't the only difference. This figure wasn't clad in a swirling black cloak. He wore a leather doublet over a white linen shirt, breeches, and brown leather boots. A fur-trimmed green cape rested on his shoulders, and a thin, silver circlet perched on his head.

Bowie's throat tightened as he stared at the figure before him. *Ah, shit.*

"I was the prince in your stories, wasn't I?" Bowie asked needlessly.

Katie nodded. "Originally."

"Let me guess," he said. "I changed into the villain the night after the pig-kissing episode."

Katie nodded and flipped the page. Instead of a static character drawing, this showed the prince battling an older, gnarled wizard. From the prince's stance and position, he was clearly trying to protect a group of villagers and his own wounded guardsmen. The wizard was laughing as he shot lightning toward the villagers with one hand and what looked like a magical chain from the other. The prince's face was skillfully drawn as it simultaneously conveyed desperation and fear, yet also stalwart bravery. The young man was clearly choosing to use his sword to deflect the lightning away from the crowd, rather than protecting himself from the evil chain snaking toward his midsection.

The prince wasn't just a pretty boy. He was noble and self-sacrificing. More than that, his look of terror humanized him. For a high-school girl's fantasy, he wasn't a teen magazine pinup but a complex character. Bowie had no idea how he would have reacted to this drawing in high school, but it certainly humbled him now.

"Why?" he asked, ripping his eyes from the page to study her.

Katie's forehead furrowed. "I'm not sure I understand your question."

"Why did you make me the prince?" Bowie asked. Was it just his looks, or had she seen something in him? Something decent and maybe even a little noble.

Katie paused and then licked her lips. "It was right before middle school."

Before middle school? Had he known Katie back then? He supposed he must have. The town only had one elementary and one middle school. He hadn't paid too much attention to class or to his schoolmates. He'd spent most of the time staring outside, dreaming of leaving Sagebrush Flats behind.

"It was summer," Katie was saying. "I'd gone with my brothers to the park near our house."

"Yeah, I know it," Bowie said. He used to go there to make drug deliveries for his father.

"The twins were at the ball field, and the older two were playing a game of pickup football with their friends," Katie said. "I never had any interest in sports, so I did what I always did. I found a quiet spot under an elm and started sketching."

Bowie wished he could remember her sitting under that tree, her face scrunched up in concentration. His first memory of Katie was of her rushing to class, half doubled over under the weight of her enormous backpack. Sawyer had pointed her out as the "little dorky nobody" with a crush on him. He'd vaguely recalled seeing her around in the past, but that was the extent of his knowledge.

"There was a group of boys," Katie continued. "Some of them were in our grade, but a couple of them were one or two years older. One boy snatched my notebook. I lunged and tried to take it back, but he just laughed and tossed it to his friend. They then got the bright idea to play monkey-in-the-middle."

"I wish I could go back in time and beat them up for you," Bowie said.

Katie smiled. "You did stop them. You came pedaling up. You paused for a second and then jumped off your bicycle, letting it fall onto the grass. You sauntered up the hill, plucked the notebook out of the air during midtoss, handed it back to me, and got right back on your bike. I've had a crush on you ever since."

"I don't remember doing that," Bowie said.

"You did," Katie said. "In my eleven-year-old brain, that bicycle was a white steed."

Growing up, Bowie had generally stuck to himself. If someone messed with him, he fought back, but he didn't insert himself into conflict. Something about Katie vainly jumping for her book must have struck some chord inside him. Most likely, it had reminded him of the games his father and his drinking buddies had played on him. Plus, it was just wrong for a bunch of boys to pick on a girl, especially if some of them were a little older.

"I didn't do things like that a lot," he admitted. "I'm glad I did, though. I just wish I could have been that guy for you in high school."

Katie's smile grew wistful. "Part of me does too. But you know what? I think it worked out for the best. Enduring what I did gave me inner strength. Plus, if you'd chosen me over Sawyer—"

"I wouldn't have Abby," Bowie said. "I know. I've thought that myself."

Katie started to speak, stopped herself, and then plunged forward. "Do you ever wish…if it wasn't for your daughter…"

"That I would have picked you?" Bowie finished her question when her voice trailed off. "Hell, yes, if it wasn't for Abby. I needed someone like you in my life back then. I might have started paying more attention in school instead of putting my energy into stupid pranks. Honestly, I think part of me started to fall for you too."

Katie straightened with interest. When she spoke, her voice was higher than usual.

"Really?"

Bowie smiled at her uncharacteristic squeak. She sounded like her teenage self. "I liked talking to you. A lot. You weren't like everybody else. You didn't treat me like I was stupid. You talked about everything—history, science, art—without dumbing anything down. It wasn't until Lou and Gretchen that anyone else acted like I had a brain in my head."

"Everyone else was an idiot," Katie said indignantly. "Any fool could see how intelligent you were, even back then. You might have been a smart aleck when teachers called on you, but you gave the best sarcastic responses. Your retorts were rude, but they were also clever."

"The principal didn't think so."

Katie laughed. "You still shouldn't have said them, no matter how witty they were. And then there were your pranks. They were diabolical, sure, but carefully planned and well executed. Sawyer and her friends weren't smart enough to pull them off on their own. I always knew you were the mastermind."

Bowie pulled her close. "There was another reason I started to fall for you back then. You had this amazing passion. I'd never met anyone who could focus on something like you can. And you were nice. To me. To others. I think Sawyer realized it. That's why she upped the timing of the pig-kissing. I was supposed to string you along for a couple more weeks."

Katie swallowed. "Did you ever regret it? I mean, back then? I know you do now."

"Yeah," Bowie said. "Honestly, Sawyer didn't

give me much time to think about it. I'd laid out the entire scheme to her and her friends when she first mentioned you. You and I hadn't even talked at that point. Since I had all the details worked out, her friends were able to get everything ready, including the pig. So when Sawyer told me everything was set up, I agreed. I felt awful afterward. I even left a note in Sawyer's locker to tell her not to run the video on the morning announcements. She claimed she didn't get the message in time, but I have my doubts now. Anyway, after it ran, you already hated me, and Sawyer's friends treated me like I was the king of the school. You know the rest."

"It was horrible," Katie said. "I'm not telling this to accuse you, but it's why I pushed you away...why I pushed men away. I'd built up this whole fantasy of you. I never thought it would come true, but when you asked me out, I experienced this whole torrent of emotions. It was so exciting, so amazing that part of me wanted to keep that joy to myself and cherish it before I told anyone. I didn't even let my mom know about us."

Bowie didn't speak. He knew this was going to be hard for him to hear, but he needed to listen. Katie deserved to tell her story, and until she did, it would always fester between them.

"I daydreamed constantly about our first kiss," she continued. "I thought it would be magical, like in the movies. I'd spin story after story. Then, it happened... or rather it didn't. This one moment I'd been dreaming about since I was eleven, and then it was with a pig."

Bowie shifted uncomfortably. He stroked his hand over Katie's soft curls. He didn't know if it was to soothe him or her. Probably both.

"I think I would have gotten over that…if it had ended there," Katie said as she stared into the living room. "Then there was the morning announcement, my journal being read aloud, the Little Orphan Annie wigs. It just didn't stop."

"You know, I'd go back in time and beat myself up if I could," Bowie told her truthfully. He wanted to punch the little punk who'd put her through all this.

Katie flashed him a weak smile. "I'd almost let you, but it wouldn't solve anything. That's why I didn't tell my brothers. Plus, I was embarrassed. The whole school was making fun of me. Even my few friends stopped hanging out with me. They didn't turn on me, but they weren't popular either and didn't want to get caught in the crossfire."

Ah, shit. Bowie hadn't known that. Guilt sliced at him. He hated that he'd done that to her. He understood social isolation, and it destroyed him that he'd brought it on Katie.

"I didn't realize," he said. "I never thought about that. I should have, but I didn't."

Katie shrugged. "I survived. It wasn't fun, but I had my family and my drawings. Honestly, it made me a more prolific and better artist. Plus, college was great. June forced me to be social, and I had plenty of friends. Everything worked out in the end."

Bowie squeezed her and pressed a kiss against her temple. "I'm glad you met June and Josh too. He and I might have had our issues, but he's a good friend to you. Both of them are."

Katie leaned her head against Bowie's shoulder. She was silent for a moment, and he was wondering what she was thinking. He leaned over and gently pressed another kiss on her forehead.

She wiggled her body so that she could watch him. "Something has been bothering me about your parents. Do you mind if I ask a question?"

Bowie brushed his lips against Katie's. He hated talking about his mom and dad, but he again sensed that she needed this. Part of him even felt warmed that she wanted to know more, that she worried about him. It was still a novel thing for him, and he kind of liked it.

"What do you want to know?"

Katie inhaled and then asked in a rush, "Did your parents... Did they abuse you? Physically, I mean."

Bowie shook his head. "Not much. It was mainly verbal. I mean, if I bothered them at the wrong time, especially if they were on something strong, they'd give me a smack or two. I guess my dad did more than my mom, but I learned pretty quickly when to lie low."

Tears glistened in Katie's eyes. Bowie brushed them away with his thumb. "Hey, now. None of that. I'm okay. That all happened a long time ago."

"What about your foster parents? Did they?"

Bowie shook his head. "They ignored me for the most part."

"Even the rancher? The one who kicked you out after you broke your leg?"

"I lived in the bunkhouse with the other ranch hands. They weren't too bad a group of guys. Some of them were drifters. A couple of old-timers. Quite a few migrant workers. I was a lot younger, so I wasn't real close to them, but they didn't bother me either."

"It sounds lonely," Katie said.

"It was," Bowie admitted.

She snuggled against him. "It makes even more sense now."

"What does?"

"Why you treated me the way you did in high school. You weren't being mean, not really. You were just desperately trying to fit in."

Bowie brushed a strand of hair from her forehead. "I wish I'd done it in a different way."

Katie smiled back at him. "So do I, but at least now I get why you did it. I wish you'd told me about your home life back then. I would have made you understand that you mattered and that you didn't need Sawyer or any of her idiot friends to make you important."

A rush of emotion charged through Bowie. He crushed Katie to him, his mouth pressing against hers. The kiss deepened. When they broke apart, she smiled, rose from the couch, and tugged on his hand. As much as he wanted to follow her to the bedroom, he shook his head. Now that he'd resolved things with Katie, he had to get back to Abby. His baby girl was hurting, and he should be with her, even if he didn't know how to help.

"I can't. Abby's pretty upset."

───∿∿───

Thoughts of sex gone, Katie's heart seemed to flip over in her chest. "Abby saw the video."

Bowie nodded. "She's feeling betrayed. She..." His voice broke. This time, it took him a second to collect himself. "Katie, she wouldn't even let me call her Abby Bear."

Once again, agony swamped Bowie's voice. Katie's heart wrenched at the pain he and his daughter must be feeling. Abby was smart enough to realize that Bowie and Sawyer had been Katie's unnamed tormentors. Since Abby was bullied too, she would project herself into the situation as Katie. Worse, Katie doubted that Bowie had told his daughter much about his past, so the preteen would have no explanation for how her loving father could have acted so deplorably.

"I'm so sorry, Bowie," Katie said. "I know how hard this must be."

"She's locked herself in her room," he said as he turned to Katie. "What am I supposed to do? I don't know what to say. I don't know how I am going to fix this."

"I do. I'll talk to her."

Relief swept over Bowie's face for the second time that evening. "You will?"

Katie nodded. "She's just hurt right now, Bowie. She's probably scared that we're going to break up and that I'll disappear from her life forever. Once I talk to her, she'll come around. Everything is going to be fine, including us."

"Did I tell you that I love you?" Bowie asked.

Katie smiled. "Many times, and we still need to mark the occasion, but first, let's get this resolved."

He nodded, and they headed out to his truck. As Katie walked to the passenger side, she noticed the broken taillight. "Matt?"

Bowie shook his head. "Mike. With his nightstick."

She whirled around. Destruction of property was

more Matt's thing. Mike was generally the calmer of the twins. "He didn't arrest you on trumped-up charges, did he?"

Bowie grinned. "No, but in retrospect, he probably just wanted to give your other brothers a chance to exact their revenge. He was the first, and he confused the hell out of me. I hadn't seen the video yet."

Katie climbed into the truck, shaking her head. "The four of them will be the death of me."

Bowie shrugged. "Just be glad you've got 'em."

Thinking about his childhood, Katie conceded his point. As much as her brothers bugged her, she loved each of them deeply.

She was trying to focus on that thought when she and Bowie heard a siren about ten minutes later. He sighed as he pulled over and placed the truck in park. "Round two."

There was not going to be a round two. Katie would see to that.

Mike sauntered over, all male bravado. Katie was not amused or impressed. Her baby brother didn't know it yet, but he was going to walk away from this encounter with a bit of his hide missing. Bowie might be okay with her siblings' treatment of him, but she was not.

"What did I tell you about the taillight and the decals?" Mike barked, clearly not spotting Katie.

Before Bowie could speak, Katie leaned around him. "Michael Harris Underwood, you broke that taillight!"

Mike looked surprised and not at all happy to

see her in Bowie's truck. "What are you doing with this creep after what he did?"

"Don't be an idiot. That was over ten years ago. Do you think I'd be with a guy who still acted that way? Stop insulting my intelligence."

Mike's mouth set in a hard line. "He's no good for you."

"Oh, for pity's sake, he probably saved my life, and he got shot doing so," Katie pointed out.

Mike crossed his arms, but before he could speak, Katie did. "Mike, we don't have time for this foolishness."

"Yeah, what's the emergency?" Mike asked, clearly unimpressed.

"Abby saw the video. Since she's been teased herself, she didn't take it well. She's locked herself in her bedroom, and she's very upset."

Mike's entire demeanor changed. "Shit, I didn't think of Abby. This has to be rough on her. That other girl in the video is her birth mother, right?"

Katie nodded. "So, if you would excuse us, we'd like to get going."

Mike took a step back, but before he moved any further, he fixed Bowie with a death glare. "Hurt Katie again, and it won't be a taillight that I smash."

"I'm not going to hurt her, Mike," Bowie said. "I happen to love her." With that, he put the truck into drive and pulled away, not even waiting for Mike's reaction.

Katie laughed. "You know, I think you're going to handle my four brothers beautifully."

"You think they'll get over this?"

"Oh yes." She nodded. "It might take time, but they'll come around. They really do like you."

"What about your mom and dad?" Bowie asked.

"I'll probably have to tell my mom a little about your past, if you don't mind. Once she knows your history, she'll be fine. I have a feeling my dad knows some of it, and that's the reason you're not bleeding more. He's worse than all four brothers combined. If you haven't heard from him, then you're good."

"That's a relief," Bowie said as they pulled into the driveway of the Victorian. When they entered the house, they stopped to see Lou first.

"Abby?" Bowie asked when they entered the living room.

"Still up in her room," Lou said. "I told her that you were gone and dinner was ready, but she thought I was trying to trick her into speaking with you."

Bowie's expression turned even grimmer. He was worried. Katie could tell. She wasn't.

He and Abby shared a strong bond, and this wasn't going to break it. Without her running interference, Bowie and his daughter would have gone through a rough patch, but their relationship would have eventually healed.

Katie walked over to Lou and bent to give him a kiss on the cheek. "Hey, Lou."

He smiled at her. "I knew you'd be level-headed about this nonsense. You and Bowie are good?"

Katie nodded. "We're more than good. We confessed that we love each other."

Lou straightened in his chair, clearly interested. "Is that so?"

"Yep. It was on the phone yesterday," Katie said.

Lou swung a mock-accusing gaze toward Bowie. "You didn't tell me."

Bowie held his hands up in surrender. "A gentleman never kisses and tells."

Lou *hrmph*ed, but Katie knew he was thrilled. He'd wanted Bowie and her together from the beginning.

"Well," she said, "I have a little girl upstairs who needs to be comforted."

"Should I come?" Bowie asked.

Katie nodded. "Yes. This is between the three of us."

When she knocked on the door, she heard Abby's watery voice. "Go. Away."

Bowie visibly flinched. Katie reached out and brushed his arm. Right now, she wanted to wring Sawyer's neck. The woman had hurt her own daughter in an effort to attack Bowie and Katie.

"Abby, honey," Katie said. "It's me."

"Katie?" Abby's voice sounded surprised and more than a bit relieved.

"Yep. Can you let me in?"

The door flew open. An angry Abby stood before them. When she spotted Bowie, her scowl deepened. "What is *he* doing here?"

Katie ignored the question. "Can we come in?"

Abby crossed her arms and glared at her father. "You can. *He* cannot."

Bowie, to his credit, stayed silent.

"Abby, how much do you know about your father's childhood?" Katie asked.

That caused Abby to drop her rebellious stance as a look of curiosity spread across her pixie features. Bowie shifted from one foot to the other, clearly agitated now.

"Katie—" He began to warn, his voice deep.

"Bowie, it's important," she said.

"What's important?" Abby asked, wide-eyed, her head swiveling back and forth between them.

"It's you or your parents." Katie addressed Bowie.

Understanding lit across his face. He clearly realized she meant that either he or Abby's grandparents would be destroyed in his daughter's eyes.

"I'm not sure," he said.

"About what?" Abby asked.

"Trust me, Bowie," Katie said.

His gaze held hers, and finally, he nodded. A rush of responsibility swept through Katie as it dawned on her that Bowie had just shared a parenting decision with her. She sucked in her breath as she prepared to talk to Abby.

"What do you know about your grandparents?" Katie asked. "Your father's parents?"

"They died when Dad was a little older than me," Abby said. "Then I guess Lou and Gretchen took care of him. Dad never talks about it."

That surprised Katie. It made sense that Bowie wanted to shield Abby from the fact that her grandparents were drug addicts and criminals. His foster-kid past, though, was different. It wasn't a shameful family secret—just in Bowie's case, a sad one.

He clearly didn't view it that way. The hurt from his childhood permeated deeper than Katie had realized. She didn't know if he refrained from telling his daughter over a hidden fear of rejection or a desire to not seem vulnerable.

Bowie couldn't miss Katie's surprise that Abby didn't know he'd been in foster care. He probably should have told Abby—maybe not when she was little, but she was mature enough now. But he hadn't mentioned it. He supposed he worried that Abby would look at him differently. His daughter saw him as strong, competent, and capable of fixing any problem. He hated telling her that he'd once been the boy nobody wanted.

"I was a foster kid," Bowie said, his voice rough. "I didn't meet Lou and Gretchen until right before you were born."

That grabbed Abby's attention. For the first time since she'd opened the door, she looked fully at Bowie, her eyes not full of venom. "You were?"

He nodded, and some of the mutiny left his daughter's face. Katie seized the opportunity. "Abby, if you let us into your room, we can tell you the story."

Abby hesitated, but Bowie thought it was more a point of pride than anything. She stepped back and allowed them to enter. Abby plopped on the floor, and he and Katie followed suit.

"Why didn't you tell me?" Abby asked Bowie.

He barely prevented a sigh. Was Katie's plan going to backfire? It sounded as if Abby might feel even more betrayed, and it still felt odd to concede a major parenting decision to another person.

But Katie loved Abby. Bowie didn't doubt that for a moment. If he wanted to make Katie a permanent member of the family, he would have to learn to co-parent. Plus, he had no idea how to smooth this over with his daughter, and Katie seemed to understand Abby.

"It's not easy for your dad to tell," Katie said,

her voice soft, "but he didn't have the best childhood."

A flare of concern replaced the recalcitrance on Abby's face as she flashed him a questioning look. Bowie nodded in confirmation.

"What does that mean?" Abby asked.

"His parents were drug addicts." Katie maintained a gentle tone, but Bowie forced himself not to wince at her otherwise blunt statement.

"What?" Abby asked in disbelief. Her incredulity only grew when Katie briefly recounted a sanitized version of his parents' deaths.

When she finished, Abby studied him as closely as she did a particularly challenging section in one of her science books. Bowie could practically see her absorb and process the new information, arranging it in her mind. As his daughter reevaluated him, he waited, his heart pounding, striking a faster beat every second.

"Did…" Abby paused, took a breath, and then asked in a tumble of words, "Did they hurt you?"

Bowie went to shake his head, but he stopped himself. Abby needed the truth. "There wasn't much physical abuse. They mostly ignored me."

Katie's hand closed over Bowie's knee, but she regarded his daughter. "They were unkind in other ways. The taunts that we faced from the kids at school… Bowie had to hear from his parents and then his foster parents."

Tears filled Abby's eyes. "You did?"

Bowie nodded. He'd never thought of it in quite those terms. It touched him that Katie had.

Abby flew at him. Bowie caught his daughter in his arms as she slammed against him and buried her face in his chest. Relief flooding him, he enfolded her in an embrace. He knew this hug. Since Abby had begun to walk, she'd run to him whenever she needed comfort and love. The gesture was full of faith. She still trusted him to hold the world at bay.

"I'm sorry, Dad," Abby said.

Bowie didn't know if she meant for his childhood or her anger. It didn't matter. "I am too, Abby Bear," Bowie said.

Abby pulled back slightly, her face wet with tears. "Why did you do it? Why did you treat Katie like that?"

It was Katie who answered—or rather who responded with her own question. "Abby, when you were little, who told you when to say 'please' and 'thank you'?"

Abby swiped at her face. Looking a little confused, she shifted slightly away from Bowie to face Katie. "Dad. Why?"

Katie didn't answer Abby's question. "And who showed you how not to be a poor loser?"

"Dad?" Abby asked, still befuddled.

"And who taught you how to care for animals and show respect to Lou and Gretchen?"

"Dad," Abby said, her tone slightly annoyed now. Katie ignored that.

"And when the kids picked on you at school, who comforted you?"

"Dad," Abby said. "Is there a reason you're asking me all this? Dad's the one who taught me everything."

"But who taught your dad?" Katie asked, her tone very light.

That caused Abby to pause. She wrinkled her nose. Then her mouth formed an O as she finally realized Katie's point. "He didn't really have a mom or dad, did he?"

"No," Katie said, letting that sink in.

"I didn't know that," Abby said sadly.

Katie reached forward and brushed back a lock of Abby's hair. "I didn't know either, sweetheart, not until late this summer."

Abby turned toward Bowie. "Did you play pranks 'cause your parents were mean, and you didn't know better?"

Bowie sighed, wishing it were that simple. "I knew it was wrong, Abby."

"Then why did you do it?"

"He was lonely," Katie said before Bowie could answer. "When the kids made fun of him because of his parents, he didn't have anyone to come home to like we did. He didn't have a family. Then a popular girl at school liked him. He suddenly had friends. He was in the in crowd, but in order to stay in, he had to impress them by playing jokes on me."

"Oh," said Abby.

"That's why I've told you not to bend to peer pressure," Bowie said. "I did. I've regretted it ever since, even before Katie came back into my life. I don't want you to live with that guilt, and more important, it's not right."

Abby regarded him solemnly. "But nobody told you that."

Bowie shook his head. "No, Abby Bear, nobody told me that."

Katie touched Bowie's arm and squeezed it gently. "Abby, you asked me what I was doing here with your father. I forgave him for what happened in high school. Yes, it was wrong. Yes, he never should have done it. Yes, what he did to me in the past was not inconsequential. But he was a kid, Abby, and he did stupid things and got in over his head. No one was there to pull him back, but he managed that on his own. That shows your dad's true character. How he raised you, the values he chose to instill in you, the way he cares for you—that shows who your dad is, not the foolish actions of a lonely boy. Everything you thought and believed about your father is true and is the real him."

Bowie couldn't help it. He teared up. Honestly, if Abby hadn't been in the room, he might have lost it. Emotions had slammed into him again and again like a relentless battering ram ever since Mike had first pulled him over. He felt pulverized. Katie's words swept over his emotional wounds, bringing a cool, soothing relief but also a joy so sharp and powerful, it almost sliced him open anew.

Katie really did forgive him. She understood his motivation, maybe even more than he did himself. She hadn't just shoved his past mistakes into some small corner of her mind where the memories could unexpectedly burst forth and taint their relationship. She accepted his cruel tricks as part of his past, part of the ugliness of his childhood, and she still loved him. It was apparent in how she described him to his daughter.

Lou and Gretchen had always supported Bowie, always praised him. It had taken a long time for Bowie to feel completely comfortable with that. Sometimes,

Lou's affection still surprised him, but he no longer doubted it.

And Abby? Well, Abby had always loved him with the sweetness and completeness that only a child could manage.

But Katie's love...

It undid him—and, at the same time, healed him.

"I love you, Dad," Abby said, squeezing him tightly, tears streaming freely down her face. He pressed her against him, unable to say more. If he tried to force anything through his larynx, he was afraid a sob would come out instead of words.

Katie glanced back and forth between the two of them. They must have looked like a watery mess. She plastered on a bright smile and slapped her hands against her thighs. "You know, I think this calls for ice cream. That's what my mom always gave us after a day like this. Bowie, do you have any in the freezer?"

He nodded. He could talk about ice cream. "Moose Tracks."

Katie nodded and scrambled to her feet. "Let's all move downstairs so Lou can join us. In fact, let's have an ice cream picnic in the zoo."

A short time later, they were sitting on the benches outside the permanent cougar enclosure. Fleur crouched behind a clump of newly planted sagebrush, her tawny black-tipped ears just visible above the silvery-green plant. Tonks sat on one of the rocks, using the shadow of the larger boulder to camouflage herself. Below, Dobby drank from his water dish, seemingly oblivious to his sisters' whereabouts. Fleur jumped first and then Tonks. Dobby, the little sneak, was ready for both of them when they landed.

Abby giggled beside Bowie as the trio tussled. The kits had grown even lankier as they edged toward adulthood. Their spots had all but disappeared. But much to the delight of the zoo visitors, the little pumas had grown even more playful as they tested their jumping, pouncing, and stalking abilities. Bowie could spend hours watching the mountain lions explore their world, not that he normally had the time.

The cougars weren't the only zoo residents joining their celebration. On their way from the house, they'd run into Fluffy lurking near Frida's enclosure. Instead of having Abby catch him, Bowie had told her to run to the zoo office and grab some honey-covered larvae. The rascal was happily munching the treat under the shade of the bench.

"This was a perfect idea," Bowie told Katie as he dug into his sundae. They'd heated hot fudge in the microwave and found some cherries in the back of the refrigerator.

"Mmm-hmmm," she said between mouthfuls of ice cream.

"So Bowie mentioned that you got a job offer out in California," Lou said.

Bowie froze at the statement. Some of his joy slipped away. He wanted to look at Katie's face. Study her. See her reaction. But he was afraid his own expression would give too much away. He and Katie might have confessed their love for each other, but they hadn't discussed the future. As much as Bowie wanted to ask Katie to marry him, he also didn't want to be the reason that she gave up her dream.

Katie swallowed the ice cream she was eating and then nodded. "Yep, I did get a job offer, but I decided on the plane ride that I'm going to turn it down."

Bowie jerked his head up at her response. He found Katie looking at him, her gaze warm and welcoming. When she spoke, she addressed him before turning to Lou. "I like running my own business, and Sagebrush has become home again. I missed all of you when I was away."

Bowie's heart took off like a cheetah after an antelope. Katie was staying in Sagebrush for good. Beside him, Abby perked up as well.

"You missed us?" she asked, glancing speculatively at Bowie and Katie.

"Of course," Katie said. "I bought you souvenirs, but you'll have to wait until tomorrow. I left them at my place."

"Does this feel like home?" Abby asked, pointing downward with her spoon to indicate the zoo rather than Sagebrush at large. As if to echo Abby's question, Tonks emitted a loud squeak as she pounced on her sister.

"Abby…" Bowie warned, worried about this line of inquiry.

She uncharacteristically ignored him and plowed ahead. "Does it?"

"Abby," Bowie said more sharply. "Katie's had a long trip, and she doesn't want to play Twenty Questions."

"But since she's forgiven you, and if this feels like home, then you can ask Katie to—"

To Bowie's surprise, it was Lou who stopped Abby from blurting out the m-word.

"Abby, that's enough," he said.

Wide-eyed, Katie glanced at all three of them. "What is going on?"

Abby was more than happy to enlighten her. "I think you and Dad should—"

Bowie jumped up from his seat on the bench. The movement was so sudden that even the pumas stopped playing to stare at him. He didn't stop to think or worry. He simply dropped to one knee and pulled out Gretchen's engagement ring.

Katie's spoon fell to the gravel. Abby squealed. Lou remained respectfully silent, but his eyes twinkled. The cubs moved to the fence. They sat in a perfect row, watching the proceedings as their tails gently swished behind them.

For a moment, Bowie froze. He might have been even more surprised than Katie as he held the ring out to her. He'd wanted to engineer a unique YouTube-worthy proposal, but when Abby almost blurted out the word *marry*, he'd just reacted. He didn't want his daughter to beat him to the question.

Then the words came. "Katie Underwood, would you do me the honor of marrying me?"

―⁓―

Katie stared at the ring in dumbfounded surprise. This time, it wasn't the high-school girl squealing inside her; it was the woman. Until Bowie had dropped to his knee, Katie hadn't realized how much she'd wanted marriage—at least marriage to him. It was right. This was what she had been missing during her trip to the West Coast. Home. Bowie was home. So were Abby, Lou, Katie's family, and even the zoo.

But Bowie was central.

He was hers, and she was his. They fit. Not in some teenage girl's fantasy. Maybe not even on paper.

But in life. They fit. Perfectly.

"Yes." Katie's answer came out as a squeak but an audible one.

At her response, a wide, bright smile instantly smoothed Bowie's increasingly anxious expression. Almost from a distance, Katie heard Abby's happy shriek. Then Katie was swept off the bench and into Bowie's arms. They were both laughing as he spun her around. Still holding her, he pressed his lips against hers in a kiss of pure joy.

When Bowie set Katie down, Abby immediately launched herself in Katie's direction. The girl almost barreled her over, but Katie managed to keep them upright. Glancing over Abby's shoulder, she spotted Lou clapping Bowie on the shoulder. Behind them, the cubs had resumed their play, their pounces even more exuberant than usual. Katie swore the honey badger even smiled at her. When Katie caught Bowie's gaze, she saw her own joy reflected there.

"I didn't think it was possible, but you look even sexier as an archaeologist than as a pirate," Katie said as she reached up to tug playfully on

Bowie's fedora. They had just finished filming a video to announce Lulubelle's pregnancy, and Bowie had dressed like Indiana Jones. Beside him, Lulubelle heaved a huge, besotted sigh.

Bowie chuckled as he patted the camel's neck. "I appreciate the compliment, Lulubelle, but you don't want to make Hank jealous."

The camel turned her liquid-brown eyes in the direction of her mate, who made a rumbling sound in his throat. With another laugh, Bowie led the duo back to the llama pen. The herd looked up briefly at their entrance and then returned to chewing. Bowie shut the double gate and extended his hand to Katie. She took it and positioned their entwined fingers so that Gretchen's ring glinted in the sunlight. Bowie watched with a smile as she gazed down at it.

"I can't believe we're engaged," Katie said. She had repeated the same statement multiple times since his proposal yesterday, but Bowie didn't care. He loved hearing the wonder in her voice.

"Me neither," he told her.

"The ring is beautiful," Katie said as she stretched out their hands to admire it. "It's so special knowing it was Gretchen's."

"You would have liked each other," Bowie said.

Katie pressed her body against his as they walked. Resting her head on his shoulder, she tilted her chin in his direction. He glanced down, and the love on her face transfixed him. He stopped walking and gently brushed back her hair.

Her lips formed a soft, sexy smile that swept through Bowie like a warm tropical breeze. "You know," Katie said slowly as she played at the lapel of his shirt, "it's after closing time, and my mom is watching Abby."

They'd stopped by her parents' ranch after their ice cream picnic yesterday to announce their engagement. If either of her parents had watched the video, they hadn't mentioned it. Instead, her mother had beamed and enveloped Bowie in a hug. Even her father seemed pleased—or at least he didn't seem upset. Bowie still couldn't read the man, but Katie said he was happy.

Katie's mom had offered to watch Abby this evening. Although Abby made some sounds of protest, Katie's mom told her that the two adults needed time alone to plan for the wedding. Since it was Friday, Katie's mom promised Abby that the two of them could stay up late watching a marathon of preteen movies.

"What do you have in mind?" Bowie asked as he dipped his head so his lips hovered mere inches from hers.

Katie's grin turned wicked. "Well, you know what these costumes do to me."

Bowie snaked his arms about her midsection. "I might have an idea."

They kissed then. It was hot and sweet at the same time, and the fire it created blazed through Bowie. Katie broke off the embrace and, with a laugh, grabbed his fedora and stuck it on her head. She looked adorable, and he reached for her again. But she slipped away and took off at a run toward the animal hospital. This was one chase Bowie didn't mind having. Letting her lead, he followed her straight to the air mattress.

She stood in the small room with a satisfied look on her face that was similar to Fluffy's when the honey badger spied a treat. Bowie's heart squeezed. He reached for her red hair, letting the soft locks slide through his fingers. She was beautiful, his Katie.

She reached up and gently undid his shirt. She took her time removing the fabric, and the heat threatened to turn him into an inferno. When she pressed her lips against his exposed skin, his eyes fluttered closed as he cupped the back of her head. She explored his body as if discovering it for the first time. His shirt dropped to the floor. He tugged at hers, and she pulled back to let him remove it. He kissed her then, long, sweet, and deep. They fell on the bed together, a tangle of limbs.

Despite the fire burning inside him, Bowie kept the pace slow, and so did she. This was a moment to savor, a slow, delicious glide into oblivion. With no more barriers between them, their lovemaking had deepened. It contained an emotional element that slipped inside Bowie and filled him with a sense of belonging he'd never felt before. When they joined, it was a completion that went beyond the physical. His release shuddered through him, cracking through his old doubts and fears and leaving him utterly replete. He rolled their bodies so they lay side by side, still pressed against each other. Katie snuggled close, her hand lightly stroking his back.

"It's never been like that for me."

He pressed a kiss against her temple. "Me neither."

"I love you," Katie said.

"I love you too." Bowie leaned over and captured her

mouth with his. As they sank into each other again, affection swelled inside him, almost undoing him. It was overwhelming, this need for Katie, yet also so comforting, so perfect, so *right*.

She propped herself on one elbow. "You know what, Bowie Wilson? I think we've started something special."

He brushed a tendril of red hair from her face, his heart full of affection. "I think so too."

—◆—

Fluffy did not leave his enclosure that night. He was staying in. He'd earned at least one night off from patrolling the zoo. After all, he'd chased away not one but two snakes. He'd even hurt his paw twice in the process.

And he'd succeeded in his long-term plan. He just knew it. It wouldn't be long until more wee ones were running about the zoo giving him well-deserved honeyed treats.

Epilogue

NOT TOO MANY WEDDINGS FEATURE A CAPYBARA AS A FLOWER girl or a cockatoo as a ring bearer, Bowie thought while the rodent picked her way down the aisle with the parrot riding on her back. But their inclusion in the ceremony suited Katie and him perfectly. Watching the bird bob her head along to the "Wedding March" as Sylvia ambled down the white runner calmed Bowie's nerves. They'd practiced this part of the ceremony for weeks. One of the hardest parts had been finding a pillow to attach to Sylvia's back that had a compartment for the rings that Rosie couldn't open.

He and Katie had chosen to get married in front of Fleur's and Tonks's enclosure. Dobby had been relocated about a month ago to a well-regarded zoo on the East Coast. His new keeper kept Bowie updated on the puma's progress. He was settling into his new home just fine and was getting along with the female. Once Dobby reached sexual maturity, the new zoo hoped to breed more cubs, since the two were a good genetic match.

Fleur's and Tonks's exhibit was on the edge of the Sagebrush Zoo, which provided plenty of space to set up chairs for the ceremony. Bowie and Katie's brothers had installed poles and hung netting in case Rosie chose to fly off. For the reception, they'd set up tables throughout the zoo. In addition to food for the human guests, all the zoo residents were getting special treats. Frida, in

particular, would be presented with an elaborate,
tiered ice treat that mirrored a wedding cake. The
whole town had turned out. The local news crew
had wanted to attend too, but Katie and Bowie had
promised to send the station a video instead. They'd
been receiving well wishes from around the world,
which had only increased Bowie's nervousness.

Sylvia trotted over to Katie's brother Mike, just
as they'd practiced. Mike bent over to give both
animals a treat. He carefully placed Rosie in a white
cage, and Sylvia dutifully plunked down beside
him, sitting proudly on her haunches. She stuck her
head in the air, looking as noble as a kidney-shaped
animal could. Bowie couldn't help the grin that
spread across his face. He swore the old girl knew
how important this event was.

Abby came down the aisle next, beaming from
ear to ear, with June following her. At the sight
of his daughter in her junior bridesmaid dress,
Bowie's eyes misted. She looked so grown up with
her gown and upswept hairdo.

Abby had already taken to calling Katie "Mom."
Katie's brother Luke had drawn up paperwork so
Katie could legally become Abby's mother after
the wedding. It pleased Bowie how easily Katie
had become part of Abby's life. He often found the
two of them giggling about something or watching
girlie movies. He never knew when he'd stumble
upon June either. At least Josh let Bowie know
when he was dropping by. He was the only one,
since Katie's family also popped in at random.

Not that Bowie minded. He liked being part of

a big family, especially since Katie's brothers were no longer gunning for him. For about a week after Sawyer posted the pig-kissing video, Katie's brothers had given Bowie a hard time. Fed up, Katie had called a family meeting. With Bowie's permission, she'd explained his family history. To Bowie's surprise, Katie's father had also come to his defense.

"Boys, you all did dumb-ass things as teenagers—a lot of them to your sister. A lot of kids with Bowie's background end up addicted to drugs, in jail, or dead. Probably all three. Bowie didn't, and I give him credit for making something of himself. He's a decent father, a good son to Lou, and a successful businessman. Your sister picked him, and your mother and I have no objections. Cease yours. That's an order."

The brothers had grumbled, but they'd relented. Personally, Bowie thought they were having too much fun making his life miserable. They evidently had a diabolical streak as wide as his. Heaven help the guy who messed with any Underwood or Wilson female, since that guy would have the five of them to contend with.

Thoughts of Katie's family fled as the woman herself appeared. Riding Hank. Lulubelle trotted behind on a lead rope. She was about two-thirds of the way through her long pregnancy and was doing well. The awkward duo practically pranced down the aisle. Both camels wore beautiful, hand-embroidered covers on their humps that June and Josh had specially ordered from the Middle East. However, Lulubelle's goofy, grinning face prevented the animal from appearing too regal.

Katie, on the other hand, looked like a princess or a queen. She rode sidesaddle with surprising ease, her train draped over one of Hank's flanks. Although Bowie had taught Katie how to ride, he hadn't seen her in her wedding dress. She'd never looked more beautiful. She'd forgone both a veil and a tiara, choosing instead to stud her hair with white roses.

But it was Katie's smile that truly arrested Bowie. The joy there reflected the happiness filling his heart. And there was peace in her expression. A comfort and a certainty that this was right. She'd turned down that impressive job offer and never looked back. Her freelance business was going strong. Her interview blitz on the West Coast had earned her several loyal clients, and after the videos went viral, she'd also gotten work from other animal parks and rescue centers looking to improve their outreach.

The Sagebrush Zoo was doing great. Their list of volunteers had swelled, and Bowie had funds to hire more staff. That had freed up his schedule enough for him to enroll in online classes. It would take time, but he was working toward a degree in zoology. They'd also received the grant money for the polar bears and were in the process of getting ready for the arrival of a cub or two.

Bowie stepped forward to help Katie dismount. She did so flawlessly. June stepped forward to hold Hank's reins. As Bowie and Katie joined hands in front of the minister, Fleur and Tonks chose that moment to peek over the boulders, which were framed by the tent of netting. The crowd gasped and then clapped with delight. Even the noise did not scare the cats away. They stared down as if wanting to watch what they had unwittingly set in motion.

And there at the edge of his zoo, Bowie Wilson married Katie Underwood, the woman who'd crashed back into his life and permanently stolen his heart.

———~~~———

Fluffy did not attend the wedding. He had more important matters to address. More important even than exploring the multitiered cake he'd spied being wheeled past his enclosure.

No, Fluffy had to deal with *her*. The interloper.

The object of his frustration stared at him. Smugly. He growled. She preened.

Fluffy did *not* like Honey—which, by the way, was a ridiculous name for a honey badger. It lacked all creativity, even for the bipeds.

Honey, however, did not appear to notice the silliness of her epithet. She was too busy getting all the treats and the Wee One's attention.

Worse, Honey thought she was cleverer than Fluffy. Up until now, he'd scoffed at the notion. But she'd performed the impossible last night.

She'd found and managed to pry open the treat cabinet—something that had eluded Fluffy for years. And she'd eaten every last honey-covered morsel. Without sharing.

This. This was war. And Fluffy fully intended to win.

Sweet Wild of Mine

"You must be new to Sagebrush Flats."

Magnus Gray reluctantly turned in the direction
of the friendly Southern drawl. The speaker matched
the rich, sexy voice. Blond. Willowy. Tall. Bonny
green eyes. Pink lips curved into a welcoming smile.

Magnus didn't trust the woman's grin, but at
least he didn't grimace in response. He chose,
instead, a neutral expression—not surly enough to
be rude, but not pleasant enough to invite further
conversation. Unfortunately, the lass didn't register
the subtlety.

Typical American.

Instead, she slid into the booth across from him.
This time Magnus didn't stop his frown. In fact, he
growled under his breath. He didn't want to chat
with the dafty woman. Couldn't she see his open
laptop?

"I'm June Winters." The woman beamed like the
desert sun.

He grunted. Under the best of circumstances, he
hated introducing himself. Even after years of practice, he always stuttered on the letter *M* in his name.

And this? This was *not* a good circumstance.

"You don't need to be a stranger, you hear?

You're welcome to join the celebration. The more the merrier!" The woman still smiled. Even for a Yank, she was a damn Cheshire cat. Without breaking eye contact, the lass waved her hand in the direction of a group of rowdy locals congregated around a rustic bar decorated with antlers. Some people might have found the decor of the Prairie Dog Café quaint. Magnus didn't. He'd given up "quaint" when he'd finally escaped his boyhood home on a remote Scottish isle in the North Sea, part of the chain of islands that made up Orkney.

Despite his silence, the woman kept blethering. "My friend and her husband just found out they're going to have twins. The whole town is just as happy as ants at a picnic. Drinks are on the house—well, all except for the new mama-to-be. She's having sparkling grape juice!"

Magnus could only stare at the woman in disbelief. This was why he hated small towns. All the endless gossip. Why would he want to know about her friend's drinking habits or the fact that she had a trout in the well? Next, the lass would be telling him just when and where her friends had shagged to conceive the bairns.

He'd hated growing up on an isle with a population of less than five hundred. No privacy. No boundaries. No peace. Even though he'd lived with his da on a speck of an island off-shore from the larger one, he'd still found himself entangled in the threads of town gossip. They'd trapped him as surely as a spider's silk did a struggling beetle. Against the odds, he'd broken free...only for his editor to send him straight into another web. A dusty, arid one, at that.

At nineteen, Magnus had penned his first book between shifts as a roughneck on an oil rig off the coast of Norway. His muscles had ached, and the constant cold had seeped so deep into his skin, he'd sworn that even his molecules had ice crystals growing in them. But despite the dogged tiredness, he'd used the precious hours meant for sleeping to write about his childhood as if he could purge it from his soul.

It hadn't worked. Not completely. But the publishing world, and then the public, had loved his cathartic musings about his formative years on a struggling, windblown croft surrounded by the ever-present gray sea. When he'd hit bestseller lists all over the world, the media had billed him as a wunderkind.

Intoxicated by his first success, he'd quickly written a second book about his adventures in Norway. While working on the ice, he'd found a pair of orphaned polar bear cubs, rescued them from starvation, and kept them alive until they could be relocated to a zoo. His fans had adored the tale.

With all the cosh he made from his first books, he'd left the roughneck life behind and headed to Glasgow. Then a few years later, he'd moved to the welcome obscurity of London. In a city of over eight million, no one cared if a man chose to sup alone. Since his author photo was taken from the back with him staring out to sea, no one recognized him. He could eat, drink, and write in peace.

But the public didn't like his wry witticisms about city life. Sales from his next two books plummeted. And that had led to the fateful call with his editor a few weeks ago. Magnus could still hear the man's rough Bostonian accent growling in his ear.

People aren't buying your urban jungle crap. You've gotten too acerbic. Too much misanthropy and too little humor. Get back to your roots. Small towns. Living creatures. I know the perfect place for you. It's been all over the internet, a zoo in a place called Sagebrush Flats. It's got the animal angle from your first books, but in a different enough locale that it'll be fresh. Go work there for a season. Write about it. That...that I can sell. The other stuff, I can't.

Because Magnus preferred to keep his current lifestyle and not go back to being a roughneck, he now found himself in the back of beyond. The idea of shoveling manure again didn't bother him. Animals and their shite he could take. But the human kind? Ay, that was the kincher.

Across from him, the bonny blond still beamed. Welcoming. Charming. Sweet. And he didn't believe any of it. She'd plopped her arse down in the booth across from him for one reason and one reason only. Gossip. She wanted to be the very first to meet the hulking stranger so she could blether to her friends about him the following morn. Magnus wasn't a chap who typically attracted the lasses, especially those as braw as the likes of this one.

"I swear none of us bite," the woman joked and waited a beat for Magnus to speak. He didn't. "We're all very friendly."

Magnus sighed and looked longingly at his computer screen.

"Come on," the blond insisted as she rose from the table. Magnus shook his head, but the lass didn't pay any attention. She reached forward and grabbed his hand. At the unexpected contact, Magnus jerked back, jamming his elbow hard against the wooden booth. He didn't like being touched, especially by a stranger. He appreciated even less the strange jolt of awareness that zipped through him.

Surprise showed in the blond's leaf-green eyes. "I beg your pardon. I didn't mean to startle you, darling."

Baws. Now it would be all over town that he was a nervous numptie. Anger and frustration whipped inside Magnus like the furious polar winds of the North. Worse, his larynx muscles tightened ominously, and he felt his chest constrict. If he tried to speak, tried to explain that he wanted to be left alone, he'd never manage to force the words out. His neck would stiffen and his tongue would feel thick and useless as it stuck to the roof of his mouth. He'd be left as helpless as a carp flopping on a trawler's deck. The welcome in those green eyes would turn to shock and then discomfort and finally to disgust, or worse, pity. Within a bloody night, the whole town would know about his stutter. They might even give him a nickname like his schoolmates had.

Magnus grabbed his laptop, the hasty movement upsetting his ale. Hastily mopping up the liquid with napkins in one hand, he shoved his computer in his messenger bag with the other. Placing the sodden napkins in a neat pile, he stood up. Although the lass was tall and willowy, his massive frame still dwarfed hers. He expected her eyes to widen at his full height. Most folks' did upon first meeting him. But instead of a flash of leftover primordial

fear, he thought he spotted something else entirely...
appreciation.

Lust speared him. Strong and heady. It was an attraction Magnus didn't want to feel, especially when it
tangled his tongue worse than driftwood caught in a
fishing net.

He pushed past the lass. He had no choice but to
brush against her shoulder since she was blocking his
exit from the booth like an old fairy stone. As his large
body collided softly with her slender one, he swore that
her heat seared him.

"Wait," the woman said, "I didn't mean to chase you
away. Let me at least replace your beer."

Magnus swung toward the lass, no longer caring how
rude he'd become. He was either going to make a fool
or an arse out of himself. And, having been both, he
much preferred the second. Asses got more respect than
jesters. Even if he couldn't find the rhythm to explain
himself, there was one phrase he could always force out.

"Fuck off."

The lass's lower jaw dropped slightly, revealing
that she'd understood his deep Orcadian Scots accent.
Instead of looking ridiculous with her mouth agape, the
lass's perfect pink lips formed a rather seductive O. Not
waiting for his body's reaction to that particular observation to become apparent, Magnus stormed from the
Prairie Dog Café. As he burst out into the twilight, he
greedily turned his face in the direction of the cool evening breeze. The restaurant had been roasting. Although
Sagebrush in early January was much cooler than he'd
expected for the desert, the air still felt thin and dry.
Aye, he missed the familiar damp of Britain.

Shoving his hands deep into his pockets, Magnus slouched as he ambled down the street. He'd been waiting all day for that ruined draught and a bit of relaxation after a long flight. Perhaps he'd have better luck in the morn at the tea shop on the corner. It looked pleasant, if a little treacly, with its lavender-painted facade and lace curtains in the windows. He'd checked the menu online. The owner claimed her nan was British, and some of the items sounded surprisingly authentic. It was one of the few things Magnus was looking forward to in Sagebrush. Knowing his luck, it probably would turn out to be the favorite haunt of the blond.

———

"What was that all about?" June's best friend, Katie, asked as she appeared next to her, a glass of sparkling grape juice in her hand.

"That man just told me to fuck off," June said, still unable to shake her disbelief at the man's rudeness. Her atypical feeling of annoyance only spiked when Katie snorted.

"Josh," Katie yelled over to their mutual friend from college who was in town for the weekend to celebrate her good news. "You won't believe it. Some guy actually told June to fuck off."

"Well, he didn't tell me to fuck off exactly. It was more like 'feck aff.'"

"Suu-uure," Katie said before she took a long sip from her flute of grape juice. "Totally different."

Josh wandered over to join them. "What's this I hear about some guy giving June the brush off?"

"My word, you'd think no one has ever been rejected before in the history of mankind."

"Oh, *we* all have, June," Josh said. "Just not you. What did this guy look like?"

"From the back, not June's usual type," Katie said. "Too hairy. Too beefcakey."

"Too rude," June added.

Katie's husband, Bowie, walked over to them and slung his arm around his wife's shoulders. "Who's a rude, hairy beefcake?"

"June's unrequited love." Katie stood up on her tip-toes to brush a quick kiss across her husband's mouth, even though they'd only been separated for a matter of minutes. June found the couple's affection incredibly sweet, especially now that they were expecting twins.

June said quickly, "Heavens to Betsy, I was just making nice to the man. I don't know why y'all are turning it into a declaration of love. It wasn't as if I was flirting."

At her last statement, all three of her friends burst into irrepressible laughter. June glared at them. Katie got herself under control first. "June, you flirt with *every* guy. It's how you interact with the entire male popula-tion of our species."

"Our species? Have you seen how she gets with the cute animals at Bowie's zoo?" Josh asked.

June popped Josh on the arm, but she couldn't argue with Katie. She was a flirt. "Well, maybe I was flirt-ing just a smidge, but I was only being welcoming to a stranger. Like Katie said, he's not my usual type." June liked her lovers to be as easygoing as herself. A romance should be as delightful and pleasant as sweet jam made from the first spring pickings. It should *not* have the drama and devastation of a fall hurricane, and Mr. Rude seemed to have the personality of a tempest, tornado, and tsunami all rolled into one godforsaken storm.

June enjoyed handsome, debonair men. In contrast, the scowling Mr. Rude looked like a grumpy Paul Bunyan after a mishap with Rogaine. Yet, when the man had stood and stared her down with his piercing blue eyes, she'd felt a thrill clean down to her toes. It hadn't been the smooth pull of attraction. No, this— this had been a searing bolt of primal energy. It was as if some elemental feminine instinct had instantly, and explosively, responded to his raw strength.

There'd been something about his face. True, his unruly hair and shaggy beard had obscured his features, but June had always possessed an eye for a person's bone structure. Her second talent after making jam was giving folks a makeover. And if anyone needed her helpful advice, it was Mr. Rude. Oh, he'd never be classically handsome. The planes of his face were too harsh. But with the right hairstyle and a trimmed beard, he'd look arresting, especially considering his cobalt-blue eyes.

"Hmmm, he may not be your type, but I'm detecting a classic June Winters glint in your eyes," Katie said.

June smiled airily. "I'm just thinking about how I'd go about taming a wild Scot."

Josh snorted. "You sound like the cover of a romance novel."

"Oooo, I wonder what June's crush would look like in a kilt," Katie added.

June was just about to retort when Bowie broke into the conversation with something blessedly sensible. "Wait. Was the guy Scottish?"

June nodded. "With a deep brogue. He only said two words, but I got that much."

"Shit. That was probably Magnus Gray. I hope you didn't scare him off. He's supposed to start work at the zoo tomorrow."

Katie turned toward her husband. "June's guy is the mysterious writer who's going to volunteer at the zoo?"

"Unless June's man is visiting Rocky Ridge National Park and was just passing through, but I doubt it," Bowie said. "It isn't tourist season, and we don't generally have a lot of Brits in Sagebrush."

"Dang blast it all," June grumbled, "*he's* Magnus Gray. I was hoping I could ask him to chat with Nan. During the Blitz, her parents sent her to live on the island he wrote about. She's been re-listening to his audiobook for years."

The teasing glint left Katie's eyes as she regarded June with a serious expression. "How is your grandma doing?"

June sighed, wishing she had something better to report. "I'm not sure. She gets confused lately. She keeps calling me in the dead of night, thinking we had some big kerfuffle and that I'm angry with her. She's just not herself."

"I know Lou can have his off days," Bowie said, mentioning his eighty-year-old adoptive father.

"I'm worried it's more than just tiredness. This horrible, haunted look comes over her face as soon as the sun goes down. It's like she's constantly fretting about something fierce."

"Why don't you bring her by the zoo?" Katie asked. "The animals always cheer her up."

"We'll give her a personal tour," Bowie promised. "I know how much your grandma loves the baby animals, and the orphaned polar bear cub is due to arrive soon. That's one of the reasons Magnus contacted me. He had some experience with the species when he was a roughneck in Norway, and his editor had heard we've received a grant from the Alliance for Polar Life."

"His second bestseller was about polar bears," June said. "Nan listened to that one too. She didn't care for his other books, though, so she stopped asking me to download them."

"His email said something about getting back to his roots," Bowie said. "I wasn't going to turn down free labor, especially from someone who has his background with animals."

"Why didn't you recognize him just now?" Katie asked.

Bowie shrugged. "I didn't know what the man looked like. Magnus is very private. I haven't even talked to him on the phone. All of our correspondence was through email. When I researched him online to check out his credentials, any pictures were taken from the back."

"According to my nan, Magnus Gray would make a hermit seem downright sociable. Part of his mystique, I suppose."

"He sounds like an ass," Josh interjected.

"My sentiments exactly," June said. "I was just being genteel. Poor Nan. She was tickled pink he was coming to town. And I thought meeting him might help her."

"I don't know, June," Josh teased. "As you always say, if you try hard enough, you can charm a snake."

"A snake, yes, but can I charm a surly Scot?"

—⁓—

Magnus rose before the sun. He wasn't meeting Bowie until ten o'clock, but even years after leaving his da's croft, he couldn't escape the rhythm of rural life. During his childhood, responsibility for the farm animals had fallen mainly on Magnus, with his da off early on his trawler bringing in the day's catch. Their Shetland sheep and shaggy Highland beef cows had been fairly self-sufficient, but the milch cows had required his attention before and after school. In the evenings, there'd always been a stone wall to repair or a barn to clean. And that was in the winter months. Work had only intensified in the spring with lambing, calving, and planting. In the summers, Magnus had helped his da on the trawler, the two of them working in silence with only the sound of the waves lapping against the sides of the boat. Life on the oil rigs had been just as constant and demanding. Magnus had spent long shifts hefting hammers and wrenches as he kept the machinery working.

When Magnus had begun writing full time, he'd found himself fighting a constant low thrum of pent-up energy. Eventually, he'd buckled and begun lifting weights, which he detested. He'd always mocked the toonsers who paid good money to work out in sweaty, smelly indoor gyms instead of earning their muscles. And then Magnus had become one of them. But it was either exercise or go absolutely barmy.

As daft as it sounded, Magnus actually looked forward to hauling feed and cleaning out pens again. It would be good to use his muscles for their intended purpose. He just wished it didn't mean dealing with the zoo's guests and all the townsfolk.

The streets seemed fairly deserted as he left his B and B. Thankfully, the Primrose, Magnolia & Thistle opened at six thirty. Up ahead, a welcoming glow seeped from a large picture window. Picking up his pace, Magnus could fairly taste the bangers and tattie scone. The fare on the menu was heavier than the food served by a traditional British tea shop, but he was in the States now. He supposed he should be grateful that a Wild West town like Sagebrush Flats even had something approaching a traditional Scottish breakfast. Although the name of it—the Hungry Scotsman Platter—made his hackles rise, he'd order the blasted thing. As long as a breakfast included black pudding and beans, he wouldn't quibble over what a Yank called it.

Magnus pushed open the door, and a little bell chimed. Two older men with sun-leathered skin and cowboy hats glanced up at his entrance. Their eyes scanned him briefly, taking his measure. Magnus bobbed his head sharply. The men returned the gesture. Their assessment of him complete, they returned their attention to the more important matter of breakfast.

Magnus turned toward the front of the tea shop and froze. Behind the counter stood the blond lass from the Prairie Dog Café. She'd wrapped her long, wheat-colored hair into a comely top knot that drew

Magnus's attention to the graceful lines of her neck. For a minute, he went utterly doolally and imagined planting his lips there. Because of his cursed imagination, he could practically feel her shiver in his arms. Baws, he'd be sporting a fair stauner if he didn't stop the direction of his thoughts.

The woman smiled, and her green eyes sparkled with an unholy chirpiness, especially given the early hour. Magnus wondered if she'd divined his thoughts. She did look a bit like a fae creature despite her height. One thing was certain. She didn't look either goosed or hungover—just happy to the point of being mental.

"Hi there, stranger." She grinned broadly. "Welcome to my tea shop."

"Fuck me. Thoo bloody own this place?" His dismayed shock had evidently startled the stutter right out of him. He didn't even block on the *P*, which generally gave him trouble. He still spoke in his Orcadian accent, using "thoo" instead of "you." It could confuse Americans, but that was one aspect of his dialect that he'd retained through the years.

To his amazement, the lass's smile didn't turn brittle at his crudeness. In fact, it stretched a little farther northward in pure glee. The barmy hen was taking delight in his misery.

"I sure do. Now how can I help you, Magnus?"

He glowered. How the fuck did the lass know his name? She must have read the confusion in his face.

"We don't get many Scots here in Sagebrush, especially in the winter. When I mentioned your accent, Bowie figured it was you."

Magnus scowled. Damn it all to hell. And damn

the nosy lass too. Was the whole town gossiping about him now?

"So," June asked, leaning across the tall glass counter, "what can I get you?"

"I'll be having the Hungry Scotsman P-P-P…" His throat closed up. He couldn't fight the tightness. He stood there, stuck on the *P*, helplessly watching the lass's face. He wondered in those long seconds of horror what her expression would be. Frustrated annoyance like his da? Amusement like his classmates? Pity like the headmistress? Discomfort like the townsfolk? He'd witnessed them all…or so he'd thought.

A light flickered in the lass's eyes as if she'd just solved a challenging riddle. Then, she stuck her arms akimbo and delivered a look a mum would give to a lad who wanted to quit football just because his team got mullered.

"Now why didn't you tell me that you were a person who stuttered?" June asked. "I would have understood, honey. Is swearing one of your avoidances? You don't need to worry around me. Just be yourself. I don't mind disfluency. And people who do can go straight to the devil."

Magnus blinked. The woman made his head spin faster than a weathercock in a gale.

"Disfluency?"

"Do you prefer another term?"

Magnus rubbed his head. He couldn't help it. What he preferred was to be left alone, but it didn't appear the fae lass would grant him that particular wish.

"What one would you like me to use? My

brother, August, is pretty flexible about terminology, but I know some people prefer certain words over others."

"Thoor brother?" Why the hell was she blethering about her brother?

"He's a person who stutters," the lass said. "I did too in elementary school, but I've been fluent for years. It's partially why I speak like a Southerner. My mama's from Georgia, although I grew up all over the world. That doesn't mean I use my drawl as an avoidance. It's how I talk naturally, and the slower cadence gives me more control over my rate of speech."

The deluge of information pelted Magnus like spray from an arctic wave. The woman could drown a body in random facts. She sounded like a bloody medical pamphlet from the National Health Service.

"So?" the lass asked, with an expectant expression on her face. He simply stared back in confusion. A bloke needed a compass to navigate her speech.

"What term do you prefer instead of disfluency?" she clarified.

"I don't give a shite," Magnus said in frustration. Why the hell would he care what she called his damn stutter? He wanted to live free of the bloody thing. Calling it something different would never fix it.

"I'm sensing you don't like talking about it."

"Aye, that's right." *Bloody perceptive of her*.

She leaned over the counter and said in quiet seriousness. "Ignoring it won't make it go away. My brother tried that for years, but August found it was easier if he just told people up front. He's a JAG officer in the air force now."

Was she giving him advice on his own stutter? Magnus

glowered. For once, the blond heeded his look. She straightened, and the welcoming smile returned. What was it about her pink lips that made him think of snogging when the woman herself was nothing but a constant vexation? She had him in a tangle.

"So," the lass said conversationally, "what would you like to order?"

Magnus opened his mouth to respond and discovered that he'd lost his appetite. The lass had ruined his ale and now his breakfast. "Fuck me."

Without giving the hen a chance to react, he turned and left the tea shop. He'd eat at the bloody B and B.

It wasn't until Magnus was halfway down the street that a realization struck him. He hadn't stumbled over his words once since the lass had started havering about disfluency. Which never happened. Especially in the company of a stranger. An annoying one at that.

───～∾～───

Magnus arrived at the zoo in a sour mood. Instead of a hearty Scot's breakfast at the Primrose, Magnolia & Thistle, he'd scarfed down weak tea and overly sweet French toast drowned in maple syrup.

Since it was the middle of the week in January, the zoo was deserted. Magnus felt his shoulder muscles unhunch as he wound his way through the animal enclosures. Finally, peace. Quiet. Solitude. This was why he'd chosen to volunteer during the winter. That, and he didn't want to haul feed under the desert sun in August.

Gravel crunched under his feet as he followed the directions the owner had given him to the main zoo building. At the sound, a pack of disgruntled llamas and two camels picked up their heads. Magnus paused, watching the animals as they chewed their cud.

He'd read about the female camel, Lulubelle, on the zoo's website. The animal park claimed she'd been love-lorn until she'd met her mate, Hank. All shite, but the public loved it. According to her profile, Lulubelle was pregnant, but even knowing nothing about camels, Magnus would have noticed she was up the duff with her swollen belly and her lumbering, uneven gait as she approached. Glancing between her hind legs, Magnus saw her udder was swollen with milk. Her bairn would be along anytime now.

Magnus scratched Lulubelle's wooly neck and something inside him seemed to slide back into place like a latch on an old metal gate. He'd missed this, he realized. The simplicity of animal husbandry. He'd never felt nostalgic for his childhood. It had been rough, dreich, and devoid of comfort…and not just because of the drafty crofter's cottage he'd called home. Yet something about the mix of hay, manure, and animal scent whispered to him. Balanced him. Perhaps this wouldn't be the hell he'd imagined.

Lulubelle emitted a contented, low, rumbling bray that reminded him of a horse's. Magnus smiled. "Thoo're a fine lass, thoo are." His stutter never troubled him when he spoke to the beasties. When his da was out on the trawler, he used to blether on and on to the cows and the horses. Aye, they'd been his first audience. If it hadn't been for them listening to his descriptions of his day, he might never have become a writer.

Magnus pulled back to stare into the camel's soulful

eyes. They reminded him keenly of Sorcha's, one
of his da's highland cows. He hadn't thought of her
in years, but she'd been his favorite. She'd come
running up to him whenever he passed the pasture,
probably because he'd sneak her treats when his da
couldn't see. In trying to bury the terrible memories of his youth, he'd discarded the good ones too.
Giving the camel one last pat goodbye, he made a
promise to himself. When he returned to London,
he was going to find himself a dog.

Walking around the bend, he spotted a bear
lounging on a fairly good facsimile of a rock.
Judging by the animal's contented expression, he
wondered if the structure was heated. He paused
for a moment, leaning up against the rail to watch
the blissful beastie. By the size, girth, and color, he
guessed the animal was a grizzly, and he was partial
to any bruin after raising two polar bear cubs.

The massive creature shifted. It turned rheumy
eyes in Magnus's direction as it sniffed the air.
Magnus grinned at the faint snuffling sounds. The
elderly animal was having trouble spotting him, but
there was no doubt he'd been scented.

"Good morning," Magnus said, and the bear
snorted in response. "I'm sorry I disturbed your
sleep."

A rumbling sound emerged from the grizzly as
it tried to settle back down on its rock. It did not
appear to be successful. After shifting for several
minutes, the animal clamored to its feet with a
beleaguered groan. Shaking its limbs, it began to
pad around its enclosure.

"I'll bring thee a treat if Bowie Wilson will let me," Magnus promised.

The bear did not appear to be impressed. It shot Magnus what seemed to be an accusing glance as it lumbered back to its rock again. It sank down, this time finding a better spot. With a happy sigh, the bear rested its chin on its massive paws.

"You're here early."

Magnus turned to find Bowie Wilson walking up the path. He recognized the zookeeper from his online videos. Magnus had spotted him at the Prairie Dog last night, but he hadn't wanted to bother with small talk. Unfortunately, he hadn't planned on the blond menace.

"Aye," Magnus replied. He could always form that word without hesitation. Through the years, he'd accumulated a library of phrases that saw him through most short interactions.

"I see you've met Frida. She's our grizzly and one of our oldest residents. I imagine you saw Lulubelle, our camel, on your way in. She's become our unofficial greeter. She's probably the friendliest animal here— although our capybara, Sylvia, is a sweetheart too."

Magnus grunted in response. He'd learned people generally liked to hear themselves talk. As long as he gave them some encouragement, they'd carry on and never notice he hadn't actually uttered a word.

"I thought we'd start with a tour," Bowie said. "You can get to know the animals, and then we can go over what your volunteer duties will be. You said you don't mind shoveling manure or lugging around feed."

"Aye."

Bowie flashed a broad smile. "That's great," he

continued. "But don't worry. This job won't just be about hauling stuff. This morning, I finally got the call from the Alliance for Polar Life."

Magnus jerked his head in Bowie's direction. He'd worked with the Norwegian branch of the APL when he'd rescued the polar bear cubs.

Magnus started to say "bear" but he could sense he was going to block on the *B*. Quickly, he switched the word. "Cub?"

"Yeah." Bowie nodded. "Oil exploration near dens up in Alaska scared off a lot of new moms. APL has too many bears that aren't candidates for rehabilitation. They're going to send us a female cub who was born late in the season."

Magnus whistled. In the wild, polar bears gave birth between November and December. Since it was early January, the bairn must be very young. Magnus started to say just that, but he felt his throat muscles tighten as he tried to say "must be," so instead he got out, "She a...wee cub, aye?"

Bowie luckily didn't seem to notice Magnus's hesitation or the slightly incorrect syntax. Instead the man nodded. "She's about a month old and the APL is struggling to provide round-the-clock care for all the abandoned young."

Magnus jerked his chin again. The group focused on research and wasn't staffed as a rescue center. Although they'd given him advice on how to care for the orphans he'd found, they hadn't had the manpower to care for the cubs. Plus, the oil rig had been too far north to easily extract the cubs. The other roughnecks had initially given Magnus a hard time about being a polar bear mum, but eventually they'd all helped. The weans had become his crew's mascots until they could be relocated to a zoo.

"The cub's eyes are open, but she's still pretty young," Bowie said. "It's going to be intense in the beginning."

Magnus responded with a shrug. He'd taken care of cubs in the middle of the Arctic while working fourteen days straight; he could handle caring for one while doing odd jobs around a small animal park. Hard work didn't fash him. It would only improve his book.

"We're not a very big zoo," Bowie said as he started walking again, "but we are growing. In the last year, we've gotten some grants, and we're starting to build our reputation for providing care for abandoned young and unwanted exotic pets."

"Aye," Magnus said. He'd done his research when his editor had ordered him to come here.

"Part of it is because of this sweet girl."

Magnus looked inside the pen in front of him. A kidney-shaped creature lounged in a heated pool of water. She looked as content as Magnus felt tucked away in a corner of a pub enjoying a good whiskey.

"That's Sylvia, our capybara, who I was just telling you about. She mothers all of our orphans."

Intrigued, Magnus stared at the odd-looking animal. He'd read her profile on the zoo's website. Strange how a member of a wild species—and a rodent, no less—could have a greater natural affinity for nurturing than many a human. Neither of Magnus's parents had shown any instinct for caring for him, their only offspring. His mum might have been the only one to physically abandon him, but his da had been more

interested in keeping their livestock alive than
he'd been in raising Magnus.

Magnus pushed abruptly away from the fence.
He started moving forward, hoping Bowie would
understand that he wanted to press on. He didn't
feel like trying to form words. Luckily, Bowie
understood the unspoken signal. They walked in
silence until Magnus turned the bend.

The next enclosure looked like an empty ten-
foot-deep swimming pool, but with red dirt instead
of cement for a bottom. Two separate sheds were
erected at opposite ends. Unlike the other pens, this
one was relatively barren with only a few balls and
other small toys.

"This is the home of our two resident honey badgers," Bowie said. "They make the goats look per-
sonable, but we love Honey and Fluffy all the same."

Magnus looked at Bowie questioningly. Orkney
did not have badgers, but mainland Scotland did.
He'd never heard them referred to as honey badgers, though.

"They're from Africa," Bowie explained,
"and they're more closely related to weasels than
the badgers you have back in Britain. They've
got similar coloration to the true badger but are
meaner. They kill cobras...for fun. Snake venom
doesn't kill them, it just temporarily knocks them
out. They're smart and extremely devious."

Now that would make good fodder for his book.
Magnus leaned over the fence as he tried to peer
into the shelter. He still couldn't get a glimpse of
the beasties.

"Fluffy and Honey are nocturnal," Bowie said, "but don't worry. You'll get a look at them. Honey-badger wrangling will be a big part of your job…and cleaning up their messes. They escape at least once a week."

"From there?" Magnus asked in surprise, jerking his thumb toward the sheer concrete walls.

Bowie nodded glumly. "Yep. They're smart. Too smart. I thought if I found a mate for Fluffy—that's our male—he might settle down. Now, I've got two of them running around, and Fluffy is ornerier than ever. Honey is always pestering him, and I think he blames me."

Magnus glanced back at the small shed surrounded by red dust. He could sympathize with the unseen Fluffy. After all, he had his own meddlesome female to contend with.

About the Author

Two-time Golden Heart finalist Laurel Kerr spent a few weeks each summer of her childhood on family road trips. That time packed into the back seat of her grandparents' Grand Marquis opened her imagination and exposed her to the wonders of the United States. The lessons she learned then still impact her writing today. She lives near Pittsburgh, Pennsylvania, with her husband, daughter, and loyal Cavalier King Charles spaniel.